The Bishop of 12TH Avenue

Ray Lucit

ISBN: 0-9720411-1-7
ISBN-13: 978-0-9720411-1-9

For Steven, whose cool idea and love of the faith has inspired the following story.

Written under obedience, August 2047.

THE WEST END

Seems like there's always something burning.

For as long as I can remember little clouds of smelly blue smoke have drifted over the busted streetlights each morning, and at night you can see a hundred little fires in the dirty windows of the tall buildings. Over on the East End I've seen smoke rising from piles of stone and rubble that have sat there for years. I never really thought about it till now, and I can't imagine what's down there, but I guess that's one thing in life I'm absolutely sure about. There is *always* something burning.

That reminds me, before I get started you might as well know that sometimes I ramble on about shit like that. That's just how I am. My brain is always remembering something or digging up stuff that makes me drift off a little. Some memories won't leave you alone until you've thought about them long enough. The story I'm about to tell you all happened in the last few months but it's filled with a lifetime of memories. I promised to write it all down just like it happened, but there's lots of stuff I haven't had time to think through yet. Hell, start to finish, this is the first time I'll be thinking the whole thing through myself, so don't be surprised if I ramble on a bit.

That first night I was living down on the West End, across from the cathedral. I know what you're thinking, but it's not as bad as it sounds. Sure, the West End has a rep for being dangerous, but you can live pretty good if you can stay clear of the dogs and the Feds. My place is right next to a compound so there's usually running water, and if you're smart, it's a good place to find food. I guess I'm eighteen or nineteen now, and there's not another kid my age in the whole city with a build like mine, not even in the gangs. I'm tall and strong, and from downtown all the way out to Twelfth Avenue, nobody's crazy enough to mess with Jake Walker.

It was a few hours before sunup and I was sleeping out on the balcony as usual. I'm on the sixth floor facing the high fence behind the compound, and I've got a good view of the street in both directions. It's a cool old building that used to have eight floors, but everything above the sixth is gone now, just concrete blocks and twisted steel beams poking up at the sky. With a Fed compound right next door, the neighborhood is even more deserted than the rest of the city. You might see a gang pass through once in a while, but only a few people still live here. In my building there's only me and a couple of old women on the first floor, so when I heard voices on the street I sat up and reached for my blades. The lights of the compound are always on, and there was enough light to see Old Joe talking with another guy on the steps of the cathedral. When I saw that it was only Joe, I almost went back to sleep.

Old Joe was the strangest character in the city, and he'd lived in that huge old building forever. Everybody knew the white-haired old man in black clothes, and most of us thought he was crazy. When I first got to the West End I thought that he was dealing something out of the cathedral because once a week there'd be five or ten people show up at the same time. They'd walk right in through the side doors like they lived there, and after about half an hour they'd leave again. I finally broke in through a basement window one night to check the place out. It was gigantic and all shot up inside, with busted statues and pieces of broken colored glass everywhere, but I think I figured out why people were coming. Joe must have been selling candles. There were lit candles everywhere, and there's nothing as hard-to-find as candles on the West End. He must have run out because as far as I could tell, Joe hadn't seen any customers in forever.

Anyway, as I looked on, Joe and a smaller guy I didn't recognize were standing halfway down the steps arguing about something.

The stranger was dressed all in black and the skinny little dude was even older than Joe. There's something funny about two old guys standing out in the open and jabbering at each other in a foreign language. I watched them for a sec, and just when I thought that the whole thing couldn't get any more bizarre, Joe dropped to his knee right there on the concrete steps and kissed the other guy's hand. He stood up again, hugged the little dude, and headed off down twelfth.

I must have fallen back to sleep, and I can't say for sure how long I was out, but I wasn't sleeping too long when I heard something coming from the street again. This time it was an ugly sound and I was wide awake after hearing it. I slipped my knives into my back pocket and leaned over the railing toward the street. Joe's friend was on the ground, just outside the big doors of the cathedral, and there were two guys standing over him. There was another one, with his face hidden inside a black hoodie, standing there watching. It took me a sec to figure out what was happening, but the two assholes hovering over Joe's friend were torturing him. They had a long *stick* or something. It was curved on one end and the tall guy was twisting it into the old man's guts. The other one had his foot on the old man's chest, holding him down. They were really putting it to the little guy, and he was whimpering like a wounded animal.

What happened next wasn't my fault. I can keep my temper as well as anybody, and you can't stay alive for very long on the West End if you don't mind your own business, but how was I supposed to just sit there with all that going on? I stepped over the railing and jumped onto the balcony next door. From there I swung down onto the lower balconies and onto the street. I've been doing it for so long now that I can get to the street within a few seconds and I can do it without making a sound. The three guys were too busy to hear me coming, and I was halfway up the stairs before they saw me.

The shorter dude turned, and when I saw him reaching for a piece I knew I'd have to kill him. His gun was an old nine, and as he brought it up I threw my knife. It was a great throw for a guy on the run. It landed dead-center in his throat and he dropped the gun and fell to his knees. The taller guy was already moving at me, swinging the curved stick at my head. I ducked, and it skimmed through my hair before I spun around and hit him. I hit him hard, hard enough to hear his jaw crack, but I swear I had to hit that asshole another three or four times before he dropped. I looked back at the jerk in the hoodie thinking he'd be coming too, or maybe going for the gun, but he was suddenly down on the other side of the street, calmly staring back at me.

It's not like me to imagine things, but I swear I never saw that guy move! It was as if the dude disappeared from the steps and reappeared again across the street. There wasn't time to think about it, so I pulled my knife from the first guy. While staring at the sneaky creep in the hoodie, I wiped the blade clean on the guy's tee shirt and stuck it back in my jeans.

I could talk for hours about my knives, their balance, how many times they've saved my ass, and why you'd never leave a good throwing-knife anywhere, but I guess that'll have to wait. When I got to the old man he was in worse shape than I thought. I walked around to his other side before kneeling down beside him, so I could keep an eye on the dirtbag on the street.

'How ya doing, buddy?'

His hands were clenched over his guts, and when I moved them to see the wound, I couldn't believe it. They must have really hated the little guy to open him up like that. He was in some *serious* pain, and it was a miracle the old dude was still alive because he'd lost a lot of blood. He didn't have long.

'I'm sorry,' he whispered. 'Tell them I was out of time.'

He must have been delirious because he smiled up at me. I wanted to get him off the concrete and into the cathedral. Nobody deserves to die on the street where the dogs can find you, but before I could do anything he reached up and grabbed my right hand.

'Take this ring, the seal of your fidelity.'

His grip was strong for an old guy, and he slid a ring on my finger. The ring was huge and it glimmered in the dull light from the compound. I figured it was his, and I smiled back at him.

'You don't have to thank me, dude.'

He closed his eyes and moaned when I tried to lift him up.

'No, stop!' he winced. 'What is your name?'

'Jake Walker. Now come on. We gotta get you off the damn street.'

'Jacob?' he asked softly.

He smiled at me again and made a funny sign with his hand, like he was drawing a big t in midair in front of me.

'With faith and love protect the bride of God, his holy Church.'

Dying men can say stupid things sometimes. I don't know what the old guy was thinking, but it must have been pretty cool because I've never seen a dying man smile like that before. The little guy was checking out, but he looked like a hungry cat that had just caught himself a mouse.

He fell unconscious as I lifted him up, and I realized that it was raining. It was a cold drizzly rain, and before I carried the old man into the cathedral, I kicked the tall guy to make sure he was still out. The shorter guy was history, so I looked out across the street one last time. The asshole in the hoodie was still there in the shadows, staring at us.

Now you're gonna think I'm full of shit, but as I was glaring down at that guy, I swear his eyes became weird and red and visible. Even through the rain, I could see his eyes from all the way across the street.

RARE AS CANDLES

After I left the old man, the West End felt different to me somehow. It wasn't all the time, and it wasn't always huge, but there was a nagging weirdness everywhere. Hey, I'm the last guy in the world to get spooked or superstitious, but I couldn't shake the feeling that something was happening. I tried telling myself that I was just weirded-out by the dirtbag in the hoodie, but that feeling never left me. It followed me home and wouldn't let me fall back to sleep. Hours went by, the sun came up, and I was just about to nod off when I heard noises out on the street again.

I stuck my head up in time to see three people standing in front of the cathedral. They looked young, about my age, and they were talking so loudly that I could hear a lot of what they were saying. They'd found the little guy's body inside, and they were standing over the dude I killed. After taking the old man into the cathedral last night, I stayed with him until I couldn't get a pulse, but it wasn't more than five or ten minutes. Being there in the dark gave me the creeps. There were some candles lit on a table up front, so I put him there before leaving. Finding him dead wasn't what these people were expecting, and they looked jumpy.

Some people just don't fit in on the West End, and as I watched these three, it became obvious that they weren't from around here. They were dressed in good clothes, I mean *really good* clothes, with backpacks and leather boots. One of them was holding a sawdi, but he looked like he never fired a shotgun in his life. Neither of the two dudes looked like much to me, but the girl was fascinating and I couldn't take my eyes off her. She was wearing jeans and a girl's shirt, one of those shirts that's tighter at the waist and comes down a little in front. She had long brown hair, and it was hanging down in a loose ponytail. Her backpack was *pink*, and from where I was sitting it also looked like she was wearing makeup.

On the West End, and anywhere else I've ever seen, females never do anything to draw attention to themselves. It just doesn't happen. Females are as rare as candles, and even if you could find one, you'd never catch her wearing makeup out in the open like that. The only females I'd ever seen wearing makeup before were gang property, and their faces weren't young and soft like this girl. I'd honestly never seen anything like her, and while I was still trying to figure her out, the guy with the gun said something about a *proper burial* and told her to wait outside. I couldn't believe they left her alone like that, and when they moved into the cathedral I started down to warn her. When I reached the road something else dawned on me. The sun was nearly over the compound, and the Feds would be arriving soon.

While I was crossing the street another idea came to me and I realized that my own clothes weren't much to look at. My jeans were worn through in places, and I remember wondering if there was still blood on my shirt. My shirt wasn't much of a shirt anymore either, being so thin and not having any sleeves, but I've never had a good reason to think about my looks before. I know I'm six-four and I have blue eyes and dark brown hair. I know I should cut my hair once in a while, but who's got time to think about shit like that? There wasn't anything I could have done about it then anyway, but I must have looked like hell because she almost came out of her boots when she saw me coming up the stairs. When I saw her jump, I stopped.

'Hey,' I started, pointing to downtown. 'You better get inside. The gangs patrol all through here, and the Feds will be here soon.'

She caught sight of my hand, and her eyes got bigger.

'That ring! Where did you get that ring?'

The little guy's ring had completely slipped my mind, and I held my hand up for a better look. It was cool, shiny and gold, with a large black stone. In the middle of the stone was a silver cross with a shinier little stone in the center.

'An old guy gave it to me last night,' I answered. 'Now get inside while you still can.'

I turned toward home, but she started talking again.

'Wait!' she called, 'Tell me what happened. Where's Fr. Kowalski? Did he get away?'

Normally I would have gone back home and ignored her. If you warn somebody about something once, that should be plenty. But this female was even better looking up close, with big green eyes, a nice mouth, and a body that was unreal. If the Feds weren't on their way, I could have stood there looking at her all day.

'We can't talk here,' I answered, nodding toward the compound. 'That's a Fed compound there, and their trucks will be here soon. We gotta get off the street.'

Her face went blank and she didn't have a clue about what I was saying.

'Every day a convoy of trucks comes into that place to pick up food and stuff,' I explained, breaking into a smile. 'They'll shoot anyone or anything in sight when those gates open.'

She looked back at the doors to the cathedral and at the ring again, like she was trying to figure something out.

'I live right over there,' I offered. 'You can come up if you want, and I'll tell you about it.'

She must have really wanted that ring back because after thinking about it another second, she started following me. She didn't seem the type to hop balconies, so I took her through the front door and up the stairs by the elevator.

It's strange, but some people make you feel self-conscious just by standing next to you. I'd walked that path a thousand times, but as we moved along I noticed a hundred things I'd never seen before. I noticed how the elevator door was half open, and the burn marks on the walls and ceilings. We stepped over the broken wood and plaster on the floor and I noticed the women who live in the old front office, how they sat in the corner, how they smelled and how their eyes followed us up the stairs. My door doesn't have a lock but it can open and close, and I noticed she left it open after we stepped inside.

'I'm Rebecca,' she said, looking around. 'Do you have a name?'

'Jake.'

She was fascinated with my place, and I watched her as she started checking everything out. I was half-expecting her to start talking again, but she wandered around looking at all my stuff. I could see her eyes scanning my stacks of books, my pile of clothes and the two pictures on the fireplace. I'd never been so close to anything so beautiful, and while she was staring at the picture of my parents' house, I moved closer.

Rebecca spun around when she felt me behind her, and I grabbed her by the arms and lifted her, forcing her up against the wall. I pressed against her, in case she decided to kick or start fighting. She was making a lot of noise, but her hair smelled so good that I wasn't paying much attention. Her body was incredible, but not all that strong, and I barely felt her struggling to get free. She was warm and amazing and I pushed my face into her hair and started kissing her neck. In a second or two she stopped squirming, but as I started working around to the other side of her neck, I felt something I wasn't expecting. She was *shaking*. When I pulled back there were tears, and she had a look in her eyes like she was terrified.

I'll say it again. I'd never seen a girl like this before, not just cause she was so pretty, but because how she was acting. No girl I'd ever seen, or even *heard of* would have acted like this. Hell, when you can catch a female that easily, you can usually bet that she doesn't mind getting caught! Rebecca was stunning, and after catching her alone and all, why was she surprised and so freaked that I'd want her? This dark-haired girl with the big eyes was different, and the look in those eyes bothered me, like I was a rabid dog about to tear her to pieces. All at once I was feeling self-conscious and stupid again, and all I could do was ease up and let her slide down the wall to her feet. She stared back at me, trying to catch her breath.

All I could think to say was, 'You want a drink or something?'

Without turning her back to me, she started moving to the door. I knew she wanted to run, but she stopped in the doorway.

'I just want to know how you got the ring, and what happened to the nuncio.'

'I don't know what a nuncio is, but I'll tell you what went down last night.'

She stood frozen in the doorway, and I sat on the floor with my back against the fireplace so I'd look less threatening. I think she was still shaking a little.

'You can sit down. I won't touch you again.'

She didn't know whether or not to believe me. She stared back at me for a long time before talking again.

'Why did you stop?' she asked softly. 'Just now, I mean.'

She was looking at the wall, where I'd been kissing her.

''Cause you wanted me to.'

Maybe she was expecting a better answer because she didn't say anything right away. There were footsteps on the stairs, and I jumped to my feet again as the two guys that were with her at the cathedral showed up behind her. They were both about the same height, dressed in khaki jackets. The chubby guy with the gun was older, in his late twenties. He had blonde hair, but the other one had hair like Rebecca's. The blonde dude pointed the gun at me and he looked scared. It always sucks when someone's got a gun in your face, but when he's more scared than you are, you've gotta be extra careful.

The dark-haired guy took Rebecca by the shoulders and looked her over, as if he expected to find her hurt.

'You ok, Sis? We heard screaming.'

'I'm fine,' she answered, turning to me. 'Jake, this is my brother, Michael, and that's Casey.'

I nodded, and when Rebecca noticed Casey's gun pointing at me, she gently pushed the barrel down.

'Jake knows what happened to Nuncio Moreau and Fr. Kowalski.'

Michael seemed alright, but Casey was an asshole. He looked me up and down, with a disgusted look on his face, like I was dogshit on his shoe.

'You're kidding, right?' he asked, turning to Rebecca. 'Does that thing even understand human speech?'

'Bite me, asshole,' I answered, leaning toward him.

Rebecca's brother burst into laughter.

'He's obviously picked up the finer points of the language!'

Nobody else heard it at first, but a low rumbling noise was coming in from the balcony. There's no real door to my balcony to block sound, just a twisted frame that used to hold glass, and I could see the smoke from the Fed convoy on the horizon.

'We need to keep out of sight.'

Everyone turned and watched as the trucks became visible. We crouched down and stayed out of the light as the convoy approached. As usual, the first truck stopped, and four guys in camo piled out with their machine guns. One guy fired a burst into the air, and they took their positions as the gate opened.

Casey asked, 'Who are your friends?'

I was beginning to think these people were from Mars.

'You guys have never seen Feds before?' I asked in disbelief. 'Those are federal agents and that's a processing facility. They package food and make the shit that keeps the government working.'

'Our Feds don't look like that in the country,' Rebecca answered softly.

She looked at me and caught me staring at her.

'Oh my God! How long have you been living like this?'

'Like this?' I laughed. 'Hey, it beats being downtown or in one of the gangs.'

'What do you eat?'

I couldn't help myself.

'Every now and then, a fat asshole with a khaki jacket and blond hair wanders into my neighborhood.'

Michael was laughing and I knew that Casey was glaring back at me, but I couldn't take my eyes off her. Rebecca's laugh was indescribable. The others disappeared, and there was nothing left but her and that smile. I might have been staring too much because she looked down and changed the subject.

'Can you tell us about last night?'

'Sure.'

I led them away from the window and back into the kitchen, but when I told them the whole story, their reaction wasn't anything like what you'd expect. For one thing, they freaked that I'd killed the asshole with the gun. At first I was a little pissed. It was as if they would have liked it better if the guy would have done me first. But after thinking about it, I think it's because they didn't like any kind of killing, no matter who was doing it. These people were odd.

I told them everything about Old Joe leaving, the dude in the hoodie, and the little old man and his ring. Rebecca completely freaked when I explained about that. She made me repeat everything the old man said, over and over again. They left me standing there and huddled together by the sink to talk about it quietly, but it was more like an argument. In no time at all I could hear every word.

'Oh, please,' Casey groaned. 'The nuncio was dying and out of his mind! It meant nothing.'

He pointed at me and laughed.

'Can't you see he's lying? He stole the ring! Look at him, he doesn't even know right from wrong.'

'He knows right from wrong.' Rebecca interrupted, looking at me. 'And he's not lying. Come on Casey, how could Jake know the rite? Everything the nuncio was clearly from a rite of ordination.'

'Listen to what you're saying, Becky. He's a teenager! He's not a priest and he's probably not Catholic. It's not legal.'

'In the early persecutions of the church there wasn't time for a lot of rules either,' she argued. 'And the nuncio was here for expressly that purpose! We've got to have faith.'

Casey started to say something, but Rebecca was too fired up to let him finish. She looked awesome and she was using words I'd never even *read* before.

'You know how things are, Casey! Over two thousand years of apostolic succession and you're willing to ignore this?'

'She's right,' Michael announced. 'We've got to assume the nuncio knew what he was doing.'

Michael was the quiet type. He didn't say much, but when he did say something, it meant more. There was silence for a minute, and they all stared at me like I was something they'd never seen before and I just crawled out from under the stove.

'Jake?' Rebecca said, turning to me. 'Would you come back with us? We think something important happened last night. We think that the nuncio did something for you and that there are a lot of people depending on you now.'

'All he did was give me this ring,' I laughed. 'I'd give it back, but it won't come off. My knuckles are still swollen from hitting that clown.'

'No Jake,' she insisted. 'Nuncio Moreau was a cardinal that came all the way from Rome on a special mission for our people. I believe he made you a bishop last night.'

I didn't know what a bishop was, but it sounded big.

'No shit?' I grinned. 'So where exactly is this place we're going?'

'We've got a place in the country with other people like us, the people I told you about. Will you come?'

'Will you be there?'

She was surprised by the question and stared back at me a second. She finally smiled a little.

13

'Yeah, it's where we live. You'll like it, I promise.'

'Ok. I'm in.'

Casey got a stupid grin on his face. He slung the gun over his shoulder, stepped up to me and bowed respectfully with his hand on his heart.

'Well then,' he said, sarcastically. 'Shall we be off, *your holiness*?'

'Hold up!' Michael interrupted, staring out past the balcony. 'I think someone's coming.'

I looked out at the street and although the convoy was gone, there were three small trucks pulling up, and a whole bunch of Feds began piling out with guns in their hands.

'The Feds are looking for someone,' I thought out loud as we watched them scatter down twelfth. 'They're going door to door!'

One of the trucks was a big open jeep. I could see the Fed driver and his passenger, a tall guy in a black hoodie. I was just thinking that it might be the same jerk I saw last night when he turned and looked up at me. It takes a lot to spook me, but when I saw those eyes, I got cold all over. I swear nobody up there had made a sound, and I don't know how he knew we were there.

'Come on,' I said. 'We gotta move!'

A TALK IN THE DARK

Did you ever wish that you'd have done something when you first had the chance? As I glared back down at him, all I could think about was how I should have killed that little asshole last night. He said something to the driver and they raced off, no doubt to the front doors of my building. Casey was already halfway to the door, and Michael was right behind him with his arm around Rebecca.

'Not that way!' I shouted, 'Over here.'

I stepped out onto the balcony and jumped onto the balcony behind mine. I held out my hand and helped Casey over, but Michael was taking so much time helping Rebecca that I got impatient. The Feds would be there any second so I stepped up onto the railings, grabbed her, and pulled her to the other side. She was still afraid of me, I think, but she must have been afraid of heights too. Once she looked down, she wrapped her arms around my neck. Even with everything that was going on, it felt excellent.

The apartment behind mine had collapsed long before I moved to the West End. The front room and most of the kitchen was nothing but a pile of concrete. It's like a cave inside without a whole lot of room, but it's a great hiding place. There's nothing left in the hallway that would make you think there's another apartment there, and you can only get inside by using the balcony. Even if the Feds were smart enough to figure out it was there, it wasn't likely they'd jump a balcony to check it out. I figured it was a smart place to hide out, but once we got inside, Casey didn't think so.

'We're trapped!' he whined. 'I thought we were leaving.'

'We're safe here,' I told him. 'And shut the hell up! The Feds are all over this place and you guys are too slow. We never would have made it.'

He started to say something, but the sound of gunfire rang out from somewhere downstairs. Then there was a scream, cut short by another burst of gunfire. I pulled a blade and leaned against the wall, next to the opening of our little cave. A few seconds later, I heard someone in my apartment, and then out on my balcony.

The gunfire surprised me. Evidently the Feds were looking for someone important. They can be ruthless as hell, but the Feds usually don't kill people who are inside and staying out of their way. I kept thinking about that guy in the hoodie and wondering if the Feds were looking for Rebecca and her friends. There were footsteps on the stairs again, this time decreasing in volume. A weird feeling hit me, knowing that the two old women were dead downstairs, and it was a long time before I thought it was safe enough to say anything. When I turned back to the others, everyone else looked like they'd been holding their breath the whole time.

'Relax,' I said softly, 'and get comfortable. We won't be able to go anywhere till dark.'

Slivers of light were streaming in from somewhere above us, but it was still mostly dark in the little apartment. I could hear everybody sitting down and taking their backpacks off. I turned away from the doorway, and let my eyes adjust to the darkness.

'Can I see your knife?' Michael asked.

I handed him the knife in my hand, and he started checking it out it in the beam of light by his foot.

'This is a throwing-knife, isn't it?'

'Yeah,' I answered. 'So, you into blades?'

'A little. I don't think I've ever seen a throwing-knife before.'

My eyes were adjusted enough to see Rebecca sitting next to him.

'Jake?' she asked. 'How'd you ever come to live here?'

'My family lived here. Not right here, I mean, but in the city. I don't remember much about it.'

'What *can* you remember?'

'Running mostly,' I laughed. 'We were always running. My dad said it was because the Feds were trying to enlist him into the service, but I don't think so. The Feds didn't want him. He could barely walk after the first war. I'm thinking the Feds were probably after me. I've heard they were recruiting eleven and twelve-year-olds if they were tall enough.'

They were all looking at me like they were expecting more details.

'The night my mom got sick he woke me up. He said he was going out to get medicine. When he didn't come back, we knew that the Feds must have found him. He should have known better. There wasn't any medicine if you weren't marked, but I guess he felt like he had to try.'

'After my mom died,' I went on. 'I spent a couple of months in the orphanage on Union Street, but when the city started burning the people that ran the place bailed. I was big for my age so I spent some time in a few of the gangs that sprung up. The other guys, most of my friends, weren't so lucky. Just about everybody I knew died in the second war, so the gangs—'

'The second war?' Rebecca interrupted,

'Yeah. When we got nuked, and the darkness came.' I explained. 'Didn't you guys get that in the country?'

Rebecca exchanged a funny look with the other guys like I'd just said something wrong or stupid.

'We got that in the country too, Jake. But I don't think it was because of a war,' she said softly.

All of a sudden nobody felt like talking. Michael handed me my knife and I slipped it back into my jeans. Even in the dark, I could feel everyone's eyes on me. I'm not sure how long it had been since I said more than a couple of words to anyone, and I was getting an uncomfortable sort of feeling.

'So what are you guys doing here?' I asked, looking at Casey. 'Why are the Feds looking for you, and why the hell would you bring the female?'

'The female?' Rebecca replied. 'Really Jake?'

She was acting like I'd just insulted her, but she didn't understand. It doesn't matter what you know, or if you're smart or strong. The West End, the whole damn city is no place for a girl. Rebecca couldn't survive here, and if she did, she'd end up wishing she didn't. I'd have tried explaining it to her, but the words weren't coming to me.

'It wasn't our idea,' Michael answered, defensively. 'Becky knows Italian and some Latin. She also knows everything about church protocols, so she convinced us to bring her with us. We were supposed to meet the nuncio and take him to Fr. Kowalski's cathedral, but when we got there his escorts were dead and the nuncio was gone.'

'Fr. Kowalski's cathedral?' I asked. 'You talking about Old Joe?'

'Yeah, Fr. Joseph Kowalski, *your worship*.' Casey interrupted. 'It's a religious title. Try showing some respect.'

Casey was one of those guys that sounds like he's calling you an idiot, no matter what the hell he's saying. I didn't know why he was riding my ass, but I'd had enough.

'Open your mouth again, asshole, and I'll stick that shotgun up your ass, sideways.'

'Any time you're ready, *your holiness*.'

The second I stood up, Becky moved in between us.

'Guys, please!' she said softly. 'This isn't helping.'

If I was better at talking with people, or if I wasn't nervous about getting her and her idiot friends out of the city, I might have handled things better. I was pissed, and I glared back at him.

'I don't need this,' I grumbled, moving to the patio.

'Where are you going?' Becky asked

'It stinks in here. I'm gonna get some air.'

When I looked out, I saw two Feds posted on the corner, on opposite sides of the street. They were facing away from the compound so I pulled my knife and jumped over to my balcony. I didn't really leave the cave just to get some air. I needed to check things out and find out what the Feds were up to.

My apartment was ok, and the lower floors of the building checked out. The Feds were still all over the street, but there was also a guy standing guard outside the back door. The Feds must have thought we made it out of the building, and I guess he was there in case we came back. The old women were dead like I'd figured, but I found myself getting angry when I saw them. The older one, the one that always wore a knitted gray thing on her shoulders, looked like she was asleep when they found her. Stuff like that never bothered me before, but I was suddenly pissed about it. There's something senseless and ugly about killing someone who wasn't a threat, someone who couldn't possibly defend herself. It may have been because I was nervous and tired, but I remember feeling different about everything I saw that day, like something had changed inside me. It was a hard feeling to ignore, even for me, but I put it aside and started back upstairs.

Everyone jumped when I landed on the balcony and stepped into the little cave apartment, but once I got inside everyone was quiet. It felt a little unnatural, and I figured that Becky must have bitched out Casey while I was gone.

I told them that we could go back to my place, and we carefully moved to my apartment again. With all the Feds out front, I wasn't taking any chances. First, I carried the backpacks over myself before coming back to help Becky and the guys. They were still giving me the silent treatment, and once everyone got settled, Becky touched my arm.

'Jake, can I talk to you?'

I looked at Casey and Michael, but they wouldn't look back at me.

'Sure.'

She started moving into the kitchen, but I opened the door to the hall.

'I got a better place.'

At the end of my hall there's a door with a sign on it. In large black letters it says *LAUNDRY* and in smaller letters there's a list of *rules for considerate neighbors*. I've always found it kind of funny. The door looks like the laundry room doors downstairs, but this one leads outside and onto the collapsed roof that used to sit high above the back of my building. I opened the door and watched the surprise in Becky's eyes when she saw the bright sunshine.

'This is my backyard. Watch your step.'

There was a drop of about a foot, and I jumped down and reached back to help her. It was nice getting my hands on her again. She was fascinated, like when she first saw my apartment, and she walked over the slanted floor and over to my snares.

'This is amazing! You trap things here, don't you?'

'Yeah, the compound processes food three times a week, and the smell attracted animals. I get crumbs and stuff from their dumpsters and use it as bait. On most days, I can get as many birds as I want, and I usually get about a dozen squirrels or coons a week.'

She turned toward me, took a deep breath, and became serious again. It was the first time since this morning that she didn't look like she was afraid of me.

'Jake, please don't be angry with Casey. Nothing has gone like we planned, and none of us expected the city to be so—'

She stopped and restarted.

'We're all a little frightened, and when Casey gets nervous he acts—'

'Like a dick?' I interrupted, smiling.

'Yeah,' she laughed. 'But he's a good person. You should give him a chance.'

'So, tell me why the Feds are so interested in you guys.'

20

'I'm not sure, exactly. The Feds aren't like this in the country,' she explained, 'but after last night, I think the Feds may be looking for you too.'

It didn't bother me that the Feds would want me, but I was surprised that they'd want Rebecca. Becky and her friends were the most unthreatening people I'd ever seen. The guys were practically lame.

'Why? What'd you do?'

'I think it's because of what we believe. We're what the Feds call *Churchers*. We believe in God. We pray and follow a faith.'

From the tone of her voice I could tell that Becky thought that she'd completely answered my question, but I wasn't getting it.

'So?'

'We're too young to remember,' she explained, 'but before the war, the government controlled religions and how they could be practiced. Religions were regulated as belief systems. Most of Christianity, Judaism, and some others were classified as intolerant faiths. The government alone decided what behavior was good or bad, and what was normal. The groups that didn't agree were labeled as hate groups. The Fed networks stirred up the people, and lots of our churches were attacked and burned. Our faithful bishops, priests, and deacons were arrested. They said it was for their own protection, but most of them were never seen again.'

I was following what she was saying but the sun was on her, and the way she looked was distracting. You could tell with one glance that Becky belonged in sunshine. As she talked she held her hand above her eyes to shield them from the light, but I could still see a few freckles, not a lot of them, just a couple around her nose.

'It was terrible, and we heard that it was much worse in the cities,' she went on. 'When the tribulation ended, things started getting back to normal in the country. A few churches have reopened, and the Feds don't bother us anymore. We knew that the cities were still bad, but we never expected it to be like this. We never expected—'

While she was still talking, I reached up and grabbed the thing in her hair. It was cool, blue and rubbery, and it held her hair back.

Her hair was soft and it glided through my fingers.

'Darn it, Jake! Are you listening?'

'Yeah, sure.'

She looked sad, and suddenly a little angry.

'Don't you get it?' she asked. 'There's so much I need to tell you. We're afraid for our lives. We've been praying about it all afternoon.'

'Praying about it?' I laughed.

'Of course! Casey and Mike don't know if they can trust you. They're not even sure if—'

'Do *you* trust me?' I interrupted.

'Yeah,' she said with a smile returning. 'But I honestly don't know why.'

'Good. Cause I'm thinking we might have got off to a bad start,' I explained. 'Maybe I shouldn't have gone for you like I did.'

'Ya think?!'

'You don't have to worry, Becky. I'll make sure you get home.'

She let out a sigh and stared back at me. The sunlight was making her eyes greener.

'Thank you,' she said softly. 'And the guys too?'

'I guess.'

I didn't realize it, but my hand was still on her shoulder, sampling the softness of her hair. Her hand came up and shoved it away.

'And keep your hands to yourself!'

If she wouldn't have said that, I might have tried harder to keep my hands off her, at least for a while, but when we got back to the door I helped her step up into the hallway again. When I put my hand on her ass and pushed her up, she spun around and glared at me.

'Hey!' she objected. 'What did I just say?'

22

'I was only helping you up.' I grinned. 'Trust me.'

THE DIVERSION

When we got back to the others, Casey and Michael were staring out at the street, watching more trucks arriving. There were Feds on every corner now, as far as the eyes could see, and there was a lot of activity at the cathedral. Both of the guys looked nervous and a little pale, and I knew they were worried about getting home. I guess I could have said something to make them feel less anxious and take their minds off the Feds, but I didn't. It's not like I was trying to be an asshole, but now that I think about it, I wasn't trying very hard *not* to be an asshole either. You could feel tension in the air, and although Becky looked like she was handling everything alright, I think she wanted to get everybody talking again.

'Is anybody hungry?' she asked, reaching for her backpack.

Michael shook his head, and Casey just kept staring out at the street. It was hard to believe they weren't hungry because I was starving.

'Yeah, what ya got?'

It turned out that Becky had all kinds of stuff in her backpack. She had strips of dried meat and hard pieces of bread that were soft on the inside. It was all excellent and I wolfed down everything she gave me, but then she pulled out something amazing, wrapped in a shiny metal kind of paper. It was the most incredible food I've ever had! It had a fun gritty feel in my mouth, but it was also sweet and delicious. She called the stuff *cornbread*, and I'm not kidding, I know people who'd kill to get their hands on something that good.

'This stuff is unbelievable!' I said, talking with my mouth full.

Becky and the guys weren't expecting me to like it so much because when I looked up they were all laughing at me. I didn't care though. It was enough to break the tension and they didn't look so nervous anymore.

'Jake?' Mike started. 'Becky says that you can get us outta here.'

'I can get you out of the city,' I said, chewing. 'But I won't know my way around once we're out.'

'I can handle that,' Casey said. 'We're heading south, but we left the boat about a mile north of here, where the lake meets the river.'

'The boat?'

'Yeah,' Michael spoke up. 'If the rain holds off and the current isn't bad, we can be home in a day and a half.'

I'd never been on a boat before, and to be honest, I wasn't looking forward to it. Learning how to swim had never been an option for me, and the way I saw it, a lake or river was just a huge wet monster waiting to swallow my ass and drown me. But after thinking about it, the idea of heading north wasn't bad. If I could create a little diversion out front, all we'd have to do was get past the Fed at the back door and we'd be home free. It would have been worse going south, past the cathedral. There's a lot more city that way, and we'd have to avoid the gangs. I shoved the last piece of cornbread in my mouth.

'Alright,' I said, standing up. 'I'm going downstairs to keep watch. There's a Fed guarding the back door. I'll be back before dark, and we'll come up with a plan.'

I looked at Becky.

'Thanks, that food was amazing. Try to sleep if you can.'

When I got downstairs I found a spot by the back stairs where I could sit on the floor with my back to the wall. It was a good place to think and keep an eye on things. The hours passed and the shadow of my feet on the railing moved left to right, along the charred wallpaper and over the broken pictures on the wall. You might think that I'd get bored, sitting there so long, but I wasn't. It was easy to think about Becky and her friends, and I was a little pumped about getting them home. If you haven't figured it out by now, I had it bad for Becky by then. It was more than that, though. It's a strange feeling, knowing that people are counting on you, and I don't think I'd ever felt that before. Everything was different and a little more intense. Suddenly I was in the middle of a great adventure, and it was my turn to do something.

The shadows were nearly gone, and there was just enough twilight left to see the elevator doors when I started back upstairs. Everyone was already standing and nervously holding their backpacks, and Becky smiled when she saw me and said, 'Hi.' As I look back on it now, maybe Casey and Michael were surprised that I came back.

Remember how I said that there's no time to think about stuff when it's happening? Well, right about then, my brain was moving faster than I ever remember it. I went into the bathroom and opened the little door under the sink. I kept some gasoline there in an old plastic bottle that says *Mountain Dew*. I lifted the lid to the busted shitter and grabbed my spare knives. They're old and nicked up, but they're too good to leave, so I slipped them in my pockets as I moved back into the front room.

'You got any room in there?' I asked Becky, nodding at her backpack.

'Sure.'

I grabbed the two pictures on my fireplace and handed them to her. She slipped them into her backpack, and looked up at me, expecting something else.

'Is that all you're taking?' she asked, surprised.

'Yeah, I sent everything else on ahead of us, with the housekeeping staff.'

She grinned, but everyone else had lost their sense of humor.

'Listen up,' I said, holding up the bottle. 'We need a little diversion on the street so I'm gonna torch one of their jeeps. When you hear noise out front, count to fifty and go downstairs and out through the back. Cross the street and head straight through the alley. If I'm not there yet, keep going north. I'll catch up with you when I can.'

I noticed Casey had the gun in his hands.

'And if anything gets in your way, *kill it*.'

I was already at the door when I heard Becky say, 'Wait!'

We were losing light fast, and I didn't want them moving down the stairs in complete darkness.

'What?!'

I've read that people who are nervous or scared can act funny, and I guess it's true because all three of them joined hands. They drew something on themselves, like a t with their right hand, just like the old man had done when he gave me the ring. Becky grabbed my hand just as Casey started mumbling something about a heavenly father and keeping us safe. They did the t thing again, and they all said 'amen' at the same time. There was just enough light for me to see their faces, and when they saw me glaring at them, they looked at me like I was the one who was crazy.

'Can we go now?!'

It's not that I've got anything against praying. I remember my mom used to do it, but hell, there's a time and place for everything.

I think the delay might have jinxed us too because I had a terrible time with my part of the plan. First, the guy who was guarding the back door was gone. I didn't know if he was coming back or not, and I was worried he'd come back just as Becky and the others were leaving. It took me longer than I expected to get across the street too, avoiding all the extra Feds. When I finally made it across, all the jeeps had moved to the front of the compound. Whatever the reason, things weren't starting out very well.

Sometimes you just have to improvise, and I finally got a diversion started. It wasn't exactly how I planned it, and I had to run a lot farther to safely cross the street again, but at least the plan was in motion. There was lots of shouting coming from the street now, and most of the Feds were already heading toward the chaos.

I was running as fast as I could, all the way down 9th. I was supposed to join the group on the other end of the alley, but since I was late, I half-expected them to be gone already. When I arrived, I heard something in the alley and I stopped. I held my breath to hear better and poked my head around the corner. Standing in the glow of the Fed's flashlight, I could see Becky and the others with their hands in the air.

It was probably the Fed from the back door, and I don't know why he wasn't shooting, but I had to act quickly and carefully. When a guy's got a gun pointed at people, you can't just kill him. The gun could go off and hurt somebody. He was about thirty feet away, and I started moving toward him.

There's only one place to aim a knife in that situation, and when the blade hit the back of the Fed's knee, he did exactly as I expected. He let out a groan and lurched backward in agony. I was behind him a second later with another knife, to grab his gun and finish him. He hit the floor at the same time as his flashlight, and it bounced to a stop pointing at his face. I forgot that Becky and the guys had a thing against killing, and I was surprised that they just stood there staring at him. Even after I flipped him over and got my knife back, they stood there like they were in shock. I finally grabbed Casey and shook him.

'Why didn't you kill him?' I demanded, looking down at his gun.

He looked embarrassed, and I shoved him out into the street.

'Wake up and move!'

As Michael passed me I handed him the Fed's gun. I took the flashlight for myself, and after turning it off, we ran from there all the way to the corner of Ontario. It was a good half-mile run, and I was surprised that there weren't any Feds around. It seemed to me that the Feds must have known that Becky and her friends came up from the south, and they were expecting us to go back that way.

We crossed Ontario Street and I pointed to the entrance to the train station at 6th. Michael got there first and started down the stairs, but he stopped cold. The moon was up, but the stairwell was a black hole, and I had to turn the flashlight on again. The guys weren't very light on their feet, stampeding down the metal stairs, and I had to tell them to shut up. When we got down to the platform, I huddled everybody together and turned the light off. We waited and I watched the street above for a light, a sound, or any sign that we'd been followed. After a minute or two, the only sound was from everyone breathing heavy. We made good time from the alley and everybody was winded.

To give you a better idea of where we were, I'd better explain that train station at 6th isn't like the nice underground station at Madison, or the big ones closer to downtown. The station at 6th is just a shitty little platform about thirty feet below the street. If it was underground, it might have been useful to the gangs, or for old people to live there, but it was out in the open and overgrown with weeds. We couldn't see much in the darkness, but there were tracks running parallel the platform, and another set of tracks off to our left.

'We can rest here a minute,' I said, taking a knee.

I pointed to the other set of tracks.'

'The freight tracks over there turn north ahead, and they lead all the way out to the shipyard and the lake. It's only a short walk from there to the river.'

We all took a seat on the long bench facing the city. We were safe for the moment, in the train-track valley below the roads, and I wanted to wait until our eyes were adjusted to darkness before moving on. On both sides of us, steep grassy slopes led up the backs of the broken building. We could see the moon to our right, and reflected in the high windows on our left. Even with an adrenalin buzz, it was peaceful and kind of cool.

'Jake?' Becky asked, interrupting my thoughts.

'Yeah.'

'You said that you were going to create a diversion,' she went on, 'and burn one of their jeeps?'

I nodded. 'Uh huh.'

'When the shouting started, I looked out front. One of the Feds was on fire. He was running down the street screaming and burning! It was horrible and...'

Her voice trailed off, and I could see her looking at me in the moonlight.

'I have to ask,' she resumed. 'You didn't really—'

'Yeah,' I interrupted. 'I couldn't find a jeep!'

I'm not sure why she asked the question, and you'd think she could have figured that one out for herself, but we sat silently in the darkness for another minute without saying a word. I was about to get up and start everyone moving again when I heard Casey's voice.

'Becky?' he asked with a laugh. 'Promise me that I can be there when you introduce the new bishop to the parish.'

HUFFERVILLE

Off in the distance, I could see fog moving into the valley, an ankle-deep mist reflecting the gray light of the moon. A real fog might have helped us stay out of sight, but this one was thin and close to the ground. When I saw Michael holding the gun I gave him, I remembered that a few minutes ago Casey got everybody captured, without even firing a shot.

'Mike? You know how to use that?' I asked.

'Yeah, it's a nine-millimeter carbine, military issue. I've fired one before.'

It was a good answer. Hell, I never knew that piece had an *official* name before.

'OK, listen up,' I said, turning to the others.

'Stay close behind me and watch for dogs. If the fog gets any worse, we won't be able to see them till they're on us. And don't shoot unless you have to, it'll attract the Feds.'

There's lots of other stuff I should have said, but at the time nothing else was coming to me. We climbed off the platform and moved over to the freight tracks. It wasn't easy going in the dark cause the ground was uneven and covered with gravel. Moving as a group is always slower, but the others were keeping up pretty well. As we moved on, the buildings above us were growing shorter, and it was hard to say if we were climbing out of the valley, or if the world around us was shrinking down to our level. The freight tracks headed off northwest, but we followed the fence along Nobottom Road. I knew a shortcut to the river.

Behind us, we could see lights from the city, and beneath the mist, we were finally walking on concrete again. The grassy valley fed into an old plant that used to make chemicals, and we were suddenly walking between gigantic white and rust colored tanks. Some of them were hundreds of feet high, and they had their own fire escapes going all the way to the top. We could see the glow of fires, starting about ten or twenty feet off the ground, and going all the way to the top of the steel cages around us.

I saw two huddled figures heading slowly toward us. I almost pulled a knife, but it turned out to be nothing but an old couple, an old guy with his arm around a woman. They must have thought we were Feds because they freaked when they saw us and ran off toward the city. I remember that the old woman was injured and couldn't run very well. They were probably going to one of the underground train stations, like Madison, where the old ones live. I've only been down to Madison once and I couldn't wait to get the hell out of there. It smelled funny and it's too weird seeing so many old people in one place. Some of the old ones must be pretty smart though because even though their old and weak, they still manage to stay alive. We watched them hurry off into the darkness until they disappeared into the mist. A few minutes later the silence was broken again by some coyotes howling back behind us. Becky was right behind me and she let out a little gasp.

'They're only coyotes,' I told her. 'Wild dogs don't make any sound.'

'I know, it just startled me,' she explained softly, 'It sounds like a baby crying, doesn't it?'

'Yeah.'

I'd never heard a baby cry before, but I didn't want to say so. Yeah it was a lie, but I didn't want to look any more *different* than I looked already. It sounded like something I probably should have known about, and I guess I didn't want to look stupid in front of her.

The fog around us was getting thicker as we moved north. I

remember cussing about it more than once because it was the damnedest fog I'd ever seen. It was like we were in a bottle slowly filling up with smoke. Hey, I'm no expert on fog, but this one was up to our waist like we were wading through water, and we could still see the moon and stars above us. There were two tall mounds of gravel off in the distance, and they stuck up out of the fog and blocked out the stars on the horizon. I felt a slight tugging at my shirt, and when I looked back, I realized it was Becky. Since the coyotes scared her, she'd been holding onto me as we walked along.

On the other side of the gravel, the lake was coming into view, and it was my turn to be scared. There's something frightening about the lake at night. It was even spookier with the fog and in some places, you couldn't tell where the land ended and the water started. The mist looked like a thin cloud, barely covering the bottomless hole in the universe. I'd never let Becky or the guys know that I was nervous, but I was told to write down everything, so I thought I should mention it. It seemed to me that Becky and the others were actually pumped at seeing the lake ahead. It meant that they were suddenly closer to home.

We were just about in the center of the plant, and we could see faces around some of the fires up above us. We could see figures walking at the base of the stairways, and someone walking toward us.

'Are there people here?' Becky whispered, doubtingly.

'Just Huffers.'

'Huffers?' Mike asked.

'Yeah, they're the low-lifes that live here. They inhale the shit in these tanks to get high. They're skin and bone, and they walk around like zombies, but they're harmless. They'll steal anything they can get their hands on though, so stay clear of them.'

I laughed and remembered, 'The guys in the gangs call this place Hufferville.'

I could feel Becky getting a better grip on the back of my shirt, and I can't say I blame her. Hufferville is a creepy place, and if you're not careful your imagination can play tricks on you. The first time I walked through here at night, I almost thought I could feel their eyes on me, and for a while, I thought I was being followed. As we kept walking north, one of them walked up to us and stopped. He was tall and skinny, with long hair and no teeth.

'Hey man. Got anything to eat?'

I didn't answer because I heard something coming from the valley behind us. It was an odd sound that I'd never heard before. Mike figured it out before I did.

'Are those dogs?' he asked, turning toward the noise.

We listened for a sec and Casey asked, 'I thought you said they don't bark?'

'Wild dogs don't bark when they hunt,' I answered. 'Those aren't wild dogs. The Feds must be tracking us, and their close!'

I'd heard of the Feds using dogs to track people, but I'd never seen it happen before. When I turned back again, the Huffer was still standing there.

'Hey man, I got a sister,' he offered. 'If you got some food, we—'

I'd had enough of the guy, so I spun around and kicked him in the face. He fell back and out of our way, and we were running toward the lake before he hit the ground. It was suddenly crazy, knowing the Feds were so close, and even the gentle Churchers didn't care that I took the Huffer out that way. If you've never seen one, Huffers are filthy and disgusting, and you don't wanna touch one if you can avoid it.

'So, where's the boat?' I asked.

'We left it in the woods,' Mike answered. 'There's a park just inside the mouth of the river. We were told to leave it there, and backtrack down the river to the back of the cathedral.'

Whoever gave him those instructions must have known the city pretty well. He had to be talking about Wade Park. It's the most desolate place in the city. The river smells so bad from the chemicals there that you can't take it for more than a few minutes. It's a smart place to hide something, and backtracking along the riverbank was smart too. By taking that route, they'd avoid

Hufferville, the Feds and any of the gangs.

I figured we were only half a mile away or so from the boat, but the barking was getting louder, and you can only go so fast when you can't see the ground. When I looked back, I could see Fed flashlights getting closer. We didn't have more than a minute or two and the dogs would be on us. Our only chance was to move faster, which wasn't going to happen, or to slow the Feds down.

I started dropping back, and I reached out to Mike.

'Give me the piece,' I said, 'and get Becky to the boat. I'm gonna—'

'No!' he said. 'We can't risk it.'

'Risk what?!' I shouted, 'Don't be an assho—'

'He's right!' Casey interrupted. 'You're the important one. This will all be for nothing if you don't make it back!'

In a few seconds, the Feds were gonna let the dogs loose and we'd lose any chance of ever seeing their damn boat, but these people weren't getting it! To make things worse, there was no time to explain it to them. I had to think of something fast.

'OK,' I said, 'When I say so, turn and start shooting. Make a lot of noise, but save some rounds if you can.'

I turned the flashlight on and set it on the ground facing straight up. The light made the fog around us light up, and it gave the Feds something to target. I caught up with the others a second later, and shouted 'Now!'

Mike and Casey both turned and opened fire, and the night exploded with the sounds of gunfire. It was like a war just started, and just like I'd hoped, the Feds stopped and fired back at the only light they could see. Sound travels better in fog, and the shotgun blasts sounded like cannons.

I shouted, 'OK, go!' and we all took off toward the park again.

The dumbass Feds kept shooting for at least another minute, plenty of time for us to reach the park. The air was toxic and smelly, but with all the adrenaline in our systems, we made it to the woods without anybody puking. Even without much light, Casey found the boat by some droopy dead trees where he'd left it. The boat was bigger than I expected, but it was amazingly light. There was a lot of stuff still in the boat too, but Casey and Mike got it to the river in seconds. Everybody climbed in except Casey and me, and he looked at me like he expected me to jump in too. I remember thinking that a boat that light couldn't possibly hold four people and all that other shit too, but I took a deep breath of the shitty air and climbed in.

Becky grabbed my arm and pulled me down into a seat next to her. I felt like I should be doing something, but all I could do was watch Casey push the boat out onto the water and climb inside. Mike handed him an oar and they started rowing the boat out into the nothingness around us. The fog was so thick by then that we could only see a few feet in front of us. Nobody said a word, and none of us realized how close the Feds had come until a few seconds later. Even though the dog's barking was still a little ways off, we could hear voices on the shore, as if the Feds were only a few yards away. As I remember it now, there must have been another team of Feds hunting us from the northeast. When we heard their voices we all jumped, and Becky grabbed my arm again.

That reminds me, if you ever get a chance to ride in a boat, I can tell you that they're a shitty way to get anywhere. They rock back and forth whenever somebody moves, and they're so damn unstable that you don't dare stand up when you're close to the sides because you'd fall right out! But, since I couldn't do anything but sit next to Becky and think, I started to realize something.

The strange fog I'd been cussing about had been more help than I ever could have imagined. It kept us hidden on the river, but it wasn't so thick that we couldn't still stick our heads up to see enough to steer. The guys kept rowing and after about ten minutes, the air didn't stink anymore. We could hear crickets chirping, so I knew we were already a good distance from Wade Park. We came around the bend and I recognized the old warehouse on Riverside. There was too much light in the sky around us, and I stood up to see what was going on. I saw the old cathedral, burning in the distance.

There were Feds on the shoreline with their flashlights pointing out on the water, but they were too far off to see us through the fog. As I looked on, the guys stopped rowing and everybody paused to watch the cathedral burn.

Every day for the last few years, the cathedral had been my horizon, as much a part of the world as mountains and stars. Now, all at once it was a ball of fire, with flames leaping fifty feet into the night air, and smoke pouring out of the broken colored windows. The whole roof was rolling in flames, and as we looked on, the part next to the bell tower collapsed, shooting more sparks into the sky. Seeing it burn made me feel shitty inside, and maybe a little pissed.

Nobody said anything, and after a few seconds, the guys went back to rowing. I could see Becky's face in the light. I thought she'd be happy, now that she was finally getting out of the city, but I think she felt shitty too. There were tears rolling down her cheeks, and when she saw me watching, she sat down and turned away.

JODIE

I've read somewhere that you can get used to anything if you do it long enough, but I can honestly tell you that that's a load of crap. There's no way I'll ever get used to being in a boat. It wouldn't have been so bad, but the last thing I wanted to do was just sit there on my ass feeling worthless, and I couldn't even see where the hell we were going. Just for something to do, I picked up Mike's gun and put it in my lap, but it didn't make me feel any better.

While I sat there thinking, something about the last few hours started bothering me. The guys were rowing only a few feet in front of us, so I leaned toward Becky so they couldn't hear me.

'Can I ask you something?'

'Of course,' she whispered back.

'When we started out tonight, I thought I was getting you guys out of the city. But after Hufferville, the guys were acting like they were getting me out. What's that all about?'

'I think you won them over.'

It was too dark to see my face, but she must have known that I didn't understand.

'When we started out, the guys had their doubts about you,' she explained. 'But now they believe in you. You saved everyone's life tonight, Jake.'

She nudged me with her shoulder.

'We came to the city to bring back a bishop,' she laughed. 'You're not what any of us were expecting, but maybe God gave us exactly what we needed.'

Casey stopped rowing and I could see him turn toward us.

'Hey, Jake?' he started, 'That Fed in the alley—'

He stopped to think.

'He came up on us from behind,' he went on. 'I would have shot, but we didn't see him in time.'

You could tell by his voice that what happened in the alley was still bugging him, but I hadn't thought about it since we left the valley.

'Forget it, man. We made it out, didn't we?'

He nodded, and a second later, he started rowing again.

I watched the sky become darker and darker as we moved south. A slight wind had kicked up by then, just enough of a breeze to wash the fog away, and I could make out the jagged banks of the river. Everyone was tired, and the sound of the oars against the water was rhythmic and kind of sleepy. I was still too wound up to relax, but Becky sat down on the floor of the boat and propped her backpack up behind her like a pillow. We were coming to a place where the river wound to the right and became narrow, and even in the dark, I could see rocks in the water ahead. I might have thought seriously about panicking, but nobody else seemed to give a shit about them. Mike pulled out a flashlight, the biggest flashlight I've ever seen, and when he set it into a mount on the front of the boat, the water in front of us lit up.

I almost said something about it too. It wasn't that long ago when we were being hunted by Feds, and a light like that would have given us away. But it was so quiet, and the darkness was so deep, that I felt that like we were the last four people on earth. The guys steered through the rocks like it was nothing, and when the boat cleared the bend, the river was a lot wider. It was a good thing that I kept my mouth shut. Although they weren't much use in the city, out here on the water Casey and Mike knew what they were doing. Once we got to the center of the river they put the oars away, and Mike moved around behind me.

I must have been too busy to notice it before, but there was something hanging off the back of the boat, and Mike lowered it into the water. It was hard to see what he was doing with it, but he moved something on top, pulled a little rope, and an engine screamed to life. I jumped to my feet and nearly fell out of the damn boat.

'No shit!' I exclaimed. 'You got gasoline? Working gasoline?'

Casey turned and laughed, and Becky sat up when I jumped.

Before I say anything else, I'd better explain that gasoline isn't all that hard to find. Hell, if you wanted some, you could get it from a thousand abandoned cars in the city. Most of it is old and sludgy though. Some of it's ok for starting fires, but it won't run anything. Working gas, gas that hadn't gone bad and could run an engine, was only available to the Feds.

'Yeah,' Mike laughed. 'We bought this from the Feds back home, but we can make our own too. It isn't good enough for big engines yet, but every week we're getting better at it.'

'Years back,' I remembered, 'we could get bad gas working again by adding rubbing alcohol and lighter fluid. But you guys can actually make it yourselves?!'

'Sure,' he nodded. 'The world's a lot different outside the city, Jake.'

I sat back down, and in the glow of the light, I saw Becky smiling up at me from her makeshift bed. The low hum of the engine was a sleepier sound than the oars made, and a few minutes later, I watched Becky fall asleep. The little motor was too cool though, and there was no way I could sleep without driving the boat first. The guys took turns sleeping and driving, and it was late by the time I took a turn. The motor could pivot back and forth, and by moving it left and right, you could move the ass-end of the boat, and point the front where you wanted to go. Boats are scary, but when you're driving they can be kind of fun. It was only a few hours till dawn and it was Casey's turn to drive again.

'You better get some sleep, Jake. We've got a stop to make in the morning.'

Staying awake all night was no accident. I figured that if I stayed up long enough, I'd fall asleep quickly and forget I was on the water. I sat on the floor in front of my seat and rested against a bag of clothes that Mike gave me. It was more comfortable than you'd expect, but when I dozed off, it was a crummy kind of sleep. You know the kind, when you're half in and half out, and it's like you can hear things around you? It was weird and restless, and I remember hearing the sound of the motor and Mike letting out a snore. There was suddenly a chill in the air, and I heard someone calling.

'Bishop?'

At first I didn't think that the voice was talking to me, but when I heard it again, I opened my eyes. Everything was the same, except for the shitty feeling in the air. Becky was asleep across from me, and Mike and Casey were now in the back of the boat, talking. They didn't hear it when the water began bubbling and foaming all around us. I looked out over the front and saw something black and muddy in front of us. Rising slowly from the water, it was in the shape of a man, except covered with gunk and mud. It stunk like burning plastic, and it was giving off smoke as if it was steaming hot. When I saw that the other guys weren't reacting to it, I knew that I was dreaming.

Even when you're dreaming, you act by instinct. I knew I was in a nightmare and one hell of a nightmare too, but I pulled a knife and I brought it up to throw.

'You're only dreaming, dear Bishop,' the voice said. 'You won't need your weapon.'

The slime oozed off of the thing, and I recognized him as he stepped onto the boat. I remember thinking how weird it was, that the boat didn't tilt or rock as he climbed on, not even slightly. It had been a long time since I thought about the asshole in the black hoodie but it was him, the same guy with the glowing eyes that watched the old man give me the ring. I kept telling myself it was all just a bad dream, but he was as real as anything I've ever seen.

When you're scared, really truly scared to death, you have two ways to play it. You can shut up and just watch things play out, or you can act like it's no big deal, and refuse to admit that you're about to shit yourself.

'So what the hell are you supposed to be?' I asked casually.

'Forgive the dramatic entrance, Bishop. I had to get your attention because I need to speak with you.'

When he pulled the hoodie back, I could see he'd been burned. His face wasn't scarred, naturally butt-ugly, but not actually injured. The whole left side of his head was kind of gone though, all crispy and mangled, and you could see that he was missing an ear. He sat down on the front of the boat, and I lowered my knife.

'You keep calling me *Bishop*,' I said, but it was more like a question.

'Of course,' he chuckled. 'Titles are everything. I wouldn't dream of not showing you the respect due your office. I've been known by a number of names and titles over the years, but you can call me Jodie.'

'Kind of a female's name, isn't it?'

He glared back at me for a sec, but then he smiled again.

'I can see that I'm going to have trouble with you, aren't I?'

I'd never met anyone in my life that was easy to hate, and I answered by glaring right back at the asshole.

'Very well,' he continued. 'Then you should know that these new friends of yours, these Churchers, are the last of their kind. I've worked too hard and too long to destroy them. Whereas they once covered the continent, from sea to shining sea, there are only five or six groups left in this land.'

It didn't matter that I knew I was dreaming. When he smiled, I felt like somebody pulled out my spine, and replaced it with packed snow.

'This remnant will be gone within the year, perhaps within mere weeks,' he resumed, 'and if you join them, then you will die too. And when *you* die, Bishop, I can assure you it will be slow and exquisitely painful. I will take the greatest care with you.'

'Like the little guy at the cathedral?'

'Precisely,' he nodded, still grinning, 'but not before you watch the others die before you.'

He fixed his eyes on Becky.

'Maybe we'll let Rebecca remain a while longer. After all, the gangs need their entertainment, don't they?'

I was growing so pissed that the little hairs on the back of my neck stood up, and I was squeezing the handle of my knife.

'You should have taken her when you had the opportunity, you know,' he sighed. 'Catholic bishops so rarely get to have any fun.'

Even if I could explain what I saw in those eyes I wouldn't write it down, but I can tell you that as he looked at Rebecca there was something filthy and grotesque and overwhelming. I felt myself coming out of my seat and going for the bastard's throat.

All at once the sun was in my eyes, and I realized that I was standing with a knife in my hand. I was awake, and so off-balance that if Mike hadn't grabbed me, I might have gone clean over the side of the boat.

'Hey, you ok?!' he exclaimed.

'Yeah,' I answered, 'must have been dreaming.'

I looked around for a sec trying to shake off the cobwebs before sitting back down. The air was clean and clear, with a pleasant kind of smell. We were in a narrower stretch of the river again, with nothing but trees on either side of us. By the looks of things I knew that the sun had been up a couple hours already. Becky had her backpack on her lap. It was open, and she had my pictures in her hands. She looked embarrassed when she saw me watching.

'I was getting ready to fix breakfast,' she apologized. 'I didn't mean to look at your things.'

'It's ok,' I said, rubbing my eyes.

She held up the picture of my old house.

'Are these your grandparents?'

I knew that the picture was of my parent's old house, but I never thought much about the two old people standing on the lawn.

'I don't know. Those pictures were on my mom's fireplace at home.'

'Well, the man has your eyes!'

Becky looked at the other picture, the one with Mom putting a shiny red thing on a Christmas tree. It wasn't a great picture, and you couldn't see all of her face, but she was smiling.

'She's beautiful,' Becky said softly. 'Is that your mom?'

'Yeah.'

Mike stopped the boat's engine, and the sudden lack of noise startled me. I must have been used to the sound of the motor, and maybe I was still a little spooked from my nightmare, but it felt foreign and strange with only the sounds of birds in the air. We were pointed to an opening in the trees, and I could see a clearing on the other side of the brush. It looked like a path ended there. An old tree was stretching over the river just ahead, and one of its branches leaned out over the water. A rope was hanging from a high branch, and the river was so calm and smooth that you could see its reflection mirrored on the water below.

As we were getting closer to the shore there was lots of moving around. Becky grabbed a canvas bag that was in the back by the gas cans, and Mike was up front with a rope in his hand. The boat was really rocking, and since I didn't have anything to do, I sat there in the center of the boat, holding onto my seat. Right before Mike jumped off onto the grass, I caught Becky staring at me. She looked surprised at first, but then her face blossomed into a big smile.

'Oh my Gosh! You're afraid of water, aren't you?!'

I'd have tried to deny it, but the guys were both looking at me now too, and by the smiles on their faces, they were really enjoying the idea. Mike pulled the boat up onto the bank, and I jumped out while they were both still laughing. I threatened to kill them, but it only made them laugh louder.

When we were all out, Mike and Casey dragged the boat all the way up onto the grass. They grabbed their backpacks and we all followed Becky over to where the path started. It looked like the path became a gravel road a few hundred feet ahead. It was overgrown and grassy now, and it wound off to our right in the distance.

Becky announced, 'This looks like a good a spot for breakfast.'

I was glad that somebody mentioned breakfast. We hadn't eaten anything since last night and I was hungry. She put her blanket and canvas bag down on the ground and said, 'Ready?'

'Yeah, I'm starved!'

I thought I'd answered for everybody, but Becky let out a sigh and smiled at me. She took my hand, and on her other side, Mike took hers. Like yesterday, just when I thought that we had a hundred better things to do, they started praying again.

Casey thanked God for getting us out of the city, he talked about God's goodness and mercy and then he grinned.

'And we thank you for our new friend and bishop, Jake.'

He added something about 'Christ our Lord, Amen' before doing the t thing again. By the looks on everyone's faces, I think they all felt better after praying, but I was still hungry.

Becky pulled a green blanket out of her bag, and I watched her spread it over the grass. Even in the morning, after sleeping on the damn boat, she looked amazing. I remember trying to shake the feeling I had, the feeling from my nightmare. I was still a little freaked by the dream, and in my mind I could still see that Jodie asshole in the boat, staring at her. As I watched Becky kneel down and try to get a fire going, I started thinking about how much I liked her.

My mind drifted back to our escape from the city, and I watched Casey and Mike for a while too. I wasn't having any luck at figuring them out though. Nobody had ever risked their own ass to save mine before, and even though they sucked at it, Mike and Casey did that last night. And although they had a thing against killing, when it came to finding a new bishop, they weren't afraid of dying either. It didn't make much sense to me.

I had nothing in common with these people, and I'd only known them for a day or so, but there was something fascinating about these Churchers. Whatever it was, I knew it was bigger than the Feds, or my dream, or the gangs and the city. For the first time, I remember getting a weird feeling that I still get sometimes, even today. It was a crazy, confusing feeling. All at once I didn't know whether I belonged to these people, or if maybe they belonged to me. Like I said, it doesn't make any sense, and I don't expect you to understand, but I wanted to mention it to you.

I suddenly had a thousand questions running through my mind, but one of them was bigger than the others.

'Becky?'

'Yes.' She turned to me.

'Why would the nuncio dude make *me* a bishop? And what's a bishop do?'

THE PUNISHED EARTH

Did you ever ask a question and suddenly it felt like the whole world turned to hear the answer? That's exactly what I was feeling, and although Mike was pretending to do something in his backpack and Casey was loading slugs into his sawdi, I knew that they were both waiting to see how Becky was going to answer.

'We don't know why the nuncio chose you, Jake,' she said, without looking up. 'Fr. Kowalski was supposed to be our new bishop, but after they were attacked, the nuncio must have changed his plans.'

Becky had a little wire grill set on the ground beside her. She was arranging twigs and kindling underneath it, but I could tell that she was busy thinking. She reached into her pink backpack and pulled out something that looked like a small candle and lit it with a match. It burned hotter than any candle, and a second later Becky had a pretty good fire burning under a coffeepot.

'As a practical matter,' Mike thought out loud. 'We need bishops to ordain priests. Our pastor is very old, and there's no one else to say Mass or administer the sacraments of the church.'

I didn't have a clue about what he'd just said. It was like listening to another language.

'Theologically,' Becky continued, 'the bishop's job and the

church's job is the same, to teach, govern and sanctify your people. The Church is responsible for the whole world, and your job is your diocese.'

'Am I supposed to know what that means?' I shrugged.

'No, but that's ok,' she replied with a laugh. 'Let's start with the teaching part. A bishop is the principal teacher in his diocese. You're responsible for preaching the Word of God to your people, Jake. It's your responsibility to make sure that the people teaching in your name, like priests and teachers, teach the truth.'

Becky paused to poke the fire.

'I run the school back home,' she resumed, 'and I teach everything from reading to catechism. Did anyone ever teach you anything about God, or the Church or the Bible?'

'I don't think so.' I admitted, 'But I've read lots of stuff.'

It was no lie. The best thing about living on the West End was that I learned to trap food there. When you don't have to spend the whole day rummaging around for something to eat, you can spend a lot of time reading, and I bet I read a thousand books over the last few years. In the city I knew as much as anybody, and I was eager to show off a little.

'I like books on history and war, and how stuff works,' I bragged. 'But I've read lots of classic shit too. I've read *The Iliad, Tom Sawyer,* and *Pet Cemetery.*'

Casey made a noise, trying to hold back a laugh, and Mike was laughing too. It always happens like that. Whenever you're trying especially hard to not make an ass out of yourself, you say something stupid without realizing it. I shot a look their way, and I was about to tell them to shut the hell up when Becky started talking again.

'You've never had *any* religious instruction?' she pressed. 'From your mom or dad, maybe?'

In my own defense, it's not like I was completely stupid about religion. I knew who God was, and that he made everything and all that. I knew a little about Jesus too. It's just that Becky and the guys were experts, and I hadn't thought about God since Mom died. I didn't want to say anything dumb again, and the more I thought about it, the more I figured I should just keep my mouth shut.

'What are you worried about, Sis?' Mike asked. 'He'll learn on the job, while he's doing it. The parish will understand. '

'No they won't!' Becky argued. 'They've been waiting a long time, and they have expectations of what a bishop looks like, and how he talks, and what he knows.'

'So why didn't you just find somebody that knows all that stuff?' I asked.

'It's not that easy,' Becky sighed. 'In our church, bishops trace their lineage back to the apostles of Christ. They must be chosen. It's one of the ways we make sure that they're qualified to teach others.'

Teach others?

I brought my hand up to get a good look at the ring on my finger. In my mind I could see the old man putting it there, and the way he smiled at me. The nuncio was older than dirt and half-dead. It was looking more and more like he'd made a mistake. If I lived to be a hundred, how was I ever gonna learn the things that Becky was talking about?

'Jake's our new bishop,' Casey said impatiently. 'The parish will just have to deal with it. What choice do we have?'

'I don't know, but we have to think of something,' Becky answered. 'It isn't fair to them, and it isn't fair to Jake.'

The coffee pot was rumbling, and it smelled so good that we all started thinking about breakfast again. Becky pulled out more of the hard rolls, biscuits and dried meat from her bag. They all prayed *again* before we ate, and she poured coffee for everyone in red plastic mugs. I hadn't had coffee in forever, and I didn't remember it being so bitter before, but it was good for dunking the biscuits. There wasn't any cornbread left though. I must have had the last of it before we left the city.

The morning was already warm, and a nice breeze was moving through the trees. You could still smell the river a little from where we were, but it wasn't a bad smell. In fact, everything here smelled great, like tall grass and flowers. It wasn't like the city at all, and no matter what direction I looked, there was nothing but trees, wildflowers, and dandelions. We packed everything up and started walking down the gravel road. I remember being tired and a little spacey, but not too tired to notice that Mike left the carbine in the boat. Casey had his gun slung over his back, and wherever we were heading, the guys weren't expecting to run into any trouble there. My extra blades were back by the boat, but my best knives were in my back pocket as usual.

'So, where we going?' I asked.

'There's a town ahead,' Becky answered. 'Casey thinks there's a drug store there where we might find medicine and batteries.'

As Becky finished talking we reached a clearing in the trees, and we could see the backs of houses in the distance. They were big houses with fences and patios. It only took a minute to walk through the backyards to the street, but with each step, the scene in front of me became more bizarre. I was weirded out, and at first I didn't even realize what was wrong, but when it hit me I was completely blown away. The houses, the whole damn street was perfect. *None of it had burned!*

It's probably hard for you to imagine, but for someone who grew up in a burning city, this place was unbelievable. While I was growing up as a kid, I guess I just naturally assumed that everywhere else was burning too, and I never once thought that there were places that had escaped the chaos and the flames. My earliest memories were about living in a house like these, perfect little houses like the ones in my mom's pictures.

'What is this place?' I asked.

There must have been something in my voice because they all stopped walking and looked at me.

'It's just a town,' Becky answered, 'like a thousand little towns.'

She looked at the house I was staring at, and then at me again.

'Jake?' she added. 'What's wrong?'

I couldn't answer. Maybe Becky and the guys had seen all this a thousand times before, but we were suddenly in a world that I'd only read about, and a world I never thought I'd ever see. We were standing on a street surrounded by faultless little houses, unbroken homes in different colors and shapes as far as you could see. It was like the street was sleeping, waiting to be dusted off and used again. There were cars in driveways and in open garages. If it wasn't for the overgrown lawns, I might have thought that we'd traveled back in time. Up and down both sides of the street it was the same story, straight mailboxes, windows with drapes, screen doors without rips, and uncracked streetlights.

It was a world right out of my books, a place where people used to live, where all day long they'd be coming and going, talking over fences, or getting in their cars to go off to work and school. But as we looked on, none of that was happening. There were no people here to do those things. We could hear birds chirping and the wind in the trees, but I remember that it felt quiet. There was an odd silence that was numbingly cold in the warm summer air.

'What the hell happened here?'

Becky exchanged a surprised look with the guys before answering.

'The world was punished, Jake.'

'Come on, Sis,' Mike objected. 'We don't know that!'

'Really?' she shot back. 'Then what would you call it?!'

'The truth is,' Mike explained, turning to me, 'we don't know what caused it. We've heard lots of ideas, everything from a nuclear warhead to a comet hitting the earth, but when the darkness came, it killed everything it touched.'

'Just like it did in the city,' I acknowledged, 'Is it like this everywhere?'

'Almost everywhere,' Casey joined in. 'Some cities were wiped completely off the map, and others were left untouched, like this one. When it was over, the survivors gravitated to the cities. You know all about that, but there are also groups of believers, Churchers that live in the country. That's where we're going, to your parish.'

I was still freaking a little, and as I started walking up that first driveway, I heard Becky's voice from behind me.

'Michael, you guys go on ahead,' she said. 'We'll meet you right here when you get back. I wanted to talk with Jake about the parish anyway, and tell him what to expect when we get home.'

The guys headed off up the street, and Becky followed me up the stairs to the porch. I opened the screen door, and we stepped into the front of the house. Although the sun was pouring in from the windows, it was still musty and gray inside. There was a faint and familiar smell in the air too, a smell that I wasn't expecting to find in these perfect little homes.

There was a big painting on the wall of a girl in a red dress sitting at a bar, and a couch and chairs, and gray carpeting on the floors. It reminded me of my mom and dad's house and I couldn't keep from checking everything out. In the hall by the bathroom there were pictures, a family of four with sandy blonde hair. There were knick-knacks in a big glass cabinet and all kinds of furniture and TVs. I didn't notice at first, but Becky was checking everything out too. I got the feeling that she'd done this before. She went through all the cupboards and shelves of every room we went into, and once in a while she'd pick something up and slip it into her backpack.

The upstairs was perfectly preserved, and even the big mirrors in the bathrooms were unbroken. There were pictures on the walls here too, and as I checked out the bedrooms, I knew right away whose room belonged to who. In one room, the small bed was undone, and there were stuffed toys on the floor, an elephant and a monkey. The thick blanket on the bed had roaring dinosaurs in bright colors, dulled now by a fine coating of gray dust.

When we got to the kitchen, there were yellow paper lists and dusty pictures stuck to the refrigerator door with little magnets, and something that used to be bread sticking up and out of the toaster. There were dishes in the sink and on the counters, all covered in cobwebs.

'The city was already burning when the darkness came,' I thought out loud, 'but these people weren't expecting it. They were surprised when it came, weren't they?'

'Yeah,' she nodded. 'They didn't have a chance.'

I stepped past her, to the half-open door at the end of the counter. There were stairs on the other side leading down to a basement, and when I opened it that familiar smell hit me again, a little stronger this time. I took a step down, but when I looked back, Becky wouldn't follow me.

'What's wrong?'

'When it came, most of the people went into their basements to hide,' she said softly. 'That's usually where we find them. I don't go into basements anymore.'

Part of me still wanted to go down there to have a look around, but I guess I've lived in the city too long for that. Even in this dead silent world, I couldn't bring myself to leave Becky upstairs alone. She pulled a chair away from the table.

'Can we talk?' she asked. 'I need to tell you all about your parish and the people who are waiting to meet you.'

'Can we do it outside? This is creepy.'

We headed to the big glass doors that led to the patio, and I unconsciously put my hand in the small of Becky's back as we stepped outside. Putting my arm around Becky felt natural to me, but she gave me a funny look when I touched her.

The patio was made out of red wood, and there were chairs stacked over by the big windows, but I took a seat on the railing where I could be in the sun. Becky didn't sit down. She had that serious look on her face, and I knew that she was thinking.

'There's a lot to tell you,' she started. 'I don't know where to begin.'

It wasn't that I didn't care about what she had to say, but she was distracting me again. She looked tired today, and I think some of her makeup had rubbed off, but in the daylight, Becky was the prettiest thing in the world.

'The people of the parish have been waiting a long time to meet you, and they're going to love you,' she began, 'but they're expecting someone a lot older. You don't look or act like a bishop, or talk like a bishop, or—'

Becky stopped suddenly and her face lit up with a smile. She reached into her backpack and pulled out something she'd taken from one of the upstairs bathrooms. It was a little plastic bottle with a square lid, and she opened it and splashed some of the stuff on her hands. She set the bottle down and walked up to me.

'Here,' she said, patting the smelly stuff on my face. 'This is something called *aftershave.*'

She took a playful step backward and sniffed at the air around me.

'That's a little better,' she laughed, 'but you still don't smell like a bishop!'

Becky looked *too good*, and all at once I needed to get my hands on her again. I knew I had to be careful about it though. Becky was a special kind of female, and the last thing I wanted to do was scare the hell out of her again, like I did back in my apartment. I'd read about girls like her, and I quickly thought up a plan. Cautiously, and acting as refined and cultured as I could be, I grabbed her around the waist and pulled her into a kiss. I couldn't have been any slower or more careful about it, but she pulled away like she'd been stung by a bee.

'Darn it, Jake!' she shouted. 'Why'd you do that?'

'Couldn't help it. Why, didn't I do it right?'

I'll admit that I don't know shit about females, but I was beginning to think that there just wasn't any way to show a girl that you like her without making her angry. All of a sudden Becky was nervous and confused, and I was confused too. Hell, it wasn't like I tried to jump her again! Even after I went slow and was being all sophisticated about it, she was still mad at me. Apparently I'd screwed up again, and the whole thing was starting to piss me off.

'You did it fine, Jake,' she said, with an edge to her voice. 'But you're making this difficult for me. You can't be kissing me like that, and you can't put your arm around me when we're walking!'

'Why? You don't like it?'

'Of course, I—'

Becky stopped herself and took a deep breath.

'That doesn't matter. Bishops don't do that!'

'They do now.' I grinned.

'Jake, listen to me, and this is important!'

I'd never seen Becky look so serious before, not even when we were running from the Feds.

'When we get back to the parish,' she pleaded, 'you'll meet Fr. Doogan. He's our pastor and he'll explain everything about being a bishop. He'll tell you what you should do, and why you shouldn't do things like that. But until then, would you please promise me something?'

'Sure.'

'Promise me that when there are people around, *any people*, you will never put your arm around me, or touch me, or try to kiss me.'

'But why should—'

'Please!?' she interrupted. 'Could you just trust me on this?'

She looked awesome, with her sunshiny eyes looking up at me. I pulled her closer again and pretended to look around us.

'Ok,' I agreed, 'but it looks like we're alone now.'

I kissed her again, and I think I got it right that time. She didn't pull away. Even when I brought her really close, Becky just closed her eyes. After a little while she pulled back like she was dizzy or out of breath, and she rested her head on my chest. She stayed there a while too, and I gotta tell you it was the best feeling in the world. I was sure that Becky felt like I did, but I knew that something was still bugging her. You could tell from her voice that she was thinking.

'Jake, this may be hard for you to understand,' she started, 'but you need to know that we can never be—'

She stopped to take a breath.

'I know that you like me, and I apparently like you too,' she said, shaking her head, 'because you're gross and disgusting, and I keep letting you kiss me. But I don't want you to think that we—'

Becky was having trouble getting the words out, but I was

enjoying myself and I wasn't in the mood to talk anyway. I think she finally decided to talk about something else because her face changed, like another idea had come to her.

'We're changing our plans!' she announced excitedly, looking up at me again. 'I should have thought of this before, but we can't take you home just yet. If we're going to make this work, you'll need to learn some things first. We need to get you cleaned up and into some good clothes. I know a place where we can do that. It's on the far end of the parish and nobody will notice us there. While we're at it, we can teach you more about behaving like a bishop, so you make a good first impression.'

'First impression?'

'Yes, and you can meet Mariam,' she added, with a smile returning. 'She's my best friend and I know she'll help us.'

Becky's shirt had crept up a little in the back when I was kissing her, and I got my hand in there and pulled her closer. Her back was warm, sweaty and kind of exciting, and she felt amazing.

'So,' I said, changing the subject. 'How much time do you think we got before the guys get back?'

Becky was surprised by the question, and that I'd pulled her so close. Maybe I brought her too close because her face was getting red.

'There's nothing shy about you is there?!' she asked softly. 'You have to promise me something else, Jake. When we get home, you can't ever look at me like that.'

'Like what?'

'Like *that!*'

'Why?'

'I think it's illegal,' she sighed. 'If it isn't, it should be.'

THE RULE OF GOLD

It was a good half-hour before the guys got back, and if it had been up to me I'd have spent that time a lot differently, but Becky wanted to check out a few more houses. She did find more things for her backpack, but I was getting the feeling that she was just keeping busy so that I wouldn't kiss her again. Mike and Casey showed up right as we left the last house, and they started running toward us carrying lots of white plastic bags full of stuff.

'Jackpot!' Casey exclaimed, holding up one of his bags.

'Antibiotics?' Becky asked.

'Yeah, and steroids too,' he answered, 'fourteen packs, plus batteries, expectorant, and asthma inhalers!'

I didn't know it at the time, but Casey told me later that some medicines are like gasoline, and they go bad after a while. From the way that Becky took the news, I knew that the guys must have done pretty well. I took a couple of their bags to carry, and we all started walking back to the boat.

While we were walking, Becky broke the news about changing our plans. I was surprised at how the guys reacted. It instantly killed their good moods and they were pissed about it. Mike and Casey were more impatient to get home than I thought, and Becky had to convince them that I wasn't ready yet. She said that I could use some time to *mature socially*. Mike and Casey didn't care much about that, but once she brought up new clothes and getting me cleaned up, they were sold on the idea. While I listened to them arguing, I realized something about Becky that I hadn't seen before. For stuff like getting out of the city, Becky was ok with letting me call the shots and running things, but for stuff like this she was in charge, and she wasn't taking any crap from anybody.

Before we reached the gravel road by the river, I turned for one last look at Northwood Avenue, the perfect little street from out of the past. The more I thought about it, the more questions popped into my head. It seemed to me that the people who lived there had everything, and I wondered what they could have done to screw it all up.

'So, Becky,' I said, starting toward the river again. 'Why was the world punished?'

'Lots of reasons,' she answered, 'but I think it all comes down to one. We forgot about God.'

'Everybody?'

'No, not everyone, but in general the people of the world put their faith in everything *but* God. We stopped looking for him. We became self-centered, and without God's help we couldn't even tell right from wrong anymore.'

'Yeah,' Casey grumbled, 'and having a corrupt government didn't help!'

'Really?! You're still blaming the government?' Mike challenged him. 'We lived in a democracy. If the people weren't already selfish and corrupt, they wouldn't have elected assholes!'

It was the closest thing to cussing that I'd ever heard from a Churcher, and it made me laugh. I remember getting the feeling that this was a topic that they'd argued about before.

'The point is,' Becky continued, 'Godlessness crept into society at every level, our governments, and even our families. The courts passed laws that were stupid, divisive and wrong. Some of the laws were obviously evil, and nobody cared. The common good gave way to selfishness and corruption. Half the people were too comfortable or too busy to pay attention. By the time they realized what had happened it was too late. Good people were persecuted, and anyone who objected was labeled a fanatic.'

Becky was fired up again, and it was pretty clear to me that Becky and the guys took all this political shit seriously, but I wanted details. I wanted to know why the cities started burning. I was about to ask about it when I heard something coming from the riverbank. It sounded like a voice, and I held my hand up to silence everybody. We all froze and I reached out to Casey for the sawdi.

Casey had barely finished handing me the gun when a Fed came through the high grass in front of us. He was an older guy with gray hair and a mustache, and he was more surprised than we were. Just as his rifle started coming up, I let go with the shotgun. The blast caught him in the chest and tossed him back, and onto his ass. At that range I knew he was through, but there was no way of knowing how many other Feds were there waiting on the riverbank. Casey's gun was all we had, and everyone else was still in the open.

I shouted 'Get back!' and dropped to a knee.

Mike grabbed Becky and everyone scattered back toward the houses. I pumped another round into the chamber and pointed the gun defensively out toward the river. I remember looking down at the sawdi and getting a terrible feeling. Casey's piece only had three shots left, and I was expecting at least two or three Feds to come blasting their way toward me at any second. It had been a long time since I felt like I was about to die, and I was pissed that I didn't make Mike take the rifle with us.

When you think you're gonna die, weird stuff pops into your brain. It's happened to me a couple times before, and there's probably some medical reason for it, but I remember thinking about my mom and dad. I thought about Becky too. While I was thinking, my body started moving instinctively again, and my right hand was already holding a blade as it steadied the barrel of the sawdi. My other knives were out and ready, on the ground by my foot.

A couple seconds passed, and I couldn't figure out why nothing was happening. The world had become still and silent again, and I glanced back to make sure the guys were in the clear. I didn't want to jinx myself and start moving too quickly, but sitting still is never a good idea when you're out-gunned. An idea came to me, and I figured that my gunshot might have surprised the other Feds. Moving left and staying close to the ground, I came around the big tree where the riverbank met the grass.

When I looked past the tree, I could only see one Fed. He was a skinny little creep holding his rifle up, and he looked scared to death. He'd taken a step toward the town, but he was stopped now, looking at his dead friend. He didn't know I was there, and he kept looking out toward the houses and then down at the dead Fed in the dirt. I was a good twenty feet away but I could see his knees shaking. Maybe that's why I didn't kill him.

'Drop it, shithead!' I shouted.

About half the time, when you surprise a guy with a gun, you can expect him to turn on you, but this dude dropped the gun and put his arms up before I was done talking.

'Where are the others?' I demanded.

'Ain't no others.'

There was a Fed boat on the riverbank painted in camo. It was no bigger than ours but it had a huge machine gun mounted in the front, probably an old M2. It looked like the little Fed was telling the truth. With that gun and all the other shit inside, there wasn't room for more than two or three Feds in there.

'What you doing here, asshole?'

'Wa, wa, we was told to patrol the river down to the Medina Bridge,' he stuttered, 'and report on anything we find. We saw the boat here.'

There was a noise behind me, but it was only Mike and Casey returning. Mike immediately grabbed the dead guy's gun and pointed it at the Fed. Becky was still standing a few yards back, by the white bags we'd dropped on the road. I stepped closer and stuck the gun in the Fed's face.

'You lying to me, shithead?'

'No, I swear!'

He looked at me and his eyes got big, as if the little Fed

recognized me.

'Excellent,' I answered. 'It looks like we got ourselves another boat.'

Becky moved closer and stepped between Mike and me. When she saw the older Fed lying at our feet, she got that sick look on her face again. Some of the shot from the sawdi had caught the old dude in the throat, and he was messy. It reminded me again that Becky had a thing about killing people.

'Mike?' I called, 'take Becky for a walk. You can come back in a couple minutes.'

At first Becky looked at me as if she didn't understand, but when I raised the gun to the Fed's head, she let out a gasp.

'Oh my God! You're not thinking of killing him?!'

'I'm not *thinking* about it,' I answered, 'He's a stinking Fed and he's gonna die.'

'He's just a boy!' she exclaimed. 'He can't be sixteen!'

I took another look him. He was a skinny black kid with big scared eyes, and that short Fed haircut. From where I was standing, I could see his mark tattooed below his ear.

Like most people in the city, the Feds have their ID branded on their head, right below their ear. Most of the time you can't notice it, but if you're black, they lighten the skin around your mark so it's easier to read, and it looks stupid. He didn't look all that young to me, more like seventeen or eighteen, but he couldn't have been a Fed for very long. I remember thinking to myself that the government must be scraping the bottom of the barrel to enlist this clown. He was too scared, and if it wasn't for the camouflage uniform and the high boots, you'd never know he was a Fed.

'He's plenty old enough,' I said, setting my sights on him again.

'Jake, no! God wouldn't want us to kill a defenseless person.'

To be perfectly honest, I was only half-thinking about killing the Fed. For some reason it wasn't all that important anymore. Five minutes earlier, I thought that I was gonna die, so I was actually in a damned good mood and feeling kind of lucky. The little asshole was shaking so badly that he was fun to watch too. There wasn't anything I hated more than Feds, and screwing with this one was irresistible.

'The Feds are always killing defenseless people,' I answered, 'so let's just say I'm doing God a favor.'

I raised the sawdi again, and the little shit closed his eyes.

'Jake, look at me!' Becky shouted.

She was really worked-up about me killing this guy.

'Life is sacred and precious,' she said, trying to keep her voice down. 'We need to show mercy and forgiveness.'

'Can't we forgive him after he's dead?'

I couldn't keep from laughing anymore, and when Becky realized that I'd been playing with the creep she got mad at me. I was only trying to lighten the mood, but she didn't see the humor in it.

She turned to him and asked, 'What's your name?'

'Devon.'

'Nobody's going to hurt you, Devon,' she told him gently.

I lowered the shotgun, and when the Fed saw the knife in my hand, his eyes got bigger.

'You're the new bishop man,' he said, trembling, 'ain't you?'

As far as I knew, Becky and the guys were the only people in the world that thought I was a bishop. It struck me kind of weird, and I stared back at the kid for a sec. Becky and the guys were surprised too.

Casey asked, 'What do you know about a new bishop?'

'It's been all over our radios. A tall longhair butchered three city agents and two civilians last night. We heard that one was burned, and the other ones were skinned alive. The Churchers made him their new leader.'

'That's ridiculous!' Becky exclaimed. 'That's not what happened at all!'

True or not, it was a cool story and it explained why the Fed was so afraid of me. I knew that Becky wasn't going to like it, but I flashed him a twisted grin and started playing with my knife, pointing it at his throat and spinning it on my fingers. I thought the kid was gonna shit himself.

'Bishop Walker,' Becky said, loudly. 'Can I see you over here for a moment?'

Becky never called me that before, and I followed her all the way back to where the road started. Her hands were on her hips and she looked angry.

'First of all, thank you,' she began. 'I think you saved our lives again.'

'Yeah,' I grinned. 'You guys are shit magnets, huh?'

She glanced over my shoulder toward the river.

'Why are you antagonizing that boy, Devon?'

'Antagonizing?' I objected. 'He's a Fed! The little bastard should be happy he's still alive.'

'Remember what we talked about?' she asked. 'You're supposed to be setting an example and teaching. When you torture someone like that, it reflects poorly on the church and Christianity.'

'When exactly was I supposed to do any teaching back there?! And I wasn't torturing him. I was just having a little fun.'

'If people hear about this—'

'What people?' I laughed. 'Outside the city, it looks like we're the only people left.'

'There are others, Jake. You'll meet some of them tomorrow. And don't forget that Casey and Michael look up to you now, and they're watching everything you do.'

I knew Becky was probably right, but I still felt like she was making a big deal about nothing.

'Alright,' I groaned. 'But the Feds don't give a shit about the truth and everybody knows it. Their story will be twice as good by tomorrow, and they'll say I killed twenty people.'

While I was still talking, some fuzz from an old dandelion landed on the corner of her mouth. The odds of something like that happening have gotta be a zillion to one, and it just stuck right there on her lip, quivering in the breeze. I think I already mentioned that Becky has a nice mouth, and the whole thing took my mind off our conversation for a sec. She watched me as I slowly picked up the fuzz and let it go floating off toward the guys. When I looked into her eyes again, she was suddenly lost in thought.

'Which one of you is real?' she asked with a sigh.

It was one of those questions that doesn't really have an answer, and I wondered if I'd done something wrong. She was staring out toward the river, and I wasn't even sure if she was talking to me.

'What?'

'It's like there are two of you,' she said, with a smile. 'One Jake Walker is so calm. He can be so gentle and even shy sometimes…'

Her voice trailed off, and she looked up at me again.

'And the other Jake Walker is the most violent human being I've ever known! How can they be the same person?'

I wasn't sure if I should say something or not, so I kept quiet. She glanced over at the river and took a deep breath.

'Jake, we have to treat everyone the way we want to be treated ourselves,' she said finally. 'It's called the *golden rule*. Jesus gave us that rule himself. You'll learn all about that when we get home.'

'Everyone?'

She smiled and nodded.

'You have to stop being cruel to Devon, and we have to let him go. It's the right thing to do.'

'I guess.'

We walked back to the river without saying anything else. Everything was like we left it, and Mike still had his rifle on the Fed.

'Ok asshole, start walking,' I told the kid. 'Get outta here.'

'Bishop Walker?' Becky interrupted. 'It's many miles back to the city. Devon will need his boat and some food for the trip.'

Becky's golden rule was becoming a pain in my ass, but I didn't want to set a bad example by arguing about it.

'Casey,' I grumbled, 'see if you can pull that M2 and all the ammo out of there. And make sure he only has enough food and gas to reach the city.'

While Casey got busy with that, I decided to check out the locker on the Fed's boat. It had loads of stuff, and I got a radio, first aid kit, tools and two brand new rifles. Casey needed the tools to get the M2 off its mount, but it only took ten minutes. When we finished up, Becky told the kid he could go.

As he walked to the boat, I grabbed the dead Fed's body and drug it over to the river.

'Take your trash with you,' I said, tossing the dead guy in with him.

Casey and Mike pushed the boat off the riverbank, and it floated slowly out into the river. It was leaning to one side where the dead guy's legs hung out. The little Fed stared at me the whole time, even after he got the engine started, and the last thing he saw before the boat passed the bend was me giving him the stink eye. I can't describe to you how much I hate Feds, and I can't explain why I let that one live. Maybe it was because how I felt for Becky, but I remember standing there wondering if I was going soft or something. Her voice surprised me from behind.

'Thank you, *Bishop Walker*.'

She turned to Mike and Casey.

'Hey guys,' she continued. 'I want to reach the Hershberger's farm by morning, and we're out of food. We need to think about catching some dinner.'

'Jake?' Mike asked, grinning. 'You ever been fishing before?'

'Hold on one minute!' Casey interrupted. 'I'd better handle this.'

'Look Jake,' he said confidently, 'If you want to know about politics or philosophy, you can ask Mike. But if you need to know anything about theology, women or fishing, I'm the man!'

Everyone laughed and Mike groaned, 'Oh, please!'

It was fun, seeing everyone laughing like that, all at the same time. A funny, crazed look came over Casey and he poked me in the arm.

'Oh, man!' he exclaimed. 'We'll be eating good tonight, Jake!'

ANNABELLE

I'm normally open to new ideas, but if you think about it logically, you'd have to be an asshole to like fishing. It's not just because I hate being around water either. Sitting in one place for too long is unnatural, and it should make any normal person feel weird and uncomfortable. Not only that, but I'd heard more than once that eating fish can kill you. Casey and Mike laughed when I told them that, and they said that the fish in the river were different than the lake fish by the city. They were so excited about getting me to fish with them that I decided to go along with it. It wasn't logical, but I'm glad I did. Going fishing that afternoon turned into one of the best memories of my life.

The guys broke out their poles and fishing gear, and we moved down river just a little ways from the big tree. Michael dug up some worms while Casey and I found a comfortable spot in the shade. I learned all kinds of shit that afternoon, all about tackle boxes, sinkers and bobbers, wrapping a worm around a hook, and something called a lure. It's a cool-looking metal and plastic thingy, but to the fish it looks like food. He said that you can also use something called a *french fry* as bait, but he didn't have one in his tackle box. We were supposed to be hunting perch fish, but we got a couple bass fish too. I caught two perch myself and one was longer than my hand.

The weird thing about fishing is that it makes you feel strangely comfortable, like everyone around you just became your best friend. In five minutes, the guys were talking about all kinds of things, people in the parish, more politics, and even girls they knew. I didn't say too much as I listened to them because it was fascinating to hear so many details about their lives. Churchers are into farming and growing stuff, and I remember being surprised at how different their lives were, compared to mine. Becky was quiet too. She didn't do any fishing but she must have known all about it because she helped me cast out, and she got me untangled a couple times. She was happy just sitting there on the bank with her toes in the water, listening to us talking.

'Jake,' Becky said, once it got quiet again. 'In the morning when we get to the Hershberger's, we have to be extremely polite, and I'll do all the talking. Mariam and her family are Amish. They're going to seem strange to you.'

'Amish?'

'Yes, they're Christians too, but they live differently, and they don't believe everything that we do.'

'Yeah, I've heard about them, but I thought our parish was Catholic?'

'It is,' she answered, 'but some of the people living with us are Christians of other faiths. We even have a Jewish couple, Dr. Weiss and his wife. After the darkness, we all came together around the Hershberger's farm. We worked together as a community. It's how we survived.'

Becky's talking caught the guys' attention.

'Father Doogan's big thing is Christian unity,' Mike added. 'He says that if the Godly people of the world would have stuck together to begin with, the world wouldn't have become such a mess.'

'You'll hear that a lot,' Casey added, smiling, 'Some days, that's all Doogan talks about.'

'But when we're at Mariam's,' Becky said, returning to her point. 'Please don't cuss. And I *never* want to hear the f word again.'

I don't remember actually using the f word in front of her before that, but I couldn't deny it either. It's not like I did it on purpose, it was just a habit and nobody ever cared about how I talked before. I've been good at cussing since before I was in my first gang. It's one of those talents you're born with. I didn't mind promising Becky that I wouldn't use that word though. She really hated hearing it, and to be honest, I still do pretty well without it.

We were out there fishing a good couple hours, but it flew by in a heartbeat. Once we'd caught enough for everybody, you should have seen Becky getting those fish ready to cook. She looked like she was born with a knife in her hand, and she had them cut up and in a pan in no time. She cooked them up in some oil she found in her backpack, and the smell was unbelievable. I was beginning to wonder if there was anything Becky didn't have in that pink backpack of hers. We had some hard rolls left, and she'd made coffee too. Casey said some prayers and we all sat on the green blanket for dinner. It was nearly covered with food, and it was the most food I think I've ever had at one time.

Maybe I ate too much because I don't remember much about that evening. After we packed up and got back on the river, I must have fallen asleep quickly. Becky and the guys weren't as tired as me, and I think it's because they don't eat like normal people do. It the city, we're used to eating everything we can, because it's hard to know exactly when we'll be eating again. But I guessed the Churchers can go fishing whenever they want, so they only eat till they're not hungry anymore.

I was so beat that I only remember waking up once that night. It was a few hours before dawn. Casey was asleep, Mike was driving, and Becky was sitting in her usual spot across from me. It was starry and clear, and the moon was high above the river. I was surprised that Becky was awake, and she was staring at something in the southwest sky. I turned to look and saw something like a star, only faint and blurry. It looked like the fuzz that I found on her lip yesterday.

'Hi,' she said, leaning close enough for me to hear.

'What is that up there?'

'It's a comet,' she said smiling. 'It's been getting brighter every night for the last two weeks.'

I rubbed my eyes. 'Aren't they supposed to have a tail?'

'I think it will soon,' she answered. 'Comets have always been messengers of change. I've been sitting here praying that any changes that come are good ones.'

There was enough light for me to see that Becky was holding something in her lap, but I couldn't see it very well.

'What's that?'

'It's my Rosary,' she said, holding it up.

It looked to me like an old woman's necklace.

'Jewelry?'

'No, silly,' Becky laughed. 'They're beads. They help me pray.'

Just out of curiosity, I watched her till I dozed off again. She looked distant, peaceful and pretty as she moved the beads through her fingers, and I couldn't help grinning. Hell, the last thing I thought Churchers would need is something to help them pray.

I didn't open my eyes again until the motor stopped. It was light out, but the sun wasn't up yet. We were in a quiet part of the river, still a good ways from the bank, and there was a dewy mist in the air. Off in the distance, surrounded by rolling fields, I could see a big farmhouse. It was older than the houses we saw yesterday, and it had a porch that wrapped around the whole front. There was smoke coming from the chimney, and the entire scene was like a picture, only surprisingly alive. The yard was huge and I could see cows behind the house. There were other buildings in the yard too. One of them was bigger than the house, and right next to that was a fenced-in area where you could see some horses. I'd never seen animals like that, except in pictures, and it was pretty cool. I couldn't stop staring at them while we floated to shore.

Nobody was talking, and it looked to me like Becky and the guys were nervous about something. I wondered why they turned the engine off so soon, before we got closer to the farm. Everybody's eyes were glued to the house as we drifted nearer.

'You think he's gone?' Mike asked Becky.

'He must be,' she answered, 'It's nearly dawn.'

When we reached the shore, Mike jumped out with the rope in

his hand, and once the boat stopped, we all climbed out too. It was getting freaky with everyone so quiet, and although I didn't have a clue about *why*, I started feeling nervous too. Casey pulled the boat up onto the grass, they grabbed their backpacks, and we started toward the house. We walked the whole way up to the porch without anyone talking.

'Hey?' I whispered. 'Why's everybody so quiet?'

'Mr. Hershberger is an important man,' Becky explained quietly. 'He was one of the founders of the community.'

'So? What's he a creep or something?'

'No, of course not!' she said, impatiently.

With a wry smile, Michael said, 'That depends on who you ask.'

Michael wasn't one to say much, and he was normally so easy-going that his words surprised me. It sounded like he was afraid of this Hershberger guy, or maybe he just didn't like him. I would have asked him about it, but by the time I thought about it, we were already up the porch steps.

The sun was just peeking through the trees on the horizon when Becky knocked on the door, and I could see movement through the window and white curtains. A moment later, the door swung open, and a girl in a long dress answered. She was dressed funny, with an apron tied around her waist and her hair tied back in a black thing. She was a little shorter than Becky, with blue eyes. She looked about seventeen but it was hard to tell. She had a women's build, but her features were so soft that sometimes she looked like a kid to me. The second she saw Becky standing there, her eyes lit up.

'Becky! You're back,' she screamed, jumping into a hug. 'We were getting worried.'

While they were still hugging she looked over Becky's shoulder, and when she saw me her eyes got bigger. I knew that I didn't look Catholic, but I guess I didn't look Amish either. Her mouth fell open and she took a step backward.

'Mariam,' Becky apologized. 'I really need your help.'

'Hey, Mariam,' Casey interrupted. 'Can we use the radio? I'd like to let Doogan know we're here.'

'Sure, help yourself.'

The guys stepped into the house, and Becky looked up at me.

'Bishop Walker,' Becky announced. 'This is my best friend, Mariam Hershberger.'

Becky turned to Mariam.

'And this is Bishop Jake Walker, all the way from the city.'

I nodded, 'Hey.'

When Miriam didn't budge, Becky laughed.

'It's a long story, but I've got to get him cleaned up before we can go home. Will you help me?'

With her eyes locked on me, and her mouth still open, Miriam nodded. Becky looked cautiously inside, past the doorway.

'You're dad's not here, is he?' she asked. 'We didn't want to make a bad first impression.'

'No, he's out tending the stable,' Mariam answered. 'Have you eaten?'

Becky answered by saying something about not wanting to be a bother, but I wasn't paying attention. I was busy checking out the place as we walked inside. It had a big front room with wooden furniture and a fireplace. In some ways it was like the houses on Northwood, but it was different too. Although some of the furniture was the same, there weren't a lot of colors or pictures on the walls, and there weren't any TVs. The best part about it was the smell. In these last few days, one thing was becoming more and more obvious to me. Churchers really know how to eat!

Mike and Casey appeared again, stepping out of a little room to our right. They put their backpacks down by the door.

'Couldn't get through,' Casey said. 'They weren't on yet.'

'Make yourselves at home,' Mariam said, 'Becky and I'll fix breakfast.'

I'm not always the first person in the world to notice stuff like this, but when Mariam glanced over to Mike, they shared a smile like I've never seen before. I didn't see Mike's face right away, but she looked at him the same way that I look at cornbread. It didn't last long, but before she turned back toward the kitchen, he was looking at her the same way. I couldn't blame him. You could tell that, buried under all those clothes, Mariam was a good-looking female.

All at once there was a loud bang from behind Mariam, like a door slamming, and everyone turned toward the noise. With everyone there, and that amazing smell in the air, the last thing I was expecting to happen was something dangerous, but all at once an enormous animal came through the kitchen door! It was a dog, a huge brown dog that was bigger that Mariam, and it was tearing toward us fast.

'*Holy shit!*'

I reached out and pulled Becky behind me. I got a blade out, but the damn dog was already halfway across the room and bearing down on us fast! I could hear its claws on the wooden floor, scrambling to go faster, and I brought the knife back to throw. Before I could get the throw off, I heard Michael yell, 'Jake, no!' and I felt Casey on my arm.

Suddenly I felt Mike hit me from behind, and Casey, Michael and me were all tumbling to the floor. I had no idea why Mike would do that, but I remember thinking that the dog was gonna rip into us at any second. Mike and Casey were trying to hold me down, and when I looked up, the damn dog was only an inch from my nose!

It sniffed at me a sec, and then it started licking my face.

With Mike and Casey on me, all I could do was get slobbered on. It was totally unexpected and kind of gross, but the damn dog seemed to like me. It was the most enormous dog I'd ever seen, but all she was doing was wagging her tail and licking me!

It was just dawning on me that the giant dog wasn't gonna eat me, and the guys let go. Becky had that look again, and I knew that I'd done something wrong. We were just getting to our feet when I heard a voice.

'Bishop Walker,' Mariam said softly. 'That's Annabelle, my dog.'

'And this is my father,' she continued, 'John Hershberger.'

Standing in the kitchen doorway was an older dude with a beard. His sleeves were rolled up and his pants were held up by black thingies that went all the way over his shoulders and attached at the waist. He was an odd looking old guy, not quite as tall as me, but his shoulders were almost *too wide*. I remember thinking that the old dude took up way too much of that doorway. His eyes were blue like Mariam's, except they had a toughness in them, and I could tell he'd been around. He was tall and wide and proud, and I remember thinking that, twenty years ago or so, this dude was a top-notch badass.

'Hey,' I greeted him, wiping the dog's drool off my face.

For a long time he stared at me. He looked over to Becky and Casey, and then he scowled at Mike. He let out a long breath before turning to his daughter.

'Catholics!'

MATCHING SHOES

When I caught the looks on everybody's faces I felt myself getting hot. Yeah, I knew that I hadn't made a good first impression, but the old man didn't have to be an asshole about it, did he? Maybe I wasn't much to look at, but he didn't have the right to talk shit about Becky and the guys. I leaned toward him, and I was just about to tell the old fart that he hadn't made such a great first impression on me either, but I felt Becky's hand on my arm. She must have known what I was thinking, and she was reminding me that I'd promised to be polite.

It was the first time I realized that about Becky. Even then, she had a way of calming me down just by being in the same room with me. When she squeezed my arm, all I could do was stand there like an idiot and glare back at the old jerk. He finally stepped back through the kitchen door and we all stood there looking at each other.

'Sorry, Jake,' Mike said, 'I never thought to warn you about Annabelle.'

Annabelle was staring up at me and wagging her tail. Casey told me later that Annabelle was a Mastiff dog, and they all grow to be gigantic like that. The wild dogs in the city travel in packs, and they're a lot smaller and skinnier. Annabelle was a pack of dogs all by herself, and I'd never seen anything like her. As I looked down, her mouth opened up and she smiled at me. If I hadn't seen it for myself, I wouldn't have believed that a dog could do that! Mariam followed her dad to the kitchen, but she stopped in the doorway. She looked back at me and smiled too.

'Father can be gruff in the mornings,' she said. 'It isn't you.'

Mariam is one of those people that looks really serious all of the time, but when she smiles, it's like everything in the room smiles back at her. I knew it was a lie and she was just trying to make me feel better, but the kindness in her eyes was real. You can't fake something like that, and I was beginning to see why Becky and Mariam were best friends.

'You can wash up for breakfast,' she added, turning to the guys.

The girls went into the kitchen, and Mike led us into a hallway by the stairs. He seemed to know his way around the place pretty well. We walked into a narrow room next to the kitchen with long shelves on the walls. There were jars and cans and sacks of things stored there, and two baskets of clothes on a little table. There was another wooden table against the other wall with a washtub and some towels. We washed our hands in the washtub, and while we were at it, I heard voices in the kitchen. I could hear Mariam telling the old man something about *being rude* before he stomped away and slammed the back door again. We got to the kitchen just as the sun started coming in through the windows. It couldn't have taken us more than five minutes to wash up, but the girls already had food cooking, and there were smells in the air like you'd never believe.

'Bishop Walker,' Mariam said as I sat down. 'Would you like to do the honors?'

I didn't know what she was talking about, so I looked at Casey.

'I got it,' he responded, lowering his head. 'Let's say grace.'

Amish people don't pray the way we do, at least they don't do the t thing before and after, and they keep their eyes closed like they're asleep. Everybody seems comfortable ending prayers the same way though, and Mariam said *amen* along with everybody else before she went back to cooking.

I was right about Churchers and food. Amish Churchers make something called *pancakes* and they're unbelievably good. They're round, fluffy and buttery to start off with, but then you pour this thick sugary stuff called *syrup* on them. It was the best breakfast ever, but I only ate three stacks. I didn't want to feel stuffed and sluggish again, and I had to leave some room for sausages. Becky and Mariam didn't eat with us. They were talking over by the door to the washroom while Becky picked at a few dry pancakes. She'd talk to Mariam for a sec, stare at me, take a bite of her pancakes, and then start the whole thing all over again. I was being polite, and I even used my fork like the other guys, but they still kept staring at me.

'He's too big for Casey or Michael's clothes, and there's no time to make anything,' Becky told her. 'What do you think?'

'Roy's things should fit him,' Mariam answered.

When we finished eating, everything started moving quickly again, and it felt like everyone knew what was happening but me. Mike and Casey took some big pots over to the sink, and Mariam started heating water on the stove. Becky and Mariam were doing a lot of mumbling and laughing with each other, and Becky took a chair from the table and moved it onto the back porch. We went outside, and a second later Mariam showed up with some scissors and some metal things that looked like little tools.

'Have a seat, Bishop Walker,' Mariam said, standing behind the chair. 'It's time for your haircut.'

'Call me Jake.'

'No,' Becky corrected. 'That wouldn't be appropriate.'

Mariam smiled. '*Bishop* Jake then.'

It's never dawned on me till right now, but they never even asked me how I wanted my hair cut that morning. They just started talking and laughing, and pretty soon they were cutting off my damned hair.

'It's so uneven,' Mariam complained, untangling my hair with a comb. 'How was this cut before, with a broken bottle?!'

When I told her I wasn't sure, they started giggling again.

Not that I'm complaining, but I was surprised that they only cut off six inches or so. I guess they liked it long. I remembered that the frightened little Fed called me a *longhair*, and I liked the idea of leaving it that way. By the time they were done brushing, and clipping and laughing, it was completely even, untangled and down to about my shoulders. Of course, I didn't get to see it right away. There aren't many mirrors in Amish places and Becky had to get one from her backpack. I stood up and brushed myself off just as Mike was coming through the back door.

'Ok,' he said, grinning. 'It's ready.'

Mariam and Becky led me back into the house, to the front room and up the stairs. They weren't saying much as we walked, and I started wondering where we were going. There was a long hall upstairs that went the whole length of the house, and at the end there was a small bathroom. When we got there, I could see that the tub was filled with hot steaming water. All the water that Mariam had been heating up downstairs was there in the bathtub, and it looked a little scary.

'Bishop Walker,' Becky announced. 'We're still working on shoes and socks, but your bath is ready.'

'A bath?' I objected, 'We just washed up an hour ago!'

Becky leaned toward me and poked me in the ribs

'Jake,' she whispered. 'The Amish bathe once a week, and they normally share bathwater. Mariam is doing this as a very special favor, and you're embarrassing me!'

You've gotta admit, washing up before every meal *and* taking a bath every week is kind of excessive, but after what Becky said, and with Mariam standing there, I couldn't argue about it. Mariam handed me some towels and turned to Becky.

'Maybe we can mend the trousers, but that shirt is—'

Mariam paused. She stared back at my shirt, completely grossed out.

'We need to sink that in the river.'

If you put Becky and Mariam together, I'd bet they weren't half of me, but I was suddenly feeling outnumbered. It was like they were moving and talking together as if they'd somehow practiced the whole damn scene before. They walked me into the muggy little bathroom and closed the door behind me.

And just for the record, the concept of a bath wasn't new to me, and it isn't all that complicated. I just didn't have a lot of experience at it. I took off my clothes while I listened to their voices from the other side of the door. They were telling me things while I looked at the steaming water, and I was growing more and more anxious. When two females are both talking to you at the same time, it blends into one loud irritating voice, and it can make your nerves a little raw.

'There's soap and washcloths by the faucet and the new clothes are on the sink. By the time you're done, I'll have some shoes for you too.'

I was just about to try putting my foot in the water when I heard Becky's voice again.

'And bring out your old clothes so we can get them soaking.'

I picked up my stuff again and walked back to the door.

Now, remember how Becky overreacted when I killed people? That was nothing next to what happened when I came through that door. I took two steps toward her and tried to give her my clothes, exactly like she just asked me to do, but her mouth fell open and Marian let out a scream. I nearly jumped out of my skin and dropped everything on the floor. They both spun around so they couldn't see me.

'Jake!' she shouted. 'Get back in that bathroom this second!'

I went back into the bathroom and got right into the tub. After seeing the girls freaking out at me, the damned bathtub wasn't so scary anymore. At first there was a lot of noise in the hall. I heard Casey and Mike running up the stairs and a second later, I heard them both laughing. There was no way of knowing why the girls freaked like that, but I knew that I'd hear about it soon enough.

Once you get used to being in heated water, a bath isn't too bad, but it's not the kind of place you'd want to hang for very long. When I was finished washing everything, I climbed out and started drying off. For a long time it had been quiet out there in the hallway, and when I heard Becky's voice, I was surprised that she was still there.

'Jake?'

'Yeah, come on in.'

'No,' she laughed. 'I'm not coming in, you idiot!'

'Why not?'

'Jake, please understand,' she explained. 'There's something called modesty and it's very important in the community.'

She kept talking while I was figuring out the suspender thingies.

'Modest people never say anything or do anything that would make anyone around you think of intimate or personal things. Nudity is unacceptable and impolite. God wants us to dress appropriately in front of others so that they aren't tempted into thinking thoughts that might be suggestive or sexual.'

I was done getting dressed, so I moved my knives into the pocket of my jeans and opened the door.

'Suggestive or sexual?' I repeated. 'What if we're already thinking that way?'

Becky was standing right outside the door holding a new pair of shoes. She cocked her head cynically to the side and glared back at me, but I could tell she wasn't really mad.

'Just playing,' I confessed in a laugh. 'I got it.'

She handed me the shoes and I noticed a balled-up pair of socks in one of them.

'I'm glad to hear about that modesty thing,' I resumed. 'For a minute there, I didn't know why you freaked. I thought that maybe you saw something wrong with me.'

I was half-expecting Becky to laugh or say something else, but she was looking at me with a strange look. She looked me up and down a couple times, like she was surprised by the new shirt and pants. As best as I could tell, the clothes fit me fine, but you'd never know it by the way she was looking at them.

'Holy cow,' she said softly. 'You clean up nicely, Bishop Walker.'

With all the excitement I must not have been thinking right

because I suddenly remembered that we were alone and I should have been working on my kissing. Before I got the chance, I heard someone jogging up the stairs. It was only Casey and he stopped short when he saw me all dressed up.

'Hey,' he grinned. 'Look at the new Churcher!'

'Bishop Walker,' Becky interrupted. 'Casey will show you around the farm, and tell you about the other farms of the parish. Mariam and I have some things to do.'

I leaned on the wall so I could put the socks and shoes on. I'd never had shoes like that before. Both of them matched, and the bottoms were thick with lots of tread. I remember thinking that shoes like that probably last forever. Becky started down the stairs, before turning back to Casey.

'We'll meet you out at the hollow in an hour.'

I put my shoes on, and Casey led me out through the kitchen again and onto the porch where I had my haircut. The farm was an enormous place to see in the morning sun, and I was looking forward to seeing the animals up close. Out near the smaller barn, I saw a boy working, throwing feed on the ground. He looked fourteen or fifteen, and he smiled and waved when he saw us. It was one of those mornings where the air is cool, and you can smell rain in the air. The sun was coming in and out of the clouds, and while we walked out toward the fields, Casey started talking.

'We have three major farms in the parish. Hershberger's is the largest and they raise everything from peas to livestock. The church and school are at Doogan's place, on the grounds of St. Lucy's parish. We've got some livestock too, and fruit trees and dairy. That's all a few miles north of here. We passed it on the river so we could get you to Hershberger's first.'

You could tell that Casey was proud of the farms. He sounded like he was bragging as he explained everything.

'The Weiss farm down by the quarry is the smallest, but not by a lot. It's all a big circle if you see it on a map.'

'This place is huge,' I thought out loud. 'How's the old man do it?'

'The people of the parish work the farms together,' he explained. 'At planting and harvest times there are lots of people here, but this time of year it's just Big John, Mariam, and Samuel. Sammy's the kid we saw feeding the chickens.'

We were coming up on a fence, where I'd seen the horses from the boat. You could smell shit in the air, but there were lots of smells on the farm. None of them were bad, nothing like the caustic smoky smells of the city. Through the big open door of the building, I saw Hershberger look up when he saw us. He looked surprised to see me in good clothes. It looked like he was fixing a railing or something in the stable, and he only paused a second before he started hammering again.

'What's his story?' I asked Casey. 'And who stuck the pole up his ass?'

'Don't be too hard on Big John. He's a good man and he's been through a lot.'

'Like what?'

'During the persecutions, the Amish were one of the most vocal religious groups in the country. They refused to be marked or serve in the Fed militaries. John had a wife and five sons. Mariam and his nephew are all that he has left now. That's why he's so protective. The clothes you're wearing belonged to his oldest son, Roy.'

We leaned on the fence and I thought for a sec while we watched the horses. It was hard to stay pissed at Hershberger. If all that had happened to me, I'd probably have turned into an asshole too.

I drifted in and out of thought as we toured the farm that morning. Farm animals are bigger than what you'd expect and a lot bigger than how they look in pictures. That's especially true with cows and bulls. I also learned that bulls are such nasty bastards that at some times during the year, you gotta keep them in their own pens. While Casey was showing me the turkeys, I remembered how Mike and Mariam were looking at each other.

'So, Mike's got a thing for Mariam?'

'Yeah,' Casey grinned. 'Mike and Mariam have been together

for two years, but Big John won't even think about it.'

'Why? What's he got against Mike?'

'It's nothing like that,' he answered sadly. 'But if Mariam were to marry Mike, she wouldn't be Amish anymore, and neither would any of his grandkids. Big John's a good man, but he's just not ready for that yet. Mariam doesn't want to hurt her dad, but she loves Mike. It's a mess, but we're all praying that John eventually comes around to the idea.'

Annabelle showed up behind us and interrupted the conversation by poking me in the ass with her nose. It seemed to me that Annabelle was the real master of the farm. She'd come and go whenever she wanted, just to see what was going on, and then she'd run off again. Hell, if you scratch her behind the ears, she'd stay with you forever.

I could spend a whole day explaining all the stuff I experienced that morning with Casey, even though we were only out there about an hour. There were a hundred sounds that I'd never heard before, cows mooing, horses neighing, and turkeys gobbling. Even the birds in the country make different sounds than you'd ever hear in the city. I also found out that some of the stuff you read about farms is a lie. For one thing, turkeys don't really gobble. If you ask me it's more like a high warbling sound, like air escaping from an old tire.

Casey explained all about the parish, the school, and the church. He finally led me onto a little path into the woods, behind the barn by the house. He started talking about stuff that I didn't know much about, like generators, wells and gas lines. I kept nodding my head so I wouldn't look stupid, but I was glad when I caught sight of Becky again. We came to a little clearing and I saw her and Michael sitting at a picnic table. I was surprised that right next to him was another female in jeans. She had blonde hair, and it was so long that it was almost down to her ass. For me it was weird enough just being around females, but all these Churcher girls were smoking hot! As we got closer, I almost couldn't believe it. The blonde girl turned out to be Mariam, but she looked so different that I almost didn't recognize her.

'Whoa!' I said, stopping at the picnic table. 'What happened to the hat and the dress?'

'It's called Rumspringa, Bishop Jake. I'm allowed to dress English if I care to.'

'Rumspringa?'

'Yes,' Becky explained. 'It's a time when Amish teenagers can wear contemporary clothing and get a taste of what life is like in the rest of the world. Mariam can enjoy forbidden pleasures until she's twenty.'

'Forbidden pleasures!' Mariam objected, laughing. 'You make it sound dirty! Wearing jeans and letting my hair down is all it is, and I don't do it all the time.'

'Only when there's company,' Casey teased. 'Right Mike?'

Michael scowled. 'Why don't you shut up, Casey?'

Casey laughed and turned back to the house.

'I'll be right back,' he said. 'I'm gonna try the radio again.'

As Casey backtracked toward the house, I caught sight of something sitting on the table behind Mike. Next to a pad of paper and some pencils, was a plate of little round things that looked like food. They were smaller and fatter than pancakes, and I went in for a closer look. Mariam must have noticed my curiosity.

'Oatmeal raisin cookies,' she smiled. 'Please, help yourself.'

I picked one up and at first it didn't look like much, kind of fat and bumpy with shriveled up black things baked in. It wasn't all that appetizing, but I gave it a sniff and it smelled amazing.

'Bishop Jake,' Mariam interrupted my thoughts. 'Becky told me about your journey back from the city. I heard how you saved everyone.'

She glanced at Mike with that *cornbread* look again and added, 'Thank you.'

I know I should have said something back to her, but I'd just taken a bite of the cookie and I was speechless. That cookie was amazing, soft and chewy, sweet and totally awesome! I stared back at the cookie as I kept chewing.

'*Holy flipping shi—*'

'It's been a long time,' Becky interrupted loudly, flashing me a look, 'since the bishop has enjoyed freshly baked cookies.'

Becky reached behind her and took the pad of paper from off the table. She must have taken down some notes with Mariam, and she started scanning them with her eyes.

'If we time things right,' she began, 'we'll arrive at the parish late tonight, but there may be people waiting to meet you. You need to know how to greet them and talk with them. Most of it is just simple courtesy and manners. I'll try to help you with any questions, and Fr. Doogan will be there too. Mrs. Thompson and the Ladies Guild have prepared a room for the new bishop in the rectory, with your own library and—'

'So, where are *you* staying?' I interrupted.

'Close by,' she answered hesitantly. 'Michael and I live in a cabin behind the school.'

Maybe I'd missed something, but when she answered that way I suddenly felt let down inside. I knew things were different outside of the city, but even in this fairytale world of the Churchers, I was expecting to be with Becky after I got her home. For the longest time I'd been looking forward to spending some time alone with her.

'I don't get it,' I complained. 'I thought we were kind of together. Why can't I live with you?'

Becky's eyes opened wider, and Mariam's mouth fell open again. Even Mike was staring back at me like he was confused, but I didn't care. It didn't make any sense. I knew Becky liked me, I could tell that when I kissed her. Why should she want to live somewhere away from me?

'I told you, Jake,' she replied, forgetting to call me bishop. 'Fr. Doogan will explain everything. When we get back to—'

'Explain what?!' I shot back. 'And what's this Doogan guy got to do with you and me?'

'Can you *please* be patient? Once we're home it will—'

'No, I'm tired of being patient and this is stupid!'

Looking back on it, I wasn't really all that pissed off. Maybe I just felt like picking a fight, but Becky wasn't having it. She was fuming and she took a step closer. That was the first time I saw Becky get truly pissed at me. She got right in my face, looked up and started bitching at me.

'You listen to me Jacob Walker! You've got more important things to worry about now. God has things for you to do, and whatever those things are, they're bigger than you and me. Stop being selfish! Forget about your hormones and start getting to know your new boss!'

Becky looks good angry, and I couldn't stay mad at her. Hell, I was wearing new clothes and shoes, and I'd eaten a week's worth of food in the last two hours. How pissed off could I be? When she saw me grinning she let out a frustrated groan. She got that faraway look in her eyes like when she was on the boat, with her beads.

'I mean it, Jake,' she said softly. 'You have to start taking this more seriously. You've got an amazing boss, timeless and ancient, and…'

Her voice faded, and she sat back down at the picnic table.

'Please believe me,' she added softly. 'You'll understand everything, but you've got to give it some time.'

'Alright,' I surrendered, reaching for another cookie. 'Hey, ya know you look hot when you're pissed.'

Mike grinned, but Mariam looked confused. She turned to him, shaking her head.

'I know I'm still learning about Catholics,' she said softly. 'But if he's a bishop, then I'm a turkey buzzard!'

It was good to see Becky laughing again, and I tossed the cookie in my mouth. I'd just sat myself back down at the table when Casey came running down the path toward us. He was worked up about something and he started shouting while he was still a ways off.

'We've gotta leave!'

'What's wrong?' Mike asked,

'I just talked with Doogan,' Casey explained, arriving at the table. 'I told him that the nuncio is dead, and I tried to explain all about Jake, but he cut me off. He says we've got trouble. He wants us home as soon as possible, and he said to keep off the main roads.'

Becky stood up.

'What kind of trouble?'

'All he'd say is that we had visitors at the parish this morning.'

Casey paused to catch his breath before glancing over at me.

'Every Fed in the country is looking for the new bishop!'

JODIE AGAIN

Maybe you've already picked up on this, but there was something seriously weird about what Casey said, and it was just beginning to dawn on everybody. I suddenly remembered the little Fed on the boat, and his story about a *killer bishop* that skinned people alive. At the time I didn't think too much about it, but I think Becky and the guys were remembering it too. All at once everyone at the picnic table was asking themselves the same question.

'How could they know?!' Mike exclaimed, throwing his hands in the air. 'The Feds on the boat knew about it too. We've been running for two days and we haven't said anything to anybody. How could the Feds know about a new bishop?'

'They found out somehow,' Casey added, 'and they beat us home!'

The strangest part was that the Feds weren't looking for Jake Walker, the street kid who'd killed some Feds and got the Churchers out of the city. They were hunting the *new bishop*, and a longhair bishop too. Yeah, someone must have seen me, but how could they have known that I was a bishop? At first I didn't see how it was possible, but when the answer finally hit me it must have shown on my face. When I looked up everyone was staring back at me like they were expecting me to say something.

'Until I met you guys, I never heard the word *bishop* before,' I admitted. 'And there's only one dude in the whole world who saw me get this ring. It's gotta be the creep I told you about, the jerk in the black hoodie.'

I could picture myself outside the cathedral again, and the nuncio sliding the ring on my finger. Off in the background, there was that weird crispy-headed asshole watching us from the street. I couldn't help picturing him as I saw him in my dream, all toasted and ugly looking. Even though it was just a nightmare, it still gave me the creeps to think about how he looked at Becky. Without realizing it, I heard myself mumbling.

'*Jodie*'

The second I said it, Mariam let out a gasp. When I looked over at Becky she looked shocked too. Everybody recognized that name and even Mike's mouth fell open.

'That man was Stephen Jodie?!' Becky exclaimed. 'Why didn't you tell us that before?'

'I didn't know it before,' I tried to explain. 'I mean, I still don't know it for sure.'

There was no way to explain it without sounding like I was crazy, so I just went with it. Hell, they were already looking at me like I was naked again anyway.

'It's nothing,' I went on. 'Once we were out of the city and on the river, I had a bad dream on the boat. He came up out of the water and told me not to join the Churchers or he'd kill me, mess me up like he did the nuncio. He said I should call him Jodie.'

All at once everyone at the table was completely weirded out. They couldn't have been more freaked if I would have said *Adolph Hitler* or *Count Dracula* instead of Jodie. With all the praying they did, I knew that Churchers were superstitious, but they all looked panicky now, just hearing that asshole's name. At first I toyed with the idea of telling them how his eyes seemed to glow, but I decided against it. The girls were taking it hard enough already. There were tears in Mariam's eyes and I heard Becky whisper, 'Oh, my God!'

'It was only a dream!' I said. 'And who the hell's this Jodie guy, anyway?'

'Since before the war, Stephen Jodie was in charge of domestic affairs at the Justice Department,' Casey explained. 'He's responsible for the deaths of thousands of Godly people, including most of Mariam's family! There isn't a Churcher in the parish that hasn't lost family and friends because of that man. I can't believe he's still alive.'

'He's no man.' Mariam exclaimed. 'He's an unholy demon!'

'But that name,' Casey thought out loud. 'How could all this be a coincidence?'

'It can't,' Mike answered. 'When the nuncio gave Jake the ring and blessed him, Jake didn't know what a bishop was, but Jodie did. Stephen Jodie knew what the nuncio was doing. He knew that we had a new bishop before we did, and long before our new bishop knew about it either.'

Becky whispered, 'Stephen Jodie really is a demon!'

'Wait a sec,' I said, trying to calm everybody down. 'There's nothing spooky about it. He was just an ugly creep in a hoodie! He wasn't so tough when I killed his buddy and punched out his other asshole friend, was he?'

At that Mariam straightened her back and her eyes grew wider, and I suddenly got the feeling that I'd said too much.

'Rebecca?' she asked, with exaggerated curiosity. 'You haven't told me everything about the new bishop, have you?!'

Becky flashed me a look before answering.

'I thought it'd be better to save the details till later,' Becky apologized. 'I'll tell you all about it while we pack.'

At that moment the sun slid behind the clouds and a warm breeze whistled through the hollow, as if we needed more drama. I'm not saying that I was swallowing all that stuff about Jodie, but everybody else sure did. We all got up and quietly started heading down the path to the farm. There was an unspoken kind of intensity in the air, like when we were back in Hufferville and we could hear the dogs behind us. It didn't bother me all that much, but I felt bad for everyone else. They were expecting their troubles to be over once they got home, but that wasn't happening.

If you watch people when they're nervous or afraid, you can learn a lot about them. I knew a lot about Becky and the guys because we'd escaped the city together, but it surprised me how Mariam was acting. She shot up and started back to the farmhouse, talking with Becky and walking so fast that it was hard keeping up with them. It was like they already had a plan and knew exactly what to do. There was a toughness in Mariam, like I saw in her old man. They split off toward the house, but Mike and Casey took me back to the stable. Hershberger saw us coming, and he came out to meet us. The old man surprised me that day too. I figured that Casey must have already talked to him, because he knew that there was trouble.

'Help me hitch a buggy,' he told Casey. 'The river is too dangerous for you now. We'll get the boat hidden after you leave and bring it by tomorrow.'

Casey turned toward us and said, 'I'll pick you guys up at the house.'

Hershberger and Casey disappeared into the stable, and Mike and me hustled back up to the house. Annabelle joined us, and while we followed her wagging tail to the back door, I realized something about Hershberger. I was pretty sure that he didn't like me, and it was obvious that he had a problem with Mike, but he was still helping us. Maybe it was a Churcher thing, or maybe an Amish thing, but helping others was automatic and natural for these people, even if they didn't like you all that much.

While we were out talking to the old man, I think that Becky told Mariam more things about me. She was looking at me differently once we got back to the kitchen. Mariam always did look at me curiously, but she didn't know what to make of me now. She also looked frightened. I think she was spooked by all that Jodie talk, and she kept looking nervously out the back window as she worked. Mike noticed it too. While she was shoving a water bottle and some rolls in his backpack, he came up behind her.

'We're taking the long path along Tinkers Creek so we can keep off the main roads,' he said. 'Don't worry, we'll be fine.'

She turned, nodded and forced a smile before going back to her packing.

I don't know if all females are like this, but it seems to me that when you tell a girl not to worry about something, she worries about it even more. I don't think they do it just to be a pain in the ass, that's just how they are.

I heard the clip-clopping sound of the horse and buggy getting closer, and I walked out through the front to see it coming. It was an open buggy, with a front and back seat, and a big brown horse was pulling it. Casey was driving, and just as he stopped by the front door, Becky and the others stepped out of the house behind me.

There isn't a lot of space inside buggies, so Mike loaded the backpacks into a black box on the back. I noticed that Casey's sawdi was on the seat next to him on the green blanket, and the carbine was on the floor up front. Becky went up to Mariam and gave her a long hug.

'Thank you! We'll let you know once we're home.'

Mike came out of the house a second later, and he took Mariam's hands and stood there looking at her. You could tell he wanted to kiss her, or put his arms around her or something, but he just stood there looking kind of stupid. He was probably worried that the old man was watching, but Mariam didn't care. When it was obvious that he wasn't gonna go for it, she jumped into a kiss.

I helped Becky into the buggy and started to climb in next to her until I heard Mariam again.

'Bishop Jake?'

When I turned, she pulled away from Mike and picked up something that had been sitting on the porch rail. It was big and round and wrapped in paper. I thought it might be a big cookie, but when she handed it to me I noticed it was heavy.

'I'm afraid you won't be having a proper homecoming. Maybe this will help. It's an apple pie.'

I took a sniff and it smelled excellent, a little like the oatmeal cookie. Then she surprised me by putting her arms around me and pulling me into a hug.

'Welcome to Nineveh. Good luck and God bless you.'

I said *thanks* and climbed into the buggy, next to Becky. Mike was up front with Casey and he said something to the horse to make it go. Mariam watched us as the horse turned around and headed south. Annabelle was sleeping on the porch, and I could see Hershberger standing next to the stable, watching us with his arms crossed. He looked like an old oak tree, except with a lot less personality. The horse took us to a path along a little creek. It was just like the river only smaller, and I could see that it snaked along through the trees ahead of us.

'Hey, Becky?'

'Yes.'

'Mariam said *welcome to Nineveh*,' I remembered. 'What's Nineveh?'

'It's biblical,' she answered. 'Mr. Hershberger gave us that name when the community was formed. It's a city that was spared the wrath of God because the people repented and returned to him.'

I nodded, but I didn't know what she was talking about.

'So,' I resumed. 'You gonna give me some more bishop lessons before we get there?'

'I don't think so.'

There was a tired softness in her voice, like her thoughts were far away again.

'You are who you are, Jake. I'm more certain than ever that God wants you here. I just hope that the others in the parish see that too.'

LIGHTNING

If you're asking yourself why I wasn't being more careful that morning, I guess I don't blame you. We knew that the Feds were after us, and that they might even be waiting for us when we got to the parish. Normally I'd have found a quiet place to hang out and let things cool down before going on. I thought about doing just that, but something inside kept telling me that I needed to get Becky and the guys home. Like I said before, sometimes you just gotta trust your instincts, and that's why I wasn't saying anything. Following your instincts is no excuse to be stupid, so I made sure that I was within reach of Casey's sawdi, and as Hershberger's farm disappeared behind a curtain of trees, I reached back and checked the pocket of my new pants for my blades.

In just a few minutes we were so deep into the forest that it was like another world. I'd never felt so far away from the city before, and it felt like I was in a picture book. Back home you're always within a few feet of concrete, steel, or a torched car, but on that little path along the creek the trees were so thick that sometimes it looked like dusk was coming on. The sky must have been thinking about storming because we heard a couple rumbles of thunder, and the trees around us all shook their leaves and branches at the same time. It was a sound like you'd never hear in the city, and louder than you might expect, but it never did rain that day. The sun popped out a few minutes later, and all you could hear was the sound of the horse and the creek again. Nobody said a whole lot as we moved along, and I think the guys were focusing on the trail in front of us.

It went on like that for a long time before Mike said something to Casey and they switched seats. Mike took a turn driving, and suddenly both of them were reaching down for their guns. It wasn't quick or alarming, but I could tell that they were anxious about something and it made me a little nervous too. The forest was thinning out on our left, and I could see that we were getting close to a city road. We didn't slow down, but while we passed, the guys were watching the road and Casey had the sawdi up. Through the trees I saw a two-lane street running parallel the creek. On the other side there was a burned out strip mall, and a grocery store with the windows smashed out. There were tall pine trees growing alongside a long driveway, and a two-story brick building set back from the road.

'Those buildings were once student housing for the College,' Becky explained. 'We're getting close to the parish.'

The guys put their guns down again and our path veered off and away from the water. There was open field beyond the trees, and I could tell that we were coming to another farm, but this was different than the Hershberger's place. It looked like the farm was in the center of a huge rectangle, and there were seven or ten little houses built around it. A couple of them were big, like Mariam's house, but most were a lot smaller and made out of logs. There were a few people working and moving around, and cows grazing on the hill. As we got closer I caught the scent of burning wood in the air and it reminded me of Mariam's fireplace. Our path ran along the backs of the houses, and I could see rippling white sheets drying in the wind.

We came within a hundred feet of a house and surprised a girl with red hair. She was in a rocking chair by her front door, holding a baby. She stood up and stared back at us curiously, and when she recognized Becky, she smiled and waved.

'That's Mrs. Mardonis and Georgette,' Becky announced. 'Wave, Jake!'

The mom was maybe twenty, dressed in a long blue skirt and a girl's shirt, like Becky's. In the warm afternoon air, the baby was dressed in nothing but a diaper. It was too little and fat to do anything but lay there in her mom's arms, but it looked like it was awake. It was the first time I'd seen a baby in person, and although it wasn't doing much of anything, it was still pretty cool to look at.

'We're back!' Becky announced. 'And we've got Bishop Walker with us!'

After Becky shouted, the door of the next house opened. It was one of those smaller log houses I mentioned, and a kid stepped out and stared back at us. He was little, maybe four feet high, and I couldn't tell how old he was. He turned back to the house and yelled, 'It's Miss Wells!'

'Miss Wells?' I asked, turning to Becky.

'That's me,' she said proudly. 'Steven is a student of mine. All the kids of the parish are mine.'

Something made me look out beyond the houses, and I could just see a horse galloping through the woods toward us. I didn't see the rider right away, but when Mike caught sight of what was coming, he elbowed Casey and pulled the buggy to a stop. I was half-expecting them to pick up their guns again, but he turned to Becky and laughed.

'That didn't take long!'

Becky looked pissed. She stood up and put her hands on her hips just as the charging horse came to a stop in front of us. It was so sudden that our horse got scared and reared up, and our buggy lurched backwards. I had to grab Becky to keep her from falling, and when I finally got a good look at the horse's rider, I wondered if I was dreaming. The only thing missing was a white rabbit holding a watch.

Sitting on top of the black horse was a girl with golden hair. Her curls hung down onto bare shoulders and fell softly onto a pale yellow dress that had ridden up, halfway above her knees. She was a beautiful kid, barely old enough to fill out the dress, but long-legged and bubbling with confidence and excitement. There was something sudden and intense about her, like a clap of unexpected thunder. She had a slight mischievous grin on her face, and when she noticed Becky scowling at her, the smile got bigger.

'Rita!' Becky scolded. 'You shouldn't be out riding without a saddle, and certainly not in a dress!'

While Becky spoke, she was moving her hands, making signs and shapes as she talked. The girl made a mockingly serious face, and she obviously didn't give a shit that Becky was mad. She turned and smiled flirtatiously at Casey, but when she noticed me, she looked at Becky again. Rita started moving her lips like she was talking, but without making a sound, and the whole time she was gesturing with her hands.

Yeah, it took me long enough, but it finally hit me. Rita was deaf.

'He's our new bishop, Bishop Walker,' Becky replied, with her hands signing. 'Now get back to the rectory this minute, and tell Father Doogan we're home.'

Rita gave Becky a dismissive look before turning to me again. She looked me up and down, carefully checking me out, and I noticed that her eyes found the shotgun sitting next to Casey. She finally burst into laughter and signed something else to Becky. She smiled at Casey again, turned the horse around, and raced back down the road.

'Wow,' I laughed, 'she's like a bolt of lightning, isn't she?'

'Lightning,' Becky repeated. 'That certainly describes my Rita.'

Something else hit me, and for a second all I could do was stare back at Becky, a little awestruck. Like most people, I'm pretty smart when it comes to the stuff I like, but Becky was smart on a whole bunch of shit that most people don't even know about! I was wondering if she'd spent her whole life studying books and learning things.

'How the hell did you ever learn to talk to deaf people?'

'It wasn't that hard,' she said. 'At first I thought I could learn from her, but Rita kept tricking me, giving me the wrong names for things and teaching me cuss words and inappropriate language. If we hadn't found some sign-language books in one of the libraries, I never would have known.'

There was something in Becky's voice, and I knew right away

that Rita was special to her.

'So, what did she say about me just now?' I asked.

That same sly smile that I'd just seen on Rita's face was suddenly visible on Becky's. She sat back down, and at first I didn't think she was going to answer me.

'I can't repeat it exactly because it was inappropriate,' She said with a laugh, 'but let's just say that Rita thinks you're too adorable to be a bishop.'

'See that Casey?' Mike teased. 'It looks like you've got competition now!'

Casey mumbled something and the buggy started moving again. With Mike grinning at him that way, I remembered how Rita kept smiling at Casey.

'So Casey,' I asked. 'You and Lightning are a thing?'

'Oh my God!' Becky interrupted, glaring back at me. 'She's barely seventeen. She's just a child!'

'Seventeen?' I replied. 'That's plenty old enough to—'

Becky shot me a look cold enough to freeze water. I couldn't tell if she was shocked, disgusted or just plain pissed at me, but I knew enough to shut up. I remember thinking that Churchers must look at age differently, because in the city you're pretty much fully-grown by seventeen. I was glad when Mike started talking again.

'Rita's had a crush on Casey for a long time now. Wherever Casey is, that's where you'll find Rita and her yellow dress.'

He poked Casey and teased, 'You should really stop leading her on, Casey.'

'Don't listen to him, Jake,' Casey grumbled, turning back to us. 'I've tried to tell Rita that I'm too old for her and that I've got other plans with my life. I even learned sign language to try to tell her.'

He grinned. 'But when Rita sets her mind on something, nothing else seems to matter.'

There was a lot of movement up ahead, and I saw three kids

playing in the branches of on an old tree. Seeing them playing there struck me, and I remember how I felt watching them. They were laughing and so carefree that I almost had to laugh when I saw them. They stopped when they spotted us, and started running toward our buggy. More and more people were appearing, coming outside or looking at us from their windows, and the kids we saw started running along behind us. When I looked back, I saw that the red-haired mom with the baby was following us too. When I took a good around, I couldn't help noticing something.

'Becky?'

'Yes'

'Where are all the dudes?'

Mike and Casey looked at each other and started laughing.

I'm not exaggerating, but by then I'd already seen at least fifteen or twenty people, and except for a couple kids, none of them were guys! As rare as females were in the city, there were plenty of them out here, and they all looked fresh like Becky and Mariam. Even the old ones in their thirties didn't have that *beat up* look of a city girl.

'The guys of the parish are busy working, Bishop Walker,' she answered, breaking into a smile. 'But it might surprise you to know that at St. Lucy's, the girls outnumber the guys at least five to one.'

'Mrs. Thompson says it is a punishment from God,' Michael added 'But she thinks *everything* is a punishment from God.'

I'd seen more females in the last five minutes than I'd seen in my whole life, and I didn't understand what Mike was talking about. Hell, how could having lots of females around be a punishment? I wondered if all the guys were missing because they were exhausted and sleeping. Living with all these females, a dude couldn't possibly get much sleep at night.

A parking lot was coming into view, and I could see the tall bell tower of a church above the trees. It looked like the cathedral's except a lot smaller, and built with older darker stones. There was a long, two-story building attached to the church. It looked like it used to be a school, but it was black and burned. It must have been torched a long time ago too because there was a thick green ivy crawling up the bricks, and snaking in and out of the shattered windows. The streets behind the church weren't like real streets. They were unpaved, just hardened dirt, and narrow. I was trying to take it all in, but Becky kept telling me to *smile and wave* to people. There was another row of little houses to our left, and a long thin building on our right with lots of windows.

'What's that?'

'That's the men's dorm,' Mike answered. 'The dorms are for people that don't have a house and no family yet. When the community started forming, most of the survivors came here alone. We still get people straggling in occasionally, and that's where they live. They're nice inside, with bunk beds and a common area. There's not much privacy, but it's safe and warm. We have three girls' dorms too, but they're over by the school.'

Right before we got to the parking lot, the buggy passed by a couple of streets that branched out in unexpected directions, and it seemed to me that the houses here were built hastily and without a lot of thought. Some of the houses were clustered together and some were set aside, apart from the rest. At the end of the street was a tiny wooden church, with a high steeple and a cross on top.

'That's Tangletown,' Becky told me. 'Most of our Lutherans live here.'

It's hard for me to remember all the things that were going through my head that day, but I do remember being surprised at how *alive* it all was. It was the first time I realized that the city where I'd grown up was a dying place, a huge and diseased old animal slowly collapsing under its own weight. It wasn't anything like that out here. I was in the middle of a living thing now, something exciting, surprisingly healthy and growing.

We went over a bump and started moving across the parking lot to the house behind the church, where the trees got thick again. It was like Mariam's place, with a big front porch, and smoke coming from the chimney. Before we got to the front door, Mike took the guns and wrapped them in the green blanket.

'That's the rectory,' Becky announced. 'Welcome home Bishop Walker!'

It's funny what you remember about things. With everything else that was happening that afternoon, I remember seeing an ancient bicycle leaning against the stairs, and wondering if the old thing still worked. Lightning's horse was there too, tied up to the porch railing, and she was sitting up on the porch in a cool hanging chair. It was long like a park bench, wooden and chained to the ceiling somehow. She was gently swinging on it, but when she caught sight of us, she jumped up and started pounding on the front door. An old man with a cane slowly walked out. He was wearing a black shirt that was so long it went all the way down to the floor.

'That's our pastor,' Becky whispered, 'Fr. Doogan.'

Doogan had a funny looking white thing around his throat, and he was bald except for some white hair above his ears. I remember thinking that he was as old and wrinkly as any person I'd ever seen. He stopped in front of the steps, and even before our buggy came to a stop, he was motioning for us to hurry.

'Be quick about it,' Doogan said, waving his arm. 'Come in, come in!'

One of the women that had been following us ran up to the old man.

'Father?' she asked excitedly. 'Does this mean we'll be having the program at the school this afternoon?'

'Yes of course, Mrs. Wilkinson,' he nodded, 'Let everyone know, and tell Pete to have the grills started by four-thirty.'

He looked at the others who'd followed us in from the woods, and he raised his voice.

'The bishop is a wee bit weary after his long journey. We'll all be getting a chance to meet him at the school tonight.'

We climbed out of the buggy, and Doogan held the door open as we walked up to the porch. He seemed in a rush about something, and I felt his eyes on me as we walked into the house. There was a tall older lady in a gray dress waiting inside, standing next to Lightning. Her hair was wrapped up in a ball on top of her head, and when she saw that I was holding the pie that Mariam gave me, she hurried up to me.

'I'll take that for you,' she said, taking the pie. 'I'm the housekeeper, Ellen Thompson, Your Grace. Welcome to St. Lucy's'

'Mrs. Thompson,' Doogan interrupted. 'We'll be needing a moment, if you please. We need to bring the bishop up to date on our situation.'

Doogan talked funny. Becky told me later that it was because of something called a *brogue*. All the words were in English, so I could understand everything, but it was still like listening to another language.

'Certainly, Father.' Mrs. Thompson nodded.

She smiled and walked off toward the kitchen, just as Casey stepped inside with our backpacks. Doogan didn't get a chance to start talking again because we heard something outside. It sounded like at least a couple of jeeps pulling up, and Mike went to the window for a look.

'It's Morrison!' he exclaimed. 'And he brought backup.'

'Morrison?' I asked Becky.

All the faces in the room fell, and I could see that Becky was frightened. Casey dropped the backpacks and hurried over to the window, and Mike grabbed the blanket with the guns. My heart started racing, and I already knew what Becky was going to say.

'Jake, the Feds are here.'

ONE LAST QUESTION

The only person in the room that didn't look worried was Fr. Doogan, and to be honest, I was starting to have my doubts about the old dude. From the way Becky and the guys had been talking about him for the last two days, I was expecting Doogan to be smart. It's no secret that some of the old ones lose their grip after a while, and by the looks of things, Doogan wasn't getting it. He looked more annoyed than scared. A second ago, he was nervous and in a hurry, but now that the Feds were outside and he should have been nervous, he looked *bored*. He let out a sigh, walked up to me and stuck out his hand.

'I'm sorry, lad. I was hoping to chat with you before they arrived. This is a poor welcome to our humble parish, but I'm Father Sean Doogan.'

'Jake Walker.'

He shook my hand and paused to stare at the ring on my finger. There were voices outside, so I pulled away and stepped over to the window.

Two jeeps had pulled up, one close to the house and the other farther back, where the parking lot met the woods. They were big open vehicles, older than anything you'd see in the city, but the far one had an M2 mounted in back. There were five Feds total, three in the back and two the front, and their leader was easy to spot. He had already climbed out and was walking up to the house. He wasn't wearing the usual uniform. He had the camo pants and boots, but he was in a solid green tee shirt, and none of the Feds were wearing their hats. They were nothing like city Feds, and none of them had rifles. It also surprised me that the leader was kind of a fatass. He was tall, with a round face and graying black hair, but I'd never seen a Fed with a gut like that. I was suddenly feeling a lot better about our situation. Hell, I knew I could have easily done this guy on my way to the woods, and way before the other Feds knew what was happening.

'Well then,' Doogan said, walking to the door. 'Let's get this over with.'

Becky's mouth fell open.

'Father no,' she objected, 'You're not going out there!'

'Calm yourself, me dear,' the old man replied. 'Bill Morrison is a member of our parish and a good man. He'll do the right thing.'

He opened the door and motioned for me to follow him.

Now I'd just met Fr. Doogan and I was still waiting for proof that the old guy's head was screwed on tight, so I didn't move right away. Maybe these country Feds were all fatasses, but I still wasn't crazy enough go strolling out there to say *hi*. Mike must have read my mind. He unrolled the guns from the blanket and started handing me the sawdi.

'Here now!' Doogan told him crossly. 'We won't be needing that.'

For a second time the old man motioned for me to follow him, and I was right about to say something guaranteed to give him a bad first impression when I caught sight of Mike again. He'd slipped behind the door, and was handing the carbine to Casey. Doogan couldn't see it, but Mike gave me a reassuring nod before they headed for the back door. I felt a little better, but Lightning had been watching us and she must have sensed trouble. Her eyes grew wide and she ran over and put her arms around Becky. They both stared silently up at me and I couldn't tell if Becky was telling me to be polite, or if she was just scared too. I took a deep breath and walked over to Doogan, but I reached back and moved two blades from my back pocket to my beltline.

There'd been a lot of talking and noise out front, but as we stepped out onto the porch, everything became quiet. There were still about ten or fifteen people hanging around, and they were watching the lead Fed walk up to the house. He was almost to the stairs, but he stopped short when he saw me.

'Bill, good to see you!' Doogan called. 'You're just in time to meet our new bishop.'

'Fr. Doogan,' Morrison nodded, with his eyes on me. 'I'm here on business.'

'Of course you are, Bill, but first things first. Say hello to your new bishop, Bishop Jacob Walker.'

Morrison wasn't sure how to respond. He stared back at me a sec, and then he watched quietly as the girls came out and joined us. Becky's arm was still around Lightning, and the kid was scowling at him.

I nodded, 'Hey'

Morrison looked me up and down again, and then he looked at the people gathered around us.

'Fr. Doogan, *seriously*, we're here on official business. That man fits the description of a fugitive that left the city on—'

'We have no fugitives here, Bill,' Doogan interrupted. 'Bishop Walker has been in the company of Becky Wells and the welcoming committee for the last three days. Certainly you're not suggesting that your daughter's teacher is an accomplice to a crime?'

'Look, this isn't about the faith, Father. We've got a problem,' Morrison insisted. 'A federal watercraft washed up near Barton Road, about half a mile from here. There was one dead officer in it, and another officer is missing and presumed dead. We believe that they ran into the same fugitive that killed six other agents escaping from the city. And this man fits that description to a tee.'

'I wish I had a choice, Father,' he added, starting up the stairs. 'I'm sorry but we have to take him in. The whole country has been notified—'

Morrison stopped cold when Casey stepped around the corner

of the house with the carbine up, and for a second I thought that all hell was gonna break loose. The other Feds all started moving and I was reaching for a blade when, down by the jeeps, Michael stepped out of the trees with the sawdi in his hands. He must have worked his way through the trees while we were talking, and he jacked a round into the chamber before the other Feds had a chance to react. There was a hushing sound like everyone let out a gasp at the same time, and all the Feds could do was freeze.

Morrison glared at Casey.

'Your dad and I were like brothers, and now you're pulling a gun on me?!'

'Sorry Mr. Morrison,' Casey replied, coldly, 'but you're not taking our bishop.'

Morrison turned toward the other Feds and shouted, 'Stand down!'

I had to smile. Hell, it's not like the other Feds could have done anything anyway, but something else hit me at that moment. It was the first time I realized that Casey, Michael and I were tight now. In the last two days, Casey had gone from being a total asshole to a good friend, and Michael had gone from a quiet, wimpy-ass kid, to a good friend too. They'd just taken these country Feds completely off-guard and I was proud of them. Morrison looked pissed. He stomped up the last two steps and leaned into Fr. Doogan.

'Father be reasonable,' he pleaded in a low voice. 'I can report that we didn't find him here, but it won't end there. Every federal outpost in the region is on alert, and the order came down from Jodie himself. Everything you've built here is in jeopardy as long as he's here!'

You couldn't see it on the old priest's face, but his voice sounded angry.

'And what if we did hand him over to you, *William*?' he asked sharply. 'This young man saved the lives of Becky and Michael Wells, and your godchild Casey. Even if he wasn't our Bishop, do you suppose for one minute that we'd allow Stephen Jodie and his city agents to murder him?!'

Morrison didn't have an answer. He thought for a sec before

glaring back at me.

'Whoever you are,' he grumbled, 'You're putting everyone here in danger!'

He turned and marched back down the stairs.

'Thank you, Father Doogan,' he said, loud enough for everyone to hear, 'but if you do run into anyone suspicious, please let us know.'

Morrison was just saying that for the other Feds, and before he got back to the jeep, Doogan's voice boomed.

'And Bill?' he called. 'Don't forget, the children are welcoming the bishop with a program at the school at four, followed by a grand barbeque. Bring the family.'

Morrison waved and mumbled something else, and the jeeps started back toward the street.

Doogan watched as the guys walked up the stairs to join up, with their guns over their shoulders. He looked surprised, and I knew that he never expected the guys to challenge the Feds like that. He put his hands on his hips and laughed.

'Is this the sort of catechism we're teaching in the cities now, Bishop Walker?'

He chuckled to himself and stepped inside, not waiting for an answer, and it dawned on me that I'd been wrong about Doogan. The old dude was a lot sharper than I first thought. A minute ago if someone would have told me that we could have gotten off that porch without killing anybody, I'd have said he was nuts. Still, I still couldn't help wondering about something.

'So, Fr. Doogan?' I asked, following him into the front room. 'What would have happened if the guys wouldn't have shown up with the guns?'

'I would have told Bill Morrison that he could have you,' he answered, grinning back at me, 'but he'd be doing it over me own dead body.'

Everyone followed us inside, and we found Mrs. Thompson standing at the window. Apparently she'd been watching everything through the curtains and she looked out-of-breath.

'Mrs. Thompson, no visitors for the next few hours,' Doogan said. 'And if you please, we'll be needing refreshments in the library.'

Becky signed something to Rita, probably telling her to go home, and the kid stomped her feet and signed something back to her.

That's another thing. If you ever get a chance to watch an argument with a deaf person, believe me it's entertaining as hell! Their hands start moving like crazy, and the looks on their faces are exaggerated and hilarious. Becky doesn't cuss, but whatever she was saying to Lightning must have been pretty good, cause she wasn't repeating it out loud. Rita finally gave in and started leaving, but she went out of her way to sidle past Casey on her way to the door. The little flirt smiled at him and squeezed his arm as she passed, and Casey got so uncomfortable that I had to laugh. Next to the priest, Casey was the oldest guy in the room, but I think the poor dude knew less about females than I did. He turned three shades of red before Rita reached the front door.

Fr. Doogan led us to a big room with lots of bookshelves. There was a smell in the air that I couldn't place right away, but I found out later that it was pipe tobacco. The walls were all made of dark wood, and there was an unlit fireplace on the far wall. A small clock was on the mantle, and I remember that the damned thing came alive and made noises every few minutes. There was only one window, but it lit the room pretty well, and there was a nice breeze blowing in through white curtains. There was a couch and lots of chairs, five or six of them, and they were all stuffed and comfortable looking. Everybody started taking a seat, and Doogan sat in the big chair by the fireplace. I sunk into my chair so much that I had to take out my knives and put them on the table by the couch, so they wouldn't cut into my pants.

'Now then, my friends,' he started, pulling a pipe from his pocket. 'Tell me all about Nuncio Moreau, God rest his soul, and your adventures in the city.'

I was still a little wound up from meeting the country Feds and I didn't feel much like talking, but Becky and the guys couldn't wait to tell the story again. While Doogan lit his pipe, they all started talking at the same time. They started off with all the stuff I didn't know about yet. I learned how they found the body of the nuncio's escorts, and how they ran to the cathedral and found the nuncio's body. Doogan said that the three escorts were bodyguards, all well-trained and well-armed, and they apparently got killed getting the nuncio off the riverbank. I remember thinking that the Feds must have known they were coming and ambushed them. Hell, the Feds never patrol the smelly end of the river, and even if they did, three armed men should have easily gotten by one Fed patrol.

I bet we talked for two hours, and we must have answered a hundred of Doogan's questions. Lucky for me, Mrs. Thompson brought in some cold tea and kept bringing in cookies so I didn't get too bored. Doogan kept coming back to the part where I got the ring, and what the nuncio said to me.

'Tell me, son,' Doogan asked. 'Do you think Fr. Kowalski got away?'

'Maybe,' I answered, 'But the West End was crawling with Feds that night. If he was anywhere around there, they probably got him.'

'What about that *stick* you said was used to torture the nuncio? It sounds like a crosier, the sheppard's staff of a bishop,' he explained, looking at Becky. 'What happened to it, may I ask?'

'I don't remember, but I wasn't really looking for it. When I left the cathedral, all I remember is that the dude in the hoodie was gone.'

Becky added, 'We didn't see anything like that when we got there.'

There was only one part of the story that I totally left out that afternoon, the part about me trying to jump Becky. It's not like I was lying. It's just that I knew it'd make her uncomfortable, and when she didn't mention it, I didn't either. We talked about everything else though, and every once in a while, Doogan surprised me by asking something completely off-topic. Even when we were talking about some important part of the story, he'd interrupt to ask something about *me*. Like while I was telling him how we got to the boat, he held up his hand to stop me.

'Tell me, lad. Being so capable with firearms, why do you carry knives?'

When someone asks a stupid question like that, you can bet he hasn't spent a lot of time in the city.

'The Feds kill anyone carrying a gun or if they find one in your place,' I explained. 'Besides, a knife is personal and it forces you to think.'

'Think?'

'Yeah. You gotta be close with a knife. Close enough to know that the guy in your face really needs killing.'

The old man also made a big deal about me not being marked. I told him that as far as I knew nobody in my family had ever been marked, and once everything started burning, nobody gave a shit about that anymore. When we were finally done telling him about the Hershberger's dog, and my dream, he leaned back in his chair and took a deep breath.

'Saints in heaven, that's an incredible story! May I see the ring again?'

I walked over, and as I held out my hand, I heard Becky's voice behind me.

'The nuncio's words were obviously from an ordination rite,' she explained. 'So we knew that Jake was our new bishop.'

Doogan didn't answer, and Becky looked nervously to Mike and Casey.

'Father?' she pressed. 'Jake *is* our new bishop, isn't he?'

The old man leaned back in his chair again.

'I haven't the slightest idea.'

'That's ridiculous!' Becky objected from the edge of her chair. 'Stephen Jodie believes he's our bishop and you don't?!'

'I didn't say that I didn't believe it, my dear. I'm saying that it doesn't matter what we think. We're talking about the Holy Church of God. We must show caution. Don't forget, Jacob is a wanted man and there are people of other faiths here that are affected by what we do. We have to be prudent.'

'Then why'd you tell Morrison that Jake's our bishop?' Casey asked.

'Partly to protect Jacob. And you didn't leave me many options, son. When you told your story to Mrs. Thompson on the radio this morning, she wasn't alone. Sandy and two ladies from the guild were with her, and they heard all about the young bishop that saved your lives. This is a small community, and within the hour Jacob was legend. Why do you suppose so many people followed you here?'

'Wow,' Mike laughed. 'And we were worried that they wouldn't like him!'

'I'm convinced that, at the very least,' Doogan continued, 'our friend Jacob is a force of nature, but we'll need confirmation from the church that he's our new bishop. Tomorrow, we'll be requesting some guidance, but before then I must ask one last question.'

He stood up, put his hands behind his back, and started pacing. His face was serious again, and every now and then he'd stop like he was about to say something. He finally stopped in front of me and looked me in my eyes.

'Son, it appears that God may wish to make use of you.' Doogan told me, 'but you must understand. It will be difficult for you here. It's taken us many years, and God's grace to build our little parish, and even now there are forces trying to destroy us. Your life will be in constant peril if you continue down this path. If the parish is able to survive at all, there will be great hardships for you, and a lifetime's worth of knowledge you'll need to acquire. To be bishop here and now would be an awesome undertaking. Are you absolutely certain you wish to do this?'

It sounded to me like Doogan was trying to talk me out of staying, but he wasn't doing a very good job of it. Hell, living here would be a thousand times better than anywhere in the city. Not only that, but Becky was here, and I already kind-of promised her that I'd take the job. When I noticed Becky and the guys looking at me, I remembered how they all risked their asses getting me here.

'Yeah, I'm sure.'

'May I ask why?'

'Because I said I would,' I answered, 'and I'm good at staying alive. It sounds like you guys could use a little of that around here.'

Without another word, the old man walked to the bookshelves next to the fireplace.

'I can't argue with that, heaven help us,' he said, picking up a small black book. 'Then until we know otherwise, we can only assume that the good God has answered our prayers, and blessed us with a bishop.'

Becky was smiling again, and the guys got up and came over to stand next to me. Doogan walked up and handed me the book.

'This is yours, your Holy Bible,' he said, 'We'll be starting instruction tomorrow after mass.'

The old man paused for a second, and it looked like he was thinking about something. He took another book from his pocket and pulled a tiny card from it. Doogan handed it to me saying, 'And this is my gift to you. It's been with me for many, many years.'

I wasn't so stupid about religion that I didn't recognize the little picture of Christmas. On one side of the card was the manger scene, with the baby and his mom, and on the other side were the Ten Commandments typed out in ridiculously tiny letters. The picture was covered in plastic and it was creased and worn, but the colors were bright and blue. It was pretty cool.

'Thanks.'

I put the card in my book as the clock on the fireplace went off again. The chiming surprised Becky.

'Oh my gosh, I've got to get over to the school!'

'Bishop Walker,' Doogan spoke up. 'We have just enough time for Mrs. Thompson to show you to your room.'

'And then,' he sighed, 'we're off to meet your flock.'.

ANCIENT WISDOM

We walked quietly back into the front room, and Doogan shouted up the stairs for Mrs. Thompson. I was glad he did. I remembered that the old housekeeper lady had taken my pie, and I was starting to wonder if there was anything left of it. While I was standing there waiting to ask her about it, I heard Casey say 'See ya later, Jake' and suddenly everyone was bailing.

I was in a weird mood anyway, from all the talking we'd done, and I felt a little deserted standing there next to the old man. After spending every minute of the last few days with Becky and the guys, I guess I wasn't expecting everybody to leave. Becky paused in the doorway when she saw me. Maybe she knew that I was getting restless, and she was worried that I might say something.

'Father?' she asked Doogan, 'Jenny can direct the choir. Would you like me to stay and help you with—'

'You run along now,' he interrupted. 'Bishop Walker and meself will be along shortly.'

Becky smiled. 'See you in a few minutes.'

Sometimes, even when there's no good reason for it, I get pissed when I'm tired. I don't know why it happens, but I remember feeling edgy and thinking that I should be leaving with Becky rather than hanging with the old ones. I had to fight the urge to mouth off again, like I did in the Hershberger's backyard. When the door banged shut, I kept watching her through the screen. Becky's got the kind of shape that looks excellent when she's walking away, and I think I spaced a little. She was almost to the woods when I heard Doogan's voice from behind me.

'You're quite fond of her, aren't you me boy?'

'Yeah,' I said without thinking, 'and that ass of hers is a work of art.'

When I turned and saw the look on his face I felt stupid and mad at myself. To make things worse, Mrs. Thompson was standing there too.

'Damn it,' I grumbled. 'I shouldn't have said that, huh?'

'Technically, son,' Doogan said, laughing, 'I don't think we're supposed to be *thinking it* either.'

He closed the door before turning back to me, and he noticed that I was still glaring at Mrs. Thompson. She had a stunned look on her face and I waiting for her to piss me off by saying something.

'Calm yourself, Jacob,' he said. 'You are amongst friends here. Be at peace, lad. We're here to help you, and nothing said in confidence shall ever leave this place. Believe me, son, you can trust Mrs. Thompson as I do, with me very life.'

After hearing all that, I figured I'd wait a few minutes before bringing up my missing pie.

Doogan scratched his head and let out a sigh.

'But we need to practice a bit of discretion in what we say, at least until your people get to know you.'

He stepped up to me, stroked his chin and added, 'Would you do something for me, lad?'

'Sure.'

'There's a wee bit of political advice that I'd like to pass on to you, if you please. It's an ancient wisdom, a rule of sorts, which has served our smarter religious for thousands of years, from popes to altar boys. I think it will help you today as we meet our parishioners. If I share it with you, would you try to remember it this afternoon?'

'Yeah, I guess so.'

'Good lad!' he said, putting his hand on my shoulder, 'Then remember, son, unless it is absolutely necessary, keep your trap closed!'

I had to laugh. Doogan's the only guy I'd ever seen who could tell you to *shut the hell up* and make it sound he just did you a favor. His meaning was clear enough though, and if I was gonna fit in with the Churchers, I knew I'd have to learn to choose my words better. For today anyway, keeping my mouth shut sounded like a good idea.

'It's a deal.'

'When I introduce you to people,' he went on, 'simply say *how do you do*. I'll be right beside you to help with everything else.'

After that, Mrs. Thompson led me up the front stairs, and as we reached the top I remember seeing tons of pictures on both sides of us. I didn't have time for a good look, but there were all kinds of them, in different sizes and frames. Some were prehistoric, not even in color, and they weren't like the pictures in the other houses I'd seen. Instead of moms and dads and families, these were pictures of big groups of people hanging out in and around the church. Some were outside at picnics, and there were other pictures taken in a big room with people dancing together. For a second I got the same feeling I had on Northwood Avenue. In another world and time, St. Lucy's was a crowded place, buzzing with all sorts of people and activity. Squeezed in between all the pictures upstairs were four rooms, and except for the bathroom, their doors were all closed. Mrs. Thompson walked to the last door on the right and opened it.

'This is your room, Your Grace.' She announced. 'I hope everything is in order.'

I had to stop when I got to the doorway. I'm not kidding, you could have slept ten people in there, even with all that furniture everywhere! It was as big as the whole front of my apartment on the West End, and there were two windows facing the trees out back, with puffy brown chairs sitting next to them. The bed was down a little ways from the door, and there was a small table next to it, with a lamp on it. The far wall had shelves, and about a million books. There was a chest of drawers with a mirror, and my pictures of my mom and the house were already leaning against the mirror, just as if they belonged there. Becky must have slipped my stuff to Mrs. Thompson while we were talking.

'There is a change of clothes in the dresser, Your Grace. Miss Wells told me that we'll have more clothes for you in a day or two.'

'You can call me Jake or Bishop Jake if you want to.'

'Bishop Jake.' She nodded, smiling. 'If there's anything else you need, please let me know.'

She walked back through the door, and she wasn't gone for two seconds before Doogan's voice boomed from downstairs.

'Saints in heaven! Isn't anyone else hungry? Let's not be all day about it!'

Looking back on it now, that first afternoon zoomed by in a heartbeat, and I hope I can remember everything I need to say about it. After Doogan shouted I went downstairs and he told me that we'd better head over to the school. At first I thought he was talking about the busted-up school by the church, but he took me out the side door and steered us straight into the woods again. It was a thin path behind the rectory, and we walked a good ten minutes into thick woods before we got to a clearing. There were a few people standing around talking, and for the first time I saw Churcher dudes that weren't Casey or Mike. A little boy that was with them ran into the school and shouted, 'They're here!'

The school building was like the other log houses, only lots bigger, with little square windows every couple of feet. It was a big place, set in a clearing of maybe five hundred feet round, but I noticed something weird about it. There weren't any *roads* leading here. The only way to the school was to use the little paths like we did. It seemed to me that this place was hidden in the forest for a reason, and meant to be kept secret. I remember wondering if this had been done on purpose. Even if they could find it, the Feds would have to leave their vehicles behind and come here through the woods, all lined up in a row. When you're outnumbered, that's a smart way to even up the odds. I didn't think that Churchers thought about stuff like that, but whoever built this place made sure that it was buried deep in the woods, and it could be easily defended. Doogan must have sensed my curiosity.

'After they burned our school, this was our first sanctuary,' he explained, 'but now, praise God, it serves as the new school.'

The guys standing by the door ducked into the school first, and when we got inside everyone in the place stood up. For some reason I can't explain, I was more nervous walking in there than when the Feds were chasing us! There must have been a hundred people waiting, and when they all got up it sounded like the whole building was shaking. There were long benches on either side of us where the people could sit, and there was an open area up front with a bunch of kids standing. They were all different in age and size, and about half of them were girls, but all of them were in white shirts and the little females wore skirts. They were all staring at me nervously with books in their hands. Becky was standing next to them, wearing a purple skirt, and shoes that made her taller. It was the first time I ever saw Becky with her hair down, and she looked amazing.

'Good people,' Doogan shouted, silencing the crowd, 'as I know you must have heard by now, we have a bishop! This is young Bishop Walker, from the cathedral in Cleveland.'

I hadn't heard anybody call the city *Cleveland* since I was a kid, but everyone must have known what Doogan meant cause they all went nuts, clapping and whistling and shouting at us.

And by the way, if you ever wanna feel stupid, try standing in the middle of a hundred people you've never seen with all of them clapping and staring at you. I didn't know what the hell to do, and Doogan finally poked me and said, 'For heaven's sake lad, smile!'

With everyone still clapping, we walked up to the front row, just a few feet from Becky and the kids. Doogan turned to the people, put his hands in the air, and everyone got quiet again.

'After the concert, we'll be meeting the bishop at dinner, but for now let's bow our heads.'

When everybody lowered their heads to pray, I stole a good

look at all the people there. It was like Becky said, the dudes were hugely outnumbered, and just as I guessed, they all looked tired. Most of them were well-fed except for a couple of the younger females. They were skinny as Huffers, even though they were smiling and otherwise healthy-looking. The other thing you should know about Churchers is that they're *clean*. The guys wear long pants, and the girls mostly wear skirts. The females wear makeup too, except for the little ones, and I'm not making this up but the Churcher girls have a smell to them.

I'm not just saying that they smell *clean* either. Even in the dark you can smell female Churchers because they smell flowery. At first I thought it might be because they wash up so much, or maybe it was something in their diet, but Becky told me later that they wear perfume. It's the female version of aftershave.

In the middle of Doogan's prayer, I caught something that made me laugh. I'd just noticed Mike and Casey, in new clothes and sitting in the row behind us, when Lightning walked into the school, barefoot and in her yellow dress. With everyone's head down praying, she paraded up to Casey's row and took a seat right beside him. When the praying stopped, Casey was shocked to find her there, and the dark haired girl who'd been sitting next to Casey looked pissed. She said something to Lightning about it, but Lightning never budged. When you're deaf, I guess it's a lot easier to ignore people.

Once Doogan said 'Amen' everyone sat down again and got comfortable. Becky stood off to the side of the kids, and they all started singing. Becky didn't sing, she just stood there, kind of waving at the kids, but it sounded great. I don't remember ever hearing singing like that before, and there was something strangely peaceful about it. It was easy to drift off, and I think I daydreamed through most of it. I remember that they sang two or three songs. It was no big surprise that all their songs mentioned God in them. One was about America America, and one of them was about a guy named Art and how great he was.

As soon as the singing was over and we finished clapping, Doogan took me into the back end of the school, where a desk was pushed up against the wall. There were white papers tacked up all over the wall there, and we stopped to have a look at them. I didn't think they were any good until Doogan said that the little kids made them. They were drawings of the church, and most of them said *Welcome Bishop* on the top.

When we got outside again, the dudes of the parish were taking the benches out of the building and setting them next to tables behind the school. There were two huge grills smoking by a tent, and the air smelled so good my mouth was watering. Everywhere I looked people were moving around, and it was fun to watch. Mrs. Thompson was by one of the grills, talking to a tall sweaty dude who was cooking the food. We walked up to the table up front, and as we were sitting down I caught sight of a little cabin on the tree line. I remembered that Becky told me that her and Mike lived behind the school and I figured it was their place. Most of the other people were still finding a seat when Mrs. Thompson and a dark haired girl named Sandy started bringing us food. She was the same girl that was sitting next to Casey in the school before Lightning showed up. Even though most of the people were still finding their seats, or lining up for food, everybody stopped when Doogan shouted 'Let us pray.'

That's something else about Churchers. Just like Becky and the guys, they're always willing to stop what they're doing and pray. It's not a big deal, because it doesn't take very long, but it's still kind of strange watching so many people praying at the same time. I lowered my head like I knew what I was doing, and after a thunderous *amen*, everyone was moving again. That was the afternoon I learned why Churchers are always thanking God before eating. Churcher food is truly amazing!

They have something called *corn-on-the-cob*, and if I knew how good it was, I never would have filled up on all that chicken. Then there were the smashed potatoes, and chicken-sauce called *gravy* that you pour on top. Doogan convinced me to try the green beans, but they smelled like old socks, so I tossed them out on the grass when nobody was looking. I noticed the kids drinking something at the next table, and Mrs. Thompson brought me some to try. She said it was a special treat called *chocolate milk*, and although it didn't sit too well with all the other stuff in my stomach, it was sweet and amazingly delicious.

And by the way, I completely nailed that *how do you do* thing.

That whole afternoon people were coming up to our table to meet me, and I didn't screw it up once. It's unreal, but if you say *how do you do*, keep your mouth shut and smile, you can do pretty well socially. After a few minutes Becky and the guys came over to our table to eat. Like clockwork, Lightning showed a second later and squeezed in between Becky and Casey.

I won't bore you by talking about all the people I met that afternoon. Hell, I don't remember most of their names anyway, but something important happened when we were doing desert. Mrs. Thompson had just given me another piece of the cake with gray frosting when a girl named Mary ran up to Doogan. She was about thirteen, and when I looked up and saw her, she looked like she was about to cry.

'I looked again, Father, and it's gone.' she complained, 'A whole basket, my mother's rolls, strudel and berry wine. It's all gone! Someone stole it, and Sadie Phillips said she saw a stranger by the back of our house this morning!'

'We have more than enough,' Doogan said calmly. 'If a stranger has made his way to us, perhaps God thinks he needs it more than we do.'

Doogan's comments only pissed the kid off. Her eyes got bigger and she put her hands on her hips.

'But it isn't fair, Father!' she complained. 'We baked all day so a thieving stranger could—'

'Mary, girl,' Doogan interrupted gently, 'we have plenty. And did you notice that Bishop Jacob can't get enough of your mint cake?'

It was like someone threw a switch and Mary's face lit up. She stared back at me, watching me chew. After a few seconds, I knew I'd better say something.

'Yeah,' I acknowledged, with my mouth full. 'This stuff's amazing!'

The kid forgot all about her missing basket. She gave me a proud and excited 'Thank you, Bishop Walker' and started making her way back to her table.

It was the first time I saw Doogan do that. It's probably something they teach in priest school, but Doogan knew his people so well that he could make them forget their problems by just saying a couple words to them.

I felt eyes on me, and when I looked to my right there was a lady in a blue dress talking with Becky. Like all Churchers she had nice clothes, and this one was wearing a hat and a long-sleeved jacket. She had big eyes and her black hair was down and streaked with gray. Holding her hand was a little girl who looked just like her, even in the same clothes and hat. The weirdest thing about her was that she was talking with Becky but her eyes never left me. Even after I made eye contact, she kept staring. When Doogan caught sight of her, he stood up.

'Beth! I'm so glad you could come,' he greeted her. 'Where's our Bill?'

'Thank you, Father. I'm afraid Bill couldn't get away.'

The woman walked up to us and when Doogan poked me, I stood up too.

'Bishop Walker,' he announced. 'This is Mrs. Elizabeth Morrison, and her daughter Judy, some of our oldest and dearest parishioners.'

I'm not sure if I looked surprised or not, but I recognized the name Morrison. I knew right away that this female belonged to the Fed I'd met earlier. It didn't make much sense to me, how a Fed could also be a Churcher, but the little girl was smiling up at me so I stuck out my hand and gave her one of my best *how do you dos.*

The woman's voice was angry, but her eyes stayed soft and brown.

'Bishop Walker,' she said crossly, taking my hand. 'My husband is facing an inquiry and possible disciplinary action because of you.'

Without taking another breath, she leaned into Doogan and added, 'We have to be careful, Father. Bill wants you to keep him out of site for the next few weeks.'

'Thank you, me dear,' he replied softly, 'You can count on that.'

Beth nodded, and with the slightest of smiles she said, 'It was a pleasure, Bishop Walker.'

At that moment it hit me. The Morrisons, or at least these female Morrisons, really were Churchers. It was cool and intriguing. These Churchers were kind of like spies, or like the double-agents in the books I've read. It was probably overkill, but I gave her another perfectly executed *how do you do*.

CHURCHER PARTIES

After the Morrisons left, a few other people started leaving, and at first I thought that the barbeque was over. Don't forget, we started that day out on the boat getting to the Hershberger's place, and with my belly full again, I was feeling beat. I was getting bored too, and about ready to nod off when I saw a whole new wave of Churchers coming at us from the woods. It was unbelievable. I don't think I've ever seen so many people together in one place before.

And by the way, when a Churcher says there's gonna be a barbeque, they're really talking about throwing a humongous party. I knew that getting a bishop was a big thing to Churchers, but I never expected everybody to celebrate like they did. Once everyone got tired of meeting me, and Mrs. Thompson and her friends cleaned up the plates, everyone began roaming around. The men started playing games, throwing horse's shoes at metal stakes, and the females traveled around in packs, talking and laughing with other packs of females. You should have seen how much fun they were having, and I'll bet I had just as much fun watching them. It was a beautiful summer night and there was a feeling in the air, something calm, peaceful and happy. In every direction I looked, there were kids playing.

There was loud talking and constant laughter everywhere, and when it got dark, the back of the school lit up with little lights, *electric lights*. The Churchers had electricity and not only that, but all the shitters in the school flushed! I flushed every one of them at least three times, and I would have figured out how they worked if it hadn't been for the two little boys there. They were staring at me, giving me the stink eye, and when it started getting weird I went back to my table.

And remember how I said that the parish was a living and growing place? Well, it was growing faster than I first thought. I bet I saw seven or eight pregnant women that afternoon. It was the first time I'd ever seen one in person, and they're fascinating to watch. A couple of them were so pregnant that they walked funny.

Females always struck me as being fragile in the first place, but it must be a whole lot worse when they're gonna have a baby. They get round, slow and wobbly, and everybody kept telling them to sit down, or rest, or take it easy. Their guys wouldn't leave them alone for very long either, and although all the pregnant girls were dressed nice and pretending to be *normal*, anyone could see that there was something delicate and special about them. As I sat there watching, something else dawned on me. It was the first time in forever that I'd seen families, real families with moms and dads and kids. I even met an old grandma lady that reminded me of the women in my old building.

The Churcher dudes also surprised me that day, and I watched them for a long time too. Every guy that was old enough to grow hair on his chin had a family, and Churcher dudes pick out one single female for life, and that's it. At first I thought that it was because their females are always pregnant and fragile, and it's enough trouble having just one of them, but Doogan told me later that God wants guys to be smart about females. He wants men to pick out one favorite girl and be done with it. It may not sound logical, with the girls outnumbering the guys so much, but I saw it for myself and the Churcher dudes all looked happy and satisfied with it.

The idea of having a permanent girl was strange and intriguing to me. Like any other guy, thinking about females is pretty much how I spend my spare time, but I never pictured anything like how the Churchers do it. When you grow up in the city, you never see girls like Churcher girls. In the city, females aren't something you can keep. The few females left in the city are empty, like something's missing from inside of them. Hell, I'd lived in the city my whole life, and after my mom died, I don't remember ever seeing a girl laugh until I met Becky. As I sat there with the Churchers that night, I wondered how a dude could ever get tired of watching girls laugh.

Maybe I was thinking too much because I messed up again. It had been dark for a while and the electricity was off, but you could still see everything because of the huge fire burning in the field behind the school. There wasn't much to do but sit and talk by the fire, but it was more fun than you might expect and the Churchers really liked it. Watching the guys pairing up with their females got me thinking. Mike, Casey, and Lightning had already moved over to the fire, so I got up and slid into the chair next to Becky.

The minute I did, the air got heavy and I knew something was wrong. Before I said a word, she shot Doogan a panicky look.

'I better get home,' she announced, getting to her feet.

By her reaction, I knew that I must have done something stupid, but I didn't have a clue.

'I'll walk ya,' I offered, 'We can talk—'

'No thank you, Bishop Walker,' she interrupted. 'I live right over there.'

It wasn't like I put my arm around her or got too close or anything like that, but in the flickering glow of the fire I could tell she was freaking.

'Hey, what's wrong? Did I do something again?'

Becky was staring at Doogan like she was expecting him to say something. She still hadn't looked up at me, and before I could say anything else, she turned and just walked away. I couldn't believe it, and as I stood there watching, I heard the old man's voice from behind me.

'Well, now,' he said softly. 'It's time we should be saying goodnight too.'

With that stupid look on his face and the way Becky ditched me, something dawned on me. It hit me that Becky didn't like me anymore, or at least she didn't feel like I felt for her. It was a crummy way to end the party, and I couldn't help wondering if Becky *ever* liked me. All I could do was stand up to leave with the old man. It was a strange angry feeling, like being pissed off, but with your heart stuck in your stomach. I'm not whining, but it's honestly the shittiest feelings in the world and I wouldn't wish it on a damn Fed.

The walk back through the woods to the rectory was quiet. Mrs. Thompson and I walked behind Doogan and his flashlight, and I don't remember saying two words to anybody. I was growing more and more pissed, but more bummed than pissed. Once we got inside, Mrs. Thompson disappeared into the kitchen, and Doogan put his hand on my shoulder.

'Son, I need to speak with you.'

'Save it,' I shot back. 'I've had enough talk for one day.'

The last thing I wanted to do was talk, and I went right up to my room and slammed the door behind me. I would have done anything to get my mind off Becky and that shitty feeling, but it wasn't an easy feeling to shake. I sat on the bed and tried to think, but my brain kept showing me all the shit I didn't want to think about.

I thought about *everything*, the people at the barbeque, the pregnant females, our escape from the city, and especially how Becky wouldn't look at me anymore. Finally, I tried paging through my new book, but everything I saw made things worse. The bible-book Doogan gave me didn't have any pictures in it, and at the first part I turned to, the guy who wrote it rambled on and on about who begot who. I'm not lying, the whole page was nothing but *begots*. It was just what I needed. Everybody was busy begetting with somebody else, and the girl I wanted wouldn't even look at me anymore! In a few seconds I'd had enough of books too, and I threw it out toward the open window. I rolled over on my side and my eyes had just closed when I heard a knock at the door.

'Bishop Jake?' Mrs. Thompson's whispered.

I got up, opened the door and found Mrs. Thompson standing on the other side. She was holding an oil lamp in one hand, and a big piece of pie in the other.

'The electricity will be going off in a moment,' she said, handing me the pie. 'If you need to visit the lavatory, there's a lantern in your nightstand.'

'Thanks,' I said, taking the pie.

I didn't know what a lavatory was, or why anybody'd want to visit one, but I didn't think to ask her about it. The whipped cream on the pie was distracting me.

Mrs. Thompson set the lamp down on my desk, and then she lit the lamp next to my bed. I was still angry, but it was nice of her to bring me the food.

'Hey, this is great,' I said. 'You want some?'

I held the plate out to her, but she smiled and shook her head.

'No thank you, Your Grace.'

There was something I'd been thinking about since morning, something that kept coming back to me over and over that day, and even though I'd been thinking mostly about Becky, it popped into my brain again.

'Mrs. Thompson?' I asked. 'This morning, Morrison said that everyone here was in danger because of me. Is that true?'

'We were in danger long before you arrived, Your Grace,' she answered, before changing the subject. 'Tell me, did you enjoy the program today?'

'Yeah, it was great,' I admitted. 'But I don't think I'll ever get used to being around so many females.'

'In many ways, it's been the most difficult part of our punishment.'

All at once the lights went off, except for our oil lamps, and in the softer glow I noticed Mrs. Thompson's gently wrinkled face. Although her brown eyes were bright and there was that constant smile, there was also something sad about the lady. She had a worn and wise look, like the books on the shelf behind her. She wasn't as old and wise as Doogan, but hell, nobody's as old as Doogan, and there was something in her voice that was familiar and reassuring.

'I don't get it,' I told her. 'Why is having so many females around a punishment?'

Mrs. Thompson gushed a laugh, and for a second, she looked younger.

'The punishment isn't having too many women, Your Grace!' she said, still laughing. 'The hardship is that God has given us so few men.'

She paused, and her eyes were suddenly distant.

'It's because of how the world was in those days,' she added, 'and the part that women played toward the end.'

I thought she was gonna spill some details, but when her face turned sad again, I knew I'd have to pull it out of her.

'Can you tell me about it?' I prompted, 'I mean, unless you gotta go or something.'

It looked like she was still thinking, and she walked over to the big chair by the curtains. She found my Bible on the floor and I half-expected her to bitch at me about it, but she carefully picked it up at placed it on my desk. She sat on the edge of the chair and turned to the window. It was black outside and the glass was like a mirror.

'It's hard to imagine now, Bishop Jake, but there was a terrible discontentment in people. Men and women were drawn into the selfishness of the age. Men had convinced themselves that they didn't need God, and women were convinced that they needed neither God nor man. They forgot their importance to the world. Women became increasingly more like men without considering how much they were losing or how they were lowering themselves. With both men and women turned from God, families became broken and disfigured. Innocence was difficult to find, even in the very young. Instead of being mankind's balance, his better part, and the love that sustains his life, women embraced all the qualities that make men so base, vile and disgusting.'

Mrs. Thompson obviously didn't think too highly of dudes, and she looked over and caught me grinning at her.

'Oh, I didn't mean anything *personal*, Your Grace.'

'No problem,' I laughed. 'Sounds like we know a lot of the

same people.'

Again Mrs. Thompson drifted off a little, and I had to say something to get her talking.

'What I still don't get,' I said, 'is that almost everyone died in the city when the darkness came. Females are smaller and weaker. Hell, almost all of the females in the city are gone. Out here, more females survived than the guys. How's that possible?'

'I don't know how it was for others, your grace, but I can tell you what happened to my Charlie.'

'Oh,' she added, 'of course Charlie was my husband.'

What little color had been in Mrs. Thompson's face drained away, and in the dull light she was pale as a ghost.

'The angel of death was in the darkness, Your Grace, cunning and evil! People tried to hide from it, but it lured them from safety by pretending to be friends and family.'

She turned to the window again.

'One couldn't bear to look at it, or hear it, and it was suicide to touch it. It came on like a swirling, drowning black storm, with the force of scream. When it came, our twins were playing at their cousin's on the other side of town, not too far from here.'

A curious look came over her.

'In many ways men are weaker than women, you know. It's so much harder for them to resist their nature. Charlie couldn't stop himself, knowing that Megan and Molly were out there. He locked me inside, and he went out to find them.'

Mrs. Thompson's eyes were misty, and I felt like shit for asking her to talk about this.

'I don't know if this answers your questions, Your Grace,' she went on, 'but when the darkness came, I think that many, many men went out to look for someone, and that's why they were taken in greater numbers.'

'Hey, Mrs. Thompson,' I apologized. 'I didn't mean to bring up something that—'

'Charlie was a good husband and father,' she interrupted confidently. 'He's found the kids, and soon we'll all be together in heaven.'

Like most of the Churchers, there was a toughness in Mrs. Thompson. The old girl stood up, picked my plate up from off the bed, and smiled.

'Will you be needing anything else, Your Grace?'

'No, I'm good. Thanks.'

When the door closed again, I sat there feeling stupid. Mrs. Thompson's story reminded me of a couple of things, and I remembered where I was and what I was doing just a few days ago. I remembered how important it was for me, getting Becky and the guys home, and that they'd risked their lives getting me here. It wasn't too dark to see my mom's picture on the dresser, and it hit me that if she was still around, she'd be about the same age as Mrs. Thompson. I knew that I should have been feeling happy and grateful, like a damn Churcher, but I was still pissed about Becky.

All of a sudden I felt anxious and smothered. I needed to think, to breathe and get some air, but most of all I wanted to see Becky again. Maybe she didn't give a shit about me anymore. Maybe she never did, but she was gonna have to tell me that herself. She owed me that, didn't she?

I saw the curtains rustling by the window, and I opened the drawer to my nightstand. I found the *lantern* that Mrs. Thompson talked about. It was really just a flashlight, but it was silvery and cool, and I stuck it in my back pocket with my knives. I went out the window and stepped onto the roof above the back porch. It was kind of like my balconies on the West End, and a second later I was standing in the backyard of the rectory, with the stars above and the darkness of the woods in front of me. The air was cool and refreshing and it smelled like the nighttime.

I was feeling better already.

THE STRANGER

There's something unexpectedly cool about being in the woods at night, and as I started back through the trees toward the school, the breezy darkness reminded me of something that I haven't thought about in forever. It reminded me of being downtown when I was a kid.

It was a long time ago, before the darkness, and there were still a lot of people and gangs in the city. I was living downtown off Union Street and I used to climb the stairs of the skyscrapers to search for food. Everywhere else in the city had either burned or was picked over, and you'd be lucky to find anything left to eat, but high in the tall buildings I'd always find something good. In the bottom drawer of a desk, a forgotten vending machine or in the pocket of a sweater stretched over a chair, there was always some treasure waiting to be found up there. I guess nobody but me felt like walking up sixty stories in the dark to look for food, and yeah the darkness was creepy as hell, but sometimes you've gotta push yourself to get something good. It's funny what you think about sometimes.

Anyway, that's what was going through my head as I worked my way back through the woods. At least *this* darkness was alive with sound, and the air was fresh and moving. I've always had a good sense of direction, but I had to keep turning the flashlight on to stay on the path to the school. In a little while I smelled smoke, and I could see firelight poking through the trees in front of me. I didn't want the whole world to know what I was doing, so I shut off the flashlight before heading into the clearing.

It was getting late, and it looked like the party must have broken up while I was at the rectory. Everybody was gone except for one guy and his girl. He was busy kissing her over by the fire. I kept to the tree line so they wouldn't see me, but hell, by the way they were going at it, I probably could have waltzed right past them without being seen. He finally let her up to breath, and when I caught a good look at them, I had to stop.

'Mike?!' I shouted.

They both shot up, and when they saw it was only me, Mike laughed.

'Jake! What are you doing out here so late?'

I jogged over to the fire to join them, and I saw that Mariam looked embarrassed. Even in the crummy light I could see her turning red. She wasn't in her Amish clothes tonight. Her hair was down and tied back, and she was in her jeans again.

'I need to talk with Becky,' I answered. 'Is she home?'

'No, she went off to say her prayers,' Mike answered. 'She's either at the church or over at the pond. She won't be long.'

'Bishop Jake?' Mariam interrupted, still a little out of breath. 'Becky was upset about something. Is everything all right?'

'Yeah, I guess.'

'Go on inside and make yourself at home,' Mike offered, pointing to the house. 'I'll be back after I get Mariam home.'

'And Jake,' he added, smiling at Mariam. 'Mariam's not supposed to be here. I'd appreciate it if you wouldn't mention—'

'I got it,' I nodded. 'No problem.'

Mike took Mariam's hand, and as they walked off toward the woods I wandered over to Becky's house. It was a little place, probably as big as the other log houses I'd seen, but it looked smaller because it was so close to the school. There were two steps up to the porch, and two white chairs and a little table sitting next to the door, but the thing that hit me most was all of the flowers.

There were yellow flowers in pots all over the place and some purple flowers too, in a long wooden box under the window.

With Becky off praying, there was no way of knowing how long I'd be waiting, so I figured I'd check the place out. I walked around back, and the first thing I found was a little garden close to the house, surrounded by white stones. There weren't any flowers in it, just leafy little plants. The fire was still burning in the field, and it shed just enough light for me to see a few more chairs in the yard, and a cool hanging bed stretched between two trees.

Sometimes you don't know how tired you are until you stop moving, and as I stood there waiting for Becky, I started to realize how worn-out I was. It always happens like that. A minute ago I was all fired up and I knew exactly what I wanted to say to Becky, but with every second that she wasn't there, I was feeling more and more beat. The hanging bed looked like a great place to wait, and although it was tricky getting into, it turned out to be way too comfortable. I never planned on falling asleep, but once I laid my head down I was out in a heartbeat.

The next thing I knew, I heard laughter, a low sarcastic chuckle that echoed in the darkness. There were trees all around me again, and I knew right away that I was in a nightmare. There was a heavy threatening feeling in the air, and it felt like I'd swallowed something cold.

I was limping and out of breath as I stepped out from the woods and into the clearing by the school. A heavy mist covered the grass at my feet, and the dew was so thick that the trees and the school were dripping wet. The school glistened in the moonlight, maybe a hundred feet in front of me, and I could see a faint light in the windows. The laughing stopped, and a voice boomed out so loudly that I jumped.

'You can't save them.'

A pain shot through my leg, and when I looked down I saw the bandage on my thigh, tied over my pants and soaked red. There were other voices, real voices, shouting words from somewhere behind me, and I heard gunfire. But the voices and gunshots were strangely far off and unimportant. All I knew was that I desperately needed to get to the school.

133

There was no wind, but the doors to the school were banging open and closed. They moved together, too loud and too fast, slamming themselves as if something unseen was playing with them like a toy. When the doors opened I saw him standing on the other side, a backlit silhouette of a man in a hoody, with his eyes glowing more brightly than the light around him. I already knew that it was that Jodie asshole. I knew it the minute the nightmare started, and I started running toward him.

'You can't save them!' he repeated.

When I reached the school the doors had closed again, and I pulled a blade and kicked them open, but I froze, unable to go on.

The floor of the school had disappeared! It was weird and impossible but right in front of me was a bottomless hole where a floor should have been. The pit was exactly the width of the school, and I could see layers of earth, and twisted roots sticking out from its walls. There was some light, but the darkness and shadows were abnormally black, with a threatening thickness, as if the blackness was animated and alive. I could see that the pit went down for miles, as though the hole gave off its own dull glow. The mist at my feet rolled over its edges, like a slow gray waterfall, and I can still remember that it smelled like dirt, freshly broken earth combined with a scent like burning hair.

I sensed movement, and when I looked up I saw something that took the wind from me and knotted up my guts. In the back of the school, where the kids sang to me that morning, I saw Mariam, Lightning, and Becky. They were all standing on chairs with their hands tied behind their backs and a noose around their necks. The ropes stretched up and disappeared into the darkness of the rafters. The chairs were unusual, tall fancy chairs with armrests and a big cross carved onto their backs. It was bizarre and unreal but the chairs were lined up in midair, as if by magic.

It didn't matter that everything was crazy and didn't make any sense. I needed to get to them, to save them. But how? They were there in the distance, staring at me with horrified eyes that begged me for help. There were tears on Becky's cheeks, and Lightning was sobbing.

The voice taunted, *'I warned you, Bishop.'*

As I watched helplessly and unable to move, the chairs flew away one by one with a loud crack, as if someone had kicked them into the bottomless hole. From left to right, with an ugly wrenching pause in between, my friends began dropping into the emptiness, until with a dull snap, the rope stopped their fall.

Off in the distance I heard someone screaming. The voice was cussing and raging away in shouts of horror and pain, and just when I realized that the voice was mine, I forced my eyes open.

I don't care who you are, a dream like that messes with your head, and when I sat up I wasn't even sure where I was. My body was dripping with sweat and when my eyes focused, I thought I was still dreaming. There at the corner of Becky's house I saw someone. With the fire dying in the distance behind him, I could see that he wore high boots and the short haircut of a Fed! I couldn't see his face but we stared at each other for a sec, and when I swung my legs out of the tree bed, he took off running. I fell out of the damned tree bed trying to get to my feet, but then I started after him.

There was already a blade in my hand, and by the time I got to the field, I was running at full speed. I was pissed that a Fed would be creeping around Becky's house, but there was something weird about it too. Why would a Fed run off like that? He was a short guy and I could tell by how he moved that he was thin, but he was also fast as hell. Maybe it was my new shoes or all the eating I'd done over the last few days, but I chased him all the way to the end of the field without gaining an inch on him. I expected him to slow down when he hit the woods, but he headed straight into the forest. The last thing I wanted to do was turn on my flashlight. If he had a gun it'd be like asking the bastard to shoot me, but I didn't want him getting away. I switched the light on and followed him into the woods.

It bothered me that a Fed seemed to know more about these paths than I did, but I kept going as fast as I could, and after about thirty feet the forest opened up into a little street with some log houses. The Fed was nowhere in sight, and I was starting to think that I'd lost him when I heard something. I didn't recognize the sound but I followed it into the backyard on my right, cautiously scanning everything with my flashlight. When I got to the back of the house, I laughed when I saw what had caused the noise.

Remember how I said the Churchers have white sheets drying behind their houses? Well, in the back of this house was a rope still stretched between two trees. The dumbass Fed must have hit the rope at full speed because he was flat on his ass, half conscious, and moaning like he'd just run into a brick wall. The chase was over, and I was already close enough to kill him.

'Try running from me again, asshole,' I said, moving beside him, 'and I'll waste you.'

When he turned toward me, I couldn't believe it. It was that same little Fed from the boat, the one that Becky let go before we got to the Hershberger's.

'Shithead?!'

He must have recognized my voice because his eyes got bigger. He sat up, but I could tell that his head was still spinning.

'What you doing here?' I asked, kicking his leg to get his attention. 'And what do the Feds want with Becky?'

'I ain't a Fed no more,' he answered. 'I couldn't go back there.'

He wasn't looking too good and he leaned away from my light. It didn't look like he was faking, but he was way too quick, and I didn't want him running off again.

'You try running again and I'll kill you,' I repeated. 'You understand?'

'Yeah, I don't think I *can* run. I think I'm gonna be sick.'

'It's just cause you hit your head,' I told him. 'If I don't kill you, you'll be ok in a couple hours.'

He glared back at me.

'Why do you hate me so much, man?'

'I hate all Feds. There's nothing special about you.'

I put the light in his face.

'So talk,' I pressed. 'What you doing here?'

'She was nice to me,' he said, nodding in the direction of

Becky's house. 'Nobody's ever been nice to me like that. I thought maybe I could try being a Churcher.'

Something dawned on me and I had to laugh. I crouched down and took a seat on the grass beside him.

'Hey! You're that thief, aren't ya? You're the one who stole the basket of food last night.'

'I got hungry, man. I had to eat something.'

Now, I know that Becky, Doogan and most of the Churchers wouldn't agree with me, but there are some people in this world that you just can't keep from screwing with. There's no denying it, the more time I spent with this kid, the more I needed to mess with him.

'So you want to be a Churcher, huh?'

'Yeah'

'You're a little late, Shithead. Churchers don't tolerate thieves,' I explained. 'They caught one last week and burned him at the stake. You could smell it for miles around here.'

'You're lying,' he said nervously, 'You can't know that. You just got here today.'

'I heard all about it,' I lied, grinning. 'And two weeks ago they caught another one, and you know what they did with him? They buried him in an anthill, right up to his neck, and poured sugar water on him.'

His eyes got big again.

'No shit,' I insisted, trying to sound believable. 'The ants ate him alive. He screamed like you wouldn't believe, and it took hours and hours for him to die.'

That's all I had to say. Shithead turned his head and started puking. When he caught me laughing at him, he got pissed.

'Why you like busting on me, man?'

'It's cause you're such a puss!' I laughed. 'How'd you ever get to be a Fed anyway?'

'Don't call me that!' he shouted, 'and there wasn't a choice in it.

The recruiters caught me and they was gonna kill me if I didn't enlist.'

'And you believed them?' I laughed. 'They say that to everybody.'

After thinking about it for a sec, something didn't sound right.

'When did all this happen?' I asked curiously. 'I haven't heard of the Feds sending out recruiters in forever?'

'It was a bad flu last spring, and lots of the older agents died. Two posts had to close and there ain't enough agents for the city patrols no more.'

'Excellent! Dead Feds are always a good thing.'

'I'm a hard worker,' he said, changing the subject. 'I'll pay back the food, and do whatever I gotta do to be a good Churcher.'

A funny feeling came over me, and for a second I almost felt sorry for the kid. A couple days ago, he'd have been dead a long time ago, but something was different now. Still, I was having too much fun to let up on him.

'We'll have to wait till tomorrow to see what the Churchers want to do with you. I'm not gonna bother waking anybody up just cause you showed up. Sometimes they like to put thieves on trial before they kill them.'

A great idea hit me and I poked him in the shoulder with my knife.

'So Shithead,' I grinned. 'What are we going to do with you till morning?'

HOLY STUFF

The voice was soft and familiar, and for a sec I thought I was dreaming. I'd been sleeping like a dead man, and when the voice suddenly got louder, I nearly jumped out of my skin.

'Jake?!'

It's the truth. Since the first day I decided to help the Churchers, I was always waking up without knowing where the hell I was! The tree bed felt strange and unfamiliar, and I sat up reaching for a blade.

Becky was right there beside me, dressed in jeans and a light blue shirt that was tied up in a knot above her waist. Like always, she looked great today, and I stared back at her while my head cleared. Her hair was wet like she'd just had a bath, and although she looked hot, she wasn't happy finding me there.

'Why are you here? Fr. Doogan was expecting you at Mass this morning.'

'I got here late. I didn't wanna wake you up.'

'Have you been out here all night?'

'Yeah, I need to talk with ya.'

Up till then, I thought I could read Becky's eyes pretty well, but this look was different, like she was sad but also nervous. She stared off toward the school and took a deep breath like she was trying to figure something out. For the first time since I'd known her, Becky wasn't sure what to do.

'Well,' she sighed. 'You'd better come inside then.'

Something was really bothering her. I remembered that I should have been pissed at her for ditching me, but I couldn't be angry when she looked sad like that. Becky walked off toward the back door, and I slid out of the tree bed and started following her. It was a cool morning, with the sun about to rise, and I remember seeing Lightning's yellow dress hanging on a white rope between two trees. When we got to the house it smelled like coffee, and there were already some pans on the stove. Without looking at me, she wrapped an apron around herself and walked over to the sink.

'Take a seat. I'll fix something.'

Becky's kitchen was different than Mariam's. It took up the whole side of her house, and you could see the back of the school through thin white curtains. There was stuff hanging everywhere, pots and pans and even a big wooden fork and spoon. There was a couch and some chairs in the other room too, and a little piano under the front window. I would have walked over to check it out, but I was busy watching Becky. I knew she was sad, but by all the noise and banging around she was doing, she must have been pissed too. She mixed up some stuff in a bowl, and started making pancakes without saying a word to me.

'So what did I do?' I started. 'Why don't you want me anymore?'

'Didn't Fr. Doogan talk to you last night?!' she shot back, spinning around to look at me.

'No, he tried,' I remembered, 'but I blew him off. Why? What's Doogan got to do with it?'

'Damn it, Jake!' she said, slamming the pancake flipper down.

She clenched her eyes closed.

'Then I'll tell you myself! Bishops don't have girlfriends! Our bishops don't take wives, ok?! We can never be together like that. It's not allowed.'

She opened her eyes again, and when the tears started, her voice got softer.

'I didn't want to tell you. Fr. Doogan promised that he'd explain it to you.'

'I don't get it. Why?'

'Because our Church doesn't permit it!' she said, shouting. 'A bishop is a full-time job, especially here and now! We're all—'

'I'm not talking about that,' I interrupted. 'Why didn't *you* want to tell me?'

She crossed her arms and glared back at me like I'd said something stupid.

'Isn't it obvious? Would I be crying if I didn't care for you? *You idiot!*'

By then I would have done or said just about anything to get her to stop crying. You can't help feeling like shit when a female is crying, and I couldn't think of anything to say back to her.'

'I know I should have told you sooner, and I never meant to deceive you.' she continued. 'It's just that I wasn't prepared for anything like you. I gave up on having a guy a long time ago. I've seen two and three women fighting over a man! Until you came along, I never expected a guy to ever want me.'

'That's stupid!' I interrupted. 'You're always clean and you've got big green eyes. And you got great hair and amazing boobs, and you always smell good.'

'You're such a charmer!' she laughed, wiping her eyes.

Becky was trying not to cry anymore. She moved over to the stove and got busy pouring pancakes.

'The few guys my age are long gone, and the ones coming of age now are so much younger. I never expected to run into you, Bishop Walker, and it was too easy for me to fall in love with you. Forgive me.'

While she was still talking, I got up and walked over to her.

'Look, Becky,' I told her. 'Don't worry about it. I'm not gonna give you up just because some old man says it's not allowed. I'll talk to Doogan.'

'There's nothing to talk about!' she exclaimed, putting her hands on her hips again, 'and this isn't Fr. Doogan's rule. It's forbidden. We can never—'

I put my hands on her face and used my thumbs to wipe away the tears. When I pulled her into a kiss she tried to get away, but I reached around her waist and pulled her in close. She wasn't expecting me to kiss her, and I wasn't either. It's just that I'd been wanting to kiss her for a long time, and something inside me didn't want to wait anymore.

The way I saw it, Becky was making a big deal about nothing, and the kiss turned out to be a good way to change the subject. It calmed her down for a while, or at least it got her thinking again. Becky didn't let go of me until the pancakes started burning, and then she did something crazy. She took the pan off the fire, looked straight up toward the ceiling and whispered, '*help me!*'

After that, Becky was acting more like herself again. She still wasn't saying much, but lucky for me, she went back to cooking breakfast. I sat back down and watched her flip pancakes and cook sausages. Everything was going ok until all of a sudden Becky stopped and walked back to me. She leaned in real close, close enough that I almost kissed her again, and then she put her hand on my face.

'Jake, this isn't the city! You're living in a world of rules now. We follow God's laws and the community's laws here, and there are some things that you can't control. Promise me that you'll try to understand that. If you can't learn to follow the rules, we're both going to get hurt. Will you promise me?'

Like I said, females complicate the shit out of things that really aren't all that difficult. I'd never let anything hurt Becky, and I couldn't believe she didn't know that by now. While I was thinking up a way to answer her, I heard footsteps. Becky moved back to the stove and a second later Mike turned the corner.

'Hey, I thought I heard voices,' he said, 'Hi Jake!'

I nodded, 'Hey.'

'Nobody was here last night when I got back, Sis,' he said,

falling into a chair at the table. 'So I guess you guys found each other?'

'No,' Becky answered. 'I found Jake asleep in the hammock this morning.'

Becky must have known that Mike was about to get up because she made tons of pancakes. Mike rubbed his eyes and poured himself some coffee. With him sitting there, I never did get a chance to answer Becky's question. Mike was still groggy from sleep and nobody said anything until Becky had all the food on the table.

'Big John said he was bringing the boat back this morning,' Mike remembered. 'I can get my poles and tackle box back.'

'Hey, that reminds me,' I told Becky, 'You remember that little Fed you let go, the one on the boat?'

'Devon?'

'Yeah, he came back. He's the one who stole the basket yesterday. I caught him sneaking around here last night. He said he wanted to be a Churcher, but I think he just got hungry.'

I took a big bite of pancakes with syrup on them, but the silence got so heavy I knew everybody was looking at me. When I looked up Becky's eyes were like saucers.

'Jake!? Please tell me you didn't…'

'Oh hell no,' I laughed. 'I didn't kill him. I tied him to that big tree over by that Tangletown place.'

'Michael?' Becky said urgently, 'you need to find him! Get him to the Church as fast as you can. We'll meet you there.'

'No hurry. Finish eating Mike.' I told him. 'He's not going anywhere.'

Mike shot up and ran upstairs, and Becky grabbed her pink backpack from behind the front door. I didn't know why yet, but I knew we were suddenly in a hurry, so I scarfed down as much food as I could. Mike was down a second later, and he headed out the back door while I followed Becky out the front.

'Hey,' I asked, 'What's the big deal?'

'We have to be careful when outsiders join the community.'

She smiled and added, 'Pay attention, Bishop Jake. This is Church business, and it's important.'

Becky passed the school and we headed through the path to the rectory. I noticed Lightning's horse tied to the porch railing again. There were a few people walking toward us from the church, and Becky said hi as we passed them.

When we got to the church and walked inside, I had to stop. It was a lot like the cathedral, except the colored glass wasn't busted out, and there were statues that still had arms and legs and heads. It was kind of cool, and bigger than it looked from outside. The colored windows formed pictures, and the sun coming in turned some of the benches different colors. It smelled like the cathedral too, and there were lots of lit candles in front of the statues, and on the table up front. On the wall behind the table was a huge cross with Jesus on it. Below that was a statue of his mom, and two other people I didn't know, and none of it was busted.

Lightning was sitting on a bench in the center of the place, and when she saw us, she ran up and hugged Becky. Lightning's hair was wet too, and like always, she was barefoot and in her yellow dress. Now that I think about it, Lightning must have had a dozen of those yellow dresses because that's all she ever wore. Doogan and Casey were sitting at the far end of the church, and they stopped talking when they saw us.

'Bishop Walker!' Doogan said, setting his book down. 'How kind of you to join us.'

'Hey, Casey,' I said, surprised to see him. 'What ya doing here?'

'He's taking religious instruction,' Doogan answered, 'as you should be doing. And in the future, Bishop Walker, when you leave for an appointment, would you be good enough to let Mrs. Thompson or meself know of it?'

'Yeah, sorry.'

'Father?' Becky interrupted. 'We have a problem.'

Becky and the old man stepped off to the side, under a tall statue of a blonde-haired girl in a long dress. They kept looking at me while they talked, and Doogan kept nodding his head. Lightning took advantage of the interruption by moving into the bench behind Casey. When I looked over, I noticed that Casey was holding the same bible-book that Doogan gave me yesterday.

'So he's got you learning this stuff too?' I grinned. 'How's he expect anybody to ever get this? It's impossible.'

'Give it time,' Casey laughed. 'It gets easier.'

'I guess,' I doubted, 'but this *bishop thing* is complicated.'

'You'll be great. It's all about finding out what God wants from you, and finding a way to do it.'

'And it's written in these moldy old books?'

'Yeah, some of it. But sometimes you'll have to find things out by asking.'

Casey nodded to the big cross and added, 'You know, it's called *prayer*.'

'I've never been any good at that,' I admitted. 'I guess I'll work on the staying alive part, and you guys and Doogan can handle the holy stuff.'

'The holy stuff?' Casey laughed. 'Praying isn't hard Jake. You should give it a try.'

Everyone jumped when the back door banged open. Mike and Shithead started walking into the church, but the kid took one look at me and froze solid.

'No way! You stay away from me!' he shouted. 'That bishop man ain't right in the head!'

I tried, but I couldn't keep from laughing.

'You're safe and welcome here, son,' Doogan assured him. 'Please come in.'

'Was he seen?' Becky asked, looking at Mike.

'Yeah,' Mike said, looking at me. 'He was gagged and tied to the tree with clothesline. Five or six people were standing there watching him, including the Kinsley girls.'

'We haven't any time to lose then,' Doogan mumbled.

Michael and the kid walked up to Doogan. I leaned quickly into Shithead as he passed, just to scare him.

'Son,' Doogan said, turning to Shithead. 'Bishop Walker informs us that you wish to join us. Do you understand that it is a death sentence to leave federal service?'

'Yes sir,' he answered, 'but I ain't going back there.'

'And you wish to join our community?'

Shithead nodded.

'Do you know anything of God or Christianity?'

'Yes sir. Well, some. My grandpa was a Baptist, and we lived with a group of Baptists up at Black River till I was eleven.'

'Then welcome, Devon,' Doogan said, smiling. 'We're happy to have you.'

'Michael, me boy,' Doogan called. 'Please get Devon to Dr. Weiss as discretely as possible.'

I poked Becky. 'Dr. Weiss?'

'Some members of the community don't think we should accept anyone who's ever been marked,' she explained. 'They believe that anyone who's been marked is evil and damned.'

She looked at Doogan.

'But sometimes we find people who were marked as children,' she went on, 'and people who couldn't know what the mark stood for. We can't turn them away because—'

'We mustn't presume to doubt the mercy of God,' Doogan interrupted. 'So we ask Dr. Weiss to remove the mark, or tattoo it away before it can be seen. This keeps peace in the community, and if Devon is ever caught by the Feds, they can't identify and execute him.'

Mike and the kid started leaving, and when Shithead passed me I leaned into him and quietly called him a puss again. He reacted just like he did last night, and the look on his face was hilarious.

There was noise behind me and I turned to see a big dude stepping into the church, coming in from a door behind the altar. He was out of breath and he'd already sweated through his shirt. He was carrying a big chair, and he called out to Doogan.

'Where do you want it, Father?'

'In the back behind the lector stand, Phil. To the right of the altar there.'

When he set the chair down and stepped back, the hairs on the back of my neck stood up. It was creepy and impossible, but it was the same chair that I saw in my dream! It was exactly like the chairs that Becky and the others were standing on, with the nooses around their necks. There was no doubt about it. It had the big cross carved onto the high back, and the arms padded in purple cloth. The whole thing was twisted and weird and I almost couldn't believe what I was seeing. My jaw dropped, and I mumbled something inappropriate. The big guy looked at me like I was crazy.

'Bishop Walker?' Doogan asked, 'is something troubling you, son?'

'That chair,' I asked the guy, 'where'd that come from?'

'It's been in storage, Jacob,' the priest answered curiously. 'It is the bishop's chair or cathedra. You see, since your arrival, St. Lucy's is a cathedral now. It is your seat during the Mass, and the symbolic throne where you preside over your diocese.'

When I didn't say anything Becky walked up to me.

'What's wrong, Jake?'

'Nothing. It's just that I've seen that before.'

There were plenty of things going through my head right about then, but I remember looking down at the ring on my finger and getting a funny feeling. *The bishop's chair?* How could I have seen that same chair in a dream? I could still hear Jodie's words, *you can't save them,* echoing through my head. As bizarre as the whole thing was, I remember that I wasn't scared or freaked about it. My instincts were telling me something else, something that I was absolutely sure about, even if it made no sense at all.

Someone or *some thing* was messing with my head.

CHANGES COMING

Doogan talked with Casey for another few minutes before we all started back to the rectory. The whole time I felt Becky's eyes on me, even after we left the church. She's smart about things, and she knew I was bothered about that big chair. I would have told her about it, but I didn't feel like bringing it up with everyone else there. Shithead popped into my mind again, and I started thinking about what Becky and Doogan said about being marked.

'So Becky,' I asked, 'what's wrong with the people who've been marked? You said it stood for something?'

Before Becky could answer, Doogan turned back to us.

'How much do you know about what happened, Jacob?' he asked. 'What can you remember about the tribulations?'

'I don't remember much of anything before the city burned,' I answered, 'except that we were always moving. My first memories are from the night my mom got sick. It's like most of my memories start right there.'

'I shouldn't wonder, lad,' he said softly. 'It was a traumatic time for you.'

He turned to Casey.

'Jacob should know this before the council. There are many

things he'll need to know.'

'The council?' Casey repeated, doubtingly. 'We're bringing Jake to the council?'

'That's ridiculous,' Becky objected. 'He's not ready for a council!'

'He has a right to be there, Becky girl,' Doogan sighed, 'and how would we explain the bishop's absence to everyone?'

It was getting annoying. Everyone was talking about me again, and I didn't know what the hell they were talking about.

'Alright,' I interrupted. 'What's a council?'

'Our monthly meeting of the elders,' Casey answered. 'The senior pastors from each faith in the community get together, and we discuss the topics that concern everyone.'

'Father?' he asked, turning to Doogan. 'This wasn't going to be an easy council before Jake showed up. We have the collection this evening, and now we've got Jake and Devon to talk about.'

'With God's help, we'll get through it.'

I could see the old man drift into thought as we walked on. We were already halfway through the parking lot, and the sun was coming in and out of trees on our left. Way off in the distance I saw Mike and Shithead walking toward the woods. Maybe it was because Shithead was in his Fed uniform, but for a split second it felt like I was in the city again. Before they stepped into the forest, he stopped and looked back at me across the lake of cracked asphalt. I started to flip him off, but something stopped me. For the first time, I realized something about this place.

No matter what else was happening around me, it was always steady and *calm* in Nineveh. You could almost smell it in the air, something quiet and peaceful. Last night, Mrs. Thompson said we were in danger, but everyone here was happy and hopeful. I heard laughter coming from somewhere in the woods and a generator humming behind the rectory. The Churchers were all starting their days as if they didn't have a care in the world. For a sec I wondered if the people here knew something that I didn't. It's not an easy feeling to describe, but I suddenly knew why Shithead was willing to risk his life to become a Churcher.

When we got to the house Mrs. Thompson was waiting at the door. She smiled slyly when she saw me, and held the door open.

'Good morning, Your Grace. We missed you at breakfast.'

'Yeah, sorry.'

Lightning elbowed Casey in the ribs and signed something to him. She was standing three steps high on the porch steps, and after poking him, she took a running start and jumped off the porch and onto her horse. In one smooth motion they were racing off toward the trees like Lightning and that horse were connected! She must have known that Casey would freak, and she turned back and waved before she disappearing into the woods.

I'm the first guy to admit that I don't know squat about females, but the look on Casey's face surprised me that morning. Nobody else noticed it, but for a guy who wasn't interested, he sure watched Lightning closely. It was an odd look, not the way Mike looked at Mariam, but it wasn't the look of a guy who wasn't interested either. It didn't make sense to me. Becky said that Lightning was too young, and maybe she was for a Churcher, but you sure couldn't tell it by looking at her. Nobody could blame Casey if he'd changed his mind and was interested now. It was none of my business, but I made up my mind to ask Becky about it the next time we were alone.

Doogan stopped at the door and told us to wait for him in the library, so we walked down the hall while he finished talking to Mrs. Thompson. It still smelled like tobacco in the library, even though the window was open, and I sat next to Becky on the couch. Doogan came in a second later and closed the door.

'I didn't want to discuss this in the church, Bishop Walker,' he started, taking a seat across from Casey. 'But tis a serious matter nonetheless.'

Something was bothering the old man. He had a scowl on his face, and while he stared back at me, he took out his pipe and started beating it against his hand.

'Bishop Walker, we are an ancient church with a rich history, praise God, but I've never heard of a bishop abducting someone who is inquiring about the faith and tying him to a tree!'

'Hey, wait a sec. It wasn't like that!' I said defensively. 'I caught him sneaking around Becky's house last night. How was I supposed to know that he wasn't a Fed anymore?'

'Becky's house?'

'Yeah, I got restless and wound up over there,' I answered. 'When I woke up, he was right there snooping around. After I caught him I didn't want to wake Becky, so I tied him up. What would you have done?'

'You slept at Miss Well's—'

'A little, but it was a wild night and there wasn't much sleeping,' I admitted. 'I didn't think about the kid again until Becky was making me breakfast.'

Doogan became perfectly still with his mouth open and holding his pipe a foot from his face. When Becky saw him, she let out a gasp and gave me a shove with both her hands.

'Hey?!' I grumbled. 'What was that for?!'

'Father Doogan!' she shouted, 'Jake slept on the hammock in my backyard!'

She turned to me and shoved me again. 'What's the matter with you?!'

Doogan exhaled a sigh and Casey and Mike started laughing. I didn't get what was so funny, but after a while, even Becky was grinning.

'My dear bishop!' Doogan exclaimed. 'There are certain proprieties we religious are obligated to observe, particularly with the fairer gender. There are rules—'

'Yeah, Becky told me,' I interrupted. 'And since you brought it up, that stuff's not going to work for Becky and me. We need to get a couple things straightened out around here.'

Becky hid her eyes in her hands and mumbled, '*Oh my God!*'

I was expecting Doogan to give us trouble, but he took it pretty well. He smiled, took a deep breath and pulled a leather pouch from his pocket. He calmly finished packing his pipe with tobacco and tucked the pouch away again. The old man leaned back in his chair, lit the pipe and we all watched the little cloud of smoke rise into the air.

'My dear Jacob, I hate to postpone what promises to be a fascinating conversation,' he explained, 'But we need to prepare you for a rather difficult council this afternoon. A moment ago you asked about the mark and what it represents. Perhaps we should focus on that for the moment.'

'So if you please,' he said, turning to Casey, 'would you like to begin, son? I find meself a bit winded.'

Casey had been sitting there with a smirk on his face, but he looked serious again and said, 'Sure, Father.'

'Jake,' Casey continued, 'the chaos that you remember came toward the end of it, and we all remember some of that. The cities burned because of the riots. People here were angry and divided, separated by race, age and every reason that you can imagine. Then there were shortages of food and medicine. It started in the cities but toward the end, the chaos was everywhere.'

'You see, Jacob,' Doogan broke in, 'many people depended on the Government for their necessities. When the economies of the cities began to fail, the governments could no longer provide these things. There was looting and rioting, and the governments deployed the military to restore order. The urban areas became war zones, ruled by federal compounds and gangs. Is this what you remember?'

'Yeah, pretty much.'

'An evil scheme grew out of Europe,' Doogan continued, 'a plan that promised to end the hunger and turmoil, and insure fairness and equality. The Western powers authorized a central body to take control of currencies, a United Bank to stabilize the economies of the world.'

'The first thing they did was to steal any real wealth that was left,' Casey added angrily, 'and ration out credit for food and wages. There was no purchase or payment that wasn't tracked, and every transaction was approved or rejected by a faceless bureaucracy that controlled—'

'Getting back to the point, lad,' Doogan interrupted softly. 'Before a person could receive a cent, they had to be registered and disfigured with the mark. Without it, people were unable to purchase even the most basic of needs.'

Doogan and Casey were becoming worked up just talking about this stuff, and even Becky looked angry.

'The mark represents an evil tyranny, Jacob,' Doogan sighed, 'a Godless communism and the end of free will and personal liberties. Entire nations were controlled by it, by poverty and the threat of poverty. The bank funded all types of blasphemy and sacrilege, but organizations and churches that held to God's truths, purity or virtue, were rejected. The Godly people who refused the mark and all the churches that railed against it were denounced as hateful, hurtful and backward. Religious thought was blamed for every problem, and the terrible persecutions began.'

'The Feds still uses the mark for identification,' Casey added. 'But most of the young people today don't know the evil that it stood for. That includes Devon.'

I heard three gentle knocks on the door. Mrs. Thompson came in and waited until Casey stopped talking.

'Father?' she said to Doogan, 'It's nearly eight thirty, and Sandy is here.'

'Thank you,' he answered, rising to his feet. 'Then we'd best be getting on with it.'

Everyone stood up like we were leaving, but Mrs. Thompson and Sandy came into the room and closed the door. Sandy was a good-looking girl, not like Becky or Mariam, but still fun to look at. She had blue eyes that didn't seem to match her black hair. She was dressed in a green skirt and a lighter green shirt, and she was wearing glasses. I don't know the last time I saw someone wearing glasses, but I remember thinking it was kind of cool.

She smiled. 'Good morning, Bishop Jake.'

Sandy walked over to the fireplace while Mrs. Thompson closed the blinds on both the windows. I was starting to wonder what was happening when Casey pressed something on the mantle and the bookshelf moved. The whole bookshelf on the right of the fireplace from the floor to the ceiling popped out about six inches! Casey pulled it open another foot or so and everyone started walking through the narrow opening. It was way cool, and we all followed Sandy through the secret door.

On the other side was a musty little room. It was narrow too, maybe five feet by ten, and there was a single light bulb hanging down from the ceiling. The walls were unfinished, plaster and wooden boards, and there were open beams above us. At the far end, there was a fold-up chair sitting in front of a table. When I got closer I saw that there was a radio on the table, a big radio with a microphone, and thick black wires that led up to a hole in the ceiling. The room barely fit everybody, and Sandy sat right down at the desk and started working buttons.

'Our antenna is hidden in the attic,' Casey explained. 'We communicate with Charlotte every Tuesday at this time, sometimes more often.'

'Charlotte?'

'Charlotte is the only diocese left in the east. We have just enough power to reach them, but they can relay messages all the way to the Holy See.'

Doogan put his hand on my shoulder.

'We have to share the bad news about the nuncio with them, and ask them about our new Bishop.'

Casey pulled the door closed behind us and we could hear static on the radio speaker. Becky leaned into me.

'This is going to be awful,' she whispered. 'It was only a few weeks ago, we were planning the nuncio's arrival, and now we have to tell them that he's dead.'

The air was getting stuffy, and I was wondering what we were waiting for. Becky must have read my mind.

'They always start at exactly eight thirty,' she told me.

Something didn't sound right to me, and I had to say something.

'Fr. Doogan?' I said, doubtingly, 'We tried using radios when I was running with the gangs. They were little walkie-talkie thingies. They're not safe. We couldn't trust them because there was always somebody listening.'

'I understand your concern, Jacob, but the Federal government uses scrambled frequencies. Bill Morrison provided us that information himself. We operate in the old amateur radio bands. It's extremely doubtful that they could know our frequency, or monitor our communications, son.'

'Yeah? You gonna tell that to the nuncio?'

A lady's voice came over the radio.

'This is KOKW calling…'

'Becky?' I asked. 'You know Chinese or something, right?'

'Latin and some Italian!' she laughed.

I pointed to the radio. 'What about the other lady?'

'Mrs. Franco is Italian. Why, what are you—'

Becky's eyes lit up when she realized what I was thinking. She looked at Doogan and the old man nodded.

'Alright,' I explained. 'Tell them in Italian to call back in five minutes, but tell them to use another channel.'

'We don't use channels, Bishop Jake,' Sandy explained. 'But I can give Becky a frequency in another band.'

'Cool.'

Sandy wrote something on a piece of paper and handed it to Becky. She let Becky sit in her chair, and a second later Becky was jabbering Italian into the microphone. It only took a minute, and when she stopped, we all stood there quietly listening to static.

Don't ask me what made me do this, but I leaned in close to Becky and reached for the microphone.

'You press this to talk?'

'Yes, and hold it down until you're finished speaking.'

I picked it up and clicked the button down.

'So Jodie,' I said, 'you ugly piece of shit. Did you get all that?'

Mrs. Thompson gasped, but Doogan shushed her with a nod. Nobody moved, and we all stood there silently staring at the radio.

After a while, I didn't think there was gonna be an answer, and I was just starting to feel stupid when we heard a voice.

'Enjoy yourself, Bishop Walker,' the voice said, coldly. 'Changes are coming. Your parish and your tenure as bishop are both out of time.'

Now, you'd probably think I'd be happy that I got an answer. It usually feels good when you're proven right about something, but that voice was *damned* creepy. I recognized that voice too, a voice that up until now I'd only heard in my nightmares. I didn't show it, but I don't mind telling you that I was freaked. It wasn't just me either because Mrs. Thompson and Sandy crossed themselves. They both looked over at Doogan and slowly made the big t.

Hell, to be honest, I almost did one myself.

THE GREEN AND BLACK

When the lady came back on the radio, we started telling her all about the nuncio and the night I got my ring. Casey and Becky did most of the talking, and you should have heard them explaining how we escaped from of the city. Hell, I thought I knew that story pretty well, but it was getting better every time somebody told it! It took our minds off of that Jodie asshole for a while, and I was looking forward to hearing how the story was gonna end. I never got the chance because Doogan asked Becky to take me back to the church and *prepare me*. He didn't say what she was preparing me for, but I didn't bother asking about it. I knew I'd be alone with Becky for a while, and that was good enough for me.

I didn't know how sticky and warm it had been in the radio room until we stepped out and into the morning air again. The day was clear and already hot, but the air felt cool and it smelled like wildflowers and pancake syrup. Becky was glad to be out of there and alone with me too. Like I figured, she'd been waiting to ask me about the bishop chair, and we were barely down the porch steps before she brought it up.

'Jake, you said you saw the cathedra before? I don't remember seeing one in the city's cathedral.'

'I saw it in a dream while I was in your backyard.'

'Can you tell me about it?'

Maybe there's a good way to tell the girl you like that you watched her die in a dream along with her two best friends, but I couldn't think of one. It wasn't something I wanted to talk about anyway, so I shook my head and changed the subject.

'I need to ask you something.'

'Ok.'

'What's with Casey and Lightning? Did you see how he was watching her at the rectory?'

'What do you mean?' Becky asked suspiciously. 'Of course he was watching her. Casey is close to Rita. He feels responsible for her.'

'I thought you said that she was too young.'

'She is! He doesn't think of her that way.'

Becky stopped walking and looked up at me.

'Casey cares for Rita, Jake, but it's different. It's not like the way you and I feel for each other.'

'You sure about that?'

'Of course I am,' she said, starting toward the church again. 'It might help if you knew how we found Rita.'

Becky got her far-away look, and she kept glancing up at me while we walked.

'I'll never forget that day,' she started. 'We were on a medicine run three summers ago, Michael, Casey, and I. It was a little town south of here on the river, very much like the town where we met Devon.'

'Rita was living in in a house behind a grocery store, surviving on cans of food that her father stashed for her. We didn't know how long she'd been alone, but her dad had been dead a long time. He was still in a chair in their front room, and the place was disgusting. Rita was sick, hungry and in rags, surrounded by books. There were hundreds of little paperbacks and romance novels that she apparently got from the store.'

'We couldn't reach her at first, but when we realized she was deaf I found some paper and a pen. We asked her to come back with us but Rita didn't understand, and at one point she even threatened Michael with a knife.'

'Casey refused to leave without her,' Becky went on. 'We stayed the whole day, and I finally talked her into putting on a dress, a yellow dress that we found in an upstairs closet. I was beginning to think that we'd never get her to leave, but on the back of a sheet of paper Casey wrote that her new dress was beautiful. He said that if she came with us, she'd never have to be alone anymore.'

'Maybe Rita took more from that little note than Casey intended,' Becky said, smiling, 'but she took his hand and came back with us, and it's the reason she's alive today. She might be lightning now, but she was a fragile little girl when we found her.'

We'd reached the church already, but Becky stopped in front of the big doors.

'Rita has been Casey's shadow ever since. She's always trying to get a rise out of him. She refuses to believe that it isn't something more, but Casey thinks of Rita as a member of his family. That's why he looks at her that way.'

When I remembered the look I'd seen on Casey's face that morning, it all made sense to me. Well, *most* of it did.

'So how's he do it?'

'Do what?'

'Well, Lightning's not so little anymore, and she's always chasing after him. Are you telling me he's never, even once, ever thought about…'

'Oh my God!' she exclaimed. 'Is that all you ever think about?'

'No, not *all*,' I said, 'except when you're around.'

Becky put her hands on her hips and tried to sound angry.

'Not all love is physical, Bishop Walker! And for your information, someone else has captured Casey's heart. Now get your mind out of the gutter. We've got a lot to do.'

She opened the door, and for the second time that day, we walked into St. Lucy's. This time it looked dark and different inside. There were lit candles up in front, but there's still something strange and scary about an empty church. It's the truth, and it doesn't matter if you're there during the day or at nighttime. For one thing, you never feel alone in a church even when they're empty. And remember that peaceful feeling I told you about? That feeling was thick and all around me in St. Lucy's that day. Churches are just built to be spooky. No matter what direction they're facing, the front door of a church becomes the back door once you get inside. Why would they do that if they weren't trying to be spooky?

It was super bright outside, and once my eyes adjusted I caught sight of Mariam sitting by herself in the front row. She was dressed Amish with her hair up, and she stood up when she saw us.

'Where is Michael?' she asked.

'He'll be late,' Becky answered, 'Bishop Walker found a new parishioner last night, and Michael took him to see the doctor.'

'I heard about that,' Mariam laughed.

She turned to me and added, 'Congratulations Bishop Jake!'

'For what?'

'On your baptism!'

Becky slid her backpack off her shoulder and onto the seat. She unzipped the top and pulled out a little white book.

'Fr. Doogan thinks that your mom and dad already had you baptized,' she told me. 'But he needs to be sure, and we need to have a record in the church.'

Becky explained that baptism is a new beginning with God and that it would only take a few minutes. All I had to do was answer a couple of easy questions about turning away from evil and following God. You'd have to be an idiot to get a question like that wrong, but just in case, Becky gave me all the right answers. Once Doogan and Casey showed up, we were done with the whole baptism thing in no time. I got cold water poured on my head, and Casey and Mariam got to be my godparents. From what I picked up on, it's a godparent's job to keep an eye on you and make sure you stay a good Churcher.

I dried off and everybody congratulated me again. Baptism is huge and important to Churchers, and I got to keep the candle that Mariam was holding. I didn't want to risk putting it in my pocket, so Becky put it in her backpack for me. The old priest motioned for us to sit down, and we all took a seat on the benches by the door. I'd already forgotten that we talked on the radio that morning, but Becky was eager to hear what happened after we left.

'Did we hear anything from Charlotte?'

'Mrs. Franco will relay the information to Bishop Gregory,' Doogan replied, 'and possibly on to Rome. We'll be listening daily, and should know something soon.'

'While we wait for our next baptism,' he continued, 'we should use the time to prepare Bishop Jake for the council.'

Some things are so damned dull to talk about that it hurts. I'm not exaggerating but that next hour might have been the most excruciating experience of my whole life. Doogan talked my ears off, telling me all about the elders of the community, what they believe and what they didn't believe. It's hard enough remembering what I believe, but I sat there trying to learn all about people I'd never met before! For a while I stayed awake by playing with the little springy things on the back of the seat in front of me. Becky said that in olden days, they were used to hold people's hats. After a while Doogan got pissed at me for playing with them, so I had to just sit there and listen. I learned everything you'd ever want to know about the Churchers of the world. I'm not gonna repeat it to you because it'd put you to sleep in a heartbeat, so I'll stick to the main points.

According to Doogan, people who believe in God and Jesus and the Bible and the church are the Catholics. People who believe in God and some of the Bible, but not Jesus are Jewish. Everybody else is a protestant. That doesn't include the Feds because they don't believe shit, and it doesn't include the Methodists. Doogan told me that from day to day, even the Methodists don't know what Methodists believe.

The old man didn't stop talking until he heard voices behind us, and we turned and watched Mike and Shithead walking into the church. Shithead had a big white bandage over his ear and it looked ridiculous. Hell, from the looks of it, anybody would have thought that somebody cut his whole damned ear off! When Mike caught sight of Mariam waiting there his face lit up like a tire fire. It was fun to watch those two. Even when there were twenty feet between them, Mariam and Mike were all over each other.

'Sorry we're late,' Mike apologized. 'Dr. Weiss showed off the farm, and Mrs. Weiss wouldn't let us leave without feeding us.'

'Becky girl?' Doogan asked. 'Please take the bishop back to the house. The elders will be arriving shortly and the bishop should remain out of sight until he can be properly introduced. We'll join you after we baptize Devon.'

I was sitting on the aisle with Mike and Shithead standing right next to me. Shithead's bandage had a little blood on it, and it gave me an idea. Becky was talking with Doogan about something, so I poked him in his bandaged ear.

'So Shithead,' I whispered. 'You ever been baptized before?'

He shook his head.

'It gonna be bloody! If I'd have known how much it hurt, I would have run off when I had the chance.'

Shithead's face fell, and he turned to Mike.

'He's kidding,' Mike laughed. 'It doesn't hurt Devon. You'll be fine.'

I leaned into the kid and quietly called him a puss again, but when I looked up Doogan was glaring at me. He was too far away for him to have heard me, but he must have known that I was messing with the kid.

It was a good time to leave, so I followed Becky back outside. There were people moving around over by the rectory and I noticed two guys setting baskets on the sidewalk in front of the house. They were big baskets, like the kind the Churchers bring to barbeques, and they were filled with bread and some of the dried meat that the Churchers make. There were four or five baskets already sitting there, and when we got a little closer, I saw one with bottles of wine, and what looked like some pies. I'd never been to a council and I was beginning to think that councils were big parties, like Churcher barbeques, but as we got closer I got the feeling that something was up. After setting the baskets down in front of the house, the two guys gave us a quick wave and hurried off through the trees. It was strangely rushed, and it wouldn't have bothered me, but I was just beginning to realize that Becky hadn't said anything in a long time.

As we reached the house, a noise roared out from the other side of the church. It sounded like a jeep with a bad muffler, and I turned in time to see a guy driving past the church on a two-stroke. In case you've never seen one, a two-stroke is a little motorcycle with high fenders, and I couldn't remember the last time I saw one that worked. The driver was a tall ugly dude with a shaved head and a full beard, and he stopped in the shade of the big umbrella tree across the street. I couldn't have been more surprised if a dinosaur had just strolled out of the woods, but when I got a good look at the asshole, I was even more stunned. There was no doubt about it. The guy was wearing gang colors!

He was in a sleeveless leather vest with two braided leather straps tied high on his arm, one green and the other black. I knew the colors of every gang in the city, even the gangs that were long gone, but I'd never seen the green and black before.

He was too far off to see if he was packing, and when I took a step toward him, Becky grabbed my arm.

'It's ok, Jake,' she said, with her eyes locked on him. 'We should get inside.'

'What do you mean it's ok?!'

'He always shows up before a collection. You'll learn about it at the council.'

'He's been here before?!'

'Yes, it's not a problem,' she insisted. 'They'll watch us for a little while and leave again.'

'They?' I shook my head. 'How many are there?'

'Please Jake?!'

There was something in Becky's eyes that I hadn't seen since we left the city, and when she squeezed my arm I couldn't argue with her anymore. We were out in the open where people could see us, but even with all the rules about Becky and me touching each other, Becky wouldn't let go of me. Maybe she didn't realize it, but she held on to my arm with both hands until we were back in the rectory.

Before we stepped inside I took a quick look at the dirtball on the bike. I could just see him off in the distance beyond the church, watching us. I got that shitty feeling in my guts again, and my instincts were screaming. It didn't matter what Becky just said, there was no way that things were *ok*. The Churchers didn't know it yet, but there was a shitstorm coming, and Nineveh had a huge problem.

I had a huge problem.

COUNCILS AND ELDERS

I'm not making excuses, but after seeing that guy on the two-stroke, I had a tough time focusing on anything else that day. It was killing me, knowing that some creep in gang colors was out there in front of the church, and I couldn't understand how the Churchers could have let this happen. It shouldn't have surprised me though. Anybody who's spent more than five minutes with a Churcher can tell you that they're not very bright about some things. If you ask me their instincts suck, and they don't recognize danger till it's about to jump up and bite them in the ass. I was beginning to wonder how these people could have survived out here so long without me.

'Becky, we gotta do something about that shitbrick out there,' I told her. 'You know that, don't you?'

'Yes, but it's complicated. Not all of the elders agree with us. We have to convince the other members of the council.'

'Convince them? What, are they stupid?!'

She was still thinking up a polite reply, so I already had my answer.

'Alright,' I continued, 'then I need to know everything about those guys. Who are they and when did they first get here?'

Becky closed the door behind us, and for the first time ever, I saw a Churcher lock a door. She forgot about the rules again, and she took my arm as we walked to the kitchen.

'We first saw them about three months ago, five young men dressed like that one, with guns. They call themselves the Crescent Knights. They told Fr. Doogan that the church and the surrounding farms were on their property. They were very disrespectful and they said that if we wanted to stay here we had to pay them. There was a big argument about it at the council, but we lost the vote. Now on the last day of every month, we have a collection. The Knights show up with their truck at about dinner time, and they collect from the rectory, the Hershberger's farm, and Dr. Weiss's place.'

While Becky was talking, I remembered back to when I lived downtown. There was a group that called themselves the Blood Knights. They were a small, third-rate gang that was run out of the city over a turf fight. I kept thinking that maybe they were the same guys.

'I can't believe you let those assholes take your food every month!' I grumbled. 'So where'd they come from? Where'd they get the gasoline, and how the hell did they find us way out here?'

'We don't know.'

We'd just made it to the kitchen when Mrs. Thompson showed up. She smelled flowery, and she was all dressed up in a blue dress with lacey white stuff on the edges. She saw the look on Becky's face and turned to me.

'Is there something wrong, Your Grace?'

'No, it's nothing.'

Mrs. Thompson didn't believe me, but she didn't say anything else about it either. She just smiled doubtingly and wrapped herself in an apron.

While Mrs. Thompson headed over to the sink I got a good look at her kitchen, and it was amazing. Mrs. Thompson had to be the best cook in the world because it was the biggest kitchen I'd ever seen. Even though there was nothing cooking, it smelled like bacon and eggs. The walls were bright and yellowy, and there was a long wooden table surrounded eight chairs. In the middle of the room was a square counter thingy with all kinds of pots and pans hanging high above it on hooks. Some of them were huge. The only thing that didn't fit was the stupid looking clock above the window. It looked like a cat, and its eyes and tail moved back and forth with every tick-tock. I was already in a shitty mood, and I remember wanting to cap it with a sawdi.

I must have been more nervous than I knew that day. All of a sudden there was a ringing, chiming sound in the air. It wasn't that loud, but it surprised me and I couldn't tell where it came from. It spooked me a little, and when Mrs. Thompson saw me jump, she leaned over and put her hand on my arm.

'It's only the doorbell, Your Grace,' she said gently. 'Don't worry. I'm sure you'll do very well at the council today.'

Mrs. Thompson must have thought that I was anxious about the council, but I was still thinking about the Knights.

Since we're talking about Mrs. Thompson, I need to stop and explain something. If you haven't spent a lot of time around females, you might think I'm lying about this, but I noticed something strange about women that day. Remember how I said that Becky could calm me down just by being in the same room with me? I don't know if all females can do this, but when Mrs. Thompson touched my arm and talked to me in that reassuring voice of hers, I felt better somehow. Hell, nothing really changed, so it's kind of just an illusion, but if you think about it, it's still pretty amazing. I'll probably never understand it, but I remember wondering about it while Mrs. Thompson untied her apron and hung it on the hook by the door. She stepped out into the hall just as Doogan, Casey, and Shithead came in from the back door.

Somebody must have found Shithead new clothes because the boots and uniform were gone. The bandage was still there, but he was wearing jeans and black shoes now, like any other Churcher. Everybody else was dressed up, and even though it was a warm day, Casey was wearing a green jacket with sleeves.

Out in the hall, Mrs. Thompson was talking to people, and there were lots of strange voices. I tried to hear what they were saying, but Mike, Mariam, and Lightning all walked in from the hallway, and after that it was too loud to hear anything. Just about every person I knew in the world was there, smiling and talking, and it should have felt like a party, but I couldn't shake my crappy mood. Shithead wasn't saying much either. He just sat there at the table, watching everybody.

Doogan looked up at the cat-clock and turned to Mike.

'Michael, you'll be wanting to take Mariam home now. You know Big John wants her home during collections. And hurry back, son. It's sure to be a difficult council, and we'll need you.'

'And Becky girl,' he went on. 'Please remind Rita that she is not permitted to be here during councils and that we have a collection today.'

Becky signed the message to Lightning, and I was surprised that the kid didn't argue about it this time. She must have been used to the routine because she just smiled and signed something to Casey. Whatever it was, Casey was uncomfortable with it. He turned red again and signed something back to her before she followed Mike and Mariam out the back door.

Doogan took a seat across from me and I noticed that the old guy was really sweating. Hell, he didn't look this nervous when the Feds pulled up at the door of the rectory.

'The council will start in a wee bit, Jacob.' He started. 'Try to learn all that you can, son, and please let Casey and meself do all the talking. We try to focus on the things that unite us. And please understand, the elders may seem cross at times but they are all Godly people. The Christians of Nineveh are working together for the common good.'

'You know son,' he rambled, 'the world would never have digressed into the terrible place it was if Godly people would have stood together. With charity, love and Christian unity, things might have been—'

'Yeah, I got all that,' I interrupted. 'But who's got it right?'

Ok I'll admit it. I was still hyped about the Knights and the dude on the two-stroke, and I guess I needed a laugh. Maybe it was wrong, but Doogan was right there asking for it, and I couldn't resist.

'Right?' His eyebrows went up. 'What do you mean, son?'

'Well, there's all these different kinds of Churchers, and they all believe different stuff. They can't all be right. Which one's the truth?'

Becky let out a gasp, and Casey's jaw dropped. Even Shithead's mouth fell open. The old man stood up and looked back at me like it was the dumbest question he'd ever heard.

'Good God, lad!' he shouted. 'Why, the Holy Catholic Church is the true faith, founded by Christ himself! You are one of her bishops now! Have you learned nothing since you've been here? How the devil can you—'

When he saw me laughing, Doogan froze. Casey was laughing too, but Becky still looked scared. I felt bad about it too. The poor old guy was so worked up that the bald part of his head was red.

'Sorry, Father,' I apologized. 'So, tell me again. If we don't believe in the same stuff, why do we meet every month?'

Doogan was fuming.

'If you'd have read the gospels I gave you last evening, *Bishop Walker*, instead of visiting the parish secretary, you might know that Jesus commanded us to love each other as he loved us! If the Protestants had shown love like that, perhaps they never would have left us. And if we had shown love like that, perhaps they wouldn't have wanted to go.'

He finally blinked.

'Now do you understand?'

I shrugged, 'No.'

I wasn't trying to be a smart ass, not anymore anyway, but for a sec I thought that the old guy was gonna come right over the table at me! Luckily Mrs. Thompson walked in from the hallway.

'Father, our guests have arrived.'

'Heaven help us!' he sighed.

We all got up and headed over to the library, except for Shithead. We left him there, eyeballing the two pies that were sitting next to the sink. Becky stopped in the hallway to get some paper from her backpack, and Casey buttoned a button on his jacket before we all walked inside. Somebody had moved all the chairs, and there were a couple of metal folding chairs there now. There was also a little table over by the fireplace with a bowl and little cups around it. I found out later that Mrs. Thompson made some pink stuff called *punch* for everybody. There weren't as many people as I expected, only about six or seven, and they all looked up and stopped talking when they saw us.

Two of the guys looked familiar, like maybe I'd met them at the barbeque, and they stood up as we came into the room. The others just sat there, looking like they were pissed at me. For being *elders*, none of them looked all that old to me either. I guess I was expecting them to be old like Doogan, but most of them were about thirty or so, and a couple of them wore black clothes like his. Over on the couch I saw the Morrison female dressed in a long purple dress, and I wondered why she was there.

'Members of the council,' Doogan announced, 'I'd like to introduce Bishop Jacob Walker.'

After that, it was pretty easy to pick out the assholes in the room. Two of the dudes got up to shake my hand and the others sat there glaring at us. One guy really stuck out. He was a short dumpy guy who was dressed in black, with blonde hair sticking out of a funny looking hat. He had such a painful scowl on his face that made me laugh.

Casey was right beside me, and I leaned into him.

'Why's that dude look like that?' I whispered. 'Was he born that way or did someone kick him in the nuts?'

Casey blurted out a laugh, and we stood by the door and shook hands with the two guys. After that everybody took turns introducing themselves and telling me the kind of Churcher they were. I wasted a whole bunch of *how do you dos*, but most of them still looked mad at me. There were two elders that seemed alright though. One was a Lutheran named Downton and the other was a Baptist named Robertson. The guy with the face was a Methodist named Kinsley. I already knew that Beth Morrison was on our side, because of what she said at the barbeque, but you couldn't tell it by looking at her. Her face was soft and neutral, but everybody else looked like they needed to use the outhouse. I knew we were outnumbered before we even sat down.

Becky sat next to Beth Morrison, and now that I think about it, Becky's job must have been to write everything down on her yellow paper. The three metal chairs in front were for us. Casey sat next to me but Doogan didn't sit down yet. He walked into the center of the room and said, 'Let us pray.'

Now you'd think that praying would be a good way to start a meeting of Churchers because it normally puts them in a better mood. I'm not saying that it made things any *worse* that day, but nobody looked any happier after we said 'amen' either.

'Before we open the floor to discussion,' Doogan started, 'we have one announcement. Dr. Weiss won't be joining us because he's delivering the Picket's first child. He's asked me to say that we have a replenished supply of antibiotics, inhalers and such. Praise God, there'll be no further rationing of medicine!'

'Finally!' a voice griped from the back of the room. 'Maybe now the Calvinists will receive the same treatment as everyone else.'

'Mr. Pine,' Doogan sighed. 'You know Dr. Weiss treats everyone equally. In his judgment, antibiotics weren't required.'

'Really?! The Wasserman boy had virtually the same injury last month, and he immediately received antibiotics! It seems our Lutherans and Catholics, have more serious looking wounds than the rest of us!'

The guy talking was a tall skinny dude with black hair. He was in a gray shirt and he didn't stand up when he talked.

'We'll bring your concerns to Dr. Weiss,' Doogan answered. 'Has Steven fully recovered?'

'Yes,' Pine answered grudgingly. 'Thank you.'

Doogan walked back to us and took a seat next to Casey, but his ass barely touched the chair when the Kinsley guy stood up and cleared his throat.

'Father Doogan,' he started. 'Speaking for myself and other non-Catholics of the council, may I remind you again that we are not subject to your church's traditions and doctrines?'

He glared at Doogan.

'Is your congregation so desperate for priests that you accept this teenager, a street thug from the city, and expect the rest of us to receive him as a bishop? The man is a wanted criminal!'

I didn't know what a thug was, but Casey was pissed. He jumped up and started bitching back at Kinsley.

'I was with Bishop Walker in the city! He saved my life and the lives of every—'

'Yes!' Kinsley interrupted, 'by sabotage and murder?'

'He's done nothing wrong!'

'And yet he is wanted by the Federal Government? How does this help us?'

In less than a minute, we went from praying to fighting. Everyone was talking at the same time, and Doogan stood up again and put his hands in the air.

'Good people!' he started. 'Our Church and the people of St. Lucy's recognize Jacob Walker as bishop to our parish and diocese. This is not debatable, and is not a matter for this council!'

That shut everybody up, but only for a sec or two.

'Then in a related matter,' Kinsley went on, 'can you deny that you've taken in a Federal Agent? An agent that witnesses say was marked only just this morning?!'

There was a lot of grumbling again, and even the two guys on our side looked surprised.

'Devon is simply a young man who wishes to join us,' Doogan answered. 'How can we not extend God's mercy to him?'

'We can't expect Catholics to know scripture,' Kinsley sniped, 'but the Bible is clear about those who take the mark! This *Devon* person is a deserter from Federal Service and yet another fugitive. You are endangering everyone in Nineveh with this decision and the matter was never brought before the council!'

'He didn't take the mark,' Casey interrupted. 'Devon was a child when the mark was forced on him. He's sixteen years old!'

'Scripture couldn't be more clear!' Kinsley argued, turning to me.

'Bishop Walker?' he asked smugly. 'Was this your idea? Perhaps you can point to a scriptural basis for your decision?'

For the record, I'll admit that I didn't understand the question, and I was fighting off the itch to give Kinsley a reason for that look on his face, but something else hit me. These elder people were so busy thinking about their own petty little bullshit that they couldn't see the real problem.

'We've got an armed gang on their way here,' I said, pointing to the window. 'And you're worried that Devon is a danger to you? Don't you understand what's happening here? Why do you think that dirtball out there on the street is watching us?'

Everybody stopped talking and Kinsley stared back at me, looking like he just swallowed a bug.

'He's a scout!' I shouted, answering myself. 'The minute the Knights figure out that you can't or won't defend this place, it's over. They'll destroy everything! That's what gangs do. We need to set up lookouts, and we need to get some firepower out on the road—'

'Firepower?!' Kinsley interrupted. 'We're Christians. We are men of peace.'

'Yeah? Then you're gonna be dead men of peace!' I shot back. 'And do I have to tell you what'll happen to your females?! You want the children that survive raised as gangsters? What kind of assholes are you guys?'

'You're overreacting, young and arrogant!' Kinsley shouted. 'We have an agreement with the Knights. There have been two collections already without a single incident.'

'They're sizing you up, waiting. And once they're sure they can win, they'll burn this place to the ground. You don't know what they'll do here.'

'Bishop Walker is right,' Casey spoke up. 'Sometimes evil must be confronted. We have to be ready to defend ourselves!'

We were so busy with Kinsley that I didn't catch Mrs.

Thompson standing in the doorway. She was pale, and everyone got quiet after they saw her.

'Excuse the interruption, Your Grace,' she said softly, 'but the Knights have arrived. They're pulling up to the rectory.'

THE COLLECTION

When I looked around, I couldn't decide if these elder Churchers were just stupid, or if they were all gutless little turds like Shithead, but either way they were useless to me. In my whole life I'd never seen people with so damned much to lose, and so worried about petty shit that meant nothing! I was growing more pissed by the sec, and I turned toward Doogan.

'Christian unity?' I asked sarcastically. 'These clowns can't even come together to save their own sorry asses!'

Kinsley started to say something, but he shut up when I shot him a look. I was really hot and he must have seen it on my face. I started moving to the hallway and I heard Doogan's voice behind me.

'Be cautious, lad.'

Out of all those guys at the council, Casey was the only one that followed me out to the front room that afternoon. Before we even left the library we could hear the council members arguing behind us again. When we reached the front of the house, I saw the knights through the tiny white curtains on the door. White curtains are cool like that. If it's bright outside you can see right through them and the people outside can't tell you're watching.

At the bottom of the porch steps I counted four big guys in colors, and every one of them was packing. Two of them were loading the Churcher's baskets into a green truck. I'd spent most of my life in gangs, and the scene out front didn't make sense to me. After one look, I knew that something stunk.

There were three vehicles parked in front of the rectory, not counting the two-stroke. I've gotta admit one was pretty amazing, a big black car with chrome wheels and silver letters that said *Escalade*. I'd never seen a car so decked out before. It was decorated with rows and rows of tiny blinking lights. I could tell that it was a gang car. Back when gas was easy-to-get, the gangs hung all kinds of stupid shit on their cars, and this one was dripping with strings of colored lights and what looked like old Christmas decorations. The car's ass-end was painted with yellow flames, and the whole underneath was lit up in a dark blue light.

When I saw the other two vehicles I felt my guts knotting up. Sitting less than ten feet from the walkway, with St. Lucy's off in the distance, there was a Fed jeep with an M2 mounted on its back. It was sitting next to a carrier, one of those little green trucks that move in and out of the city's compounds every day. The back of the truck was covered in green camo, so I couldn't tell how many guys might be inside. Something else hit me as I looked on. Every one of those dudes had a new piece, a Fed nine with matching holsters and shiny new clip bands. Everything was brand new, and it was all Fed issue.

'Where the hell did they steal all that shit?!' I wondered out loud.

A voice spoke up softly from behind me.

'The Southern posts ain't got nothing like that, man.'

I turned and saw Shithead standing next to Casey. He must have wandered out of the kitchen and they were both watching the Knights through the curtains of the front windows.

While we looked on he added, 'That's all from a city post.'

I heard the two-stroke's engine revving, and the bearded creep on the bike pulled alongside the others Knights. He turned off the engine but stayed on the bike as he talked with the others. He said something that I couldn't make out, and they all started laughing and cussing. They split up again and I watched the two smaller guys pick up the last two baskets and start walking them over to the truck. The tall zit-faced Knight in dreads looked familiar to me. He was bigger and louder than the others, and when he smiled his teeth were all over the place. The details weren't coming to me, but I knew I'd seen him before. He snatched a bottle of wine from the basket as it passed, and busted off the corked end on the truck's bumper. After gulping down half the bottle, he started laughing and pointed to the house.

'Hey,' he shouted to the others, 'ya think Green Eyes is in there?'

They all laughed, and the biker dude nodded.

'She's in there, but she's got a big Churcher with her.'

'So?'

He took another mouthful and started coming up the porch steps.

'Hey Green Eyes!' he bellowed, banging on the front door. 'I got something for ya.'

Suddenly the house went silent. Everyone at the council heard the shouting and banging. When I looked back, I saw Becky's green eyes looking at me from just inside the library door. Doogan and Beth Morrison were right behind her.

'Come on out here!' Snaggletooth shouted, taking another hit from the bottle. 'It's party time and I wanna show you something!'

An hour ago, I'd watched Becky lock the front door, but with all the visitors coming and going, it wasn't locked anymore. The doorknob turned and I watched the door slowly swinging open. The dirtbag popped his face inside, but before he could take another breath, I put my blade to his throat.

There was just enough pressure on my knife to get his attention, and the bottle fell from his hand and crashed to the porch floor. I knew I had to be careful but I didn't have much of a choice. There was no way I was letting this snaggletoothed inbred inside, but I didn't want to start anything either, not with all that firepower outside. He finally thought about going for his gun but when he reached down, it was already in my other hand.

'Are you lost or something, dick nose?' I asked, twisting the knife.

He didn't move. I felt blood dripping onto my hand, but I was obviously taking it easy on the creep. Hell, I could have killed him three times already, but I had to be smart and careful. Anything I did now might start a war, and it was a war we couldn't win.

'Get lost, asshole!'

With the butt of the gun I shoved his face outside, and he stumbled back all the way to the porch steps. His friends were watching, but they must have been taken by surprise because none of them had their guns up. The door slammed shut and I flipped the lock down.

Casey called, 'Jake!' and when I turned, he handed me a sawdi. He'd already pulled the guns from the closet, and he had the carbine up, resting on his shoulder. I tucked Snaggletooth's nine in my pants and took the sawdi, and I remember being surprised that Casey had the guns ready. At least one guy from the council had my back, and I was glad Casey was with me.

At first, the zit-faced creep just stood there, stunned, but when he realized he was bleeding, he wiped his face and looked at the blood on his hand. He saw that all his friends were watching, so he decided to grow a pair.

'Somebody give me piece!'

The biker dude shook his head.

'Bacchus ain't ready.'

'I ain't taking that from no Churcher!'

'Yeah, you are,' the biker said coldly. 'You know what Bacchus said. We wait for Jodie.'

Snaggletooth turned back to the house. We could see that the frustrated asshole wanted to do something, but he couldn't figure out *what*.

'I'll wait!' he shouted. 'But you're gonna pay for that, Churcher! You hear me?! You're dead!'

He stormed over to the truck and grabbed another bottle of

wine. At first it looked like he was gonna launch it through the front window, but he decided to open it instead. He guzzled down a long drink before grumbling something to the others. Three of them got into the jeep, and Snaggletooth climbed into the black car. A second later the Knights were pulling onto the road. We watched silently until they turned toward the river, and the black car disappeared behind the trees.

'Did you hear what he said about Jodie?!' Casey asked nervously.

'Yeah.'

It was unreal hearing Jodie's name again, and suddenly it was easy to guess where the Knights were getting the vehicles, gas, and hardware. Knowing that Jodie was somehow behind all this changed everything, and a zillion questions were going through my head. I unconsciously handed my sawdi back to Casey but he didn't put it away. He leaned both guns against the back of the door.

'We'd better keep the guns out,' he explained. 'Quarry Road dead-ends at the Weiss farm, and they'll be passing here again when the collection is over.'

It's amazing how suddenly unimportant the elders and the council had become. I'd almost forgotten about them and when we turned around, they were all standing behind us, packed into the hallway and watching. Becky was standing with Beth Morrison, next to Doogan. The rest of them were dead to me.

'Look, Father,' I told him. 'We can't wait till these people wake up. We have to be able to defend this place.'

The Downton guy, the Lutheran dude that had been sitting next to Kinsley, pushed his way through the others and stepped up.

'What do you propose?'

Before I could answer, Kinsley mouthed off again. He was already halfway to the kitchen door, and I think he was about to bail, but he stopped when he heard Downton's question.

'Problems aren't solved with violence! Those who live by the sword—'

'What's with you?' I cut him off. 'If you're not gonna help, shut the hell up and get out of the way!'

Kinsley grunted something, and after giving everyone a shitty look, he left through the kitchen. Just about everyone else at the council followed him out too, even some of the guys I thought might be on our side.

It was just us now, Casey, Shithead and Doogan, along with Downton and the females, but I already felt better about everything. Hell, it's always better being with a few people you can count on, rather than lots of spineless clowns that you can't trust. Maybe everybody was thinking that way. They were all looking at me like they were expecting me to say something but it was Doogan who finally broke the silence.

'Well now,' he sighed, with a grin starting. 'Sure and it's time for a visit with the Reverend Mr. Jamison.'

Casey and Beth Morrison laughed, and even Becky broke into a smile. Everyone was feeling better just knowing that the Knights were gone and the council was over. I'd met a lot of reverends that day, and I didn't remember the guy Doogan was talking about, but I figured he must still be in the kitchen because everyone headed straight for it.

When we got inside, the kitchen was empty except for Mrs. Thompson. She was cutting up some bread over by the sink. The old priest went right over to the cupboard next to the stove. He reached way back inside, behind the pots and pans and pulled out a tall skinny bottle. Doogan dusted off the bottle and motioned for everybody to sit down.

Mrs. Thompson let out a disapproving sigh when she saw what he was up to, but she stopped working and went over to the pantry. She pulled out a tray and loaded it with tiny clear glasses. She brought it to the table just as Doogan got there, and he started filling the little glasses. In big letters, the label on the bottle said *Jamison Irish Whiskey*, and it finally dawned on me.

'The Reverend?' I laughed. 'You're talking about hooch?'

'No, Bishop Walker,' he answered, filling the tiny glasses. 'Henry Fitzherbert Jamison was a real man, God rest his soul. He was an Anglican Pastor and one of the founding elders of

Nineveh.'

As he filled each glass, he pushed it one by one to everyone around the table.

'On the first anniversary of his murder,' he went on, 'we found an entire boxcar full of Jamison Whiskey in the rail yard. Cases and cases! In the civilized Christian world, and to old Irish priests, that's what we call a miracle!'

'In blessed memory,' he added, holding up his glass.

At first I wasn't gonna try it. Most of the alcohol I've ever had before tasted like crap, and even if you're not fully shitfaced, it makes you slow and stupid. This *Jamison* stuff wasn't bad though. I knocked down a shooter, just to be polite, and I remember feeling my insides getting warm. Everyone there was a lot more relaxed and talking easily again, but there were still things I had to cover with Doogan.

'Fr. Doogan, we've got things to do,' I told him.

I turned to Beth.

'We need guns. Can Morrison help get us guns?'

'No,' she shook her head, 'but he has his own store of ammunition. I'll talk with him.'

'It looks like Jodie is supplying the Knights,' I explained. 'That's where they're getting the vehicles and weapons. Can you find out exactly what he's given them?'

Becky let out a gasp, and everyone in the room looked surprised. Casey nodded his head.

'We heard them talking,' he confirmed. 'It's the truth!'

'We'll do our best,' Beth answered. 'Please excuse me, I should be leaving.'

Even though it was warm outside, Beth pulled out a fuzzy purple hat and put it on. It was a stupid looking thing when she held it in her hand, but it looked kind of nice on her head. She nodded 'good evening' to everybody and walked out through the back door.

Mrs. Thompson set a plate down on the table with a huge pile of sandwiches on it. There was blue jelly on them, and I'd had that before, but there was also some light brown stuff that smelled amazing.

'This is the last of our peanut butter so enjoy it!' she announced.

Mrs. Thompson turned to me and lowered her voice.

'I've been saving this, Your Grace. It's a rare treat and impossible to find anymore. I think you'll like it.'

Looking back on it, Doogan wasn't in the mood to talk about the Knights that afternoon. I think he must have figured that everything could wait till later. Everyone grabbed a sandwich, and that peanut butter stuff was so delicious that nobody talked for a while. We were all busy scarfing down the food while Doogan rambled on about the hooch.

'Ted, have you noticed?' he asked, turning to Downton. 'The Baptists won't touch a drop, poor souls, but our Mormons sure know the good of it, don't they? It'd be a sin not to drink their health.'

The old man raised his glass just as the back door opened. Mike stepped inside and laughed when he saw Doogan.

'Wow, the council's over already? What did I miss?'

He took a sandwich and fell into the seat next to Casey. Becky and Doogan told him all about the council, the Knights, and hearing Jodie's name again. I don't know how much time went by, probably half an hour. Doogan and Ted did another round, but Mrs. Thompson had lemonade for everybody else. When I saw there was only one sandwich left, I snagged it. I wasn't all that hungry but Shithead was eyeballing it, and I was afraid it might go to waste.

We heard the sound of a horse galloping onto the pavement outside. It came right up to the kitchen door, and at first I didn't think much about it. I figured it was probably Lightning coming back, but when the door slammed open, the Hershberger kid, Sammy, was standing there. He was out-of-breath, sweaty and excited. Tears were rolling down his face and everybody stood up when we saw him.

'They took her!' he said. 'They got her!'

Doogan asked, 'Who's taken—'

'The Knights!' Sammy shouted. 'They shot Annabelle and beat Uncle John unconscious! They drug her off and put her in the black car!'

When his eyes found me, he ran up to me and grabbed my shirt.

'They've taken Mariam!'

NO ONE ELSE

It felt like everyone in the room just got kicked in the guts at the same time. Becky whispered, 'Oh my God' and put her hand on her stomach like she was about to be sick, and Mrs. Thompson ran over and put her arms around Sammy. Doogan clenched his eyes closed and set his glass down, and even Ted Downton and Shithead looked like they'd had the wind knocked out of them.

I guess I was feeling all that too, but I was also dealing with something else. Remember the funny feeling I mentioned, that feeling that somehow the Churchers belonged to me? Well that feeling hit me again, except stronger than ever, and this time it was cold and personal, like a fist in the teeth. Mariam was the first friend that I'd made after coming to Nineveh. Before she even knew me, she fed me and helped Becky get me cleaned-up so I could meet the other Churchers. I was more than just *pissed*, and even though we were outnumbered and outgunned, all I could think about was killing Knights and bringing her home. What I'm trying to say is that everything that happened that day was my fault. If there's any blame in it, you should know that the Churchers only did what I told them to do.

'Casey?' I called. 'You said that they gotta come back this way?'

'Yes, there's only one road to the quarry.'

'How long have we got?'

184

He turned to the kid and asked, 'Did they turn back this way or—'

'No!' Sammy interrupted, 'they went toward the quarry.'

'Then they're still collecting from the Weiss farm!' Casey said, excitedly. 'They won't be back this way for about twenty minutes.'

'We need guns, sawdis, anything!' I said, 'With as many rounds as we can get our hands on.'

'Leave that to me!' Doogan answered, turning to Downton. 'Ted, would you give me a hand, son?'

They disappeared around the corner, and we could hear their footsteps echoing down the basement stairs.

'We need more people,' I continued, 'people who can shoot.'

Becky's eyes lit up.

'Sammy,' She interrupted. 'Ride as fast as you can to Mrs. Mardonis' house. Tell her to bring the deer gun, and hurry!'

'Mrs. Mardonis?' I asked.

'She's the best shot in Nineveh!'

Sammy bolted out through the back door, and Casey turned to Shithead.

'Devon!' he said, with his eyes on the cat-clock, 'Run to the men's dormitory and tell whoever's there what's happened. Someone needs to fetch the doctor for Mr. Hershberger, and tell the others to get here as soon as possible!'

'Your Grace!' Mrs. Thompson interrupted from the hallway, 'It's Michael!'

Things were happening so quickly that nobody'd realized that Mike wasn't in the room anymore. I moved past Mrs. Thompson and out to the front room. The outside door was open and I could see Mike slowly walking by the church. He'd found the guns leaning by the door and he had one on his shoulder as he walked steadily out toward the road. Even after I called out to him he just kept going, as if he was sleepwalking. I started running over, calling out to him the whole time, but he never looked back.

'Hey!' I shouted, finally catching up with him. 'What the hell are you doing, man?'

'Mariam,' he answered. 'Getting Mariam.'

With one glance you could tell that Mike wasn't all there. His eyes met mine but they were dazed and not seeing me. In my whole life I'd never seen a guy lose it that bad, and never over a female before. Mike cared so much for Mariam that the poor dude's brain wasn't handling her being gone. His face was pale and twisted with worry. I always looked at Michael as the cool, brainy Churcher, and it was spooky seeing him so messed up. If there'd been more time, maybe I might have thought of something better to do, and I still feel bad about this, but I ripped the sawdi from his hands.

'Wake up!' I shouted, slamming the gun's stock into his guts. 'If you want her back get your head out of your ass!'

He stayed doubled-up for a sec before glaring up at me. When I saw him getting angry, I knew his head was clearing up. In the distance I could see Becky and Mrs. Thompson watching from the porch, and I put my hand on his shoulder.

'I need you to focus, Mike,' I told him. 'We'll bring Mariam home. I promise.'

He coughed, 'How?'

'I don't know yet, but you can't help me if your head's somewhere else.'

Mike looked ok after that, but he didn't say anything right away. Once he caught his breath we started moving back to the rectory. It was getting busy there, and there were already a few Churchers waiting at the house. Most of them were holding shotguns. They were hunting guns, too long for city fighting, but for what we were doing I was glad to have them. I was still a little worried about Mike, so I figured I'd give him something to do. It's a trick I learned a long time ago in the gangs. Even when a guy's head is seriously messed up, putting him in charge of something forces him to start using his brain again.

'Keep everyone here,' I told him once we reached the house. 'Get the guns loaded and have everyone ready to move in two minutes.'

I left Mike with the others and I headed inside. Becky and Mrs. Thompson followed me in from the porch, and when got to the kitchen Casey was holding a gun like I'd never seen before. It had a wide barrel like a sawdi, but it had a big round thing sitting on top and a pistol grip. It was extremely cool, and there were two more just like that one on the kitchen table.

Casey grinned when he saw me.

'You're gonna love this, Jake! Thirty rounds in the drum and they shoot as fast as you can pull the trigger!'

'Thirty rounds?!' I said, amazed. 'Where'd you find them?'

Doogan grinned proudly.

'We couldn't allow the government to confiscate everything, could we?' the old priest explained. 'I've had these hidden in the cellar. Like meself, they are relics of a different age.'

It took a minute or two, but Doogan showed us how to load and work the drum-guns. For a holy guy, he knew a lot more about weapons than you'd expect. The old man also brought up a whole basketful of shells. It was sitting on the table and nearly overflowing with enough rounds for a small war. Doogan surprised me that day, and so did Mrs. Thompson. Next to the basket was a pile if ammo-bags. They looked like little cloth sacks with a shoulder strap, and I didn't know what they were for until Mrs. Thompson started filling them with shells. Casey slid his jacket back on, and stuffed his pockets with rounds too. As I watched, something dawned on me. It looked like Doogan and Mrs. Thompson had done this before.

When we got outside there were seven or eight guys already waiting with Mike. Casey knew everybody a lot better than I did, so I let him decide who got the drum-guns. He passed out all three, and one of them went to Ted Downton. For what I was gonna do I was fine with a sawdi, and I wanted the Churchers to have the extra firepower. I was looking out at the road just beyond the Church, thinking up a plan, when I heard Becky's voice behind me.

'Ginny! Thanks for coming.'

When I turned, Becky was hugging the little female that we met my first day in Nineveh. Ginny Mardonis was the red-headed mom that followed us to the rectory, and she was holding a long gun, a bolt-action rifle with a scope on top. The gun was bigger than she was and wondered how she could handle a piece like that. I already had my doubts if the Churchers could fight or not, and seeing that tiny female with the long gun wasn't helping.

'How far out can you hit something with that?'

'If you can see it, Bishop Jake, then I can hit it!'

The confident little redhead may have had a rep for being a good shot, but she was still a Churcher, and a female Churcher.

'But can you shoot to kill?' I pressed. 'If we're gonna do this, I need to know—'

'Mariam is a sister to me. I won't miss!'

Shithead showed up next, coming in from the woods with two more Churchers. The sun had just passed the top of the church and I could see the shadow of the bell tower on the ground where they were walking. It gave me a great idea.

'Ginny, I need you up there in the tower,' I explained, pointing to the church. 'Take whatever shots you can, but there's gonna be a jeep with a machine gun on the back. If the Knights get to that gun, we'll lose people. Your job is that jeep, ok?'

Ginny nodded and headed straight into the church. I didn't know how much time we had left, but I knew I had to hurry.

'Now look,' I shouted, turning to the others. 'Stay out of sight until the two-stroke goes by, and nobody fires until I do. Mariam's in the black car. When the shooting starts I want all the tires flat. Just the tires, I don't want Marian getting hurt! I'll handle whoever's inside, but whatever happens, that car stays here. Take out the other vehicles any way you can. Start by shooting through the windows, and kill any Knight that you see.'

A hush went up through the guys, and a voice rose up.

'Kill them, Bishop Walker?'

'Listen to me guys,' I groaned impatiently. 'We're outmatched and outgunned. The only advantage we have is surprise. I'm not *only* asking you to kill them, I'm asking you to kill as many as you can, as fast as you can! If you don't, people you care about are gonna die, and the Knights will get away with Mariam. If you can't do that, then tell me right now!'

Nobody said a word, so I kept talking.

'There's gonna be at least two or three guys riding in the back of the big truck. When the shooting starts keep pumping rounds into that green cover, and remember they can slip out of the truck on either side. Their guns are fully auto, so if you let them, they're gonna send a lot of shit your way.'

'Casey, you'll be up front,' I said turning to him, 'take out the driver's window first, and anyone that—'

I had to stop. Maybe this isn't all that important now, but while I was talking I noticed two brothers standing by the porch steps. They were about twenty-five with blonde hair, and exactly alike. I'm not just saying that they *resembled* each other either. These guys were like both sides of a damn mirror, and dressed in the same kind of clothes too! Nobody else was freaked by it, but I was so weirded-out that I stopped talking when I caught sight of them. Becky told me later that they were *twins*, and that twin people aren't that unusual, but at the time it was way too distracting so I made up something for them to do.

'You guys,' I pointed to them. 'I need you to stay back here, out of sight. If any of the Knights get by us, take them down and protect the house.'

After that we started moving to the road. I wish I could remember the names of all those guys that were with me that day because they did great, every last one of them. We were nearly to the street when I noticed Becky behind me. I don't know where she got the damn thing, but she was holding a long double-barrel. I stopped and let the others pass.

'What are you doing?' I asked, edgily. 'Get your ass back in the rectory and stay there.'

'But I can help! I'm not such a bad shot myself—'

'Just do it, ok?!'

189

We were running out of time, and with all the other shit I had to worry about, Becky was suddenly pissed at me.

'Bishop Jake!' she exclaimed, trying to keep her voice down. 'You're behaving like a sexist!'

'Religion's got nothing to do with this,' I argued. 'I just need to know you're safe inside somewhere.'

Becky started to say something, but then she let out a sigh.

'Be careful,' she whispered, 'alright?'

I nodded, and for a second I got distracted watching her walk back to Doogan and Mrs. Thompson. When Becky's walking, a dude would have to be dead, *not* to be distracted.

When I joined everybody down on the road, we positioned the Churchers on both sides, in a long crossfire. Casey knew everybody, and he was good at giving orders and explaining things. We split up the guys with the drum-guns and Casey took his place in the clump of trees near the sidewalk. I was still unsure about Michael's head, so I kept him with me. I wasn't expecting this, but Shithead asked me for a gun so he could help. Maybe I was crazy, but after thinking a sec, I gave him the nine that I took from Snaggletooth. Then I set him next to Mike where I could watch them both.

We were ready, or as ready as we were ever gonna get, and things got really quiet. I was going over everything again in my head, trying to think of anything I'd missed, and something came to me.

'Where's Sammy?' I asked, poking Mike. 'I don't remember where we put him.'

'He left for home,' he answered. 'The Amish don't believe in violence.'

'Believe in it?' I laughed. 'So how's that change anything?'

Mike didn't get a chance to answer. The sound of the two-stroke was suddenly in the air and growing louder. I took a quick look back and my Churchers were all in position and out of sight.

The ugly asshole on the bike rode into view. He slowed up a

little as he passed the church and I could see the other vehicles a hundred feet behind. The jeep was first, followed by the truck, and lagging back another thirty feet, the black car.

I watched the jeep until it was only about twenty feet away. The driver had a guy next to him, and another dude riding in the back, but nobody was on the big gun yet. The Knights weren't expecting trouble, and I set my sights on the jeep's driver. Holding my breath, I waited till they reached the perfect spot on the road and I squeezed off my first shot. After that, the world around us exploded with fire and smoke.

The two Knights in the front of the jeep were dead before they knew what hit them. Their bodies shook with the red splotches from the shotgun blasts, and the jeep started veering off to the right. When the driver of the truck saw what was happening he sped up to get around it, but the jeep drove right into his side. At that moment, Casey blew out the windows of the truck, and both vehicles skidded to a stop. The Churchers pounded the Knights with everything they had, and the damned Knights never had a chance! There were flames coming from under the truck's fenders and so much smoke in the air that it was hard to see.

The tires of the black car disappeared, and there was nothing left of them but little pieces of black stuff on the road. White smoke began spewing out of the car's grill, but the dumbass driver still tried to get away. He floored it, riding on the rims until I stepped out onto into the road and put a round through the driver's window. I took a chance stepping out into the open like that, but I knew Mariam was in the back of the car, and I didn't have a safe angle for my shot. After that, the car lurched to a halt in the grass, with the front rims spinning in the dirt.

Oh, and there were six Knights in the bed of the truck, a lot more than I expected. One of them never made it out and they didn't find him till later, but the rest of them bailed and tried to scatter when the shooting started. Somebody rolled out of the truck's passenger side too, and started shooting blindly into the woods. Even with all the bullets flying, he was able to get to the crippled jeep. He jumped onto the back, and the second he touched the big gun, the whole top of his head blew off!

I'll admit that I had my doubts about the little redhead in the bell tower, but both times one of the knights got close to that big gun, she took him out with one shot! And remember the asshole on the two-stroke? While he was safely watching next to the bridge, at least five hundred feet away, she suddenly took him out with one shot too! I've never seen anyone shoot like Ginny, not even in the city. Since then I've heard from a couple of guys that you should never piss off a redheaded female. It's the truth, and although there's no way of knowing for sure, I'll bet she saved a lot of Churcher lives that day.

The whole firefight only lasted a minute or two and there was still a lot of smoke in the air when both of the car's back doors flew open. The Knight on my side had his hands in the air like he was giving up, but I couldn't see what was happening behind him so I dropped him as he was climbing out. There was another Knight right behind him with a rifle, and once the first guy fell, Michael took him down before he could fire.

All at once it was quiet again, and through the clouds of smoke we saw the snaggletoothed asshole standing on the other side of the car. He had Mariam out in front, holding her by her hair, and he had a nine to her head. She was in her Amish outfit and she looked scared to death, but it didn't look like she was hurt. Snaggletooth moved her slowly out into the open, pulling her hair back so hard that her face was looking up. My Churchers started coming out from cover, with their guns on him.

Churchers aren't the kind to shoot without thinking, but just in case I shouted, 'Hold your fire!'

'Back Off,' Snaggletooth screamed, 'Back off or I'll waste her!'

Michael was already moving toward Mariam, so I told him to stay put and handed him my sawdi. I grabbed the nine from Shithead and started walking toward Snaggletooth.

'Shut your mouth, asshole, and let her go!'

He was looking around like he couldn't believe what he was seeing. My Churchers were all around him.

'Listen up, creep,' I told him. 'I'm gonna make this easy for you. Let her go now and you walk. Otherwise I'll take three or four days to kill you, and I'll start off tonight by making you a girl.'

I only said that to scare him. Hell, nobody's twisted enough to take four days to kill somebody.

Snaggletooth looked around nervously.

'Bacchus is gonna kill me!'

I laughed, 'So what?'

'You don't understand!' he pleaded. 'Bacchus is a prophet. He talks with God!'

'Yeah? So how come God never told him about me?'

I'd had enough of this guy, so I cocked the nine and pointed it at his right eye.

'Time's up dirtball. What ya wanna do?'

'Ok ok!' he shouted, dropping the gun and throwing his hands up. 'Look, I'm letting her go! Just like you said!'

Mariam ran straight into me, hugging me so tightly that I almost shot Snaggletooth by accident. Michael was there a second later, and she wrapped her arms around him and started crying.

Hell, as you can imagine I was suddenly feeling pretty damned good about things, and I think the other Churchers were feeling it too! Snaggletooth was standing there with his hands up, and the rest of the Knights were lying dead on the road. But just when it started looking like it was over, I felt movement behind me and a terrible hush went through my Churchers.

In my whole life I'd never seen anything that caused me to freeze. I've seen plenty of nasty shit too, and I guess I always figured that nothing could shake me, but when I turned I saw something that'll stay burned into my eyes forever.

It was Lightning, standing on the path to the church, but the scene was ugly and unreal, worse than a nightmare. Her yellow dress was streaked red, by the same thick redness that covered her hands and arms. And those arms. They were reaching out for me, grasping for me as if her legs refused to bring her any closer. Some of Lightning's once-golden hair was matted down and glued to the scarlet side of her face. Her eyes were wide open, too open, and filled with panic and horror. Her mouth was frozen in a silent scream, with a force that made her whole body tremble. When my mind finally grasped what I was seeing, I realized something else. The blood wasn't hers.

Before I could react, Lightning's bare feet brought her to me, and she seized my hand and started pulling me toward the walkway. I followed automatically, past the burning truck and over to the path to the rectory. Once we turned the corner, I knew where we were going.

We got to the place where Casey should have been. We found him lying just beyond it, almost to where the sidewalk meets the street, and I suddenly remembered the shots I'd heard when the Knights were bailing from the truck. When I got to him, I knelt down in the blood and turned him over. He groaned, still conscious, but the holes in Casey's side told me that it was over.

I propped him up against me, but I couldn't think of anything to say.

'Is Rita alright?' he asked weakly. 'She stepped out from the trees and into the open! She didn't hear us. Is she ok? Did I get there in time?'

'She's fine, man,' I told him. 'You did good.'

'Thank God!' he exhaled. 'Mariam?'

'Good too.'

I saw Lightning behind us, crying in Mariam's arms.

'Get her out of here!' I screamed. 'And the rest of you, give us room!'

Michael was on his knees beside us, and he shouted, 'Run! Somebody get Doogan!'

Ted Downton ran off toward the rectory, but Casey grabbed Mike's hand.

'There isn't time—'

His voice was failing, and he turned to me. I was trying to stop the bleeding in his chest, or maybe I was just trying to keep myself busy.

'Please Jake, the papal blessing? It's a special blessing for the dying. It's in my pocket.'

'Doogan's coming,' I told him. 'I can't do that. He'll be here in—'

'Yes you can. Any priest or bishop can do it.'

Mike reached into the high pocket of Casey's coat and pulled out a little black book.

'The Urbi et Orbi?' Casey asked him. 'In English.'

I looked back to the house but nobody was coming yet.

I stalled, 'Doogan will be here in a sec—'

'Quickly, Jake!' Casey groaned.

'But I don't—'

Michael gave me a hard shove, returning the favor that I gave him earlier.

'Damn it, Jake, just do it!' he told me. 'No one else can.'

Mike handed me the book and came around so he could see over my shoulder and help me. It only took a minute and I swear I did everything Casey wanted me to do. I read all the words by the sunlight slicing down through the trees like yellow shards of broken glass. They were more than just words to Casey. As I finished, he smiled and said *amen*. It was the same unreal smile that I saw on the nuncio's face before he died. A moment later, Michael reached over and closed Casey's eyes one last time.

Something in my brain stopped working. I was sad and furious, and so damned numb that I didn't even know why I was pissed. The air smelled like smoke and blood, and I could feel the Churchers' eyes on me. I could barely think, or even breathe, but a question still forced its way into my brain.

'How did he know?' I shouted, turning to Mike. 'Who the hell has a prayer like that in his pocket? How did he know he was gonna die?!'

Mike looked at me, surprised.

'Casey was taking instruction, Jake,' he answered. 'It was part of his coursework, I thought you knew.'

I shook my head. 'Knew what?!'

'He was our seminarian,' Mike replied. 'You were going to ordain him next spring. Casey was going to be our priest.'

Like I said, my head was broke, and there were way too many things going through it to think right. I kept remembering the look on Lightning's face, looking up at me with her hands soaked in blood. Suddenly this storybook land of the Churchers, this world of thick shirts, females and endless food, was ugly and ruined. In the last few minutes I'd transformed it into something bloody and terrible. Without knowing exactly how, I'd screwed it all up.

I remember watching Doogan arrive, running and out of breath. He was praying even before he knelt down beside us. I set Casey's head down on the sidewalk and got to my feet. Becky, Downton and some of the others were running toward us from the rectory, but all I could do was turn and start walking in the other direction.

For the longest time, all I can remember is walking.

OVER MY HEAD

Just so you know, I wasn't crazy or geeked-out like Mike became after the Knights took Marian. Sure, I was pissed as hell as I walked away, and yeah I wanted to kill something, but I can handle normal feelings like that. It's just that my head kept racing through everything that had just gone down, and I couldn't figure out how everything turned to shit so quickly. No matter how I looked at it, I knew I'd let the Churchers down. I'd managed to get my friend Casey killed, their would-be priest, and on top of everything else I kept remembering Lightning. How could anyone ever undo what I'd done to Lightning?

Since I'm being honest, there was something else bothering me too, the *religion* thing. As he was dying Casey asked me for a blessing, and even as I read it, I didn't understand what I was doing. I'd only been a bishop for a couple of days but I was already a miserable failure. I wasn't worth a shit at keeping the Churchers alive, and I didn't know enough about God to help them die! And where was this God of theirs anyway? Why couldn't he have helped us out, and how could he let Casey die like that? I knew less than nothing about this religion stuff, and the more I thought about it, the more obvious it became. I was in over my head.

My memories of that time are a little screwy, but I know it was nearly dark before I turned around and headed back to Nineveh. I remember stopping at the creek and trying to wash the blood from my hands and face in the darkness. It was like I was walking in one

197

of my nightmares and I kept remembering Jodie's words *you can't save them*. I was crazy-pissed remembering how that ugly little bastard supplied the Knights with guns and vehicles. I never wanted anything like I wanted to kill that man.

Once I saw lights up ahead, I kept to the darker shadows by the tree line. I wasn't ready to return to the rectory just yet, but I wanted to check things out and see what was happening by the church. I crossed the street and moved onto the old bridge where I see the Churchers through the trees. There was a good spot about halfway across, and I sat down with my back against a rusty light pole. It was on the sidewalk side, and on the other side of the railing, I could hear the river moving below me in the darkness. There was a lot of talking and shouting going on at the church, and I knew that the generator behind the rectory was still on because the house was lit up.

They must have taken Casey away while I was gone, but I watched as the Churchers took the bodies of the Knights into the burned-out school. Doogan and a bunch of Churchers went inside too, and from what I could hear, I think they prayed over the Knights. It pissed me off at first. If it were up to me I would have dumped their asses down a hole somewhere or burned them, but knowing the Churchers like I do, I figured they probably had a golden rule for dead people too. After that, the Churchers started splitting up, and I caught sight of someone walking toward the bridge from the rectory. I watched the thin silhouette coming straight for me, backlit by the Knight's truck still burning on the road. At first I thought that she knew I was there, but then she stopped. After studying the darkness from every direction, Becky turned and started for home.

All at once it was quiet and peaceful at St. Lucy's again. It must have been late because the moon had crept over the treetops, and I could see waves shimmering on the white water below. Maybe my head needed to shut down for a while, or maybe it's because I could smell the burning truck from my spot the bridge, but I closed my eyes and fell asleep. The burning truck was a familiar kind of smell, and even though I didn't feel tired, it helped me unwind and drift off.

When I opened my eyes again it was light, and I knew I'd slept too long. The sun had been up for a long time already and there were noises coming from the old school. I knew something wasn't right. I never *ever* sleep so late, especially out in the open, and my instincts told me that I wasn't alone. As I was reaching for a blade, I heard Shithead's voice.

'It's just me, Bishop Man!'

He was standing on the sidewalk against the railing, and when he saw me put my knife away he took a cautious step closer. I propped myself up against the light post and rubbed my eyes.

'What do you want, Shithead?'

'She sent me out last night to find you. Everybody's worried 'bout you.'

The sound of the river was deafening, so I got up and leaned closer to the edge for a better look. It was a good sixty feet down and really moving. There were huge rocks and boulders sticking up everywhere. The old bridge was surprisingly cool in the morning light and a scary place to wake up. It was like I was sitting in a long metal cage, wedged between two shale cliffs. Once my head started clearing up, I had questions.

'Where's Snaggletooth? What happened after I left?'

'He jumped on the dead guy's motorcycle and rode off.'

'When the other Knights hear about last night, they're not gonna like it,' I told him. 'Why isn't anyone keeping lookout, or guarding the road?'

'I dunno.'

We were so high up that I had to lean over the railing and spit. I watched it float slowly down and into the misty water.

'So, why didn't you kill him?'

'I can't do that, man,' he replied, softly. 'I ain't like that.'

'I know,' I laughed. 'It's cause you're a puss!'

Busting on Shithead usually put me in a better mood, but it wasn't working that morning. I noticed bicycles and horses over at the rectory, and people walking in front of the church.

'You gotta come back,' he explained, glancing over his shoulder. 'Everything's crazy now. They're burying Casey, and Fr. Doogan says he needs you.'

I was still a little spaced, and I stared down at the river without saying anything. The look on my face must have told Shithead that I didn't want to go back yet.

'It wasn't your fault, ya know,' he said.

'What the hell do you know about anything?!'

'I know what I saw, man.'

I figured it was time to go back. It was either that, or stay there on the bridge and have to listen to Shithead, so I started walking to the rectory.

Shithead followed me passed the Knights cars and past the church, and we were almost to the rectory when we saw three young Churcher girls leaving the house. They were wearing black dresses and one of them was crying. Something made me look down, and although there wasn't any blood on my hands anymore, my shirt was totaled. Even so, one of the Churcher girls smiled when she saw me.

'Good morning, Bishop Walker.'

As far as I could tell my brain was working normally again, but you're gonna doubt it when I describe what happened next. Looking back on it, it doesn't sound so bad now, but at the time it was freaky and unreal. We jogged up the front stairs to the rectory and opened the screen door, but when I got a good look around, I couldn't believe what I was seeing.

There were at least ten or fifteen people hanging around, dressed in dark colors and talking quietly. A hushed stillness filled the air, and the whole place smelled like flowers. Some of the furniture had been moved out, and on the other side of the Churchers I saw something that made my skin crawl. They had Casey's body cleaned up and laying in a box where the sofa should have been! I'm not kidding, he was there on a table about waist-high, dressed in clean clothes and with a white pillow under his head. There was a cross on the wall above him and two Churcher females kneeling in front of the coffin, praying. There were even two rows of fold-up chairs set up, so the Churchers could sit and stare at the body! It was creepy and weird, and I bet my jaw dropped halfway to the floor.

'Are you catching all this?' I asked, poking Shithead.

'What?'

'This!' I repeated, trying to keep my voice down. 'They've got a dead guy on display in the front room, and it's Casey! You don't think this is nuts?!'

'You ain't never been to a wake before?' he grinned. 'What kind of a Churcher are you?'

The question reminded me that I didn't know what I was doing, and I wasn't in the mood.

'*This kind,*' I replied, elbowing him in his bandaged ear.

Becky was sitting in the front row near Casey, and I recognized her when she turned toward us. There was a golden-haired girl sitting next to her, and when Becky stood up, so did the girl. It was the first time I'd ever seen Lightning in anything but yellow. They were both in black dresses that went down to their knees, and Lightning looked like hell. I recognized the look of shock on her face, and she was holding tightly onto Becky's arm. Her cried-out eyes were misty, and when they met mine, I recognized that look too. She hated my damned guts.

Becky signed something, and Lightning fell softly back into her chair and hid her face in her hands. Becky began working her way through the other Churchers and over to Shithead and me, and at the same time I saw Doogan and Mrs. Thompson stepping into the room from the hallway. Becky reached us first, and although her eyes looked glad to see me, her voice sounded pissed.

'Are you ok? Everyone's been sick with worry about you!'

Before I could say anything Doogan and Mrs. Thompson joined us. When I got a good look at everybody up close it hit me. I was probably the only person there that got any sleep that night.

'There's much to do, lad,' Doogan explained, 'and we have the funeral in a few minutes. You should be getting cleaned up and—'

'No,' I interrupted. 'I need to talk with you.'

Mrs. Thompson leaned closer.

'There's a change of clothes on your bed, Your Grace,' she whispered, 'and you'll have enough hot water for a shower in a few minutes.'

She added, 'Excuse me' and headed for the stairs.

Doogan motioned for me to follow him. I knew that Becky wanted to come too, and see what I was gonna tell Doogan, but she kept looking back at Lightning.

'I have to get back to Rita,' she sighed. 'I'll see you after the funeral.'

We left Shithead by the front door and I walked with Doogan down the hall and into the library. The old man closed the door behind us, and for the longest time we stood there looking at each other. I knew what I had to do and what I had to tell him, but I couldn't find the right words. The old man was going to be disappointed with me, and I didn't want to hit him with all this right now, especially since we'd just lost Casey. I fumbled around for a sec, but I finally just came out with it.

'I can't be your bishop anymore!' I told him. 'I'll help you fight the Knights, but I can't do the bishop thing.'

'Calm yourself, son,' He replied softly. 'We're all hurting now and sorting things out. Surely, you don't doubt that you were meant to be our bishop. How can you not believe—'

'Just because I *believe*, doesn't mean I can ever do this!'

The old man took a deep breath and motioned for me to sit down. We moved over to the big chairs by the window and took a seat. Doogan looked more tired than I'd ever seen him, and he started searching his pockets for a pipe.

'We can only do what we allow God to do through us, Jacob,' he explained. 'You should trust that God will help you, and—'

'Yeah?' I interrupted, 'like he helped Casey?!'

I saw the surprise light up Doogan's face, and he gave me a long look. He'd found his pipe, but after beating it against his hand for a while, he set it down on the table.

'I see,' he sighed. 'You're angry with God, aren't you lad?'

I wasn't ready to admit to something like that, especially to a holy guy, and when I didn't answer, he smiled.

'It requires faith to be angry with God,' Doogan said softly, 'but it also means that you don't know him. Our God knows what he's doing, Jacob! He's smarter than we are and he has reasons for everything he does.'

'Casey was supposed to be a priest!' I shot back. 'How come I never picked up on that? I feel like an idiot!'

'You've been busy. We've all been busy, heaven help us!' Doogan laughed, 'And our Casey never behaved like a priest, did he now? Casey was a headstrong and impetuous young man. That's partly why everyone loved him so.'

'And did you see Lightning?!' I shouted. 'She hates my ass and I don't blame her! It's like I killed them both last night.'

'Rita is young and grieving. She'll understand in time.'

He reached over and put his hand on my shoulder.

'Casey died saving Rita, and rescuing Mariam,' he said proudly. 'He's with God now, and God has his reasons for taking him so soon.'

Looking back on it, I should have explained more stuff to Doogan. I should have been honest and told him that the religion thing was starting to scare me. I should have told him that losing Churchers was different than losing friends, and I should know, I'd lost plenty of friends. It's just that my instincts were telling me to run, to get the hell out, and I always follow my instincts. Maybe I was tired of talking, or fed-up about everything, but I stood up and let Doogan's hand slide off my shoulder. I slid the ring off my finger and held it out to him.

'I quit,' I told him. 'Kinsley's right, I'm a reckless thug. The Churchers need someone who knows how to do this stuff.'

Like I figured, Doogan was disappointed, but he was pissed too. He looked at the ring and shook his head.

'You have your free will,' he said coldly, 'but I'll be having no part in this! If you wish to resign, you can tell the people of your parish yourself. All the Catholics of the community will be at the funeral in a few minutes. They'll be expecting you to give a homily as it is. If it's not too much to ask, you can resign at that time.'

'Casey was your friend,' he added, rising to his feet, 'and God knows, the man who believed in you most!'

I knew that Doogan was just saying that to make me feel like shit, but it was working. It's probably something else that they teach you in priest school.

'Fine!' I grumbled.

I slipped the ring back on and stomped out of the library. Without looking at Casey, or anyone at the wake, I went right up the stairs and into my room. It was done. I was quitting the bishop thing, and all I had to do now was to tell the Churchers.

So why'd I feel like I was screwing up again?

THE FUNERAL

There were fresh clothes on my bed like Mrs. Thompson promised, and I picked them up and went right into the bathroom. It was a lot like my bathroom on the West End, except it was super clean and everything worked. I figured out how to work the shower, and while I was getting cleaned up I kept wondering what Becky and the other Churchers were gonna think about me quitting. They'd probably think that I turned chicken, and in a way, they were probably right. Maybe they'd all be silently pissed at me like Doogan, or hate my guts like Lightning.

I started remembered things like the kids singing at the school, the barbeque, and how important bishops were to Churchers. I also remembered Casey and Mike back on West End, and how they thought they were getting *me* out of the city. I walked back to my room, and while I was buttoning my shirt, Mrs. Thompson knocked on the door.

'Your Grace?'

Once I opened the door, I could see that the old housekeeper lady was mad at me too. She walked right past me, holding a light blue shirt with a collar and lots of buttons down the front.

'There's a reception following the funeral Mass,' she said, almost too softly to hear. 'I thought you might like to wear this after the ceremony.'

Mrs. Thompson must have known what I told Doogan. She wasn't looking at me while she talked, and there was an edge to her voice. She put the shirt gently on the bed before looking up at me.

'Excuse me, Your Grace,' she said, trying not to sound pissed. 'But may I ask you something?'

'Yeah, sure.'

I was half-expecting her to give me shit about getting Casey killed, or running out on my bishop job, but something else was bugging her.

'Do you have a problem with *prayer*, Bishop Jake?'

I didn't have a clue what she was talking about.

'I heard how Casey died last night, and I'm sorry,' she continued, 'but you seem to be afraid of talking to God for some reason? How can that be?'

If it had been anyone else, I would have told her to shut the hell up, or mind her own business, but I didn't. You know, I've always liked Mrs. Thompson.

'No, there's no problem with it,' I answered. 'It's just that I put my faith in things I can control. When I trust in other stuff, things don't go so good.'

Mrs. Thompson's eyebrows went up like she wanted details.

'The last memories I have of my mom is her praying,' I remembered. 'She prayed constantly, day and night toward the end. She wasn't doing it right, or maybe nobody was listening, cause after a full two days of it, she died.'

Mrs. Thompson looked surprised.

'No one was listening?'

She didn't look mad at me anymore, and she put her hand on my elbow.

'You don't know a thing about mothers, do you?'

Her voice changed as if she was about to tell me a secret.

'In difficult times like those,' she said, 'moms don't pray for themselves, Your Grace. They're too busy praying for the ones they love. If I know anything about mothers, I suspect your mom was praying for you.'

Mrs. Thompson let go of my arm and walked to the dresser.

'And now', she resumed, picking up my bible-book, 'you're in warm clothes, you have a warm bed that you *don't use*, and you're bishop to the wonderful people of St. Lucy's parish.'

'Forgive me, Your Grace,' she added, smiling. 'But it sounds to me as though every one of your mother's prayers have been answered.'

Churchers have a way of looking at things, even shitty things, and Mrs. Thompson is good at putting stuff into words. Sure, maybe it was all just a load of crap, but I had to smile back at her.

'Ok,' I said. 'I'll think about giving the prayer thing another try.'

I watched as another idea came to her.

'You'll be expected to say something nice about Casey, you know,' she thought out loud. 'Has Fr. Doogan helped you with that?'

'No, he's pissed at me.'

'*Men!*' she sighed, opening my bible-book. 'Well, if you find yourself at a loss, you can always start here.'

There's a red ribbon and a blue ribbon hanging from the top of my bible-book. None of my other books had anything like that, and it's a cool way to keep your place when you're reading something. Mrs. Thompson laid the red ribbon between the two pages and pointed to the second paragraph on the page. She handed it to me, and as I was scanning down through the words, Doogan's voice echoed up from downstairs.

'It's time! The procession is waiting.'

I told her 'Thanks' and slid the book into the pocket with my knives. I'm not sure why it was suddenly so important, but before I got halfway down the stairs, I stopped and looked back up at Mrs. Thompson.

'Hey Mrs. Thompson, you coming to the funeral?'

'Of course,' she smiled, 'after I finish a few things.'

I'd only been upstairs for a few minutes, but everything was different and a whole lot creepier once I got downstairs. Doogan was holding the screen door open for me, but the front room was empty and dark, and Casey's coffin was gone. The chairs were folded up and leaning neatly against the wall by the cross. I stepped out onto the porch and saw that the sky had turned gray, and there were dark-bellied clouds racing across it. There were at least twenty people standing around with their shirts and dresses rippling in the wind, and some of them were crying.

They had Casey's coffin lying in something like an Amish buggy, except long and open. The buggy had big spoked wheels like a bicycle, and every part of it was painted black. The coffin was sitting in the back and closed now, and there was a huge cross of white and yellow flowers lying across the top. Two black horses were hitched to the buggy's front, and I recognized the driver as the guy who was cooking the food at the barbeque. With everyone in black and the sky being so gray, the flowery cross looked like the only splash of color left in the world. I helped Doogan into the front of the buggy, and once we were both in, the wagon started moving toward the church.

The church was right across the parking lot, but those big horses took their damn time getting us there. The people walking behind us had enough time to sing two whole songs while we clip-clopped along. As we got closer, I saw Mike and some other guys waiting at the doors of the church. It was the first time I'd seen Mike since Casey died and although he smiled and nodded, I didn't get a chance to talk with him. They started carrying Casey's coffin in through the front doors, and when I went to give them a hand, Doogan stopped me.

'This way, Bishop Walker.'

The old man took me around back to a smaller door around back, and it led inside to a secret room. It had the smell of a church, only stronger, and it had a sink and closets, and wooden drawers built into the walls. Like I said before, churches are built to be spooky, and straight ahead through another opening, I could see the back of the church's altar.

Doogan wasn't saying much. For the first minute or two all I could hear was the sounds of people moving around in the church. He took some long curtains out of the big closet and set them on a chair. At the same time, two kids walked in from the church.

'Bishop Walker,' Doogan announced, 'This is Mark, and that lad there is Tobias.'

The kids smiled at me and I nodded, 'Hey.'

The old priest was still pissed at me, but he lightened up once the kids showed up. He was busy at the sink, filling a small glass bottle with water, but he turned to the boys.

'I once knew a young Jesuit priest,' he said to them, grinning, 'who was convinced that the souls of our beloved dead are permitted to attend their own funerals before moving on. Let's remember that, and make our Casey proud today.'

The boys were maybe ten or twelve, but they seemed to know what they were doing. They grabbed some black and white robes from the smaller closet and started pulling them over their clothes.

'Those are your vestments and miter, Bishop Walker,' Doogan said edgily, nodding at the chair. 'Tis the best we could do.'

Doogan stared back at me like I should have been doing something, but I couldn't believe that the old guy wanted me to wear *curtains*. I kept looking around, expecting the two kids to start laughing at me, but apparently it wasn't a joke. It wasn't until I watched Doogan slide into his own set of curtains that I started putting on mine.

The bigger problem was that my *vestments* also included a hat that came to a point two feet above my head! It was easy to see why they had some a hard time finding bishops. If people knew up front that they had to wear this stuff, who'd want the job? I might have bitched about it or refused to wear the thing, but I was still feeling guilty about getting Casey killed and quitting. When I was done getting dressed, Doogan lined us all up with the kids in front, and we walked out into the church.

The people in the Church stood up and started singing again, and I knew right away that we were doing something important. Casey's coffin was in front of the altar with lots of flowers around it, and even though the place was full, nobody laughed at my costume. Mike and Mariam were in the front row next to Becky and Lightning, and the kid wouldn't even look up at me. She just kept staring blankly out at the coffin as we marched in. Mariam was dressed Amish today, and Michael was holding her close beside him. Shithead was sitting right behind them, and in the back of the Church I caught Beth Morrison and her daughter rushing in like they were late. They squeezed into the front row, next to Mrs. Thompson, and started singing too. There were a lot of people crying, and even some of the singing people had tears in their eyes.

As usual, the only person in the building that didn't know what he was doing was me. Everyone else knew what Doogan was gonna say, and how to answer. My job was pretty much just following Doogan around, and the old man told me where to stand and when to sit in the bishop's chair. The two kids helped him with everything else, and they stood next to my chair when nothing else was happening. To the left of the altar was a stand with a gold bible-book on top, and people took turns coming up to read from it.

Everyone stood up when Doogan walked us over to give his speech. He crossed himself a bunch of times and started reading, and when I heard what he was saying, I started to freak. Out of all the things in that bible-book, he read the same saying that Mrs. Thompson gave me to say!

'Greater love hath no man than this, that a man lay down his life for his friends...'

Yeah, he might have spiced it up a little, but there was no doubt about it. Doogan stole my saying! Suddenly I was getting panicky about what I was gonna say about Casey, and while I was still trying to think of something, the old man turned to me and called, 'Bishop Walker?'

I've never been so frustrated, and at that moment quitting the bishop thing was all I wanted to do. I was standing there with nothing! I wanted to say something to make the Churchers feel better, something to help them remember Casey, but I'd gone empty inside. Watching Doogan and seeing the funeral Mass proved that I wasn't cut out for this stuff. What was happening around me was important and special to the Churchers, and it was meant for a better kind of person than me.

I knew I'd better get it over with, say something nice about Casey and quit, but when I walked up to where the bible-book was open, I couldn't get started. For the longest time I looked down on Casey's coffin, and the only sound in the place was from people sobbing. I had my little bible-book ready in my hand, but instead of opening it, I held it up.

'Hey, you guys know this stuff better than I ever will,' I started. 'But even I know that Casey's death last night was all about that *greater love* thing.'

I swallowed hard.

'Casey knew that—'

I stopped when the back door of the church banged open, and I was surprised to see lots of people on the other side. I watched as Mr. Hershberger limped in with Sammy, and I noticed that the big man's left eye was swelled shut. He took off his hat and his head was wrapped in a white bandage. He glanced over at me before turning and walking past the water bowl by the doors. He just stood there against the back wall, looking at me with his arms crossed. By now, all the Churchers were turned around, and they watched as more and more people marched in.

And guess who came in right behind Hershberger? It was Kinsley, with his wife and daughters, all dressed in black, and his poor little girls had that same nasty look on their faces! Behind them was Ted Downton, and some people I'd never seen before. As we looked on, it seems to me that every Churcher in Nineveh was coming to the funeral, and the back of the church became so packed that some people were standing along the walls below the colored glass. I could see an older guy with a black beard standing outside looking in. I found out later that it was Dr. Weiss. He's an Orthodox Jewish Churcher and he's not allowed to come into churches. Hell, I can't imagine what he must have done. He's the only person I ever heard of that isn't allowed in church.

Don't get the wrong idea either. The Lutherans were still Lutherans, the Methodists were still Methodists, and the Presbyterians were still whatever the hell Presbyterians are, but they were all *here*. They were here because of what Casey had done.

There was something in their eyes, a sadness and maybe an anger. As I watched them pile in, it hit me. Casey's death did more than a thousand councils could ever do. By bleeding out on the street last night, saving Mariam and Lightning, he woke everybody up. After the door closed again, I realized that everyone in Nineveh was looking at me and expecting me to say something.

'And ya know what?' I went on. 'Casey loved Lightning and he loved Mariam, and not because one was Amish or one was Catholic but because he just loved them. He had that *greater love* thing going on, like it says here in the book.'

'Casey was the first one out there last night. He knew that if we couldn't find a way to stand together, then Jodie was gonna win. Casey got that, and he knew that the things we believe together, the things that we love, have got to be more important than the things we can't agree about.'

I could see by the looks on the Churcher's faces that everyone got the message, but I still think everybody would have taken me more seriously if I hadn't been wearing the hat. I went back to my chair and sat down, and a second later Doogan went on with the funeral. I'm not sure if something had changed inside of me again, or if I got distracted by everyone coming in that way, but I remembered something as I sat there.

I forgot to quit.

BIGGER PROBLEMS

Now that I'm thinking about it, maybe something did change inside of me that day. It must have. When the funeral started, I was all fired-up and focused on quitting my bishop job, but by the time it was over I wasn't even thinking about that anymore. While I sat there, I remembered Doogan saying that *God knows what he's doing*, and all at once it hit me. If the Churchers were finally together now, maybe this was what God had up his sleeve the whole time. Maybe Casey's death was God's way of getting the Churchers to wake up.

It was beginning to make a little sense, and if God was calling the shots, what was I so worried about? God knew the kind of bishop Nineveh needed, didn't he? And did it matter what the Churchers called me? Bishop or street kid, it didn't change what I had to do here. The Knights would be coming back and somebody had to keep these people alive. God still had Doogan for the spooky stuff, and now that the Churchers were together, my job was helping them fight Jodie and the Knights. Hell, that's probably what God was thinking when he had the nuncio give me the ring! It was deep stuff, and the more I thought about it, the more everything seemed to fit. There was just one thing I couldn't get my head around. I couldn't understand why God took Casey away when we were so short on Churcher dudes.

Since we're talking about deep stuff, now's a good time to bring up the sendoff my Churchers gave to Casey. In the city, nobody cares when you die, and the only thing you can expect from people is that they'll pick your pockets after you're gone. Churchers know that people are more important than that, and they go all-out once you're gone.

And yeah, I still think *wakes* are kind of strange, but the funeral was surprisingly cool and a good way to say goodbye to a friend. The Churchers sang and they prayed and they read from the biblebook. Doogan had a shiny silver thingy on a chain too. There was something burning and smelly inside of it. He swung the ball around and put smoke on everybody, and it made the whole church smell like perfume. I'll bet the funeral took a good hour or more, and by the time it was over, even the elders who acted like they hated Casey's guts when he was alive were praying for him. If Casey did show up like Doogan told the kids, and he stayed for the whole funeral, I bet he got a kick out of that.

When the funeral was over, Doogan blessed everyone in the church again, and we started down to Casey's coffin. Mike and the other coffin-carriers were coming toward us, and it looked like we were about to take Casey back outside. All at once Doogan froze up halfway down the altar steps, staring at Beth Morrison. Nobody else saw it, but her hand was up like she was about to cough, and her finger was pointing to the back of the church. Doogan must have understood the sign, and he gave her a nod.

'Good people,' he announced, once the singing stopped. 'Bishop Walker and meself won't be joining the procession to the cemetery. Members of the council are kindly invited to remain for an impromptu meeting.'

It was my first funeral, but I knew right away that something wasn't right. Lots of people were whispering to each other and looking around. The singing started again, and Mike and the others began walking Casey slowly outside. Becky said something to Mariam, and I saw Mariam putting her arm around Lightning.

'Here now,' Doogan asked me above the noise. 'You're still *Bishop* Walker, aren't you, son?'

'Yeah.'

'Good lad,' he said, grinning. 'Then you have time to change into your street clothes if you wish. We'll be receiving information from Bill Morrison in a few moments.'

Nobody had to tell me twice, so I took my hat off and tossed it to the Tobias kid. A second later, I'd pulled the robes over my head and thrown them to Mark.

'Take care of this, will ya guys?'

They were both laughing and Doogan was laughing too. He nodded 'Thank you boys' and the kids headed back into the secret room.

Out front, I caught Mariam and Lightning stepping out into the main aisle as the coffin passed. They walked along behind it, and all the other Churchers got into the line as Casey went by. I watched Shithead, Sandy, and just about everyone I knew follow the coffin outside, even the non-Catholics who showed up late. Becky stayed back, and she walked across the aisle to Beth and Judy Morrison. It took a while, and the place was nearly cleared out when I noticed someone still sitting in the back.

Bill Morrison was in the last row by himself sitting with his head down, and I almost didn't recognize him. He was dressed in civilian clothes, and he looked more like an Amish guy than a Fed. He stood up with an Amish hat in his hands, and he watched the last of the procession walk out. The whole idea of Morrison disguised as a fat Amish guy almost made me laugh, but I'm glad I didn't. When the doors of the church echoed shut again and he started walking toward us, I caught the look on his face. Morrison was taking Casey's death worse than anybody.

The elders followed slowly behind him, talking to each other as they walked, and I got a little worried when I realized Morrison was walking straight toward me. He looked a little messed-up, and I was thinking he might be pissed at me for getting Casey killed. I would have had a blade ready, but I could see that he wasn't packing.

'Bishop Walker,' he said, stopping in front of me. 'I want to thank you for all you did for Mariam and my godson. We appreciate it more than you know.'

It was one more thing I'll never understand about Churchers. Morrison wasn't blaming me for Casey's death either, and before I could say anything he turned to Doogan.

'Father,' he started, loud enough for everybody to hear. 'Your information is correct. We've received confirmation that the Knights are working with Stephen Jodie, but that's not the worst of it. Jodie's planning to use the Knights for an all-out attack on Nineveh. He's planning on destroying us forever.'

Morrison's words echoed through the church, and it got so quiet that we could hear the wind outside. His family moved beside him, and Morrison put his arm around Beth. The elders of the council circled around Doogan, and Becky was suddenly standing next to me.

'Why the Knights?' I asked. 'Jodie's got his Feds in the city. Why doesn't the little bastard come out here himself?'

'Language, son,' Doogan warned, poking me with his elbow. 'Remember, we're in God's house.'

'Things have changed,' Morrison explained. 'Age and disease have reduced the federal ranks in the urban centers. Recruitment has become impossible, and many of the remaining Feds have been moved to the larger coastal stations. The city posts have equipment and arms, but not enough men. It's easier for Jodie to let the Knights do his dirty work.'

'He's a demon!' Beth exclaimed. 'I thought it was finally over and we could live in peace, and now this!'

Doogan sighed. 'Nineveh has been drawing Godly people to her for years. Jodie has waited with inhuman patience. He's waited for the perfect time to strike.'

'Stephen Jodie has agreed to give Bacchus Taylor half of the city's arsenal,' Morrison went on, 'five weaponized jeeps, two transports, rifles, small arms and anti-personal munitions. It's enough to destroy Nineveh five times over.'

'Anti-personal?' I asked, 'you talking about Bleeders?'

Morrison nodded and Becky looked up at me.

'Bleeders?'

'The Feds use them in the city,' I told her. 'They look like rubber balls, like toys a little bigger than your fist. They explode into hundreds of tiny wiry pieces designed to maximize bleeding.

216

And it's like impossible to stop it.'

Becky closed her eyes and whispered. 'Oh my God!'

'Back up a sec,' I said, thinking. 'Who's this Bacchus guy?'

'Bacchus is a lunatic,' Morrison answered, 'a power-hungry madman, medieval and brutal, and the perfect partner for Jodie. They've established a camp at the old Crescent City Mall, outside the city. Bacchus has convinced his gang that he's a messenger from God, and he's grown his cult by collecting strays and defeating other gangs. He gives notice when he's about to destroy you, and his enemies are offered the choice of joining him or being tortured to death. I've seen his work, and the horror he'd wreak here in Nineveh is unthinkable!'

Ted Downton had a black-haired girl on his arm. She looked a little older than he was, but tall and nice-looking with brown eyes. I found out later that it was his wife.

'We have the Knight's guns from last night,' Downton remembered, 'and Fr. Doogan's scatterguns, and—'

'It's not nearly enough,' Morrison interrupted, glancing at me. 'At most, we have forty men of fighting age, and some of them don't believe in violence. My intel says the Knights are sixty men strong, and they'll be heavily armed.'

Fr. Doogan walked slowly over to the first row of seats and sat down. You could tell he was thinking, and he looked like he was gonna be sick.

'Dear God, we'll have to abandon Nineveh!' he said, shaking his head. 'There are pregnant women and children, and our elderly. We must find a suitable place to relocate—'

'It's too late, Father,' Morrison interrupted. 'We have barely enough time to make a run for it. Jodie is delivering the rest of the weapons Friday morning. He knows we're vulnerable and he's ordered the knights to strike immediately. They'll be here sometime Friday afternoon.'

'Oh my God,' Becky said again. 'That's the day after tomorrow!'

The Churcher's faces all fell and nobody talked for a sec. Everyone was already in a crappy mood from Casey dying, but

Morrison's news was crushing and scary.

'What about hiding out in the old college dorms?' Morrison suggested. 'It's always been our first contingency, and it's better than nothing.'

Downton shook his head.

'They're too close. When the Knights start searching for us, it's the first place they'll look!'

'You got a better idea?' Morrison challenged.

It's not like Morrison was being a jerk. Downton was right and the college dorms were a shitty choice. I remembered passing them when I first got to Nineveh. They were too close, and right out in the open.

'We gotta do better,' I interrupted. 'We've gotta be farther away and impossible to find. And we need to get rid of all the food. If we can't take it with us, we can hide it in the woods.'

Kinsley spoke up. 'Hide the food?'

'The Knights won't stay long if there's no food. Whatever we can't hide or take with us needs to be burned.'

'Ted?' Doogan called. 'Can you assemble a team and coordinate moving the infirm? And Reverend Kinsley, could you organize the search, a suitable place for women and children?'

'We'll need more than one,' I told him. 'The more we split them up, the better odds they'll have for survival.'

Something came to me while I was talking.

'Churchers know the river, don't they?' I thought out loud. 'I mean, we can get to places by boat that are harder to find by jeeps.'

'That's a marvelous idea,' Kinsley said excitedly. 'There must be dozens of such places. We'll look into it straight away!'

'Fr. Doogan,' I said, turning toward him again. 'I'll need the guns we took from Shithead's boat, and the weapons we got from the Knights last night.'

'It's all in the Garage, son,' he answered. 'But why?'

'We need to set up a defense. If the Knights come early, or if people aren't gone yet, somebody will have to buy them time. And I need to know how many of our men are willing to fight.'

Things were happening quickly again, and I was feeling irritated and rushed. When I noticed that everyone was still standing there, I shouted, 'So come on, let's go!'

'One more thing, Father,' Morrison interrupted, holding up his hand. 'It concerns the parish.'

He gave me a look and said, 'Sorry' before pulling a white paper from his back pocket. He handed it to the old man and we all watched as Doogan stood up and began reading.

'The federal government has re-established communications with the church in Charlotte. They have signed an outline of mutual cooperation, and Bishop Gregory has issued a statement.'

A shocked look came over the old man.

'The Diocese of Charlotte recognizes no other bishopric in the central regions. Bishop Gregory is the sole representative of the Church between the Virginias and the state of North California. Anyone outside the diocese claiming Church authority is an imposter.'

Everyone was looking at me, and Doogan slowly folded up the paper and slid it back in his robes.

Morrison added, 'It looks like someone's gotten to Bishop Gregory.'

'We're not accepting anything until Sandy hears this directly from Charlotte,' Doogan replied. 'But if this is true, we must respect Bishop Gregory's decision until we can appeal this.'

I'd almost forgot that Becky was in the church with us, but after Doogan said that, she completely freaked. Her eyes got wide and she went off.

'Bishop Gregory wasn't there when Jake got us out of the city!' she shouted. 'He wasn't there when the nuncio put that ring on his finger! He doesn't know what's been happening these last two days and—'

'Rebecca please,' Doogan sighed. 'This isn't over. I will appeal this all the way to Rome, even if I have to take it there meself.'

'So what's it matter?' I grumbled. 'Don't we have bigger problems?!'

I was acting like I didn't give a shit, but I gotta admit I was a little pissed about things. When it was my idea to quit my bishop job, it didn't bug me so much, but now that I'd been canned, it felt like someone just kicked me in the head. There were questions spinning around in my brain again too, and I was feeling anxious and closed-in. I was about to ask Becky to take me to the garage when something else surprised me. Kinsley looked like he swallowed a bug again, and he walked up to Doogan.

'Fr. Doogan, as a member of the council, may I propose that we wait, and not make that announcement public?'

'But this is church business,' Doogan objected. 'Why would I—'

'Sean,' Kinsley interrupted softly. 'Our people have enough to worry about, don't they? They've come to trust in Bishop Walker. They'll need hope in the days ahead. God willing, couldn't they learn of this later?'

The old man sighed.

'Alright then,' Doogan nodded. 'Until the danger has passed, the people of Nineveh will have their bishop.'

I never expected to hear all that from Kinsley, and maybe I should have said something, but I was dying to get out of there. We needed to get some firepower positioned out by the road. I forgot that I shouldn't be touching Becky and I put my hand on her back.

'Show me the garage?' I asked. 'And I need to talk with you.'

BACCHUS' OFFER

We left the church by the side door, and the second we stepped outside I saw the rickety old garage at the far end of the parking lot. It was off by itself like it didn't belong to the church or the rectory, and that's probably why I hadn't noticed it before. The tired old building had three big doors, and it leaned slightly toward the woods. We headed straight for it, and as we crossed the parking lot, a light rain began to fall. I still had my hand on the small of Becky's back, and I might have been pushing a little as we walked. It wasn't on purpose. I was feeling rushed and angry, and I walk fast when I'm pissed.

'Ok, explain something to me,' I griped. 'If a bishop works for God, and God can help out whenever he wants, why's all this happening?'

'Of course God is helping us! He gave us a bishop and a leader, someone to help—'

'Really? Well, it looks to me like God gave me this ring and brought me all the way out here so I could watch Casey die! And now we gotta leave and run off like chicken shits while the Knights torch Nineveh. Hell, we don't even know if I'm a bishop anymore. Every time I think I've got things figured out, I screw things up and everything turns to shit.'

'Jake, listen to me,' she said, pulling me to a stop.

'You didn't do anything wrong, but I think you've got the wrong idea about bishops. Being a bishop doesn't mean that you won't make mistakes, and it doesn't mean that bad things won't happen. It means that God has asked you to do something for him. It's an awesome responsibility but it's up to you. We've had thousands of bishops through the centuries. Most of them have been good men, and some have become great saints, but we've had our share of bad ones too.'

'Great!' I grumbled. 'I feel loads better.'

'Jake, trust me,' she smiled, starting for the garage again. 'Have a little faith and pray for guidance.'

'You sound like Mrs. Thompson,' I griped. 'You people think that prayer can fix anything, don't you?'

'Yes, we do,' she fired back, 'and when prayer is all you have, it's even more powerful.'

I'd had enough of the theology lesson, so I let out a groan and started walking again.

We walked around to the back of the garage, to a small door facing the woods. It had a rusty lock hanging on it, and Becky reached down and pulled a key from under the rock by the door. The building was surprisingly black inside and it smelled a little like gasoline. Becky found an oil lamp hanging on the wall, and matches in a tiny box below it. Churchers can light oil lamps faster than most people blink, and a second later we were walking into an amazing place. From the outside, nobody'd ever have known what was going on in there.

The whole back wall of the garage was a high bench. There were tools laying around, power tools, hand tools, and some electrical gizmos with their wires hanging out. The windows were boarded up, preventing any light from getting in or out, but there were long lights hanging over the workbench, and I realized that the garage had electricity when the rectory's generator was on. There were pieces of bicycles hanging from the ceiling, and wheels for Amish buggies, and all kinds of gas engine parts scattered across the floor.

'What's all this?'

'Phil's garage,' Becky answered, setting the lantern on the bench.

'Phil?'

'Our caretaker,' she explained. 'He fixes things and keeps the parish running. He's an engineer and he's very smart.'

There was a wooden desk in the corner with stacks of books and papers on it, and a cup filled with yellow pencils. My eyes were drawn to the two framed pictures hanging above it. Churchers love their pictures, and whenever I see some, I have to go check them out. Pictures always tell a story, and they say a lot about the people who keep them, so while Becky looked around, I walked over for a closer look.

Phil was the big guy that I met the day I got baptized, the dude that carried the bishop chair into the church. He was in the big square picture, only younger and thinner, standing next to a pretty female with light brown hair. She was holding a baby and there was a little boy with them. The smaller picture was taken later. Just the kids were in it, and they were in the church, up by the altar. The little girl was in a white dress and a veil, and the boy had his arm around his little sister.

'Here they are,' Becky announced.

When I turned, Becky was standing in front of a big open chest by the boarded-up window. Right on top was the M2 that we pulled from Shithead's boat, and next to it, the guns from the Knight's jeep. There were also dozens of handguns, shotguns and rifles, all wrapped by themselves in oily rags.

'Jake, I've been thinking,' she said. 'Bacchus will most likely be coming over the bridge on Friday. It'll take more gas, and an hour longer if they come any other way.'

'Cool. Then we know where to put the guns.'

Becky's idea reminded me again about how smart she was, and I felt a little crummy for having bitched at her. Something else came to me as I pulled the M2 out of the box. It suddenly felt like I hadn't been alone with Becky in a hundred years. She looked damned good too, with her shirt all wet and clingy from the rain, and I set the gun down on the workbench. I reached around her and pulled her tightly against me, and before she could say anything, I kissed her.

I wasn't planning on kissing Becky, it just kind of happened, and now that I'm thinking about it, maybe all the best kisses start that way. I could feel the warmth of her body through her wet shirt, and suddenly I wasn't thinking about bishops or Knights or Bacchus or anything. Becky must have felt it too because although I was half-expecting her to pull away at any second, she just kept holding on. She finally stopped, let out a laugh, and moved my hand from her ass. I didn't even know that I had it there, but Becky acted surprised by it. It seems natural and automatic to put your hand on a girl's ass when you're kissing her, but I guess they don't always see it that way.

There were footsteps behind us and I turned to see someone in the doorway. Even though he was backlit and shadowy, I recognized the bony little creep.

I shouted, 'Take a hike, Shithead.'

'But Doogan says I'm your *assistant* today,' he argued. 'He says I gotta follow you 'round and do whatever you tell me.'

'Cool. Go jump in the river.'

'Come in, Devon,' Becky laughed, elbowing me in the side. 'I was just leaving. When Michael gets back, I'll send him to you with more workers.'

She added, 'See ya later' and headed outside.

I picked up the gun again and handed it to Shithead. We paused for a sec so I could watch Becky walk back to the rectory, but after that we got right to work. For the next five or six hours we busted our asses, and we didn't get one break, not even to eat. After we got both of the M2's and their mounts to the road, Mike showed up with two other guys. We found a good spot facing the bridge, but the only cover was a couple of trees, so we built bunkers by making a ton of sandbags. It was hard work in the rain, and once the sky cleared, it was hot and sweaty. We could see that the other Churchers were busy too. All day long, there were groups of people moving in and around the church and rectory.

Kinsley showed up just as we were finishing the bunkers, and he wanted to show me the places they found on the river. He'd found four excellent spots to hide the Churchers, all set back and away from the roads and easily reachable from the water. It was strange because Kinsley had to have known that they were great places, but he still took me to every one of them *by boat* to show me. It was the last thing I wanted to do, but it was important to him that I liked them. A lot of the Churchers wanted approval that afternoon. Everyone was a little scared and they wanted assurance, someone to tell them that they were doing good. Hell, I didn't mind telling them what they already knew.

It wasn't till dusk when we made it back to the church, and I headed straight to the bridge, to check out the new bunkers. We'd posted four guys there, two on each gun, and I was making sure that Shithead brought them enough ammo. As I got closer I was surprised that there were some Churcher guys working out on the road. There were two teams moving stuff from a flat buggy to the bridge. To buy us more time, the Churchers were using their stuff, furniture, suitcases, and chairs, to barricade the bridge. It was a good idea, and they'd already blocked one of the two lanes, and in some places the stuff was stacked ten feet high.

There were also four or five females standing by the bunker, and one of them looked like she was bitching at Shithead. She was a tiny little thing with brown shoulder-length hair and brown eyes. You could smell the attitude on her, and when she spotted me, everybody stopped talking,

'Hey, bishop man,' Shithead shouted when he saw me. 'Mrs. Thompson says you gotta eat something. She's got fish sandwiches waiting at the house.'

I was starved, but curious about the females standing around. The little one with the brown eyes didn't waste any time. She stepped right up to me and stuck out her hand.

'Bishop Jake, I'm Ella Laurence,' she said, shaking my hand. 'We'd like to speak with you, and appeal to your reason.'

It was an odd way to greet somebody, and I didn't even have time for a *how do you do* before she started bitching at me.

'Why are you splitting us up and making us leave our homes?!' We have over a hundred women who can fight, and we have our own guns! The Knights only have fifty or sixty men.'

It was hard not to like Ella. I knew what she was feeling, but she didn't understand what was happening.

'It's not about who's fighting,' I explained. 'I'm not letting anyone get into a war we can't win.'

'But we outnumber the gang!'

It was bizarre, seeing females so eager to fight. None of the females I'd ever known before were into fighting, and most of them would do anything to avoid gangs.

'The Knights are hardcore fighters,' I answered, 'and they've got five jeeps, big guns and Bleeders. They'd be through us in ten minutes, and then you'd have worse shit to worry about.'

'But shouldn't that be our decision?' she pressed. 'The elders refused to discuss it. It isn't fair that—'

'Bishop Jake!'

Ella stopped when one of the men on the bridge shouted at me. The sound of an engine was in the air, and I could see a vehicle approaching from the other side. The guys on the bridge were suddenly retreating toward us.

'Get back,' I shouted, 'behind the sandbags.'

There was a single vehicle heading to the bridge, traveling parallel the river. It was a green ragtop, one of those old cars where the roof folds back, and it looked like there was something on the hood. The car turned slowly toward us, through the unblocked lane of the unfinished barricade. It was halfway across the bridge before I saw the white flag sticking up. There was a loud gasp from the Churchers behind me, and I heard the men getting the guns ready. As the car drew closer, I saw what had the Churchers so freaked.

Remember that Snaggletooth asshole, the Knight that took Mariam? Well, he was hanging on the front of the car, his legs spread-eagled and tied up near the windshield, and his head dangling off the car's front, almost touching the road. He was dead and all nasty looking, with about a hundred holes shot through him, and the birds had already gotten to his eyes. Gang stuff like this never bugged me in the city, but it didn't belong out here with my Churchers, and I was growing more and more pissed as they edged closer.

The driver and his passenger were two bearded assholes, in sleeveless vests and Crescent Knights colors. They had tangled black hair and they could have passed as ugly twins, except the passenger dude wore a dirty yellow headband on his forehead. He stood up on his seat waiving the white flag and started yelling.

'We ain't armed and we've come in peace! We got a message.'

I already had a blade out, and we watched as the car crept to a stop about twenty feet away. The guy with the flag just stood there in the car, waving the flag, but the driver got out and took a step closer, right next to Snaggletooth. He wasn't packing, and all that he had in his hand was a rolled-up piece of paper. When he saw me pulling my nine, he repeated, 'Hey man, we've come in peace!'

I pointed the nine at his face and waited, but I knew why they'd come. He didn't like being there unarmed, and he kept looking nervously back and forth between the bunkers and me. He finally unrolled the paper and started reading.

'The great Bacchus has foreseen your treachery,' he started, glancing down at Snaggletooth's body. 'He has purged the weakness from within his Holy Knights and in forty-eight hours you shall witness his glorious victory and the destruction of his enemies. Even now, in Bacchus' benevolence, he will spare those who fall to their knees and serve him. In his mercy you will find—'

He let out a howl and dropped to the road when my knife sailed into his thigh. I took a step toward him as his friend started shouting again.

'Hey! We ain't armed. We ain't armed!'

In two more steps I had a clear shot, and I shot that one just above his knee. He screamed too, and flopped over onto the driver's seat. I knew that Churchers don't like killing, but it was almost impossible to keep from killing these guys. I also knew that there was no way I could let these two clowns leave here *healthy*. If I did, they'd be back here Friday, helping Bacchus take Nineveh. I kept the nine on them as I walked up to the driver.

'I know you're unarmed,' I laughed. 'Maybe I just like hurting you assholes! I guess your prophet forgot to tell you about that, huh?'

He screamed again when I reached down and twisted my knife free.

'The only reason you're alive is that I've got a message for your boss. You tell Bacchus that he's a piece of shit and I'm looking forward to cutting his throat! Now get out, and if I see you again, you die.'

It took a while for the creep to limp back to the car. The other guy was in worse shape, still trying to stop the bleeding, but they finally got the car turned around and headed back over the bridge.

It had all gone down so quickly that I didn't have a chance to look back at my Churchers. When I finally did, I was stunned by the looks on their faces. Shithead had the same stupid look as always, and the men were slowly getting back to work, but the females were looking at me like I was a monster. Ally's mouth was open in shock, and one of the other female's eyes were misty. Even after I let both of those guys live, the girl Churchers were grossed out and disgusted with me.

A minute ago these females were fired up and ready to fight, but as I took a step closer Ally stepped back, like she was afraid of me. It was weird and awkward and I couldn't think of anything to say to her. Without another word, they all slowly turned and walked away.

'Son of a bitch!' I grumbled, watching them leave. 'They're more afraid of me than the damned Knights.'

'Yeah,' Shithead nodded. 'They don't know no better. They don't understand what's coming, man.'

'Hey bishop man, you hungry?' he added, eagerly. 'Can we go eat now?'

THE LAST NIGHTMARE

I t's probably a dumb time to bring this up, but ketchup is awesome stuff. After we got to the rectory, Mrs. Thompson made us fish sandwiches and they were even better than the fish we caught in the river. She cooked them up with a brown crunchy coating and put them between slices of warm bread. It was delicious to start off with, but then Shithead suggested putting *ketchup* on them. It was a thick red sauce that Mrs. Thompson had in a bowl by the salt shaker. I spooned some on like he did, and the sandwich was even more amazing. It turns out that you can put ketchup on everything from chicken to scrambled eggs and it always makes the food taste better. I'd always suspected it, but there was no doubt about it now. Mrs. Thompson was the best cook ever.

Ketchup wasn't the only surprise waiting for me in the kitchen that night. There were ammo sacks hanging from the hooks where Mrs. Thompson hung her apron, and four sawdis leaning up against the wall by the door. I watched the housekeeper lady as I finished my fish. She looked tired and worried, and for the first time since I got here, there was a dark cloud hanging over Mrs. Thompson's kitchen. Once I got over the ketchup thing, my mind started wandering and a twisted thought came to me.

'Hey, Mrs. Thompson?' I asked. 'You don't think that this Bacchus dude can really talk to God, do you?'

229

She was doing something over by the sink, but when I asked the question she turned with fire in her eyes. It was the only time I've ever seen Mrs. Thompson so angry.

'That's ridiculous, Your Grace!' she fired back. 'Do you think God is so weak that he needs gangs or armies? God wants people to find him of their own free will, out of love and wonder, not because some unwashed bearded imbecile threatens them with death or torture!'

It was fun seeing Mrs. Thompson so fired up, but more questions were coming to me, and I was suddenly thinking about Casey again.

'So why does God let dirtballs like Jodie exist at all? Why'd he let Bacchus' men kill Casey, and why doesn't he help us kick the Knight's asses, instead of just watching us run away?'

'Your Grace!' she objected, laughing. 'God helps us constantly, in ways we can't begin to comprehend. And if God gives mankind a free will, then Bacchus must have it too. We mustn't blame God for the evils committed by people like Bacchus and Stephen Jodie.'

'Yeah,' Shithead added, looking up from his sandwich. 'My grandpa said there's all kinds of evil in this old world, but if we're saved, we'll walk the streets of glory with Jesus!'

Mrs. Thompson gave him a smile, but it sounded like he was showing off, so I poked him in the ribs with my fork.

'Did anybody ask you?'

Mrs. Thompson suddenly looked uncomfortable. At first I thought she saw me poking Shithead, but something else was bugging her.

'Your Grace,' she started, like she was busy thinking. 'Perhaps it isn't my place to say this, but there is something you should know.'

'What?'

'Some of our people are refusing to leave. This afternoon, Marian stopped by and asked Fr. Doogan to look in on her father. He's there now with Michael and Becky. Big John won't abandon the farm. He said he's too old and tired to fight anymore. Mariam said he hasn't been himself since the attack.'

'Head injuries can do that,' I assured her. 'He'll be better in a day or two.'

'There are others, Your Grace,' she answered sadly. 'Even Rev. Robertson is refusing to leave Nineveh, and he's on the council. He says he's placed his faith in God, and he believes God will deliver them.'

'*Them?*'

'Our Baptists, Your Grace.'

'I don't get it,' I said, scratching my head. 'We've got places on the river to hide, don't we? Staying here is suicide!'

Mrs. Thompson is one of those people who's always busy doing something, and it was a little strange when she paused and walked over to our table. She pulled out the chair between Shithead and me and she sat down. Her voice was tired and apologetic, like she didn't want to answer my question.

'Bishop Jake,' she said softly. 'In many ways, leaving Nineveh is also suicide.'

I glanced over at Shithead, and he was more confused than I was.

'There's not enough time to move the livestock and feed,' Mrs. Thompson explained, 'and if we leave before the harvest, there won't be enough food to get us halfway through the winter. Without a miracle, many of us will starve to death by spring.'

When her words hit me, I felt stupid and angry. It was the first time that I realized how important the farms were to the Churchers. Their food and their existence, the pancakes, eggs, and ketchup were all from the land! Leaving their farms would be devastating, and I wondered why I hadn't seen it before now. As it all began to sink in, I remembered talking with Ella over by the bunkers, and I understood why even the females were so eager to fight rather than leave Nineveh.

'And God's ok with all this?!'

'We mustn't blame God,' Mrs. Thompson repeated. 'We must pray and trust in his—'

'So all the work we're doing isn't going to save the Churchers at all, is it?' I interrupted. 'It's just changing how soon they're gonna die?!'

'I'm sorry, Jake,' she answered, 'I thought you had a right to know.'

It felt like my whole damned head was about to explode, and I needed to get up and get walking again. Mrs. Thompson touched my hand, quietly stood up, and took our plates over to the sink. When I moved to the back door, Shithead got up to follow me.

'Where do you think you're going?' I sneered.

'I'm your assistant today, bishop man,' he reminded me.

I was about to tell him to get lost, but I knew it wasn't a good idea for anyone to go walking around alone anymore, not even me. I tossed him one of the shotguns and picked one up for myself.

We started out by the bunkers again, but we wound up drifting all over the place that night. Walking usually helps me think, but there were no options anymore, and no chance of stopping the shitstorm that was coming. While I kept trying to think, the moon kept coming in and out of the clouds, and with every step we took, I felt more frustrated and helpless. I couldn't shake the feeling that I was missing something, that there was a way to save the Churchers but I was too stupid to see it. We must have walked halfway around Nineveh, all the way out to where the creek bends back toward the river, and not a single idea was coming to me.

We only stopped once, when we heard a sound in the air. It was a faint noise, almost too low to hear above the crickets, but we followed it into the forest and to a small cabin. The place was buried in nighttime, so surrounded by trees that no moonlight could reach it. The sound was coming from a female, a mom softly singing to her baby. It was a cool thing to hear, standing there in the darkness. It floated gently through the candlelit window, and although her voice was calm and steady, it made me feel worse. I remembered what Mrs. Thompson said about starving, and what Jodie said on the boat. He told me that *this remnant will be gone within the year*. I understood Jodie's plan now, and it made me wanna puke. I'd seen plenty of people starve in the city, but never females or children before. My Churchers all believed that killing is wrong, but after hearing that mom singing to her kid that night, I could have killed Jodie and a thousand Knights without blinking, and afterward I would have slept like that girl's baby.

We were almost back at the rectory before I realized that Shithead was still with me. I felt a little weird about it too, because I'd forgotten he was there. By the way I'd been acting all night, he probably figured I'd gone a little crazy. I'd been cussing and shouting a lot, and at one point, I look up to the sky and yelled, 'So, what are you gonna do about this?!'

Cussing, shouting and stomping around is pretty much how I work out tough situations, but if you didn't know any better, it might look like I was being immature and stupid. I finally reminded myself that I didn't care about what Shithead thought, and when I noticed that the lights were already off at the rectory, we headed over to Becky's.

Neither one of us had remembered a flashlight, and the moon had been gone for a long time, so it was a slow go through the woods behind the rectory. As we stepped into the clearing I saw that Becky's house was dark too. I knew it must be late, so I went right into the backyard and over to her tree-bed. When we got there, I had to laugh. I don't know how she figured out that I'd wind up there that night, but Becky left two blankets sitting on the tree-bed for me.

'Blankets!' I thought out loud. 'She thinks of everything.'

I was dead-tired and I crawled right into the tree-bed, laying the sawdi beside me. I started covering up with a blanket, but before I could close my eyes, I heard a voice.

'Hey bishop man, where am I supposed to sleep?'

'Who cares?'

A minute went by, but when I opened my eyes, Shithead was still there.

'Why don't you go sleep in one of those white chairs by the house?!'

'Alright.'

Another minute passed, and when I realized that the little creep still wasn't moving, I started getting pissed. I couldn't see his face in the darkness, but I knew he was there staring at me, so I sat up, picked up the sawdi and pointed it at him.

'Do I gotta shoot you?!'

'I was just wondering.' He answered nervously, 'You gonna use that other blanket?'

I tossed it to him and groaned, 'Why are you such a puss!?'

My eyes closed, but I was still too worked up to sleep. Maybe I was angry with myself, or God again, or Shithead, or the helpless feelings I had, but it would have been better for me if I'd stayed awake that night. When I finally did nod off, I drifted right into another nightmare, and this one was the granddaddy of them all. Part of me still thinks that Jodie was using my dreams to mess with my head. I know it sounds crazy, but you can judge all that for yourself after you hear about it. Believe whatever you want, but even in dreams, I know when somebody's screwing with me.

This dream started off a lot like the last one. I was limping through the parking lot between the church and the rectory, right before dusk. There was gunfire behind me, but it was strangely far off, and I wasn't bothered by it. My leg was aching, and when I looked down, I was bleeding through the bandage on my thigh. This time I noticed Phil's garage in the distance, but something was wrong with it. The big doors were missing, and the roof was gone. The whole building was a weird shell without its siding, not like it was blown up or burned, but as if it just blew away in the wind. I couldn't stop to think about it because I had to get to the school.

I hurried through the woods, and when I broke into the clearing it was just dark enough to see a light on in the school. As fast as I could, I limped straight to the front door, but there was suddenly a familiar voice behind me.

'Hey Jake!' he called, 'hold up a minute.'

When I turned I saw Casey, but he was all shot to hell, exactly as he looked laying on the sidewalk that night! He just stood there on the grass, smiling at me.

'I need to tell you something.'

In some dreams, you don't act anything like yourself. In real-life I probably would have shit myself seeing Casey standing there, but seeing him alive again wasn't a big deal in my dream. Something inside of me kept saying that I couldn't stop to talk, even to Casey, so I turned back to the school. Before I could take another step, I heard his voice again.

'Bishop Walker!'

This time, when I turned, Casey was dressed all in white, the brightest white you've ever seen. He was all cleaned up too, better than at the wake, and his face was deathly serious.

'Things aren't what they seem, Jake. Remember, he knows what you love!'

I didn't understand what he was saying, but I knew that I had to keep moving, so I gave him a nod and turned back to the school. As I slammed the doors open, his voice echoed behind me.

'Remember, Jake!'

The school was surprisingly normal, and this time it had a floor. There wasn't any furniture inside, except for a single chair, a fancy bishop's chair in the center of the room. There was someone sitting on it, but I couldn't tell who it was because they were completely covered with a long white sheet. When I saw Becky's pink backpack leaning against the chair, my heart fell into my stomach.

'Becky?!'

At the sound of my voice, the sheet began shaking back and forth, and I figured Becky was there, tied up and gagged. My instincts were going nuts, and I moved cautiously toward her. Even though the school was empty, I remembered what Casey said and I wasn't trusting anything. I even found myself scanning the rafters above me as I moved.

If Jodie was using the dream to mess with me, this was his best shot ever. As I got within arms-length of Becky, the sound of a sawdi-blast filled the air, followed by another, and then another. With every blast, the white sheet became stained red, and the tattered fabric pressed itself against her, sticking to the open wounds from the gunshots. I looked frantically around, but there was no one there to fire and no weapons visible anywhere! Becky was torn to bits as I helplessly looked on. I wrapped my arms around her to shield her, but her body still shook. She rocked back and forth taking shots from every direction, even after her body went limp in my arms. Above the sound of my shouting and the gunfire, there was a sick twisted laughter, and a familiar voice saying *you can't save them!*

Like I've said before, I promised to write everything down and I have, but this is something I don't talk about. The dream happened exactly like I just told you, and I won't be talking about it again.

Don't even bother asking.

IN THE MOMENT

W hen I forced my eyes open, I found myself sitting up, facing the light-blue beginnings of sunrise. My shirt was soaked and sweaty, and I was pointing my sawdi aimlessly out toward the woods. Nightmares can leave you in a lousy mood, even the normal ones, but I knew that *this* dream was gonna stick with me forever. I let out a deep breath and after setting the shotgun down beside me, I heard Shithead's voice.

'Hey man. You always wake up screaming like that?'

He was standing cautiously in the distance, halfway between the house and me, and I remembered that he'd seen me wake up like this before.

'Shut the hell up.'

I let myself fall back into the tree-bed, and I stared up at the sky. Through the shadowy rustling leaves, I could see a few bright stars above me, but the stars on the eastern horizon had already faded into daylight. The morning breeze felt good against my sweaty face, and when my heart stopped racing I looked back at the house. There was a light on upstairs, and it looked like someone was moving around in the kitchen. All I could think about was seeing Becky, so I rolled out, grabbed the sawdi, and headed to her back door.

As I passed him, Shithead slid his gun over his shoulder and followed along behind me. When we got closer, we could see that Becky's place was different today. We couldn't have seen them last night in the darkness, but there were three baskets on the back porch, just like the baskets that the Churchers used for collections. One had clothes in it, but the other two were filled with jars of jelly, pickles, and food. Through the screen door, I saw a small lantern burning next to the sink, and a few more baskets on the table, but no one was in the kitchen anymore.

'Becky?'

The second I opened the door and stepped inside, Lightning walked around the corner from the front room, holding a basket of clothes. I'd never seen Lightning in a ponytail before, and she was wearing a long blue tee-shirt that went almost to her knees. For a sec, it looked like she was feeling better, standing there in her bare feet, and I almost smiled when I saw her. She was surprised, finding someone in the doorway, but when she recognized me her eyes grew wide and furious.

The basket fell from her hands, spilling clothes everywhere, and she grabbed the big metal pancake pan that was sitting by the sink. It was leaning against some other dishes, and when she seized it, they went crashing to the floor. Raising the pan threateningly over her head with both hands, she took a step toward me. If there'd been any doubt that Lightning hated my ass, it was gone now. She was about to try busting my head open when Becky showed up behind her.

'Rita!'

Becky rushed in between us and started signing. It looked like Lighting was glaring at me the whole time, instead of listening, but she finally lowered her hands. Her eyes filled with tears, and when Becky stopped, Lightning tossed the pan into the sink and stormed off into the front room. After my nightmare, I didn't think I could be in a shittier mood, but seeing Lightning coming at me like that was a kick in the nuts.

'I guess I should have knocked.'

'She's confused, Jake,' Becky explained. 'She needs more time.'

Becky noticed my wet hair and shirt.

'Hey, are you alright?'

'Yeah.'

Mike came rushing in from the hallway. The noise must have woke him up, and he looked surprised to see me.

'Jake? Hey, is everything ok?'

'Yeah,' I grumbled, 'just perfect.'

Becky knelt down to clean up the dishes and Shithead came in from the back door. Suddenly, Becky's little kitchen was crowded.

'Have a seat, guys. I'll start breakfast,' she said, dumping the broken dishes in the trash. 'Excuse the mess. We'll be moving later this morning.'

Becky scooped up Lightning's clothes and set her basket on the counter. We hung our guns on our chairs and started moving the baskets from the table to the back porch. When I stepped back inside, I had to stop when I finally got a good look at Becky.

I hadn't noticed in all the excitement, but Becky looked amazing today. Her hair was down and fluffy, and she was already wearing makeup. Her eyes were big and she had a pretty green shirt on too, but the reason I stopped dead in my tracks was the shorts she had on. They looked like they were once jeans, but the legs were cut off, and I'd never seen so much of Becky's body before. Most female legs are fun to look at, but Becky's legs were long and clean and smooth, and Becky was as beautiful as I'd ever seen her. I can't explain why, but seeing her so hot-looking was even more frustrating. I sat down and watched how her ass moved while she cooked, and pretty soon I was feeling like I wanted to kill something.

'I heard that Big John and Robertson's people aren't leaving.'

Becky recognized something in my voice, and she stopped working and turned to me.

'Remember to live in the moment, Jake. We mustn't lose hope.'

'In the moment?'

She picked up the pancake flipper.

'In Nineveh, we've learned to live in the moment, being thankful every moment for God's blessings and trusting in his providence.'

'Providence?! I'll try to remember that when I'm watching everybody starve.'

'How can God possibly be ok with this?!' I added, throwing my hands up. 'This doesn't make any sense. I gotta be missing something. We're so damned close!'

Mike looked up. 'Close?'

'Yeah! We've got the right numbers and some guns, but we need something more, something big! We'd have a fighting chance if only we had Bleeders or grenades or bombs, explosives or something that—'

'There's dynamite out at the quarry,' Shithead interrupted casually.

Shithead hadn't said one word in the last half-hour, so the interruption surprised everyone to begin with, but after he mentioned dynamite, even Becky stopped to stare at him. I wondered why the little turd wouldn't have told me this sooner, and I was fighting the urge to elbow him in the mouth.

'Dynamite?'

'Yeah, Dr. Weiss says that's why the shed's painted red, down by the water. He says there's dynamite in there.'

'If Dr. Weiss had explosives,' Mike argued, 'he would have told the council. It must be a mistake.'

'That's what he says,' Shithead insisted. 'Before I got baptized, you was talking with Mrs. Weiss, and the Doc showed me the farm. Remember?'

Mike was still trying to wake up and he didn't answer, but I'd already heard plenty.

'Then let's go,' I said, jumping to my feet. 'Show me!'

Becky spun around and shook her pancake flipper at me.

'Not so fast!' she interrupted. 'It'll have to wait till after breakfast.'

I was all fired up about the dynamite, but Becky looked like she meant business with that pancake flipper. The smell of bacon was in the air too, and there's no better smell in the world than bacon cooking. As I sat back down, Becky took a clear plastic thingy out of the cupboard and handed it to Shithead.

'Devon,' she smiled. 'Would you do me a favor and fetch a pitcher of water from the well? It's just out front, behind the school.'

'Sure.'

Once Shithead left, I knew that something was happening. Becky was suddenly lighter and happier, and I knew she wanted to say something. She took the pan off the stove, fluffed her hair, and walked up to the table. She stood there staring at Mike for a sec. When he finally looked up and saw her glaring at him, he grinned and stood up too.

'I'll be right outside,' he said, moving to the door, 'getting some air.'

Becky waited for Mike to step out, and once the screen door closed, she sat down beside me and took my hand.

'Speaking of being *in the moment*,' she started, excitedly. 'I know that I'm being selfish, and we're all super busy, but we can't do any work after it gets dark anyway, can we?'

Before I could answer, she added, 'And it may be dangerous now, but this might be our last chance, right?'

Becky looked at me like I was supposed to understand what she was saying. I didn't get it, but she looked awesome and I didn't want to interrupt her. She was happy, in a way I'd never seen her before.

'Now that you're not a bishop anymore,' she resumed softly, 'not officially anyway—'

She finally took a deep breath and held it.

'Would you take me out tonight?!'

'Out where?'

'Out!' she laughed. 'Out to paint the town!'

Becky looked so pretty and happy that if she'd have just asked me to shoot myself in the head, I would have said *yes.*

'I don't know what that is,' I laughed, reaching up to touch her hair. 'But I'll take you anywhere, Becky.'

For the first time since we met, Becky put her arms around my neck and kissed me right on the lips. Yeah, I know I'd kissed her a bunch of times, but this time it was all her idea.

'We're having Italian!' she said, pulling away a little, 'and dress to the nines! Your taxi will be at the rectory at seven-thirty.'

That kiss of Becky's, and knowing that I'd be with her that night, changed everything. When Becky kissed me that way, I felt wild and alive, like an adrenalin rush. It was another one of those mysterious things that girls can do, and I was suddenly pumped and indestructible. I guess Shithead's story about Dr. Weiss' dynamite may have had me fired up too, but I was feeling more hopeful than I'd felt in forever. Becky heard footsteps on the porch so she got up and went back to making breakfast.

We prayed and ate, and I can't remember what we talked about after that. I only remember that we had sausage *and* bacon because Becky wanted to use it all up. And I'll never forget the smile Becky gave me when I stood up to leave for the quarry.

On my way to the door, I said, 'See ya later' and grabbed Shithead by his collar.

'Let's go,' I said, pulling him up out of his chair. 'Show me the quarry.'

We grabbed the sawdis and Shithead snatched a blueberry muffin on the way to the door. While he scarfed down the muffin, he led me outside and out to the woods behind Becky's.

There was an extreme weirdness everywhere that day, and it wasn't just because of my dream. When we passed through Tangletown, it hit me, and I was shocked at how empty it all was. The sky was clear and beautiful, and there were some people still around, and a few buggies, but it was still spookily quiet. Most of the Churchers had already been moved, and there weren't any children in Nineveh anymore. For the first time since I arrived, I saw more dudes than females that morning. There's an odd and unnatural emptiness without females and kids. All at once, I felt like I was back on the West End. Hell, even if you'd only spent ten minutes in Nineveh, you'd have known that something was horribly wrong that day.

The Weiss farm was farther away than I expected too, and it took forever to get there. I was anxious about the dynamite, and tired of hanging with Shithead, so I guess that's why the time dragged. He led me past the apple trees and through more woods, and at the end of a huge cornfield, a farmhouse finally appeared at the bottom of a hill. There was a little blue lake sitting behind the farm, like something you might see in a picture book, and a couple old buildings on the other side of the water, but nothing else around except hills and pine trees. A gravelly road started at the farmhouse and headed down toward the river, but I remember thinking that this place was truly out in the middle of nowhere.

The farmhouse was an older home, like the rectory, except it was big and white, and it had long pillars on either side of the front door. There was a barn and some animals on the right side of the house, but the farm wasn't nearly as big as Hershberger's place. As we got closer, I got a better look at the old buildings on the far side of the water. They were a good distance from the farm, old and crumbling, and one of them was long and high. Most of it had collapsed into jagged gray piles of rubble, but there were still metal pipes connected to the taller parts, and snaking around to the water, a lot like the buildings in Hufferville.

There was a black dog sitting in front of the house, and when he saw us, he shot up and started barking. He was running toward us with his tail wagging, and Shithead ran over to meet him. I'd just caught sight of the other buildings by the water, and one stuck out like a stick in the eye. It was a small building, smaller than Phil's garage, and way off by itself. I couldn't help but get psyched when I saw it. It was halfway around the water, and just like Shithead said, the whole thing was painted red.

A HUNDERD FEET

Before I tell you about the quarry and the dynamite, you should know that I didn't make a good first-impression on Dr. Weiss. The doc is a great guy, and he's helped me out a lot since then, but we didn't hit it off when we first met. Remember, all I knew about him was that he was an Orthodox, Jewish, Doctor Churcher, and that he wasn't allowed in a church. How could anybody *not* have doubts about a dude like that? I was still worked-up about the dynamite too. If there was truly dynamite at the quarry, it could change everything. I'll admit that I'm not the most patient guy in the world, and I might have been a little too eager to get my hands on it.

Shithead was still on his knees, playing with the dog, when the door opened and Dr. Weiss stepped out onto his porch. With one look, I was even more suspicious. The doc was a short, chubby guy with a heavy black beard. He had dark eyes lurking behind thick black-rimmed glasses, and when they looked at you, it looked like his eyes were too big for his head. As we got closer, we could see that the doc's clothes were strange too. He was wearing a gray tee shirt, and sticking out of both sides was a cloth thingy that hung down on his hips. If that wasn't mysterious enough, he had a little black thing on his head. It was way too small to be a hat and not nearly big enough to keep the sun off his melon. It just sat there, stuck to the top of his head, and it was impossible not to stare at it. Weiss was the first doctor I'd ever known, and I had no idea that they dressed so funny.

Mrs. Weiss followed him out, but she was surprisingly *normal* looking. She was a pretty, black-haired lady with perfect teeth, and when she smiled you could see tiny lines appear on the sides of her eyes, like Mrs. Thompson. She was wearing a long gray Churcher dress, and a scarf tied over her head. It reminded me an Amish hat, only black, and from a distance, it almost looked like her hair.

'You must be Bishop Walker,' Weiss said, sticking out his hand. 'Good to meet you.'

His voice was loud and confident, especially for a short fat guy, and after shaking my hand, he turned to Shithead and grinned.

'And how's the ear mending, young man?'

'Fine thanks,' Shithead nodded politely, still petting the dog.

'So, to what do we owe the pleasure?'

'I told the bishop man about your dynamite and he wants to see it.'

'Yeah,' I added eagerly, 'how much have ya got?'

The smile dropped from the doc's face.

'Oh my, that's quite impossible!' he said, shaking his head. 'You can't use the dynamite at the quarry.'

My head cocked, and I took a longer look at the old dude. Weiss obviously had dynamite, but for some reason he wasn't going to help us.

'What the hell are you saving it for?!'

'No, you don't understand!' he explained, nervously. 'The dynamite at the quarry is old. It can't be used. It's completely unstable.'

The hairs on my neck were standing up, and I'd had just about enough of this guy.

'You wanna see unstable?' I asked, leaning toward him.

'Young man!' he protested, 'when dynamite becomes old and isn't stored properly, it undergoes a chemical change. It sweats and becomes nitroglycerine! It can't be moved safely. The slightest touch or movement could cause an explosion!'

His story sounded like a load of crap, and I wasn't buying it. I knew that medicine and gasoline turns bad and worthless after a while, but this guy was trying to make me believe that dynamite becomes more powerful and dangerous when it gets old. He must have thought I was stupid! I was through wasting time, so I shoved him out of my way and started down toward the water. I could hear Shithead and the doc trying to keep up with me, and Weiss was pissing and moaning the whole way down to the red shack.

The red shack was even smaller than it looked from the house, just a square of about twelve feet, and not much taller than I am. There was a wooden latch on the door, and all kinds of warning messages in big letters. I lifted the latch, but the creaky old door wouldn't move till I slammed it open with a kick. The early morning sun was visible in the dusty air inside, streaking in through cracks in the shed's walls, and I knew right away that *this was it!* Right in the middle of the place were two square wooden boxes with DANGER and DYNAMITE stenciled all over them. Each dust-covered box was a couple feet wide and almost as high. I felt a rush of adrenalin, and I knew that I was finally looking at a way to save my Churchers! My brain was already thinking up ideas about how to use the stuff, but before I could move inside for a look, the doc stepped in front of me.

'You damned fool! Are you trying to kill us all?!'

Like I said, I might have been a little excited. There was so much riding on the damned dynamite that I wasn't listening. I grabbed the doc by his shirt, and I was right about to knock him on his ass when I felt Shithead grab my arm.

'Bishop man, listen!' he exclaimed. 'Doc is a good man and he lives here too. Why would he lie?'

'Be reasonable!' Weiss pleaded. 'You won't get a hundred feet! There'd be nothing left of you but a crater in the ground!'

The doc's face was sweaty and scared, and I felt my heart sink. Shithead was right. There was no reason for the doc to lie, and it looked like the panicky old man was telling the truth.

'A hundred feet?' I asked.

'Perhaps,' the doc exhaled, shaking his head, 'Dynamite in this condition is highly unstable. You'd be lucky to get a hundred feet. Any shock, sudden change, or even static electricity could blow you to bits!'

'What if I'm careful?' I argued. 'I only need to get it out past the church.'

'Your church is more than two miles from here!' he shouted. 'It'd be a miracle to get it out of the shed! Only God knows why you haven't set it off already!'

I let him go, and Weiss spun around and carefully closed the door again. I probably should have apologized to him, but I was too pissed. I know I say that a lot, but this was a different kind of pissed, frustrated and desperate. It was the biggest letdown of my life, as bad as Casey dying, and it felt like a rope was tightening around my throat. For about the millionth time since I joined the Churchers, just when things were looking up, someone pulled the rug out from under me!

'I don't believe this shit!' I shouted, 'Does God want the Churchers to survive or not? It's like he gave me the dynamite just so he could take it away! When's he gonna make up his mind? Whose side is he on?!'

'God doesn't change, young man,' Doc answered softly, 'Before the world began, he's known that we would be here. Perhaps it's not about what we expect from him, but what he expects from us.'

What he expects from us?

Churchers are always saying weird shit like that. Most times, I'm pretty good at ignoring it, but this time Weiss' words tripped something in my brain. I was suddenly wondering what more God could possibly want from me! I brought my hand up and looked at the ring on my finger. Ever since the nuncio put it there I felt like I should be doing something, and every *something* that I did only made things worse. This terrible that the Churchers belonged to me, and depended on me, was *killing me!* I was worn-out and as fed up as I've ever been, and I guess something snapped in my brain. All at once an idea hit me. As ideas go, it probably wasn't my best, but we were out of time. If I was ever gonna help the Churchers, I had to do something *now*.

I started back to the rectory, and after Shithead talked to the doc for another minute, he caught up with me near the cornfield. There were even fewer people moving around the parish now, and the few houses that we passed were quiet and empty. The whole way back I felt Shithead's eyes on me. I'm not sure how he picked up on it, but he must have known that I'd settled on a plan.

'What you gonna do, bishop man?'

'What the hell do you care?'

'Maybe I can help.'

'You?!' I shouted. 'Why would I need help from a little shit-for-brains puss like you?'

When I caught the look on his face, I wished that I'd kept my mouth shut. I don't know why I do it sometimes, but when I'm tired and angry, I turn into an asshole. I didn't hate Shithead half as much as when I first met him, and all he was doing was trying to help. Going off on him that way was a rotten thing to do, and for the rest of the way back, he looked like somebody elbowed him in the mouth.

We shouted at the house as we went by Becky's, but nobody was home, so I took the long path through the woods. I wanted to check on our bunkers at the bridge. Everything was spookily quiet. Someone had brought the guards something to eat, and after talking to them a while, we headed over to the rectory. Once we got past the church, I noticed two buggies tied up in front of the house. One of them was the funeral buggy, except without any flowers on it, and it was so full of Doogan's furniture and boxes that they needed ropes to hold everything down. The other buggy was shorter, with only one horse. Mrs. Thompson and Sandy were busy moving boxes to the porch, and the old housekeeper looked glad to see us.

'Your Grace!' Mrs. Thompson greeted me. 'Could you give us a hand?'

I didn't know it then, but when a Churcher asks you to *give them a hand*, you'd better think twice, cause after we said yes, we spent the whole day packing and lifting and taking things apart. I didn't care though. I'd do just about anything for Mrs. Thompson, and my head was busy anyway, working out the details of my plan.

Mrs. Thompson put Shithead to work loading boxes into the short buggy and Sandy asked me if I wanted to help her move the radio. I'd rather have stayed outside and helped load boxes, but Sandy's eyes looked so tired behind her glasses that I couldn't say no. It turned out to be a huge pain in the ass too. She led me into the secret room off Doogan's den and showed me how to take everything apart and pack it up in boxes. The worst part about packing up the radio was the antenna in the attic. It must have been a hundred degrees up there, and the antenna was all wires and poles and tiny screws. It was cramped too, with long planks of bare wood on both sides of us. It took a while, but we got it apart without busting anything, and then we had to stack it on the short buggy with some of Mrs. Thompson's stuff.

When both buggies were full, we started out for the river. One of the twin dudes, George, came by to drive the funeral buggy, and Doogan drove the short buggy. Sandy rode with George, but Mrs. Thompson said she had to stay and pack some more. We followed the road in front of the church down to a place on the river, right next to Hershberger's. It was the first time I'd been to Mariam's house using the road, and it was good seeing the farm again. Waiting there for us on the water was the strangest boat I'd ever seen. It was wide and flat, like a big wooden floor, and it was sitting on two long silver thingies floating on the water. Hanging off back, I recognized the same motor that Casey and Mike used to get us out of the city. The flat boat didn't have any seats, but it held all our stuff, and once I was sure that wasn't gonna sink, I took a seat on some boxes.

It was a long way to Doogan's new place, but the water was calm and it felt good to rest on the boat for a while. The big boat was just as scary as any other boat, but we weren't on it all that long. The old priest's new rectory turned out to be a county library a few miles downriver. It was just off the water but completely hidden in tall trees. We carried everything in from the boat and started putting the antenna together upstairs, in a huge walk-in attic. The library was in awesome shape and unburned, with books and cool stuff everywhere. On any other day it would have been a great place to explore, but there wasn't time. It took forever to put the antenna together, and hook it up. When we were finally through, Sandy had to make sure that the radio worked before we could leave.

It was late in the afternoon before we got back to our boat. Sandy and George stayed at the library to finish unpacking, but Doogan and I headed back up to Nineveh. I got to drive the boat too, but it wasn't as fun as I thought it'd be. The old priest looked sick, and I was growing worried about the old man. When you're as old as Doogan, you don't have to do a lot of work to be tired, and he'd done way too much that day. He didn't say two words to me on the way back either. He just sat there on the floor of the boat with his eyes closed. I thought he was sleeping until I saw the beads moving slowly through his fingers. Priests get bigger rosaries than normal Churchers do. His rosary was way longer than Becky's, with big black beads. While he was still praying, all at once he opened his eyes and pointed to bend in the river ahead.

'We'll be stopping ahead there, son.'

I was figuring on going home, but Doogan wanted to stop at two of the other Churcher hiding places. He said that we needed to check in on them, but all we did that afternoon was smile and walk around so the other Churchers could see us. The whole time, Doogan grinned and laughed like he didn't know what was happening, like he'd never heard of the Knights. It was kind of a lie, but the Churchers were lighter and happier after we hung out for a while. I felt better about it too, because we had jelly sandwiches, and I got to watch the kids playing on a tire swing. I don't know why, but watching kids playing always makes me laugh. We stayed as long as we could, and the sun was going down by the time got back to the boat. It took us at least another hour to get back to Hershberger's and finally get the buggy back to the rectory.

The church parking lot was darker than I'd ever seen it before. The generator wasn't on, and there weren't any lights on inside the house. But even though most of the rectory had been cleared out, Mrs. Thompson was sitting on the porch swing, with a lantern glowing at her feet.

'Mrs. Thompson?' I called, pulling the buggy to a stop. 'You're still here?'

'Fr. Doogan needs his dinner.' She smiled. 'And I knew that you had plans for the evening. I wanted to see you off.'

'Shit!' I remembered. 'I'm painting something in a town with Becky tonight.'

'You have plenty of time, Your Grace,' she assured me, handing me the lantern. 'There's enough hot water left for a shower, and everything you need is on the sink in the bathroom.'

THE COMET'S LAUGH

At that moment, if someone had told me that the best night of my whole life was about to happen, I'd have told him he was crazy. I was hungry, spent and edgy, and now that the work was over, my brain kept reminding me that the Knights would be arriving tomorrow. On top of all that, the only plan I had to save my Churchers was probably gonna get me killed. I didn't feel much like painting anything that night, but I knew Becky was counting on me. I couldn't wait to see her too, so after tying up the horse, I thanked Mrs. Thompson and headed inside. I couldn't have known it as I plodded up the dark rectory stairs, but since then I've thought about that night every day of my life.

The rectory was shadowy and unrecognizable by lantern light. Everything was creepy and different, and I couldn't wait to get out of there. The pictures were gone from the upstairs hallway, and my room was empty except for a few papers on the floor. While I'd been busy with Sandy, someone had moved my bed, desk, and all the books from my room. I found the change of clothes waiting in the bathroom like Mrs. Thompson promised, and when I closed the door, my blue shirt was hanging on the back doorknob. There was no way I was spending any more time in there than I had to, so I took a quick shower and got dressed.

While I was jogging back down the stairs I heard a familiar voice outside, and when I stepped out onto the porch, I saw Michael sitting in a buggy with the reigns in his hands. It looked like the same buggy that first brought us to the rectory from Mariam's house, except it had lights burning on the front of it. They're kind of like the headlights on a car, except bigger and not as bright.

'Come on, Jake,' Mike called, grinning. 'We're a couple hours late already.'

He was wearing a gray collared shirt and a jacket, and his hair was brushed back. We were both kind of dressed-up, and it should have made me suspicious, but I guess I was too tired to notice. I handed my lantern to Mrs. Thompson and climbed in.

'You look nice this evening, Your Grace,' Mrs. Thompson said. 'Have a nice time!'

I'd never painted anything before, but from what I knew about it, I wasn't expecting to have a *nice time* doing it. Looking back on it now, Michael and Mrs. Thompson knew more about where I was going than I did. Before Mike could get the horse started, Doogan stepped up to the buggy.

'Son,' he called, holding his hand up. 'We're having our last mass at St. Lucy's in the morning, and then a prayer service. Your people will be expecting you there.'

'Sorry Father, I've gotta be somewhere early tomorrow.'

Suddenly it felt like Doogan deserved a better explanation, and I realized that I might not be seeing the old man again.

'Look Father,' I added. 'I've got a kind of plan. It's half-assed and a little crazy, but I gotta try something.'

'We'll pray for your plan then,' he assured me, 'But surely, lad, shouldn't you be there praying with us?'

'You know I'm no good at that stuff,' I shrugged, 'but I'll be there if I can.'

The buggy lurched forward, and the horse turned toward the bridge. I smiled at Mrs. Thompson, knowing that I might not be seeing the old housekeeper lady again either.

'Jacob,' Doogan's voice boomed behind us, 'Sooner or later, you must learn to pray!'

The horse took us down to the bridge, and we waved to the guys in the bunkers as we passed. At the stop sign, we turned left and followed the road along the creek out past the college. It was too dark to see much of the road in front of us, but I could see our lanterns reflected in the dirty windows of the buildings we passed. After about a mile, we came to a little square with lots of old stone buildings. The buggy bumped over some thick wires from a fallen streetlight, and I noticed that the town was in excellent shape, with lots of shops and stores with unbroken windows.

'Jake,' Mike said, interrupting my thoughts. 'I haven't thanked you yet for saving Mariam.'

'You were there too,' I answered. 'We all saved Mariam.'

'Yeah,' he said doubtingly, 'but if it wasn't for you, Mariam would be gone and I'd be dead.'

'Forget it, man.'

The sky was moonless and dark, and it was one of those nights where the stars are so bright and so low that you feel like reaching up and grabbing a handful. It was peaceful too, and I was getting pumped about seeing Becky. We were coming to the center of the town, and everything we saw was strange and intriguing. There was a drugstore, a sheriff's house, and a place on the corner with the letters YOGA in the window. It was like a tiny version of the city with just a couple of main streets and shorter buildings.

'It's so empty,' I said, turning to Mike. 'Since I've been with you Churchers, I've forgotten how deserted the world is.'

The horse's footsteps against the road and the chirping crickets helped me relax a bit, and when it's quiet and peaceful like that, random stuff pops into my brain.

'So Mike,' I asked, still thinking. 'Doogan says that he has to *appeal to Rome* to see if I'm a real bishop or not. That's where the leader of the Catholic Churchers lives, right?'

'You mean the Pope?' Mike laughed. 'Yeah, but it's complicated. Before the tribulations, the Pope fled the Vatican when Rome was overrun. Some people say he was murdered, but after a short time, a new leader took control. He wasn't elected by the church as usual, but because of his position in the church, he was thought to be a good man. Doogan told me that he wasn't interested in keeping the tenants of the faith, and the church suffered terrible changes. Things were so bad that in some churches, the mass wasn't celebrated anymore. If it weren't for good bishops and priests like Fr. Kowalski and Fr. Doogan, I don't know how the church would have survived.'

'So who's boss?'

'I'm not sure,' he shrugged. 'Most of the faithful cardinals and bishops are still in hiding, and we can reach them by radio. But there's hope, Jake. We heard that the new king of France is moving on Italy. He's Catholic, and he's already taken most of Europe. Last month, he captured England, and he's promised to liberate Italy soon and restore the throne of Peter.'

'The what?'

'That means the Church will have a Pope again,' he laughed. 'And you'll have a new boss.'

'Before the city burned and the darkness came,' I remembered, 'there were people *everywhere*. Sometimes it's still hard to believe they're all gone.'

'I've heard, there weren't many Godly people left in those days,' Mike explained. 'People were different after they turned away from God. One time, Fr. Doogan told Casey and me that men forgot how to be men.'

'That's nuts!' I laughed. 'How could a dude forget to be a dude?!'

'He said that they forgot how to be strong, how to think for themselves and lead. They forgot the roles that God had given them. The spirit of man, the passion for freedom, individualism, truth and exploration dried up inside of them. Doogan told me that in those days, you couldn't tell the difference between men and women anymore.'

'That's hilarious,' I chuckled, 'and you believe that?'

'Yeah,' Mike nodded, laughing. 'Fr. Doogan saw it with his own eyes.'

All at once there was a sound in the air, a faint noise above the clip-clop of the buggy. The road ahead leaned right, and there was light, the glow of electric lights creating an outline of the rooftops on the next corner.

'We're here!' Mike announced.

We turned onto a cobblestone street that dead-ended in trees, and when I saw where the noise and lights were coming from, I was completely blown away.

It was an old restaurant place, except it was lit up and working! There was a glowing sign above the front door that said *Café Roma*, and a red brick patio in front, lit by strings of burning lightbulbs hanging high above the patio. There were two square tables on the patio, covered in red and white checkered cloth, and plates and knives and forks, and tall fancy glasses set out. In the light from the sign I saw a tiny bucket on each table, with a bottle of wine sticking out. The shops around us were lifeless and dark, and the Café Roma was like a single star, hanging out when all the other stars had gone to sleep.

There must have been a generator running somewhere, but we couldn't hear it. The noise in the air turned out to be real music playing! It wasn't the loud thump-thump shit that the gangs used to play either. It was slow, like the songs that the kids sang to me at the school, except with lots of musical instruments. It sounded old, probably from back when music first started, and it was coming from a cool machine by the restaurant's window. It was sitting on a smaller table, leaning against the glass and glowing in bright blinking colors. There was an old phone too, like people had in the old days, connected to the machine by a bunch of white wires. Together, the machine and the phone were pumping light and music into the air, and the whole patio and most of the street out front were bright as day.

There was already another buggy parked across the street, and we tied up next to it. We jumped out, and as soon we crossed the street to the patio, the girls showed up. They stepped out from the restaurant's front door and stood there in the light where we could see them. They were all dressed-up and wearing makeup, and their hair was down. Becky had long thingies hanging from her ears and Mariam had something shiny holding some of her hair back. They looked so good that Mike and I had to stop when we saw them. I swear, you'll never *ever* see two more beautiful females.

Becky was in a short black dress, but at first I thought it was painted on her. It fit her perfectly, clinging to every curve and falling midway to her knees. It had a split in it too, and as she walked closer, I could see even more of her legs. She had crazy black shoes on that made her at least two inches taller. The top of her dress didn't even cover her shoulders, and it fell loosely along the top of her breasts. I know that Churchers are into the modesty thing, but if you ask me, Becky couldn't have been hotter if she was standing there naked! I guess it was modest enough because everything was pretty much covered, but hell, there wasn't anything hidden either.

'Holy shit,' I blurted out, stepping up to her. 'You look amazing!'

I leaned in close, so Mike and Mariam couldn't hear me.

'If you knew what it's doing to me, you wouldn't have worn that dress.'

She put her arms around my neck.

'Think so?' she laughed. 'You poor naïve man!'

Before I forget, you should know that Mariam was something to see that night too. Her dress was dark blue, and it looked like the whole dress was made from one piece of cloth because it wrapped around her, held together with a sparkly silver belt. The top dipped down from her shoulders in sort of a v. I heard later that Marian got that dress from Becky, but don't think Mike ever saw it before, cause his jaw fell halfway to the ground when he saw her in it. For a sec, he had that stupid dazed look he had when she was being kidnapped by the Knights! I can't blame him though. When your girl looks like that, there's no way a guy can think straight.

Becky let go of my neck, and Mariam came up and hugged me. She gave me a kiss on my cheek and said, 'Thank you.'

Before I could say anything, she turned and asked, 'Michael, would you help me bring dinner?'

They disappeared into the restaurant, and Becky took my hand and led me to the table farthest from the music machine.

'Hey Becky, before you make me forget,' I remembered. 'I've come up with a sort of plan for tomorrow and—'

'I know,' she interrupted. 'Devon told me.'

'How the hell does he know?!'

'We're not talking about that tonight.'

'But you need to know about it. If it doesn't work out—'

'Stop it, Jake!' she shouted. 'Stop it right now. Don't make me cry, you'll ruin everything.'

I stared back at her wondering what hell could be wrong. Her eyes were suddenly misty, and she was fighting back tears. She picked up the corkscrew on the table and shook it at me.

'Look!' she went on. 'Tonight I'm wearing a little black dress and heels, and I'm somebody's girlfriend! There's dinner and wine, and I'm going to dance with the guy I love! Don't you dare try and steal that away from me!'

Becky was only shaking a corkscrew at me, but with that look in her eyes, it might just as well have been an ax. I needed to see her happy again, and I knew that she'd find out about my plan soon enough anyway, so I changed the subject.

'I've never danced before.'

'You'll do fine,' she said, smiling again.

I was already having an amazing time, and I would have been happy just sitting there trying to look down Becky's dress, but Mariam stepped through the door carrying a pan of something. It must have been hot because she needed huge puffy gloves to carry it. Mike was right behind her with a bowl of lettuce and some warm bread, but Mariam's pan smelled so good that it I zoned in on it. Mike walked up to our table and opened our wine bottle with the corkscrew. While Mariam set out little round bowls in front of us, Mike filled our glasses. It was getting a little weird, and I had to say something.

'Hey, what the hell is all this anyway?'

'You're our guests tonight, Jake,' Mariam answered. 'Michael and I got the restaurant working this afternoon, and Becky and I did the cooking. It isn't much, but it's our way of saying thank you.'

Mike and Mariam went back inside, and Becky reached across the table for my hand. They were back a second later, carrying their own suppers, and they sat at the table by the music. Mike pressed a button, and while the music was stopped, we prayed grace together.

The smell from the pan was incredible, and I couldn't wait to dig in. There's only one thing in the world that could have taken my mind off Becky that night, and even then, only cause I was so hungry. It's called *lasagna*, and it's so good that there's almost no good way to describe it. It's like a brick of noodles, cheese, and red sauce, and it's warm and gooey and unbelievable!

And by the way, I'm no expert at fine dining, but why would anyone eat lettuce or bread when there's something like that on your table? If you ever get the chance, head straight for the lasagna. Trust me, even if your girl keeps giving you looks or says you should *please try the salad*, it isn't worth it. Just remember to lean in close, cause if you eat fast like me, you'll get it on your shirt if you're not careful.

Things were getting better by the minute, and I felt like I was in a different world that night. We ate, we laughed and we drank wine, and when Mike and Mariam were done eating, they pulled their chairs next to our table. We talked and laughed some more, and Mike had to run inside for more wine. It wasn't the food, or the music, or how beautiful the girl's looked. I swear, there was something in the air that made everything else disappear, and the only place left in the whole damned universe was the Café Roma! If somebody ever tells you that there's no such thing as magic, take it from me, he doesn't know what the hell he's talking about.

I don't know songs, so I wasn't paying attention to the music, but Becky and Mariam knew all about it. While we were talking a new song started playing, and they suddenly stopped, let out a laugh, and jumped to their feet. Before we knew what was happening, the girls were dragging Mike and me out to the center of the patio.

Dancing isn't as frightening as you might think either. Hell, all you gotta do is hold on to your girl, and lean back and forth. Once I got my hands on Becky, I wasn't even aware that I was moving, just how she felt leaning against me. When you're dancing, females don't mind how close you hold them, and one time, I even leaned in and kissed her neck. We danced and talked the whole time, only stopping to get another drink or talk to Mike and Mariam. We talked about everything and anything too. It was all light and fun, and nobody dared mention what would be happening tomorrow. I understood why Becky shook the corkscrew at me. The Churchers call it being *blessed*, but when you feel as lucky as I did, with the food and friends and Becky in that dress, you'd be an idiot to do anything to kill it. It was maybe the one night in my life that I was living in the moment, and I didn't want it to end.

While we were dancing, something behind us caught Becky's eye, and she stopped suddenly. I turned around, about to reach for a blade, but Becky was only staring at something high in the southern sky. It was that comet, the same comet that we saw on the boat, except this time it had grown a long curvy tale. Mike and Mariam stopped to stare at it too. It was cool to see way up there, and nobody said anything until the song was over. And when the next song came on, something scary happened.

The new song was fast, more like city music, and the girls let out a scream and ran over to each another. I didn't know it then, but when fast songs come on, girls dance with other girls. It's really something to see too. I stood there with Mike watching them laugh and dance and bounce around, and pretty soon we were laughing too. Another fast song came on after that, and we stood there watching the girls and passing the wine bottle. Maybe it was the wine, but I swear that the stars and that comet, the buildings, and everything on that damned street were laughing with us.

I don't know how much time passed, but the girls had just finished another round of fast songs. Becky and I were dancing again when suddenly Mike and Mariam were standing next to us, and Mariam was holding her backpack.

'We've gotta leave, guys,' he announced.

I figured that we'd be leaving too, but we didn't. Becky held my hand while Mariam and Mike packed up the leftover lasagna and bread. We helped them carry everything over to the buggies. It was kind of sad, but kind of exciting too, because I realized that I was about to be alone with Becky again. Mariam gave me another hug before she climbed in with Mike, and we watched the lights of their buggy head down the street, and wink out as they turned the corner.

Even with the music going, it felt quiet for the next few minutes. Becky and I danced another song or two, but when I kissed her, I think it gave her an idea. She grabbed my hand, took me over to the music machine and grabbed her backpack from under the table. As usual, Becky had thought of everything, and she reached in and pulled out her green blanket. She led me around the corner, and spread the blanket on the grass, in the shadow of the Café Roma. We could still hear the music, and I could still see Becky pretty well. Maybe I saw her too well because when she laid down on that blanket, I think I went a little crazy.

Thinking back on it now, I guess Becky was expecting us to kiss some more, or look at the comet again, or maybe talk for a while, but when I saw her lying on that blanket something came over me. As beautiful as Becky looked in that black dress, I spent most of the next hour trying to get her out of it. It was impossible not to touch her, and when we kissed, it was as if I lost consciousness, only to wake up with her telling me *no* again. I couldn't help it, and for the longest time, she kept pulling the top of her dress back up, or the bottom of the dress back down. Her skin was hot to the touch, and I was like a moth, unable to keep from burning up in the fire. My brain didn't want to think about anything else, and all I wanted was getting more of Becky.

I'm pretty sure that Becky's brain was fried too. It wasn't nearly as bad as mine, but she seemed surprised at the progress I kept making. More than once I figured that she was tired of saying no, and just when I thought she was about to give in, she'd snap out of it and get covered up again. It happened again and again, and every time I'd get a little closer. She finally sat up, breathing heavily, and glared down at me.

'Jake!'

'What?'

She closed her eyes and waited, trying to catch her breath. We were both a little worked up and sweaty, and she looked amazing.

'This is just a night out, our first real date,' she explained. 'It's supposed to be innocent and—'

She stopped and closed her eyes again.

I didn't get what she was saying, but it looked like Becky needed a rest. Her back was toward me, and it looked inviting in the darkness. She was holding the front of the dress up with her hand, but I could see how her back gently curved in, and then out again. Just above her hair, I could see the comet in the sky above us.

'I love you,' she sighed. 'I want you to know that I love you, even if we can never be together.'

'I love you too,' I laughed. 'And what are you worried about? We're already together!'

I was tired of resting, so I rolled onto my back, lifting her up by her waist. Like I'd figured, the top of her dress couldn't keep up very well because she had to steady herself. She let out a gasp, and before she had a chance to react, I pulled her on top of me.

'Jake!'

CHOOSING SIDES

Ok, before you let your imagination go running off and get twisted, you need to know that Becky never stopped telling me *no* that night. Not that it's anybody else's business, but she said it wouldn't be right. I've gotta tell you, it felt damned right to me, but she kept saying that we'd gone too far already. When I tried arguing, she just said that *no means no!* What the hell kind of an argument is that anyway? She wouldn't talk about it anymore either, or give me any details about why she thought so. Maybe it's a Churcher thing, or a female thing, but there's no way any normal person can win an argument that way! Still, I'm not complaining. Nothing could have spoiled that night at the Café Roma, and I think I figured out why Becky wouldn't give in to me.

I could be wrong about this, but I think Becky was hung up on the idea that I was still a bishop, even though the guy in Charlotte said I wasn't. She figured that maybe I was still working for God, and she didn't want to mess that up. She'd never admit it to me, but I think that if I was just a normal Churcher dude, it might have been a lot different that night. If I was just someone to stay with her, work with her, and give her babies like any other Churcher guy, Becky and I might still be out there on that green blanket.

Anyway, we didn't get back till way late, and I don't remember if I slept or not that night. I only remember kissing Becky on her back porch and watching her and that dress walk inside and up the stairs. I watched her window from the tree-bed until the light went out.

When the eastern sky was just turning yellow, I was already heading down to the quarry. I kept thinking about Becky, so I wouldn't try to talk myself out of my plan. By the time I reached the cornfields, I knew that someone was following along behind me. It didn't bug me though. I knew right away who it was, cause there's only one person on earth who could make that much noise trying *not* to be heard.

'Shithead,' I called. 'What do you want now?'

He stepped out from the tree line.

'Doogan says to keep an eye on you, in case you need help.'

'So what are ya sneaking around for?'

'Yesterday you said you didn't want me helping.'

'Forget all that. I was just pissed,' I explained. 'Get back to the rectory.'

I continued down to the water and when I passed Weiss' house I was glad that the dog wasn't barking. When I reached the shed, I carefully lifted the latch and pushed the door open. Suddenly I heard his voice again.

'Hey man, what ya doing?!'

'Get lost, Shithead. I mean it!'

He was standing right behind me, and when I looked back, I was surprised that he wasn't backing down.

'So, what are you gonna do, man?'

It hit me that telling someone about my plan wasn't such a bad idea, especially if it wasn't going to work.

'Casey once told me that I needed to find out what God wants me to do, and then find a way to do it. Well, since I got this ring, all I can think about is saving the Churchers. As I see it, the only way I can save the Churchers is by getting this dynamite to the bridge.'

'But the doc says it'll blow up!'

'He says it *might* blow up.'

'No, man!' he objected, with his voice rising. 'He said it was a miracle that you ain't blowed it up already!'

'Then if God wants to save the Churchers, he'll have to help me, won't he?'

Shithead's eyes got wide, and he started freaking.

'You're crazy!' he shouted. 'You're playing chicken with God! You're daring him to—'

'I'm not daring anybody!' I shouted back. 'But I need to know whose side he's on. I gotta know if he put this ring here, or it was just a gift from a dying old man.'

'But, what if you blow up?'

'Then I'll have an answer, won't I?'

He looked so stupid and panicky that I had to laugh. I stepped inside, held my breath, and picked up the first box of dynamite. Shithead gasped as I moved back into the morning air.

'Don't just stand there looking stupid,' I told him. 'Run ahead and keep everybody away. And if you see Weiss, tell him I'll be back for the other box.'

'You need both of em?!'

'Yeah, I think so.'

He stood frozen there with his mouth open, so I moved past him and started up the hill. The dynamite was heavier than I thought, and I was trying to keep the crate steady. By now the Weiss' dog was going nuts, and I saw a light come on in the house. When I was halfway up the hill I wondered why he hadn't passed me, and when I turned back, I got the biggest surprise of my life.

Shithead was walking just a few yards behind me, holding the other crate of dynamite! Even in the early light, I could see his face sweating. His eyes were open wide, and his lips were moving like he was talking, but without making a sound.

'What the hell are you doing, man?'

'Don't talk to me!' he answered. 'I'm praying.'

'You don't have to do this, Shithead! Our chances suck, and—'

'You ain't the only one who wants to save the Churchers!' he interrupted. 'And Doogan says I gotta help the bishop.'

As he walked past me, I realized that Shithead wasn't the gutless little turd that I thought he was. Most times I'm a damned good judge of people, but right from the start I'd been wrong about that guy, and I was glad I hadn't killed him yet.

'And you can't be calling me a puss no more!' he added, 'ya hear me?'

There was a loud noise near the house and suddenly a horse came tearing out of the barn. Weiss had seen what we were up to, and he was going on ahead to warn everybody. Before we reached the cornfield, I figured I'd better say something.

'If I don't get a chance to tell ya later,' I told him, 'thanks Devon.'

Those crates got heavier with every step we took, and we had to stop more than once to rest. Shithead's a bony little guy too, and I was surprised that he was handling his crate so well. We couldn't risk setting them back on the ground either, so we rested by leaning against trees and letting the crates rest on our knees. You'd be surprised at how slowly the time passes when you're carrying explosives, and it took forever to make it through the cornfields, past Tangletown and over to the bridge. We stayed left along the creek, to avoid the church and rectory, but we could see people standing outside the church with Dr. Weiss. They watched as we came closer, and by the time we reached the bunkers, our arms felt like they were about to fall off.

Mike came running up to us, but I shouted for him to stay back.

'I need to talk with Phil, the engineer guy,' I shouted. 'We can't risk moving this stuff again. We need volunteers too, as many as possible, and we'll need Ginny. And we've gotta clear the barricade and get one of the bunkers moved into the woods, on the other side of the bridge!'

'Clear the barricade?' Mike asked, doubtingly.

'Yeah, I want a clear a path for Bacchus and his Knights.'

COLD BLOODED

The Churchers all say it's a miracle that we got that dynamite safely back to the bridge that morning, but let's face it, Churchers like to exaggerate about stuff like that. The truth is, I had loads of help that day, and I know that God had my back more than once. I don't know much about miracles, but I started that day wondering if God was gonna help with my plan, and now I'm pretty sure that God had a plan of his own.

Shithead and I were still catching our breath, resting on the bridge and leaning against the sidewalk railing. I'd just slept here a couple nights ago, but I was studying the old bridge as if I'd never seen one before. It was like a thousand other bridges, and a lot like the railroad bridges in the city, a long rusty cage with just enough room for a lane in each direction and a thin sidewalk on the church side. In the early sunlight there was something ancient and tired looking about it. The morning mist was still thick on the noisy water below us, and I was getting pumped, trying to convince myself that my plan had a chance. Mike was shouting orders over at the church, and when I looked up I saw Phil walking toward us. There weren't many people left in Nineveh, and I was surprised that he was still here.

'Bishop Walker, you wanted to see me?'

Phil stepped casually up to us, even though we were holding crates marked EXPLOSIVES.

'Yeah, thanks for getting here so fast,' I told him. 'I'm glad they haven't moved you yet.'

'My family's here, Bishop Walker. I can never leave St. Lucy's.'

'Your family?'

'In the parish cemetery.'

I looked him up and down, in his overall jeans and rolled up sleeves, and I remember thinking that Phil was a dangerous old dude. In the city we used to call guys like him *dead eyes*. When a guy isn't afraid of anything anymore, and he's got that sad look in his eyes, he's usually a little crazy. Maybe it was rude of me to change the subject, but Shithead and me were still holding crates of dynamite.

'What do you know about bridges?'

'Some,' he said, looking at the crate in my hands. 'What do you need?'

'Doc Weiss said that this stuff can blow a big hole in the ground. Can I blow a big enough hole to block the bridge?'

He gave me a curious look. 'Block the bridge?'

'Yeah, kind of,' I nodded. 'I wanna blow a hole in each end of this thing and trap the Knights on it. How do we do that?'

He glanced back at the bridge, and back at us again.

'This is a typical truss bridge,' he explained. 'The deck is concrete and mesh. There's plenty of dynamite here to blow through it.'

'The deck?' Shithead asked.

'Yeah, you know, the road's surface.'

Phil pulled out a pocketknife and started prying open the lid on my crate.

'But why would you want to trap the Knights on the bridge?'

'Who gives a damn about the Knights?' I grinned. 'I want the jeeps and weapons that Jodie gave Bacchus!'

Phil laughed approvingly at my plan. He popped open the lid

and a strong smell escaped, like old cleaning fluid or polish.

Phil's jaw dropped and he whispered, '*Holy mother of*—'

'This is too hot!' he restarted, 'I don't know how you made it here alive, but we have to be extremely careful with this. I'll show you where to set it down.'

'Cool,' I nodded. 'But we need to save some to kill the Knights. We've gotta end it today. We've got to kill them, or hit them so hard that they'll never come back.'

'Not with this stuff, Bishop Walker,' Phil said, apologetically. 'It's too dangerous to split up.'

He thought for a sec, and added, 'But I've got some black powder at my workshop. I could make a couple of decent powder bombs with buckshot and nails.'

'How many?'

'Two, maybe three. Will that work?'

'It'll have to.'

Like I said, I had plenty of help that day, and since Phil knew what he was doing, it was easy to trust him. We put the crates on either end of the bridge, on the metal thingies called *access covers* between the lanes. It felt good to finally be free of the damned dynamite, and by the time we were done talking and planning, teams of Churchers started showing up. Mike and Shithead had them clear the barricade, and we moved all the wood and furniture over to the bridge's sidewalk.

I'd bet every guy in Nineveh volunteered that day and lots of females too. It felt good, seeing everyone working together. Kinsley and Downton showed up with their people, and they busted ass, clearing the barricade and moving more stuff to the bridge. The twins and all the guys I met at the barbeque were helping, and as usual, Doogan walked around talking with everybody. Becky and Lightning showed up later with Mariam and Mrs. Thompson. They made sure that everyone had water and food, but I was too spooked about the dynamite to let them too close to the bridge.

And you wanna know something crazy? They did all that work without ever asking what I was planning. Everyone worked for hours, never questioning what we asked them to do, and they never asked how I was expecting to stand against Bacchus and his Knights. They just believed. It's a damned good thing too, because for the longest time, I had questions of my own. How were we going to set off the dynamite? What was I going to do with the Knights once they got stuck? Hell, I wasn't even convinced that the dynamite would trap the Knights on the bridge! I guess you could say I was winging it.

It took a couple hours for Phil to finish his powder-bombs, and the rest of us used that time to make sandbags and stack more Churcher stuff on the bridge's sidewalk. I wanted to give the Knights as little room as possible, and since I didn't want them getting too comfortable, we soaked it all with old gasoline. When Phil and Mike showed up with Phil's powder-bombs, I couldn't help but be disappointed. There were only three of them and they were nothing but pipe-bombs like we used to make in the city. Phil promised that they'd be loud and powerful, but they didn't look like much against weaponized jeeps and fifty or sixty Knights. I'd never let anyone see that I was having doubts, but the Knights would be coming soon, and I still didn't know exactly what to do about it.

We planted the bombs on the sidewalk, hidden in the stacked-up wood and furniture, and once I noticed that the sun was above the church, I knew that I'd better start picking out the volunteers that were staying to fight. Phil and I were talking about how to set off the bombs when I heard a voice behind me.

'Bishop Jake, you sent for me?'

Ginny was standing behind me with a stalky dude with dark hair. He wasn't any taller than she was, but he was barrel-chested with wide shoulders. He was carrying her long-gun over his shoulder, and he stuck out his hand.

'This is Jim, my husband', Ginny said. 'How can we help?'

'Ginny, this is a lot to ask,' I started, taking Jim's hand, 'but I need you in the tower for three shots.'

Ginny's husband glanced up at the church tower.

'Why's it a lot to ask?'

'Cause if my plan turns to shit, you'll need to get her out of there fast!'

'Just give me three shots,' I asked again, 'and get to safety as fast as you can. Phil will give you the details, and I'll be in the bunker at the bridge, between you and the Knights. If they make it off the bridge, I promise we'll give you as much time as we can.'

'But, what about you?'

'If they make it past the bridge,' I repeated, turning to Jim, 'You need to haul ass!'

It was getting late, so we left Ginny and Jim with Phil, and I started back to the rectory with Mike. I picked out four teams of four men to stay back with me. If the Knights did pass the bridge, the people I chose were probably gonna die, so I kept only enough men to work the bunkers. Mike was planning on manning the bunker on the far side of the bridge, but I gave that job to Robertson. Mike was super pissed when he learned that I was sending him back with the others. I know it was a crappy thing to do to a friend, but if we weren't gonna make it, I needed someone I could trust to lead my Churchers.

As if I wasn't nervous enough, Mike, Doogan, Becky, Lightning and Mrs. Thompson all waited until the last damned minute to leave for the river! More than anything, I wanted to talk to Becky that morning, but we never got a chance. I could tell that she wanted to talk to me too, to say something about last night, or just give me a hug, but with Doogan around and everyone watching us, it never happened.

Mrs. Thompson didn't care though. When you're as old as Mrs. Thompson, you can hug whoever the hell you want, no matter who's watching. She came right up to me, and for the first time, she pulled me into a hug.

'Be careful, Jacob.'

While they were getting in the buggy, I noticed that Lighting was becoming a problem for Becky. Rita was confused and refusing to climb in with Mrs. Thompson. Lighting was back in her yellow dress, and she looked like the old Lightning, except angry and stubborn. I went over to help, but with one look, she let me know how much she still hated my ass. Hell, I've known lots of dudes that hate my guts, but only a female can communicate that much hatred in just one look! Lightning is a fairly young female too, so I guess that's another one of those mysterious abilities that females are born with.

Once everyone left it got quiet again, *super quiet*, and the silence got even worse after my teams got into their bunkers. Ours was set up right across from the bridge, and I remember looking up at the church and seeing the barrel of Ginny's long-gun sticking out of the tower. Phil and his team were off to our right, about two hundred feet away and closer to the church. I had Shithead and George with me, along with a kid named John. It's confusing, but sometimes I think that every other Churcher in Nineveh is named John because there's so many of them. This one had blonde hair and a longer-than-normal beard for someone younger than me.

As the time ticked away, the air started getting heavy. When you're waiting a long time for something, and nothing happens, it can make you jumpy. John was becoming shook, and when I noticed him trying to keep his knees from shaking, I figured I'd better loosen things up.

'Hey Shithead,' I asked softly, 'you know what just hit me?'

'What?'

'Maybe Weiss' dynamite is all duds.'

'Duds?!'

Everyone turned toward me, stunned, and Shithead had that funny panicked look on his face.

'Yeah, think about it. We carried that dynamite all the way from Weiss' farm, through the woods, and the cornfields and it never went off. Then we set it on the bridge with everyone working around it all morning. Yeah, I'm thinking those crates are loaded with duds!'

I saw John swallow hard and turn his eyes back toward the road.

'Ya know, Shithead,' I went on. 'I'd feel a whole lot better about this if your crate had blown up while we were bringing it here.

Maybe I should have tripped ya.'

I kept a straight face for as long as I could, but everyone was staring at me, and once I cracked a smile, even Shithead was laughing.

'You're cold-blooded, bishop man!'

We were still laughing when a sound rose in the air, just above the low rumblings of the river. Across the gorge and trailed by a long cloud of dust, the Knights were racing toward the bridge.

BACCHUS

I remember thinking *that's a whole lot of shit heading our way.* There were five weaponized jeeps driving toward us, followed by a long carrier truck and a big white car. The truck's cover was off, and it was packed with at least thirty Knights. The car was just like the one Snaggletooth used to take Mariam, except a dirty white, and without any Christmas decorations. When they reached the bridge, I was worried that they might see the bunker we'd built in the woods behind them. If they did it could ruin everything, but my Churchers kept quiet and low, and the Knights drove past without seeing a thing.

The convoy tightened up as they turned onto the bridge. The lead jeeps used both lanes as they sped toward us, and the vehicles behind them were only ten or twenty feet away. About halfway across, the Knights in the truck all stood up and started shouting and yelling, firing shots in the air. When they spotted our bunker they opened fire, and we could hear rounds pounding against our sandbags. John and Shithead were on our big guns, and I put my hand on John's shoulder.

'Hold your fire.'

Bacchus' Knights were bearing down on us fast, and they were only a hundred feet from our side of the bridge when Ginny took her first shot. Her long-gun sounded different than the Knights guns, and before the sound echoed up from the river, our end of the bridge exploded in a thunderous blast of smoke and flying concrete! Before the smoke blocked our view, I saw the windshield of the leading jeeps disappear, and what was left of the front-seat passengers blown back and into the jeeps behind them! The bullets that Phil gave Ginny worked perfectly, and the bridge lurched to one side with the steel beams above the blast twisted upward like an old tree.

The convoy skidded to a stop, and although we couldn't see much from our bunker, it was obvious that the Knights couldn't get any closer. Before they knew what was happening, Ginny took her second shot, and the other end of the bridge disappeared in the black smoke of another explosion. I breathed a sigh of relief, now that Ginny had set off the dynamite, and for a few seconds we could hear the bits and pieces of concrete raining down around us. Suddenly there was a stunned silence everywhere. The cloud of smoke on the bridge was too thick for us to see anything, and all I could do was hold my breath and listen.

Shithead looked up and asked, 'What we waiting on?'

'Ginny's third shot,' I answered. 'We can't see the whole bridge from here, but Ginny can. If we hear a third shot, it means the Knights are stuck on the bridge.'

'And if we don't?'

I was about to tell him that his question was stupid when we heard a scream coming from the bridge. The Knights had apparently taken more injuries than we could see from our bunker. It was a windless summer afternoon, and it took forever until we finally heard Ginny's third shot. When it came, I felt like the luckiest man alive.

'Fire!'

From both sides of the bridge we lit up the Crescent Knights with everything we had! For a full two minutes we sent thousands of rounds into their stranded convoy as they scrambled for cover. I know that we killed a few more too, but I was only trying to let those assholes know we were there. We stopped, and I waited till it got quiet again before sticking my head up.

'Bacchus?' I called. 'Hey Bacchus, listen up!'

'Maybe you already know this, cause you're a prophet and all.' I laughed. 'But we found a busload of dynamite, and I decided to close the bridge.'

Yeah it was a big fat lie, finding all that dynamite. I know the Churchers aren't into lying, but it was all I had. It was the best lie of my life too, and I paused for a sec, so they could think about what I'd just told them.

'This is where it gets fun,' I resumed. 'If it were up to me, you guys would be dead already, but my Churchers don't like killing people, not even dickheads like you! So you can climb over to the road and leave the way you came, but leave your guns and weapons on the bridge. Our big guns are on you, and I'll cut anyone in half who's leaving with a piece in his hand.'

The Knights didn't think much of my offer. Before I was done talking they started cussing and shooting at us again. I turned toward Phil who was watching from his bunker and after I nodded, he ducked out of sight for a sec. He reappeared holding a bow. Yeah, a bow as in *bow and arrow!* I'd never seen one before, and in a world of weaponized jeeps and boats, you might think that it's a stupid weapon, but Phil knew what he was doing. He loaded an arrow, lit the end, and fired it off toward the bridge. I'm guessing the Knights never saw a bow and arrow before either. They stopped shooting when the flaming arrow sailed over to the bridge's sidewalk in a perfect arc. In a flash, all the wood and furniture we'd stacked there roared into flames.

The fire spread quickly along the bridge, and we couldn't see what was happening through the smoke, but then we heard Phil's bombs going off. The bombs blew within ten or fifteen seconds of each other, and we were close enough to hear the buckshot and nails slamming against the bridge and the stranded vehicles. I don't know what Phil put in those bombs, but I watched one Knight get blown over the railing and sent screaming into the river below. There was plenty of cussing and shouting from the bridge, and I knew we'd taken out more Knights, but I was getting nervous. We were out of bombs, and we still had a bridge full of Crescent Knights right in front of us.

Suddenly there was an odd burst of shots from the bridge. It was back a ways and only a few rounds. While we were still wondering what was happening, and trying to see something through the smoke, we caught sight of two Knights walking on the other side of the bridge with their hands in the air. From our bunker we couldn't see much at first, but after the first couple of Knights left, the rest of those assholes were leaving too! A bunch of them were limping or being helped out by other Knights. My bluff, my big fat lie, worked better than I imagined, and the Knights were bailing.

Maybe forty Knights walked off that bridge that afternoon, and the whole time, every guy in our bunkers was laughing and jumping around and feeling damned good about things. When I figured they were all gone, I took a carbine and stepped out onto the road.

'Come on Shithead!'

The whole center of the bridge's deck was gone, and we could see all the way down to the river, but there were a bunch of narrow places where we could walk onto the bridge. Phil ran out and joined us, and we moved past the first of the Knight's jeeps. They were pretty messed up, but their guns looked like they were ok. We headed straight to the white car, and I was surprised to find the back doors both open, and legs sticking out. It must have been Bacchus. He was a small dude dressed in long purple robes, and as best as we could figure it, he'd been shot in the head by his own Knights. There were six or seven other bodies on the bridge, but they were all just ugly nobodies in Crescent Knight colors.

Everything had gone better than I planned. We not only got the five jeeps, but we also got a huge stash of weapons from the truck! There were boxes and boxes of rounds and rifles, and two sniper rifles like Ginny's. There were two long cases filled with Bleeders, some smoke grenades, and a ton of handguns too. Even though two of the jeeps were toast, Phil couldn't believe that all this firepower was suddenly ours. Hell, he looked like a guy who was about to eat his first lasagna!

Rev. Robertson and the two guys from tree-bunker showed up, and we were all laughing and celebrating when I noticed something out on the road. In the distance and watching the last of the defeated Knights walking past, there was a Fed jeep. There was only the driver inside and he was watching us and talking on his radio. After we watched him for a few seconds, he turned the jeep around and sped off.

Now, I hadn't slept in a long time, and maybe it was just something in my head, but all at once I got a strange feeling. For a split second, it felt like I just drank something cold, and I felt that Casey was standing beside me. While I was still trying to shake off the weirdness, I heard something. Maybe I felt it more than I heard it, but the message couldn't have been any louder if Casey was shouting in my ear.

I turned and shouted, 'Phil?!'

When he saw the look on my face, Phil's smile dropped away.

'How fast can we fix the bridge?'

'Fix it?!' he shouted, 'Why the hell would we—'

'We gotta get this stuff off the bridge, and now!' I interrupted. 'We're gonna need it.'

Shithead stepped closer. 'What's happening, bishop man?'

The shadows of the church had just reached the sidewalk, and although I didn't know how I knew it, I knew we had to hurry. I raised my voice so the guys in the bunkers could hear me too.

'Jodie's coming!'

READY OR NOT

I've never told anyone that before, about hearing Casey's voice on the bridge that day. It's no big secret, but at the time, I couldn't have told my Churchers. If you want people to follow you, they've gotta be able to trust you. Would you trust anyone who says he's just heard from a dead guy? Hell, I wouldn't, and there were lots of things we needed to do.

'Shithead,' I shouted, 'Go get the other Churchers. We need the volunteers back, and bring back anyone who can load or shoot a gun.'

Phil was staring at me like he wasn't sure about something. He finally turned to the other guys and said, 'You heard the man. Follow me!'

There was an odd *urgency* everywhere, and no matter how fast I was going that afternoon, it wasn't fast enough. Shithead headed off to the river, and the rest of us started moving whatever we could carry from the Knight's truck over to our bunkers. Then we grabbed the big guns from Robinson's bunker and brought them over to our side of the river. Phil's team found some long planks of wood somewhere behind the church, and they were stacking them by the bridge. We were shorthanded, but we got a lot done before the first group of Churchers showed up to help.

Doogan and Becky were there with the first group, riding on the funeral buggy, and I stopped and waved when I saw her. They were just reaching the church when we heard a car on the road behind us. There was a vehicle racing toward us in the distance. I brought my nine up at first, but as the little red car got closer I heard Phil's voice behind me.

'It's alright, Bishop Walker. That's Beth Morrison.'

The car screeched to a stop in the church parking lot, and Beth and Judy jumped out and ran toward us. I could see that Beth had been crying cause her makeup was running down from her eyes. It looks creepy when that happens, and it was the first time I'd seen Beth and Judy when they weren't dressed up and in the same clothes. Judy looked scared to death, and although Beth looked like hell, her voice was strong and serious.

'Bishop Walker, I need to speak with you!'

'What's up?'

'Three of Jodie's men came to our home this afternoon. They were there until a short while ago,' she announced, stopping in front of me. 'They've taken Bill away!'

Doogan and Becky joined us, and Becky put her arm around Judy.

'Bishop Walker,' Beth continued, 'they're coming here tonight to destroy Nineveh! Bill gave me a message for you. He said to keep everyone away from the church. He said they have a *Peacemaker*, and the first thing they'll do is raze the church.'

'Raze?' I asked, looking at Doogan.

'It means they'll destroy St. Lucy's, son,' he explained, 'level her to the ground. But what in heaven's name is a Peacemaker?'

I hadn't heard that word in a long time.

'It's what the Feds call one of their smart bombs,' I remembered. 'They used Peacemakers back when there were still fighting in the cities. It's fired from the shoulder, and it has its own onboard computer. It knows the best way to destroy its target, and it'll take down anything from a building to a helicopter.'

It figured that Jodie would do something shitty like that. Destroying the church wasn't gonna change the battle one way or the other. The asshole was just being cruel, hurting my Churchers by taking out something they loved. A Peacemaker was more than enough to do it too, and I wasn't going to say it, but St. Lucy's Church didn't stand a chance.

'Bill also asked me to give you this,' Beth added, holding out her hand.

She handed me a small rubbery thingy, about twice the size of a button on a Churcher shirt. It had a thin little wire hanging off of it.

'What's this?'

'It's a comlink. With it, you'll be able to hear all of the attack force's communications.'

'Cool!'

'Judy,' Beth said, turning to her daughter, 'Would you please wait for me in the church, dear?'

Judy nodded, and Beth waited until Judy reached the church's sidewalk.

'I overheard them talking!' Beth resumed, turning to Doogan. 'They will demand that we surrender the bishop, and when we refuse, they'll destroy everything and murder everyone here.'

I scratched my head.

'Why are they so sure that the Churchers won't give me up?'

'It's only a pretext. They will destroy this place if they capture you or not!'

Tears were rolling down Beth's face again, and her voice was cracking.

'Bishop Walker, they're going to murder my husband! No matter what else happens, they're going to kill Bill!'

'Why would—'

'It's how they work!' she sobbed. 'Bill has never cooperated with Stephen Jodie, and that monster will make Bill an example to the others. It will be Bill who demands your surrender, and Jodie will force Bill to destroy the church. It's his sick revenge!'

281

She grabbed my shirt and cried, 'Please help us!'

I can't speak for other dudes, but right then and there I realized something about myself. When a female is crying, I turn into the biggest, dumbest dumbass on the whole planet!

I heard myself say 'Don't worry about it. We'll think of something.'

'Take a stroll with me, Beth,' Doogan offered, putting his arm around Beth and pulling her off me. 'There's a drop of something in the rectory to ease your mind a wee bit.'

'Hey, Beth,' I interrupted, holding up the comlink. 'Can I talk to Bill on this thing?'

'Yes, when he's in range,' she said, wiping her eyes. 'But it isn't private. Every man in the attack force will hear you, including Jodie!'

I tucked the comlink in my shirt pocket as Becky moved beside me.

'Hey,' I griped, 'did I just promise to help one of the Feds that are coming here to kill us all?'

'Of course you did,' she smiled. 'Mr. Morrison is a good man, and so are you!'

Phil let out a laugh and started back to the street, and once we were alone, Becky grabbed my arm.

'Everyone's talking about how you defeated the Knights!' she said excitedly. 'They're saying it's a miracle!'

'Marvelous.'

'Becky,' I grumbled. 'When the fighting starts tonight, I want you as far away from here as possible. And you can't wait till the last minute to leave either. I want you gone from here!'

'Don't worry. Rita, Mrs. Thompson and I will be with Fr. Doogan at Mariam's house. We'll have a boat ready, just in case, and we'll be waiting and praying for you.'

'I don't know how I know this,' I confessed, 'but it's gonna be over after today. It's all coming to an end tonight.'

It was the truth and another thing I learned after hearing Casey's voice on the bridge. I didn't know how it was gonna end, but I knew that we were about to finish it.

We didn't get a chance to talk after that because Mrs. Thompson shouted for Becky. The old housekeeper lady needed help over at the rectory. I couldn't have talked anymore anyway cause Mike and Shithead were finally back. We saw them walking back from the river with what looked like every dude in Nineveh! There were loads of females too. All my Churchers except the kids and moms were back and working by suppertime, but there was no time to eat. We were all busting ass again, building a defense in front of the Church.

If I was a different kind of guy, I could go on and on bragging about our defenses that afternoon. The way I set up my Churchers was a work of art! I didn't have had a clue about what to do about the Peacemaker or saving Morrison, but I was pretty sure that we could handle the Feds. We outnumbered them, and with all the weapons we'd captured from the Knights, I was pretty sure we had more firepower too. Before the sun started setting, we'd built a huge roadblock on the street, just beyond the bridge. We used sandbags, more furniture, and even the burned-out jeep we got from the Knights. On top of all that we had four bunkers defending the church, with two big guns each and plenty of rounds! We found a good spot for Ginny too, in the upstairs window of the rectory where she had a great view of the road. All through the woods, along the creek, and around the parish, we had an armed Churcher behind every tree! Hell, it's not bragging when you're telling the truth.

Before I forget, you need to know that Phil is a damned genius. His team found long heavy boards that they used to get the Knights vehicles off the bridge. They laid the boards across the holes in the deck and created just enough of a road to drive the jeeps off. A couple of those jeeps were mint too, with extra gas! And since I didn't want to tip my hand to the Feds, I had Mike move the good jeeps behind the church. They couldn't be seen from the street, but we had them in case the Feds broke our lines.

Phil reminded me that most of my Churchers had never fired a carbine. I already knew that Churchers don't know squat about fighting, but there was lots of other stuff we had to teach everyone. We didn't have much time either, so Phil, Mike, and Shithead brought everyone together in front of the church so I could talk to them. I stood on the top step where everyone could see me.

'Listen up,' I shouted. 'These city Feds have never fought outnumbered before. They'll be more scared than you are, but you've gotta stay alert! They've got Bleeders. If you hear a high-pitched sound, like a cricket chirping, get flat on the ground! Bleeders explode *up*, so you'll be safer in the dirt. You only have a few seconds to react, so pay attention!'

I saw Ginny and her husband in the group, and I remembered my promise to Beth.

'And if Morrison is in trouble, help him if you can. He's one of us!'

We answered a question or two, and before we split up, Mike remembered to say a prayer. I could tell that they were all serious about it too. You can tell when a Churcher is praying extra hard. It's not always in their voice or on their faces, but you can still tell.

Becky, Doogan and Mrs. Thompson had already left, and I was feeling pretty good about everything. The sun was still up, and I had a little time to walk around and make sure everyone was ready. I gave everyone a stupid grin too and said something light, like Doogan might do.

We'd set John, the kid from my old bunker, about a mile down the road in the woods. I knew that the Feds couldn't use the bridge, so we put John there to fire a shot in the air when the Feds were coming. It was another long hour or so, and the sun was just above the horizon when we heard that shot. As we looked on, the Feds were driving toward us in the distance. There were only four jeeps, but there were men already on their guns. There was a large carrier too, like the Knights had, and it looked about half full of foot Feds. In the rear of the Fed convoy was a black four-door jeep, and when I saw it my heart began racing.

Jodie was here.

CUTTING THE DEAL

As I watched them speeding closer, I got a funny feeling that something wasn't adding up. Was this all that Jodie had? Yeah, I figured that we had more firepower than the Feds, and more people too, but did Jodie really think he could beat us with four jeeps and some foot Feds? Hell, it even looked like there were some Crescent Knights mixed in with the foot Feds on the truck. Apparently Jodie's Feds were spread so thin that they had to pick up some of the straggling Knights on their way here!

The outnumbered convoy didn't seem to notice our roadblock or our bunkers pointed right at them. They slowed to a stop and lined up about fifty feet behind our blockade. The black four-door, Jodie's car, had its blackened windows up, and although we couldn't see inside, I knew he was there. We watched as he pulled off the road behind the jeeps and stopped on the grass. We were all expecting something to happen, but the Feds were just sitting there watching us with their engines running. I was in the first bunker on our side of the roadblock, with Shithead and the twins, and we were all scratching our heads, wondering what the Feds were up to.

Shithead whispered, 'What they waiting on?'

Suddenly on the horizon we saw two more vehicles approaching. One was just another open jeep, but the other one was big and scary as hell! It was low, painted in dark green camo, and instead of wheels, it rode on metal rollers like a tank. The huge barrel of some kind of cannon stretched out of the front turret, and I heard myself mumbling *holy crap.*

I poked Shithead. 'What the hell is that thing?!'

'That's an assault vehicle, man!' he said, excitedly. 'I didn't think the urban posts had those no more.'

All my planning and the Churchers hard work had been for nothing. The assault vehicle changed everything, and on top of that, I'd called almost all of my Churchers back from the safety of the river to fight! We were all here and vulnerable, and suddenly our chances of survival were zero! It was the biggest shit-sandwich of my life, and I was as close to panicking as I've ever been.

The assault vehicle pulled ahead and drove past the other Fed jeeps. Without even slowing down, it drove straight through our blockade, crumpling the sandbags and wood, and effortlessly shoving a burned-out jeep out of its way. For a second I thought that it was gonna run through our bunker too. It came to a stop only about sixty feet away, and the big gun on top spun around and aimed right at us.

Through the huge new hole in our blockade, the open jeep drove through. There were two guys inside, Jim Morrison and someone I hadn't seen since the nuncio gave me my ring. It was Jodie's man, the tall blonde-headed asshole that I punched out in front of the cathedral. Both of his eyes were still black from the ass-kicking I gave him too. Morrison was driving, and the blonde-haired creep was in the seat behind him. Morrison pulled the jeep parallel our blockade and stopped right in front of St. Lucy's. It looked like the creep was talking to Bill, so I put the comlink in my ear.

Morrison stood up, and the jerk behind him immediately handed him the Peacemaker. I'd never seen one up close before, and it was smaller than I expected, just a long tube about three feet long painted camo green. It had a large black sight on top and a sling, and Bill hung it on his shoulder. In my ear I heard the asshole tell Bill to 'Move!'

Bill marched toward us, and he didn't stop till he was about halfway between us and his jeep. He could see me staring back at him from my bunker, and I saw him swallow hard. He pulled out a white card from his shirt pocket and started reading.

'By order of the Justice Department, and its regional representative Stephen Jodie, martial law has been declared in this county. You are hereby ordered to surrender the criminal fugitive known as Jacob Walker. You have ten minutes to comply.'

Beth was right. The guy sitting behind Morrison was standing now, with his carbine pointing at Bill's back. Morrison wasn't supposed to live through this.

My head was spinning, trying to come up with something, but Jodie was holding all the cards. As bad as things were, my shit-sandwich was about to get bigger. There was a noise behind me and when I turned, I saw Becky running toward us. It looked like she was coming from the rectory, moving bunker to bunker! I was too stunned to be pissed, and when she finally reached us, I reached out and pulled her inside.

'What the hell are you doing here?!'

'Rita is missing!' she cried. 'She ran off, and I think she's headed this way.'

'Well, we can't go looking for her now!' I shouted, 'Get back to Hershberger's before the Feds—'

I stopped when, over Becky's shoulder, I saw Lightning galloping toward us along the creek. It was strange and unreal. Rita looked exactly like the first day I saw her. She was on that damned white horse of hers, with her yellow dress hiked up, and her hair blowing back in the wind! We all turned to watch, and Becky whispered 'Oh my God!'

Maybe Lightning didn't understand the danger, or she was too angry to give a shit, but her horse slowed as she came to the blockade. She rode casually along the Fed's line, glaring at the Fed jeeps. She finally stopped between our bunker and the assault vehicle. Lightning gave a killing glance to Morrison before bringing up her arm and then her hand. As we watched in disbelief, she started parading back and forth along the Fed line, giving them all the finger!

There was something about Lightning that threw everything into chaos, and I think it may have helped us. I don't know what those city Feds were expecting, but it sure wasn't a young blonde girl on a horse. The stunned silence in my comlink told me that the Feds had never seen anything like Lightning, but it was only a matter of time before someone opened fire. Someone had to get the kid out of there, so I stuck a nine in the back of my pants and started moving out to get her.

Shithead grabbed my shirt. 'They'll shoot you on sight, bishop man!'

With my back turned, Becky bolted out to get Lightning. It felt like everything around me was falling apart, and I heard a voice in my comlink.

'Morrison?!'

Bill Morrison stood frozen and dripping in sweat as he watched Becky run up to Lightning and start signing. In my ear, I could hear the asshole in the jeep.

'I told you to take out the Church, Morrison. Do it *now!*'

Bill slowly brought the Peacemaker to his shoulder and turned toward the church. I knew I had to buy Becky more time, and an idea came to me. It was another dumb idea that was probably gonna get me killed, but I couldn't just stand there anymore. I grabbed the comlink from my ear and showed it to Shithead.

'How do I talk to Bill with this thing?!'

'Just talk,' he answered, 'but it's gotta be in your ear.'

I screwed the damned thing back into my ear, put my hands in the air, and started walking out to Morrison. It looked like I was surrendering, and I could hear the gasp from the Churchers behind me. Even Becky and Lightning turned to look. It's not easy, walking slowly when you're expecting to be shot at any second, but I took as much time as I could. While I did, Becky must have convinced Lighting to leave. She reached up and I saw Lightning pulling her up and onto the horse. Then the horse galloped off along the creek, and all I could see was Becky's backpack bouncing up and down. The whole thing had gone down in a heartbeat, and when I looked back at Bill he looked scared.

'Have you lost your mind, kid?!'

Standing there with the assault vehicle on my left, and seeing Bill with that Peacemaker on his shoulder, a great idea came to me. I needed to let Bill in on it, but I had to be careful. Whatever I said in the comlink would be heard by all the Feds. In my head I came up with just the right words, but I had no idea that the Feds would react so quickly. I'd barely finished my sentence when Bill's eyes got big and pissed. At first I thought he might shoot me himself, but then everything exploded into motion. There was all kinds of shouting in the comlink, and I whipped around and made a break for the bunker!

It was like the world went into slow-motion. The blonde-haired asshole in the jeep raised his gun to do Morrison, but before he could get a round off, a shot rang out from behind us. In a splash of red, the tall guy's head exploded, and he tumbled over the side of the jeep. Morrison didn't miss a beat. He spun around and fired the Peacemaker into the assault vehicle!

When that thing blew, it was the most amazing explosion you've ever seen! It started out as just a few yellow and red sparks shooting out, but then it detonated in a blast that rippled out like waves. I had just reached the bunker and as I jumped, the blast blew me straight over the sandbag wall! My comlink was instantly dead, and the blast was so loud I thought I'd never hear again. I knew that it knocked Morrison over too because I saw him jumping back to his feet and running for cover. Maybe it's cause I couldn't hear yet, but for a split second there was only the crackling sound of the assault vehicle burning. Then the air around us lit up with gunfire and the Fed jeeps started rolling.

The lead jeep came right through the hole in our roadblock, and it was a huge mistake. Hell, all our firepower was already focused there. Our big guns butchered those guys, and the jeep flipped over in a ball of fire. Without the assault vehicle, the Feds were outgunned and outnumbered again, but Jodie must have ordered them to attack anyway. They split up, two heading along the creek bed, and the other ramming through our blockade on the river's side. Jodie's car followed right behind it, and I watched it speed down the road and disappear past the church.

I would have gone after Jodie right then, but there was a yellow flash in the air behind the Fed line. The foot Feds were getting ready to attack, and they were launching a wave of Bleeders into the air.

'Bleeders!'

We heard a deep thumping sound before the Bleeders bounced onto the grass and parking lot around us. After a few seconds of mechanical chirping, the air crackled with a thousand explosions. They sent two waves of Bleeders at us, and when I popped my head up again, the Feds from the truck were rushing us. It looked like the Churchers followed my instructions and we didn't take many injuries because when the foot Feds charged, we gave them so much fire that they had to fall back and take cover. Hell, we dropped five or six of them on the street, and at least three Feds were running off in the other direction!

I didn't see how it happened, but one of their jeeps was able to cross the creek. It was coming around behind us, and while we were getting the guns turned around, our hidden jeeps roared out from behind the church. It was Mike, and he was amazing on that M2! Robertson was driving, and he went straight at the Feds like he was playing chicken. The Fed driver and gunner were done in seconds, and that jeep flipped and burned not far from the spot where Casey died.

Without the assault vehicle, and with so few Feds, the fight was pretty much over before it started. I grabbed my carbine and a nine, checked for my blades, and started falling back to the church.

'Come on, Shithead!'

'Where to?'

'We're gonna find Jodie.'

Two of the Fed jeeps were still attacking from behind the creek, and the foot Feds were firing from where they were pinned down, so there was still gunfire everywhere. We kept low and worked our way around to the front of the church.

'Stay alert,' I told him. 'He's gotta come back this way to escape.'

We were losing light, and we stuck to the tree line as we passed the church to stay hidden. We'd gone less than a mile and we were still within sight of the bridge when we had to stop. Jodie's car was sitting in the middle of the road, and there was a Fed standing next to it. When I got a good look, my heart fell into my stomach. Next to the road, Lightning's horse was lying dead on the grass! There was a lot of blood and it looked like someone had put a round right between the big animal's eyes. There couldn't have been two horses in the world like that, and I knew that Jodie must have caught up with the girls as they were heading to Mariam's.

The Fed must have heard us because he whipped around with his carbine up, but Shithead dropped him before he could pull the trigger. We ran over to the car and moved around to the back doors. There's no good way to check a vehicle like that cause you're in the open, and it's a damned good way to get shot, but we had to find the girls. With Shithead covering me, I threw the door open.

In the failing daylight I could see that the car was empty, but just as I realized it, two Bleeders fell from the seat and bouncing to the ground at my feet! My ears weren't working right yet, and I guess Shithead's ears weren't working either. He didn't hear the Bleeders or see them rolling toward him. He just stood there like a dumbass, and when he didn't move, I spun around and dove toward him. For a split sec I thought I got there in time, but just as I knocked him to the dirt I felt pain ripping through my left leg.

Once I rolled off him, I could feel the blood soaking through my pants and down my leg. Shithead was winded, but when he got up and caught a look at my leg, he freaked. If there's a good thing about taking a wound in the ass, it's that you can't see how bad you're bleeding! He ran over to the dead Fed and found some bandages on the guy's belt.

'Oh, man!' he said, frantically helping me wrap my leg. 'We gotta get you to the Doc's.'

It was the first time I've ever been stung by a bleeder, and I was suddenly feeling shitty. It was like I'd just woke up, and it was becoming hard to think. As I tightened the bandage around my leg and stood up, I felt sick in my stomach.

'Get over to the Hershberger's,' I told him. 'Find out if Becky and Lightning made it there. And watch out for that other jeep.'

'Where *you* going?'

'The school,' I told him. 'I think Jodie's got them in the school.'

'You don't look so good, man,' he objected. 'We should stick together, and then—'

'Just do it, Shithead!' I shouted. 'I'll meet you at the school.'

He knew we were burning time, and he got right into Jodie's car and sped off toward the river. I started moving to the Church, but it was slow going at first. Even though I hadn't eaten in a long time, I had to stop and puke in the bushes behind the St. Lucy's sign. My head was so screwed up that I'd forgotten my carbine, and all I had was my nine and my blades.

My ears were getting better, and I could hear gunfire in the distance, so I crossed through the woods to avoid any fighting. It was getting harder to think, and there was more shooting coming from the street now, but it was strangely far off. We had plenty of firepower to handle the fighting, and I tried to stay focused on making it to the school. The sky was nearly dark, and I limped through the parking lot by the rectory. I could see red bleeding through my bandage, and when I looked up again I noticed Phil's garage. It was just a shell, and I realized where Phil's team found the long boards he needed to patch up the bridge.

It wasn't until I made it through the woods and saw a light on at the school that I remembered my dreams. It was bizarre and scary like I was living in a nightmare, and I pulled my nine. I took a deep breath and paused outside the doors, hoping that the adrenalin would clear up my head.

When I stepped past the door I saw a single lantern on the floor. It was sitting in the middle of the dark room next to Becky's pink backpack. Just like my dream, the backpack was leaning against a chair, and she was on the chair and covered with a white sheet.

'Becky?'

At the sound of my voice, Becky started moving frantically under the sheet. I carefully limped closer, scanning every shadow and even the beams of the ceiling. I remembered Casey's warning, and even though my head was screwy, I examined every inch of the school as I drew closer to Becky. I was looking for any signs of Lightning or anything suspicious. In my head I kept repeating that this wasn't a damned dream, and I couldn't let Becky or Lightning get hurt!

When I reached the chair, I slid the nine back into my pants. I pulled a blade, so I could cut Becky loose. There was a noise in the back of the school, and my eyes locked on the darkness as I reached out and grabbed the sheet. As I threw the sheet back, there was a sharp crippling pain in my guts, and I heard myself let out an involuntary groan. My head cleared with the sudden pain, and when I finally understood what hit me, I realized that I'd just made the biggest mistake of my life. It wasn't Becky at all under the sheet, but Stephen Jodie!

I was standing there facing the little bastard, completely helpless. My left hand had a hold of his wrist, but it had been too late. The knife in his hand was already buried in my gut. My other hand had instinctively brought my knife around to attack, but Jodie held my wrist too, in an inhuman grip. The pain was unreal and so sharp that I couldn't breathe.

'You're pathetically weak and predictable,' he sneered. 'Threaten what you love, and you rush into the trap like a fool! You've been more trouble to me that you know, dear bishop, but without you, I'll have these people rounded up and dead within weeks!'

His blade twisted, and his charred face grinned when I let out another groan.

'I want you to know that I have Rebecca and Rita bound to a pipe in the boy's lavatory, and after I watch the light leave your eyes, we'll be going to a party with the Crescent Knights! I'll introduce them as friends of yours, so I know they'll be very popular.'

Now, I knew that the wound in my guts was lethal, and I was out of time. The black fuzziness was already filling my eyes. Still, I remembered how God helped me out with the dynamite, and I knew that my only chance was to pray.

If I'd been a smarter Churcher, I'd have prayed for my soul or forgiveness or something, but none of that was coming to me. And even though I had nothing to offer God, I cut a deal with him anyway. It was quick and done in a heartbeat, cause I didn't have time to ask for a lot. All I asked for was strength and another thirty seconds.

As Jodie leaned in, twisting the knife again, I reared back slightly in pain. Then I quickly slammed my head forward again, smashing my forehead into his face. It was a good shot, and breaking his nose surprised him just enough for me to jerk my hand free. I brought it up and buried my knife just below his ribcage. I didn't stop when I felt the warmth covering my hand, but I pulled back and hit him again the same way. I knew it was over. He glared back at me, stumbled back a step, and dropped to the floor.

It may sound strange, but I can't remember if his knife was still in me or not. I only remember falling to the ground next to him, and even though it hurt like hell, I reached back and pulled the nine from my pants. I knew that the asshole was already dead, but for some reason I put two slugs in the back of his head anyway. Maybe my brain was still messed up. I only remember footsteps getting louder, and I remember looking up at Shithead.

His eyes were big, and he looked sad.

'Oh, bishop man!'

'Shut up and go find the girls,' I told him. 'He's got them in the back somewhere.'

The weakness in my voice surprised me, and I realized how damned tired I was. I could smell smoke in the air, probably from a jeep or the assault vehicle, and I remember thinking to myself that *there's always something burning*. I knew that Shithead would find the girls and they'd be coming right back, but I couldn't keep my eyes open anymore. I wanted to tell Becky some stuff too, but I've never felt so tired, and even after I heard more footsteps, I had to close my eyes.

OLD JOE

This shouldn't come as a big surprise to anybody, but I didn't die that night. The unbelievable thing is that I didn't wake up again for eight whole days! Doogan said that I woke up a couple of times after Dr. Weiss operated on me, but I don't remember any of that. He said that Mike and Rev. Robertson made three different medicine runs to find antibiotics, and for a long time nobody knew if I was gonna live or die. Pretty soon, everyone in the whole parish was praying for me. Doogan said that even our two Jehovah Witnesses came to the prayer meetings at the church, and that's what finally sent God over the edge. After five days my fever broke and it looked like I was gonna pull through.

When I finally did open my eyes I saw a blurry face above mine. She had blue eyes, and I thought that it might be an angel, but when I focused I recognized Lightning. She studied my eyes for a sec, and when she realized that I was awake, she bolted out of the room. I fell asleep again after that, but I remember knowing that I was in my room at the rectory. It was the first time I'd ever slept there.

The next time I woke up, the whole place was packed with people. Mike was grinning at me with his arm around Mariam. There was Doogan, the Morrisons, Shithead and Mrs. Thompson. Phil was standing in the back with Robertson, Ginny, and her husband. Hell, even Kinsley and his family were all there smiling. Becky was sitting right beside me, in the chair by my bed. Lightning was there too, and I was surprised at how she smiled at me. My throat wasn't working, and it took a sec to get my voice loud enough to say anything.

'Lightning's not pissed anymore?'

'No, lad,' Doogan laughed. 'She's been helping take care of you this last week or so.'

Becky started signing, so Lightning could follow what we were saying.

'She insisted on it,' he added grinning, 'and it's a good thing too. You were feverish and shouting in your sleep. With your language, son, only a deaf person could have survived it!'

Everyone let out a laugh, but I could barely move. It was hard to breathe, and it felt like every part of me weighed a thousand pounds. Once my head cleared up, all kinds of questions were coming to me.

'So what happened at the church? How many did we lose?'

'Not a one!' Doogan exclaimed, 'but there are a number of us who are still recovering. The worst is Jeff Jacobs. He was wounded by one of those terrible Bleeder devices. We thought he might lose a leg, but Dr. Weiss worked another miracle. He'll be back on his feet in a few months.'

'Jake,' Becky interrupted, 'what happened at the school? Devon said that he found Jodie dead, and you dying on the floor!'

Now, I wasn't feeling all that great anyway, and I didn't want to tell that story in front of everybody. It was embarrassing as hell, getting cut by that little bastard, and I didn't want everyone knowing about it. When I shook my head, Doogan started talking again.

'Well now,' he sighed, 'we should be letting the bishop get his rest.'

Everyone left except for Doogan, Becky, and Lightning, and as the others piled out, they stopped by my bed and said, 'See ya later, Jake' or 'Glad you're feeling better' or 'See you soon'.

Once everyone else was gone, I told Doogan what happened in

the school. I told them all about the fight with Jodie, and how he hid under the sheet pretending to be Becky. Then I told them how I was careless and got cut, and how I thought I was gonna die, and I told them how I wound up praying.

'Wow!' Becky exclaimed. 'You learned to pray?'

'Yeah, but it wasn't just praying,' I admitted. 'I kind of made a deal.'

'What do you mean?'

'Becky, I told God that if he'd help me stop Jodie and get you and Rita safe again, I'd do whatever he wanted. I'd be his bishop, or sweep the floors of the church, whatever he wants, whatever he decides.'

'That's funny,' she smiled gently. 'Every day while you were hurt, I prayed that God would bring you back to us, even if it meant that we could never be together. It looks like he's answered both our prayers.'

I think I dozed off after that, cause I only remember how Becky was looking at me.

After that day, I started healing lots faster. I still slept every couple of hours, and it took a few days to get used to food again. And speaking about that, Jewish Churchers make the world's greatest soup! Mrs. Weiss, the doc's wife, brought it to me by the gallon and I never got tired of it. Pretty soon I could move around, and it seemed to me that whenever I was awake someone was stopping by to see me. Mrs. Thompson would leave my window open too, so I could hear kids playing outside. Everything was different, and there was peace in Nineveh again. I could see it on the faces of everyone who came to see me, and even though I was weak and sort of worthless, I could smell it in the air around me.

You should know that everything about being sick isn't so bad. I've got a wicked nasty scar now, and some cool and disgusting stories about the first couple of times I used the bathroom. Doogan doesn't want me telling you about that because he says that it's *irrelevant*. Maybe so, but when the boys in Becky's First Communion class visited, they loved that story, and if you ask me, it's way more interesting than some of the other stuff I've written about.

Anyway, one morning about two weeks after I first woke up, Doogan came into my room. I could tell right away that he was excited about something.

'Jacob?' he asked, excitedly, 'are you up to seeing a special visitor? It's a friend from your old neighborhood. He arrived yesterday with many other Christians from the city.'

I couldn't remember any friend from the city that was still alive, so I was kind of pumped.

'Yeah, sure.'

Doogan wanted to bring the visitor upstairs, but I told him that I'd be down in a sec. My room and the bathroom were the only places I'd been since getting cut, and I felt like I needed to stretch a little.

Going downstairs took longer than I figured. It was fun seeing all the furniture and pictures back where they belonged, but I was still sore, and Mrs. Thompson was pissed when she found me on the stairs. She hurried up to me and made me lean on her until we got to the library. When we stepped inside I couldn't believe it. Doogan was there, but sitting next to him was someone I hadn't seen since the night I got my ring.

'Old Joe?!'

It was Old Joe alright, sitting in the big chair by the window, and he stood up when he saw me.

'I don't know that we've ever met, son,' he said, sticking his hand out, 'but it's my pleasure.'

He looked good, younger than I remembered, and all cleaned up in his black clothes. Mrs. Thompson led me over to the couch, within reach of the oatmeal raisin cookies that she'd set out. As I sat down, I noticed the big curved stick, the crosier thingy from the night I got my ring. It was leaning against Joe's chair. I couldn't help noticing something else. Joe had a ring on his finger, and it was even bigger than mine.

'I'd like to tell you and Fr. Doogan a story, Jacob,' he started. 'Some of it you already know. It's about the night you saved

Nuncio Moreau outside the cathedral.'

I snagged a cookie as Joe started talking.

'When the nuncio reached me, he was already seriously wounded. He insisted that we perform a brief ceremony in the cathedral, and after he ordained me, I left to get a doctor from Madison Station.'

'Madison?' I asked, surprised. 'Where the old ones live?'

'Yes,' he said, grinning. 'Many of us are older, but we have a doctor and a nurse and the nuncio desperately needed medical attention. I'd only traveled a few blocks when I saw Jodie's car heading south on 12th. I hurried back to warn the nuncio, but Jodie and his men had already dragged him from the Cathedral. As I watched and prayed, I saw a young man appear from nowhere. I watched him overpower the federal agents, and I saw the nuncio put the ring on his finger and bless him.'

'Hold up a sec,' I interrupted. 'If I'm following all this, he did you first. That makes you the bishop, right?'

'Yes, I'm the bishop of this diocese,' Joe answered, stroking his chin. 'But there is a complication. You see, the nuncio placed his own ring on your finger, the ring of his parish. In some diocese, it is acceptable under church law to ordain bishops that way, by passing the ring from generation to new generation. The words he used suggest to us that he made you a bishop that night too.'

'You see, lad,' Doogan explained. 'You may be the bishop of the nuncio's diocese in France.'

'French Churchers?'

'Yes, and we don't believe that this is mere coincidence,' Old Joe went on, sounding more serious. 'The king of France is preparing to enter Rome. Even now, Henry is assembling the Cardinals that have survived, and he has promised that the Holy See will elect a successor, a new pope! The seat of Peter will be filled again.'

He looked at me curiously as I grabbed another cookie.

'You are quite a resourceful young man, Jacob, and it may be God's will that you assist in that effort. I cannot stress the importance here! It's been prophesied that, with Peter back in Rome, the world will be granted a period of peace. This may mean the fulfillment of that prophesy!'

I was listening as well as I could, but it wasn't easy stuff to follow. Joe finally came out with it, and he gave me a huge job to do.

'To that end, we have already inquired to Rome on your behalf. Bishop Gregory, Fr. Doogan and I have appealed to Cardinal Raphael for a ruling. I received a response yesterday, and Cardinal Raphael has asked that you provide a full accounting of your experiences since that night at the cathedral.'

'The Cardinals want to hear the story in your own words, me boy!' Doogan added. 'But not to worry. Becky, Mrs. Thompson and meself will help you with all the details.'

'If I gotta go to France,' I objected. 'Who's gonna watch my Churchers? They're shit magnets! What happens the next time some gang—'

'Jacob!' Doogan interrupted with a laugh. 'While you were unconscious, Michael and Bill Morrison raided the Federal armories in the city. He brought back truckloads of weapons, gas, and ammunition. With the vehicles that you've captured from Jodie and the Knights, St. Lucy's is now the most formidable fighting force in nearly two thousand miles!'

Now I had no way of knowing it yet, but laughing was painful as hell, and after I started, I couldn't stop.

'So,' I laughed, holding my sides. 'My Churchers are badass?!'

Joe and Doogan were laughing too, and when we stopped I'd laughed so hard that I was laying sideways on the couch.

Mrs. Thompson came in and got pissed.

'That's enough for now!' she told Doogan. 'Jacob needs his rest.'

Joe came by every few days for the next week, wanting to talk some more. I found out later that both Joe and Doogan had to write a report about me. I figured that maybe those dudes in Rome were suspicious and wanted to make sure our stories matched.

They asked me lots of the same questions, about what happened with the dynamite and with Jodie. Most of it is stuff I've already told you about, but Joe asked me some religious questions too. He seemed especially interested in what I knew about praying. The last time we got together, that's all he talked about.

'One thing more,' he asked, 'Fr. Doogan has told me that you've been praying more now, and leading prayer services as well.'

'Yeah, I guess,' I replied. 'Heck, I pray all the time.'

'Can you tell me what you've learned about it?'

It was one of those questions that you gotta think about first, and I couldn't tell from his face if I got the answer right or not.

'I've been paying attention,' I explained, 'and it seems to me that there are two kinds of people who pray a lot. One kind prays because they're good and kind, and friendly. They're warm and caring and concerned and helpful. Heck, they're just naturally good Churchers.'

Joe grinned and nodded.

'And the other group?' he asked.

'We pray because we're not.'

YOUR EMINENCE CARDINAL RAPHAEL

S o, I guess that's it, Your Eminence.

Like they told me, I've written down the whole story so Fr.
Doogan can send it to you. He said to tell you exactly what
happened in my own words, even the dull stuff. While I
was healing up, Becky told me to read lots of books, so I could
learn new words, and that's probably why I write so good. While I
was getting better there wasn't anything else to do anyway, so I
read books on history and science, and the church, and the Saints,
and Harry Potter, and one on comets. Those first few weeks Becky
had to read to me because I was tired all the time, but I'm feeling
like myself again now. You wouldn't believe how long it took me
to write everything down, and Becky's had to fix my spelling and
take out the shit that's offensive or inappropriate, but the story is
all here, just as it happened.

I guess it's up to you and your friends in Italy to decide if I'm a
bishop or not, and I'm good with whatever you have to say about
that, even if I have to go to France and help the Churcher army.
Don't worry, I'll stick to the deal I made with God. I owe him. I
could have handled just about anything that night, even dying, but I
couldn't have lived with myself if Jodie had taken Becky and
Lightning. Doogan was right, God helps you if you ask him. He
really does, even if you're just getting to know him. He helps ex-
Feds too. Maybe Doogan's already told you, but Shithead's talking
about becoming a priest. When I first heard that, I figured that he

was just saying that to get attention. He told me once that he was a Baptist, and everybody knows they can't be priests. I don't want to be the one to tell him though, cause he's been real serious about it. He's been studying with Doogan and me for weeks. If he pulls it off, I might have to start calling him by his real name, especially in public places. Devon's a good guy though, and St. Lucy's could do a lot worse.

I'm writing this last part by myself, without Doogan or Becky seeing it, because I wanted to add a couple of private things. First off, Bill Morrison is a hero around here because of how he took out the assault vehicle, but there's something you should know about that. Everybody here thinks that I used the comlink to tell Bill to blow up the assault vehicle, and I sort of did that, but that's not the whole story. What I actually said was *watch where you point that thing, Bill. I've got Beth and Judy tied up in the church.*

Morrison's a good guy and he'd probably have done the right thing anyway, but I wasn't taking any chances that day. Like I said, Bill's ok, so please keep that to yourself.

The other thing you should know is that sometimes I think I'd be ok *not* being a bishop, so Becky and I could be a thing. If you could meet her you'd understand. She's a lot like the song we danced to after we ate lasagna. She plays again and again, over and over in my head sometimes. Every day since the lasagna, and about a million times a night, I close my eyes so I can have my arms around Becky once more. She won't let me touch her much now, because of the bishop thing, but I'll never forget the warmth of that black dress in my hands or how Becky felt wrapped around me that night. Doogan told me that I shouldn't dwell on stuff like that, but I don't know how to stop it. Hell, I don't know why I'd ever want to.

So let me know what you guys decide as soon as you can, ok? It'd be great if you could let me know before spring. Doogan told me not to get my hopes up about that. He says it took you guys five hundred years to figure out that Joan of Arc was a saint. I just finished a book about her and I was a little surprised to hear that. Yeah, I know you guys had other stuff going on, but I gotta think you dropped the ball on that one.

Oh, and Doogan says there's a group of Churchers south of

here that have contacted us and asked for help. They're led by a group of Godly females called *Sisters* and they're having trouble with a gang, just like we did. Fr. Doogan says they're in a city not too far away, a godless hole he called *Cincinnati*. We're taking a couple jeeps down there tomorrow to check it out, but I don't think we'll be gone long.

Other than that, I guess you'll know where to find me.

FROM THE AUTHOR

Thanks for reading The Bishop of 12th Avenue. If you enjoyed getting to know Jake, Becky and the Churchers, please take a moment to leave a review at Amazon or your online retailer.

I'd love to hear from you so feel free to contact me at my website. While you're there, check out my blog and social media links. Don't forget to sign up for my newsletter so I can let you know of new releases and other news.

Ray Lucit
http://www.raylucit.com